COEUR D'ALENE WATERS

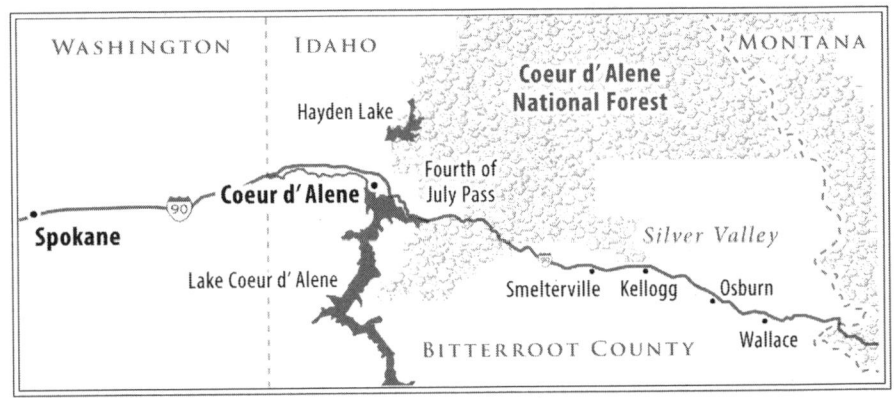

BITTERROOT COUNTY, Northern Idaho, 1988-1989

COEUR D'ALENE WATERS

NED HAYES

PROSPERO BOOK GROUP

P

PROSPERO BOOK GROUP
www.ProsperoBookGroup.com

244 Fifth Ave, Suite 45, New York, NY 10001
United States of America

Printed in the United States of America

ISBN: 978-0-9852393-8-1
1. Historical—Idaho. 2. Mystery—Pacific Northwest.

First paperback edition published December 2013.

The name Prospero and the [P] mark are the property and trademark of the Prospero Book Group, Inc. All rights reserved.

For Jill

And in memory
of the ninety-one
who died in the
Sunshine Mine disaster,
May 2, 1972

AUGUST 1988

THE GIRL *felt hope leave her as the road went dark. Night lapped across the valley and seeped over the mountains, an approaching tide. She turned her head and saw a light far away on the hill. Even as she looked, it faded into the depths. The darkness would swallow her.*

Ahead of the car were only acres of water, an emptiness that roiled slowly against the forest and the mountains. She rolled the syllables around in her mouth, a name her father had taught her: Lake Coeur d'Alene.

Her father was gone. And when she peeked into the front seat, all she could see was the strange pair of muscled shoulders soiled with dirty ink and weird pictures.

She closed her eyes, willing this strange man to go away. She tried to go to sleep, tried to pretend that none of this had happened. But even as she closed her eyes, she remembered seeing him for the first time.

That afternoon, the man had opened the car door quietly, as if he did not want anyone to see him. At first, she wondered if it was someone she should know, the man her mamma talked about, the one who would come to get them both someday. But when she saw this man's shoulders, she knew immediately this was not anyone she knew. This man had bent dragons written all over him, his skin was dirty as sin.

Heat waves vibrated up from the pavement, blurring the entrance of the building her father had entered. The dirty man looked around the parking lot quickly and then ran his hand over the steering wheel, finding the keys right where her father had left them. The girl watched the man with her eyes slit nearly shut, willing him not to get into the car.

But he did get in. He swung a small knapsack and a rolled-up sleeping bag onto the seat next to him and slammed the car door closed. He didn't even look in the backseat. It was as if the car already belonged to him. Then he turned the key. No one came out of the building.

In the backseat, the girl slid down to the floor. She gripped her doll tight in her free hand. She imagined that she was invisible with her eyes shut, that no one could see her there, curled up next to her doll. She imagined that when she opened her eyes, her father would be sitting in the front seat. She would climb over the seat to sit beside him and watch the road.

Then, a few minutes after the dirty man drove the car away, he glanced in the rearview mirror. His eyes saw her tennis shoes first, and then caught the edge of her dress, and then jumped up to lock on her face.

"Well, now I got some fuckin' leverage, don't I?" he said. Then the dirty man reached in the backseat and pulled her over, gripping her hand sideways in a lopsided hold, hard enough to hurt. Numbly, she tried to straighten herself out on the seat.

Then the dirty man opened the car window. He began to throw her father's books outside. His muscles clenched and moved tightly on each book.

Behind the green car was a litter of broken things, her daddy's church things. Quickly, she placed her doll in the gap between the seat and the window, pushing down until the doll's face disappeared from sight. She looked behind the car and saw the books falling. She imagined herself falling to the road, her skin ripping open like a book cover, the thin tissue inside tearing like pages against the black tar road.

Without warning, he spoke to her. "You ever been underground?"

She thought of worms and bugs. Dirt. She shook her head, but he was still talking.

"It get into your skin and your mouth, an' you never get it off, you got that shit coming out of your pores for fuckin' ever. You go underground, you'd know."

"No," said the girl tremulously. "No, I've never been underground."

The blackened chain around his neck bounced toward her, the red thing hanging on it like something alive. "It's hot too, y'know—it's hot ten thousand feet underground, like you're a little nearer to hell. It's like you gonna suffocate in some big womb.

"An' the air blast comes rushin' in like a freight train—that motherfucker is like fuckin' demon breath." He shuddered and slapped the wheel with the flat of his hand.

"I don't want to go underground," she replied.

Nervously, she stared outside for hours. There was only an infinite blur of motion. Fragments caught by the roaming headlights: wiry bushes, the outline of trees, pieces of light poles and old road signs. She began to count the poles, but they went by so fast she lost track. The lights in the distant houses fluttered by like anxious moths, melting into the night.

For none of us liveth to himself alone,
and no man dieth to himself.
—The Burial of the Dead, *The Book of Common Prayer*

THE TUNELESS noise of an old truck echoed across the Bitterroot Range. It was a rasping music, composed of the scratch of old windshield wipers, the cough of corroded valves, the whine of a rusted exhaust pipe, the thin buzz of a wire against the road. As the brown truck moved across the Idaho Panhandle, the gears shifted heavily, sliding down a scale made of metal and grease, skipping notes as gravel rattled against the undercarriage.

In late summer, the mining towns strung along the highway glimmered in the dusk, blighted jewels on a vast, stripped neck of mine tailings and blackened earth. The lights that blinked on top of the mine slag conveyors became flickering motes in a dense and dusty haze. Ore from deep underground drifted down, falling like heavy chunks of darker snow.

At night in the mountains, the ragged grunt of an engine could be heard from miles away, could be mistaken for some distant underground explosion. But the mines in the Silver Valley no longer ran at full capacity at night. The mountains resounded with the hum of heavy half-tons that carried an endless stream of equipment and supplies to the tourist destinations in Priest Lake and Coeur d'Alene, on the flat side of the Bitterroot Range.

The old truck with the bad engine took the road less traveled. It came out of Coeur d'Alene, went over Fourth of July Pass into the Bitterroot, and headed east toward Missoula, Montana. At the curve of Independence Loop, the truck briefly turned north, accelerating past the ghostly shadow of the Cataldo Mission. It went east again at the Sunshine Mine, and finally ground to a halt at the only remaining stoplight on I-90 between Boston and Seattle: Wallace, Idaho, former silver-mining capital of the world.

At Albi's Bar and Grill in Wallace, Matt Worthson found a table as far from the bar as he could get. The barkeep sauntered over to him, and stood there for a long moment. Old Albi's unsurprised expression never changed, no matter how many times Matt went dry. The possibility of a drink was always there, and as always Matt waited for a moment, the thirst for it turning, a worm of want impaled on a hook inside him.

"A cup of coffee," he said finally. "Black."

Albi gave a sardonic grin. Matt held up a sudden hand, silencing him, taking hold of the cup of hot coffee, a hungry man with a meal. He was not worried about the comments Old Albi had saved up to torment him with. He needed to think.

In fact, although Matt did not know it yet, these moments in Albi's Bar and Grill were the last moments he would have to think for weeks to come. If he had known, he might not have cared. Just then, his thoughts were an affliction, they would not give him peace.

Matt took a slug of hot coffee into his mouth and closed his eyes. The day before, he'd finally worked up the nerve to talk to the chaplain about his accident—previous to that conversation, no one except his best friend, Russ, had known what had happened. Telling a priest what he'd done was a big step. That's what they used to say in AA. So to keep his nerve up as he talked to Father Arlen, Matt had downed whiskey like water. Looking back, what he could remember of his conversation with Arlen made him feel ashamed. Telling someone about the accident hadn't helped. In fact, now he couldn't even remember exactly what he'd said, the latter hours of the night seemed as blurry as an alcohol-fueled fire. Ashes of memory.

For all he knew, he had busted up the place or insulted God or something. He had to have done something to have made Albi look at him now with such weary, cynical eyes.

But despite the embarrassment he'd made of himself, Arlen would still listen to him. The guy was a priest, a police chaplain. And besides, there was no one else he could tell about his son leaving town. He took a long swallow. The coffee burned on the way down.

After Doug had told them he was leaving, Matt had begun to feel an overwhelming sense that he couldn't hold it together anymore. It seemed like his world was busting into little shards and broken bits all around him. Just like after the accident and the election, four years back.

He'd talk to Father Arlen again. That's what he'd do.

Matt put his empty mug down and stepped to the door. Nothing ever changed: here he was, coming out of Albi's again, after eleven o'clock at night. He was only fifty-seven, but sometimes he felt like his life had ended a long time ago.

◇　◇　◇

The blue neon sign for Olympia beer blinked behind him. Someone yelled from inside to shut the goddamn door. Outside the Bar and Grill, the endless traffic on the highway was a rumbling murmur, it cut through the darkness.

Matt walked down the sidewalk, zipping his windbreaker closed to cover the Sheriff's Department uniform. It was late, but maybe he could still find Father Arlen. The man wouldn't turn him away.

As he turned the key and the engine came to life, the radio sputtered with sound. "Five-oh-seven," it hissed. "Come in, Lieutenant Worthson? Five-oh-seven—urgent call for five-oh-seven."

His head ached and his eyes were bloodshot with weariness, but automatically Matt reached out and picked up the microphone.

"Yeah, this is five-oh-seven," he said. "What is it? This is Matt—but I'm on my way home."

There was a crackling buzz, and then the thick voice of Sheriff Andrew Merrill punched through the static. "Matty?" he said. "Thank God I got ahold of someone. I need a lieutenant over at the Coeur d'Alene Resort—and I need you here fast. I got a body."

Matt swallowed dryly. Four years since he had last supervised a major crime scene. Why was Merrill calling him, of all people?

"The resort? Jesus, they won't like the bad publicity," said Matt. Even acts of God—rainstorms in July—seemed a personal affront to the tourist hotels in Coeur d'Alene. "What's—"

The sheriff's voice crackled over the radio. "Just get your ass over here, Matty. I need someone to be in charge, someone who won't fall apart on me."

There was a click and the radio went dead. Matt massaged his tired eyes, ran his quivering hands over the wrinkles on his face. The tremble had stayed on his hands ever since the accident. Even now, the accident and the way Matt had abdicated the election for Bitterroot county sheriff were connected for people who knew him only from the newspapers. Those in town who had known him for decades discounted what the newspapers had said about him then—the rumors, the innuendo, her subsequent death.

But Matt knew the truth.

He couldn't get rid of it, even four years after. Snow blowing across the road as the car slid sideways, the woman beside him moving, the sounds she made as her head collided with the glass, the shaking in his hands as he tried to pull them both out of the wreck. The snow falling all around, like stars melting into him as the engine popped and burned. Snow melting on her skin. Always with him.

He felt like getting rid of himself half the time now, he hardly cared why anymore. He thumped his fingers on the steering wheel, willing them to be still. In the neon light from Albi's Bar and Grill, the veins on the backs of his hands twisted darkly like paths running into his skin, a road map of journeys begun, destinations unreached.

The Coeur d'Alene Resort rose like a ridged needle over the lake. As Matt's old truck came down the long hill, the lights glittered far ahead. They sparkled indistinctly against the darkness of the lake. A mist was rising off the water, a thin fog that surrounded the media vans, the tourists with cameras, the police officers holding the line.

Matt knew the glossy advertising brochures by heart. Each luxury suite was the parapet of a customizable castle, each room was bathed in a fine glow of calibrated light, each and every balcony extended far enough to see the floating golf course a thousand yards out in the lake. He knew the brochures, but he'd never stayed in the damn place: few who lived in the city by the lake could afford the price of a room.

At eleven thirty that night, he had picked up his trainee deputy at the sheriff's station. Matt waited until they were near the resort to check the equipment. He turned his head and looked at the trainee, Jerry Kelberg. "You got everything we need?" he said.

Jerry touched the top of an oversized thermos, it stuck out of the camera bag on his shoulder. "Java is here. Notebooks, pens, tapes," Jerry said. "Camera and film."

"Right." Matt drummed his fingers on the steering wheel. "I wonder if Merrill called the chaplain, if he got hold of Father Arlen yet."

"What for?"

Matt glanced sideways at the kid. "Dead body. Family. Usually, folks need a chaplain. Why don't you try to raise Father Arlen?" Matt leaned across and rummaged through the glove box. "I got the priest's pager number here somewhere. He never minds getting called late at night. Doesn't bother him, as long as he's helping someone."

Jerry did not move forward. "What dead body?"

Matt killed the siren as they came closer to the resort parking lot, the sound murmuring away across the vast expanse of water. "Merrill treats you like a kid." Matt said it as a fact. "Why do you put up with that?" Jerry shook his head, as if he did not know.

"In Merrill's book, no one from outside Coeur d'Alene is worth a plugged nickel. Especially guys like you." The seething crowd of reporters and camera crews surged forward as the car came to a halt.

"You're from out of town too," Jerry said.

"Uh-huh. Silver Valley, wrong side of the mountains," grunted Matt. "Silver Valley. My pop was a miner too."

Jerry did not say anything in reply. Droplets of water streamed down the windows of the car. Their lights strobed over the waiting people, and then throbbed out.

The crowd of media moved with them as Matt and Jerry walked toward the resort. Questions peppered them from either side. "Any comment for us, Lieutenant?"

Flashbulbs spattered their faces with light. "What can you tell us about the dismembered body, Officer?" Matt waved the questions away, wordlessly.

Inside the Coeur d'Alene Resort, the floors were a deep maroon color. It reminded Matt of some ancient color, royal blood. The place was expensive enough for royalty: benches were carved from solid maple logs, fixtures were brushed titanium, the chandeliers hand-blown Chihuly glass.

"Call the chaplain," Matt repeated as they came around the corner. "Let me take a first look at the scene."

The corridor in front of the restrooms no longer looked royal. The hallway was strung with overlapping lines of yellow police tape. The center of the carpet was covered by a roll of plastic tarp, taped indiscriminately to the walls, the floors, and the maple benches. A sheriff's deputy was waiting for them at the restrooms, along with a man who was sitting on the floor, wearing a soiled Resort Security uniform.

Matt looked at the man on the floor. "I'm Lieutenant Worthson. You can call me Matt." He held out his hand, and then removed it when the man didn't look up. The security guard got to his feet slowly. Then he brought his coffee up close to his face as if he needed the heat more than the liquid.

"Robert Allen Fosworth." The man finally looked up at him. "Bob."

Matt took a notebook and a tape recorder out of his briefcase. He flicked the switch.

"The deputy told me over the radio that you're the one who found the body. Would you mind going in the bathroom with me—tell me what you did in there, what you saw?"

The security guard nodded at the tiny tape moving. "You gonna go with me, right?"

Matt nodded reassuringly and motioned them forward. Bob spoke in a vague mutter. "I mean, I didn't sign up for this, I just work for Tri-State . . . Jesus Christ, this week was supposed to be slow . . . I saw that—thought the toilets might be leaking again . . ."

On the floor there was liquid, a dark reflection glimmering on the maroon tile floor. It seemed to spread from the edge toward the drain in the middle of the room. The security guard pointed. "So I looked underneath the stalls—see where it was coming from . . ."

The doors of all the stalls were firmly shut. Matt bent over, craning his neck to see under the doors. In the first stall, he could see feet. Black wingtips with thin dark socks.

He straightened up and looked at Bob. "What did you do then?"

"I said . . . I said, ' 'Scuse me, the public areas of the hotel will be closing soon . . . 'Scuse me, sir' . . ."

Matt's shoes felt sticky, like he'd walked through hot blacktop on his way to work.

The security guard kept talking, his voice higher now, wavering with anxiety.

"I thought maybe he's drunk. 'Nother sleeper. So I went out first, give him time. But he didn't need the time, because he wasn't there anymore. Jesus Christ, what a way to die. See, I know him—that's what makes this so hard—"

"Before you saw the body, when you went out, did you see anyone else?"

"Let me think. No, I don't think I did." Then Bob slowly pointed upward, as if it took effort to think, effort to move. "Wait, yes. I saw Valerie Herrick, standing inside the elevator. You know her—hotel manager?"

"I know her," Matt said dryly. "She's not just the manager. Company president."

The guard nodded slowly. "One other—cleaning lady—name is May Brue, or Bruce or something. She musta been passing through too. Only folks I saw on my rounds."

Matt wrote the names in his notebook. "Okay, I got that. Thanks for the detail."

"When I come back, I tell him I'm a'gonna open the door, ask him if that would be okay." Bob shook his head again, mournfully. "But he doesn't say anything."

"And then you opened the door."

"It was locked."

"Locked? From the inside?"

"Sure was. Someone had fun doing this one." Bob's voice trembled for a moment. "So I tell the gentleman I'm gonna open the door, and I reach up underneath, my face almost touching what was on the floor, and I fumble away at the lock. And then . . ."

Matt looked again at the black wingtips. He pushed gently on the door and it swung open, a soundless motion.

The feet stayed there. The whole thing stayed there. Two feet in shoes on the floor, legs in soiled gray pants bent awkwardly, unnaturally, onto the seat of the toilet, and a pair of hips that projected crazily, out of the loop of a rawhide belt. Above the left pocket of the pants a shred of white hung down from a piece of mostly detached skin. At the beltline the bones were rounded and streaked with something purple and yellow, and for a moment he couldn't think what was the matter with the legs in front of him, and then he saw the stump of a backbone projecting an inch above the tattered, whitish, pinkish insides, and there was nothing above them.

Suddenly, he felt the nausea come over him. He dry retched, and pulled the door sharply closed again. The security guard was babbling away, which didn't seem to help.

"Goddamn, that's a bad thing to see, sir, goddamn, sir, are you all right?"

"Sure, I'm fine," Matt said, but he could hear that his voice was high and strange, and then he retched again, and this time he could taste it. He hung desperately to the door of the stall he was at and bent over so anything that came out wouldn't get on his uniform.

Jesus Christ, first serious case in four years, and he was going to pass out. He was going to pass out on the floor, in the cold sliding blood on the floor, with only a nervous security guard with him. He bent his head down, holding his elbows up and closing his eyes, willing himself not to pass out. For a moment, all he could hear was the blood rushing in his ears, the thrumming sound of surf.

Matt had pushed the next unlocked stall door open when he had bent over, and he turned now to get some toilet paper to wipe his mouth, to clean himself off. Balanced on the toilet and against the wall behind it were the missing parts. Not all of it, but enough to matter. The wall was streaked and splashed and blotted with red, as if it had taken a great deal of labor to balance that torso up there. The arms on the torso were twisted awkwardly, painfully, to hold the body up in the stall. The toilet paper beside the bowl was soaked through. It hung in thick chunks of bloody sodden paper from the holder. He did not want to look at what it was that overflowed the bowl and strung itself all over the seat of the dirty toilet. An ugly half inch of spine stuck up out of the dead white neck. He began to retch all over again, tasting the dry bitter bile coming up and dirtying his uniform shirt.

"Goddamn," the security guard was still muttering. Matt tried to steady himself, but the wet floor seemed to sink out from under him, as if he was lying on his back looking up at it. He lunged in the wrong direction and bumped hard into a post between the stalls. The doors of the first few stalls vibrated from the impact, all of them slowly swung open.

In the third stall, hair and forehead barely visible over the rim of the open toilet bowl, was the head.

Matt could feel a cold sweat start out on his chest, and then the heavy perspiration went all over his body, a sickness spreading. Under his fingers, he could feel the solid metal of the tape recorder case. He hefted his notebook like a charmed thing. Behind him, the security guard had never stopped saying "Goddamn, goddamn, goddamn" over and over until it was like a rosary.

"You said you knew the dead man?" said Matt hurriedly. "You know him?"

The security guard looked at Matt with haunted eyes. "Don't you know him too? It's the chaplain—Father Arlen, cut up in pieces. Arlen Bowman is dead, right here."

CHAPTER

◇ **2** ◇

Disappearances, apparitions . . . a thing will happen that
remains so unresolved, so strange, that someone will think
of it years later . . . in the dusk and silence, staring out the
window at another world.
   —John Haines, *The Stars, the Snow, the Fire*

ON THE west side of the Bitterroot Range, there was no sudden sinking of
evening into mountain and valley. Across the mountains, the twilight faded
slowly into the great waters of the lake, the sun settling softly across a hundred
thousand flat and fertile acres of wheat.

Although he did not know it, Kev Macht was driving his stolen car across
the land where the French and English first settled. They came to the great
lake to fish the depths, harvest the fields, cut down the trees, trade liquor for
land, and pillage the natives. But the natives drove hard bargains—the traders
said that they were sharper than most. Indeed, their hearts were thought to be
as hard as an awl: the French called them *Coeur d'Alene*. The white men had
thrown away everything they'd had before in order to make a new place for
their faith, and they were frustrated to find that they were unable to take the
land away from the natives.

White men still came to this part of the country thinking they could achieve
something they'd never known before. Kev Macht had done the same. He dis-
avowed his family and changed his name when he went to the Aryan Nations
compound in Hayden Lake. *Macht* meant *power*. That's what he wanted. He'd
shaved his head, cut his skin with a sign, thrown away everything he ever
cared about.

Yet since he'd left the Aryan Nations, he wasn't sure who he was anymore.
Kev had stolen a Walkman, snuck out at night, got on a Greyhound bus to
Coeur d'Alene, and then everything had changed. Something had gone wrong
after the bus station.

Now he had the old green car—he'd kicked some guy's ass in the station,
and the keys had somehow just ended up in his hand. But for some reason the
fight hadn't been that satisfying. Afterward, everyone else had gone away, even
the priest.

Kev could still hear the little man's voice in his head, the memory was like a vapor trail drifting with him over Fourth of July Pass, seeping out of the Silver Valley.

Somehow, even after all these hours alone, Kev couldn't escape the sound of that voice, each of those words still echoing inside, like floating leaves on the current of dark highway draining out endlessly behind him.

The little man on the bus had worn a disheveled suit. He slept with a yellow blanket under his head, leaning against the bus window. He was thin and bookish, overdressed and out of place on the late-night express from Missoula to Spokane. His tie was askew and the wrinkles in his suit looked permanent. He slept with his mouth open, the breath flickering against the window like a dusty flame. Each exhalation steamed and faded away as the bus moved through the valley. A crooked ornament on a chain bounced on his slight chest, swinging back and forth with each salivating snore.

As the bus accelerated out of Wallace, the inside aisle lights flickered out. The bodies within nodded into the darkness before twitching unevenly awake. The intermittent glare of headlights slanted over the gray faces within, faces that winked in and out of life.

When the snoring stopped, Kev slit his eyes open. There wasn't any fear in the little man's eyes at the sight of Kev, which was a surprise. The little man smiled and folded the yellow blanket more firmly under his head.

Kev remembered smelling her too, a dark elderly woman in the aisle of the bus, someone shuffling toward the rear.

"Stinks," he muttered. "Damn john stinks enough without a mongrel in there." He moved one boot toward the aisle, to block her passage. The bus bounced unevenly across a pothole. The old woman in the aisle hesitated.

Out of nowhere, the man next to him slid against his shoulder. Kev flinched as if at a spark. The little man nodded, as if he agreed with everything Kev had been thinking. Day-old gray whiskers littered his jaw. Veins filled his eyes with red. Kev decided there was nothing to him.

But when he spoke, it was something different again.

"So?" he said. "We might all stink some on the bus like this, huh?"

"Wha—?" Kev turned to the right and pulled the dead headphones off his head. The man's eyes were a striking blue, sharp as stones. Close at hand, the dark woman slid past in the aisle, hugging the other side.

"What're you saying? You saying I stink?" Kev clenched his fist so that the muscles and the scratches on his arm bulged out. Two weeks ago, he had taken a needle and a broken fountain pen and marked a swastika into his arm. It had hurt like hell, and the sign was still swollen, angry and red. He looked from under his brow at the little man. "You saying I stink?" Kev repeated.

The little man glanced at his arm and grinned. "Hey," he said. "Sure, I stink, you stink, we all stink. I'm just saying we all stink a little." The man's eyes flickered around, as if to take him in and everyone in the bus. As if they were the same. It was unsettling.

"Stink different too," he continued. "I'd agree with you there. Seems to me that we gotta put up with each other's stinks. After all, we all got our own, don't we? Because we're each one of us God's children. That's all I'm saying. We're all God's children."

Then he turned and looked directly at Kev. The little man didn't seem to care about his rage, how important it was. And because of that, it was as if the engine turning over inside Kev had gone into vapor lock. Something was gone from him.

Kev rubbed a hand over his face and looked away. "Huh," he said. "Whatever floats your fuckin' boat."

But the man just grinned again, as if he were pleased Kev had spoken at all. He held out a hand. "I'm Arlen," he said. "Father Arlen Bowman."

"Who the fuck you the father of?"

Arlen stopped talking. "I have a little girl. She's not here," he said. Then he grasped reflexively at the thing on his chest, holding it up for a moment. "But I'm also a father in a different way. I'm an Episcopalian priest. Some people like to call me Father."

Kev leaned closer, looked at the thing on the chain. It was a cross, a wooden cross. "Father?" he said. It made him see the little man differently: a priest, a father.

The priest let the cross fall to his chest and shook his head. "Just call me Arlen. And you are?"

Kev looked down the aisle and ran a hand over the bristles on his head. "Fuck who I am," he muttered.

Now he looked out the window of the green car, remembering that moment, staring again at his own face, reflected as a vacant blot.

Kev downshifted as he came out of Idaho into Washington State, where construction barriers and flashing signals marked the transition between the new highway and the old route of Interstate 90. Near the turnoff for Rathdrum, the words glimmered on a green highway sign with a broken light: Spokane 26 Miles.

If he let his eyes close for a moment, he could see the little man's blue eyes staring at him, unblinking and clear. His voice was strong, he held out his hand again.

"So," said the little priest. "What's your handle?"

Father Arlen was like no one Kev had ever met.

"Kevin Macht," he said, and then he took the father's hand into his. "*Macht* means 'power' in German. I go by Kev." But he still gripped the little man's hand hard, cracking the knuckles and bringing tears to the man's eyes.

Arlen grinned, and rubbed his knuckles. It was unsettling to Kev. In school, they only wanted to keep you quiet and brainwashed. In juvie, all anyone cared about was how fucked up you could get, and out at the shelters they only cared about how strong you were—if they could fuck with you or not. And in Hayden Lake, at the compound, it was how angry you could get, and who did you hate worse: the Jews or the mongrels? But the little preacher didn't seem to care about any of that. What did he care about?

As the night drained on, his voice never faded. Even as the grinding monotony of the highway reverberated up through the axles and the shocks into the undercarriage, rocking the people around them into uneasy slumber, Arlen stayed awake, wrapped in his yellow blanket. He asked questions about Kev, more and more of them. And before he knew it, Kev was talking too, telling the little man things he hadn't told anyone in a long time.

"See, some kids got their folks coming to see them in the joint all the time. But not me—no one ever visited me except for my friend Doug Worthson." He had no one anymore. But he didn't have to admit it. "See, this guy, Doug, he's the only guy stood by me. He's coming to pick me up at the bus station tonight . . ."

Kev's voice trailed off. Someone was moving forward in the aisle, swaying from side to side. Her hand glanced across his shoulder on its way to the next seat.

"I understand," Arlen was saying. "It's not fair. Every one of us needs . . ."

And then Kev realized that he hadn't even reacted when the mongrel bitch touched him. All the shit he'd been saying had made him weak. His reaction was delayed, like voltage that sings across the circuit, bouncing you off the wire. The burn comes after.

"You think you know it all, dontcha?" Kev blurted. "You think you know every fuckin' thing I'm going through! You don't know anything!"

Father Arlen stopped talking. He turned toward Kev again, his eyes empty of feeling. "No," he said calmly. "You're right. I don't know anything."

Kev knew right then that they were in a different place. But he couldn't stop talking. And Arlen stayed there, looking at him. It was as good a reason as any to tell him to go to hell. "Fuck you, Mister Know-It-All, if you got all the fuckin' answers to life."

Arlen shook his head wordlessly, as if to emphasize that he did not have answers. Suddenly, Kev felt as if he were trying to talk himself into something. And he didn't have the stomach for it anymore.

Kev raised his voice in frustration. "Tell me this then, why the fuck you here, *huh*, if you know it all? You're just a loser on some godforsaken bus-to-nowhere, with all the shitty bums and the whores—why the hell're you here?"

Arlen sighed. "You want to know why I'm here." It was a flat statement, but it seemed to provoke something in the little man. He turned his face toward the window, his eyes blinked rapidly. Kev wondered if the little priest had finally flipped his lid.

Then Arlen spoke out loud. His voice hadn't changed. "I guess it's only fair. You're here because you're running away from something, and I—"

"See, you got it wrong already," interrupted Kev. "It was *those fuckers* that—"

Arlen held up a hand. "As far as I can make out, you're leaving Hayden Lake on your own, am I right? You wanted to hear my story, so let me *tell* you. I'm here because I guess I'm not running away. I guess I'm running to someone, to something. I'm not sure what yet. I was helping someone. And it kind of turned sour." Arlen sighed. "He, uh . . ."

"What did he do? Who was this?"

"I told you," Arlen turned to face him. "It went sour—he started calling me. Called me all the time. I think he was asked to do it. Wanted some information. It was in a notebook I had. He did some juvenile things at first. Broke windows in my church."

"I woulda fucked him up," muttered Kev.

Arlen nodded, as if the thought had crossed his mind. "But things changed then. I got him talking about his situation. He talked some, I listened some, and he seemed to hear me when I talked. I think I was kind of helping him for a while. Maybe if I listen to him more, we can get him to a place where he's willing to bring in the police. See, he's not the guilty party at all, instead it's—"

"Dude." Kev leaned forward, glowering in the priest's face. "You haven't answered the question. Why the hell are you on this bus?"

"Well, I got him to agree to meet me. In person."

"How'd you do that? You gonna pay him off or something? You got money?"

Arlen blinked in surprise. "Yes, I suppose I do," he said slowly. "I have money—I hadn't thought of paying him something." He touched his front pocket, where the bulge of a wallet rested. "But no, he's meeting me because he's going to get something else."

"What's that?"

Arlen gave a slight grin and hitched the blanket up on his shoulders. "I told him I had the notebook with the information he's been looking for."

"So, you got the notebook with you?"

Arlen shook his head. "No, actually, I'll explain the situation to him when we meet—I'm sure he'll understand. We can go get it. For safekeeping, I gave it to a friend."

Arlen hunched his shoulders again and sighed, as if ashamed of what he was about to admit. "See, he anted it up a notch earlier today. I was over here in the Silver Valley, with my friend, and with my daughter. But then he took her. He stole my car, and my little girl."

Kev remembered Father Arlen's face changing after that part of the story. The terror welled up in him, his voice grew shrill and fearful when he talked about his girl. Up close, his face was pressed with reddened wrinkles. Even at the memory of the hitch in Arlen's voice, Kev could feel his nerves going jittery. Sure, he was going straight-edge, but he needed just one more pill.

"I can't let anything happen to her," said Arlen suddenly. "God, he can't hurt—"

"So this guy who took your car, he's like someone you know?" said Kev. "A bud?"

"No, not really," said Arlen hesitantly. "The only way I can get through this is to think of him as . . . my neighbor. God will help me, God will—"

"Well, if this guy is your 'neighbor,' he's a shitty one, that's for sure. He's torturing you, man. Messing with you. Calling you all the time, he broke the windows in your church, now he took your car, with your little girl. He's fucked up. He's fuckin' *you* up."

Arlen rubbed a finger slowly on his jawline as he looked out the window. He looked haggard now, any belief in his future stripped from his bones.

"Yes, you might be right," he said. "But he's not going to hurt her. He's just a little anxious right now, and I have to stay calm, I can't get too—"

"Dude. This guy is *fuckin'* with you. And now he has your kid, and—"

Then Arlen looked at him, his sharp blue eyes filled with an impenetrable answer. Despite the residue of speed in him, Kev suddenly felt a shiver, something that got through his skin and deep inside. Somehow, Arlen knew more about the insides of people than any of the blustering Aryan kids at Hayden Lake.

Kev looked down at his own chest and tensed the muscles in his arms. The shirt he wore showed a death's-head with horns, eating a bleeding woman tied up with chains made of snakes. The snakes bled too. Somehow, it hadn't made the impression he'd hoped for.

Arlen touched his jaw again and looked back out the window. After a moment, he spoke once more, as if he were continuing an interrupted thought. "So I'm going to get my child back, yes, but also I need to talk to him. He needs something no one seems to have given him yet. Redemption."

"What the hell do you mean by that?"

"A way to move on." Arlen looked at him, blinking his blue eyes. "Hope."

"A way to move on," muttered Kev, remembering what Arlen had said on the bus. "Yeah, wouldn't I like some of that now too."

The light poles outside the windows of the car floated past, disappearing as they reached his reflected face, flickering on the windowpane. They sank out of the wake of the car, as if they were satellites, revolving ceaselessly.

Kev pulled a hand over the sharp bristles on his skull. He remembered wondering if the little priest had just made it all up. Maybe the little girl was just the last rotten residue of some bad meth leaching out of the little man's brain. He remembered thinking that maybe the priest would even leave his thick wallet unguarded.

Kev looked down at his bloody knuckles gripping the wheel. Damn, it hurt to punch someone that hard. He'd been willing to fight. He'd proved that, in spades.

He'd told the priest, straight out, after he swallowed the reddy. "You meet up with this fucker at the bus station, I'll take him out for you."

The priest didn't want him to make trouble. "I don't need you to fight for me," he said. "You're a son of God, I wouldn't want you to do that to another."

Kev rubbed his palm across his aching bloody knuckles. "Ain't nobody called me no son of God," he said. "I been called a son-of-a-bitch plenty, but never no son of God."

But after the priest said that, it had all gone sideways.

When Kev took the reddy, he'd decided it was time to fuck someone up, even as Father Arlen held on to that little wooden cross and kept talking. "Once she's safe, I'll be able to tell everyone. I'll tell you now, this is the true story . . ."

The only minister Kev had ever met before was Reverend Butler at Hayden Lake. This one had been different though. He was a fuckin' righteous piece of work.

Kev recalled opening his eyes when the shriek of the air brakes woke him. Then he stared through the glass of the bus window, seeing if there was someone he could scam a ride off. Doug wasn't here, no one was here for him.

While the people picked up their coats and shuffled past, Kev heard Arlen's breath come in hurried uneven gulps. The little man moved as he slept, turning his head nervously as if to see through closed eyelids, twitching his hands, holding someone off. When Kev moved his arm, the body of the little man jumped, as if from an electric shock.

In that moment, Kev glimpsed a face on the other side of the bus window. Down in the station. A little girl. The expression in her eyes burned into him, fear grown into a vast exhaustion. Kev's hair prickled on his scalp. The girl was real after all.

She came toward the bus, dragged close beside a man with dragons tattooed on his arms. Under the fluorescent lights of the station, her face gleamed a stark white.

As Father Arlen twitched and shivered next to him, the thought came to Kev that she was in the wrong man's nightmare.

She swayed back and forth, stepping to a dance only she could hear. The dress was close to her skin, it moved when she did, shimmer in a dark dream.

Kev stroked a hand across the swollen swastika on his arm. Then he took hold of the little man's shoulder, shaking him until there was a sound, a choking rattle in his throat.

"Good God, what is it?"

"Hey, Arlen," Kev said. "Is that her? That your little girl?"

What happened after he saw the girl was something Kev tried to forget. The memory stayed with him in the car. Part of him remained there forever, watching her dance in the thin and wavering light, as if the rest of his life never happened at all.

The dead person must undergo certain ordeals that
concern his own destiny . . . he must also be recognized
by the community of the dead and be accepted among them.
—Mircea Eliade, *The Sacred and the Profane*

THE IRON taste of blood was pungent in the closed air of the public bathroom.
Matt helped Jerry set up his camera equipment in front of the line of stalls. It
was as if they were waiting for someone to emerge.

Matt had washed himself off as best he could. His head was clear now as he
opened the stall doors, taping them back so that the camera would have a clear
line of sight.

It was after he'd been working for a half hour that he realized he'd left the
other deputy sitting in the hallway without instructions. Instead of busywork,
he should be telling other people what to do. He wasn't used to being in charge.

He handed Jerry the camera tripod. "Start taking pictures," he said. "I've
got work."

Outside the bathroom, he saw that the deputy sitting in the hall was Dustin
Hartman. Hartman's eyes were red and swollen, his face streaked with tear
tracks.

As Matt approached, Hartman spoke. "Valerie Herrick said wait for the officer in charge . . ." His voice began to shake. Matt looked at him, waiting for
him to get a handle on himself. "Do you know who that is, because I'm just—"

"That's me," said Matt. "And don't look so damn surprised, Dusty. So you
left all this hanging so I could take care of it? And you're taking orders from
Valerie Herrick? Have the Herricks been blabbing to the media? I heard—"

"No, no—Valerie said . . . she said . . . I mean . . ." The deputy trembled
around the mouth again. "I know the guy, the guy who's dead. How can Father
Arlen be dead?"

"I hear you." Matt put a hand on his shoulder. "You've been here awhile,
right?"

Hartman nodded. "Too damn long. First deputy to get here after Lieutenant
White. And the lieutenant is over on the other side of the Resort now, checking
on witnesses."

Matt opened his mouth to ask why Lieutenant White hadn't been put in charge of the scene, and then it came to him. Russ White was married to the owner of the Resort. Matt was surprised though that Sheriff Merrill had recognized the clear conflict of interest—Merrill wasn't known for such distinctions.

Hartman was still talking. "We've been holding the fort down, waiting for you to show up. What took you so long?"

Matt ignored his question. "Look, I want you to hold yourself down right now, pull yourself together. That's your job right now, you hear me?"

Hartman shook his head. "Hell, this is all wrong. He was our priest, Matt!" Some of the spit on the deputy's lips spun out toward Matt. "A fuckin' man of God!"

Matt glanced at the security guard sitting shell-shocked in the hallway. "Get a grip on yourself," he said quietly to Hartman.

He'd give the man a job, that would calm him down.

"Go tell Valerie Herrick—if she's still here—or the night manager, whoever it is, that we need a ground-level hotel room. Need it all night."

The deputy gathered himself. "Sure thing, Lieutenant, but I think they're sold out."

"Well, get me a storage closet with a phone—anything," said Matt. "Check in with the backup lieutenant—let Russ White know where they put us. We've got to interview the staff before they leave for the night. And get some of those deputies to rotate in here, I need someone who can hold himself together. Hell, just go find Lieutenant White, okay?"

Hartman nodded again, his jaw quivering. He swallowed hard.

Matt put a hand on the deputy's arm. "There's more to do here. A lot more. And I need you focused, on target. You'll be okay, just shake it off."

Dustin shook off his arm angrily, and Matt saw that Hartman was embarrassed now, he was enraged by Matt's attention.

Hartman turned and moved past him, barging blindly down the hallway. The young man would not forgive him for seeing his weakness. Matt shook his head wearily. In the silence, he could hear the subdued click of Jerry's camera, the whirr of the advancing film. The security guard spoke to Jerry then, his voice echoing in the hallway.

"You know there's bodies in there, kid."

Matt looked down at the older man and saw that his hands were still shaking. His voice had a thin, hoarse edge.

"People got cut up."

"I know," said Jerry. But Matt couldn't catch his eye quick enough to stop him talking about what he'd seen. "There's not as much blood as I'd expect for a dismembered body. From what I can see, the stalls are pretty banged up, and there are slide marks there on the floor in the blood. Found a shoe print in the corner, untouched, not the deceased's. Got a good shot."

"Those must be my shoes there. I slid on the floor. Got myself red all over," said the security guard. "Goddamn me . . ."

Matt was making a list of deputies when he heard a voice he recognized. Russell White. Matt shook Russ's hand with a sense of relief. "So you got the staff covered? Hartman told me you were talking to witnesses?"

Russ shook his head. "Jesus, Matty, do I need to hold your hand on all these things? You took forever to get here. And now the word is, you can't hold your dinner, you pansy-ass little—"

"Save the insults for your mother." Matt laughed. "At least I got you to clean up my messes. Until you retire, eh?"

Russ grinned wearily. "Look, I just wish you could have spared me this one. I got plans for the future. I don't need this on my mind." He sighed and straightened his shoulders. "But hey, you need help, I'm your man. I think we've already found some folks who might have seen the perp. I'm starting with the staff—you need the staff interviews completed, right?"

Matt nodded.

"No problem. I'm all over it," said Russ. "And we already have the artist working on a composite. I got a description from the staff here at the resort, and some guy at the twenty-four-hour pharmacy says he saw a guy wearing those clothes."

"All right—sounds like things are moving along. Need anything else?"

"Well, Nancy Ferreday is helping me do the interviews, so that'll be quick and easy." Nancy was a psychologist employed on criminal cases by the county.

Russ grinned and pointed toward Jerry, who was still snapping pictures of the floor. "We left the bathroom for you to examine, of course. You and the CA from Spokane—some young guy named Storgen—you guys will cover the dirty work for us."

"Thanks a lot!" Matt held out a pair of gloves. "Here—take a look with me?"

Russ waved off the gloves, laughing. "No way, not before the election!"

"Yeah, like you'll win anything. Andy's never lost before."

"Screw the fat guy—I'm gunning for him in January."

Matt looked quizzically at Russ. "Hell, I never took you seriously about that." Andy Merrill had been in the office so long that for most people, Merrill and the office of sheriff had become synonymous. In the summer, the Spokane papers had exposed a kickback scheme, and afterward the County Commissioners had censured Sheriff Merrill and mandated a special election for January. But no one had prohibited Andy Merrill from running for his office again.

But then Russ grinned and asked the same question.

"Whattaya think—seriously—do I have a chance against Merrill?"

"Snowball's chance in hell," said Matt. "Nobody'll ever beat Andy for sheriff."

"You never know." Russell smiled and clapped a hand on Matt's shoulder. Then the grin slipped off his face. "Jesus, Matty, this is wrong from one end to the other. What did we do to get stuck with Father Arlen's death? What did I do?"

Matt grimaced in reply. "I hear you—this is the last thing I need in my life right now. I told Merrill a few months ago I needed a lighter load, what with Pop's health problems and all. I can't work fifty to sixty hours a week right now."

Russ glanced at his notes again. "Last thing I need is a time of death. Do you have that yet? Nancy and I need to pin these people down as to when and if they heard anything. If there was just this one guy involved, or if more than one person did this. Bathroom gets banged up like this, someone has to have heard something."

Matt shook his head. "I wish I had that for you. But things are a bit confused with the body—you might have to wait for the Spokane coroner's office to figure that one out."

"Sounds like this is going to depend a lot on what the Spokane techs tell us. But I gotta tell you, so far this looks just like the Metaline Falls thing. Same guy might have stopped by Coeur d'Alene. The FBI thinks they're tracking a serial killer over there."

"They would." Matt shrugged. "I'm gonna sort this out a bit before I go with that."

"Hey, it's your ballgame," said Russell. "Just keep in mind you'll have to tell those damn reporters something. They'll be asking about that. You saw them—even the TV stations from Spokane are here."

If Merrill showed up, he'd want to have a statement ready to read. He liked to press the flesh and be seen on television. And he liked to have all the answers in front of him before he spoke. So there was that to do as well.

The bathroom was crowded. Jerry took pictures and the coroner's technician measured dents and splashes of blackened stains on the walls. Matt was dusting the bathroom door handle with ninhydrin powder.

Each print emerged as a round spiral, seeming to rise up from the depths of the metal. Matt thought most of the prints were Robert Allen Fosworth's.

He turned his head at the sound of a booming voice. Someone was pushing through the barrier of deputies at the entrance, laughing and talking with them as he moved forward.

It was Sheriff Andy Merrill, finally arriving at the scene. When he got down the hallway, the sheriff squatted down in the hallway beside Matt. His breath puffed out, the fingerprint dust steaming off the handle in a miniature black cloud.

"So, you got the guy in custody yet?" said Merrill. He looked at his watch. "I've left you here for—what?—three hours. You must have got the case wrapped up by now!"

Matt reached down with the fingerprint brush. The handle was done. He began dusting the area of the door just above the latch—often hands grasped this part of a door to swing it open. He did not answer.

"So," said Merrill. "When are the Feds due to come in? I figured I'd show up just in time to meet them."

"Actually," said Matt. "I haven't called them."

"Whoa, what the fuck're you playing at? I mean, deputy called in, said the lead on the case is losing his lunch here, what's that about?" said Merrill. "And you haven't called the FBI yet? Russell said we got a serial case here. Murder, dismemberment."

"Yeah, I can see that, Andy, but . . . ," Matt looked up at Merrill, and the pig-gish glee in his face. It made him angry, gave him some sort of unlooked-for resolve.

"Look, I think I can handle this case on my own," Matt said. "I'm fine now. I can do this thing."

"Well, that's good to hear, at least. Maybe something good will come out of this after all. I could use a breaking case with the media." Merrill put his head back in the bathroom. "Jeezus, lots of picture rolls. How many pictures Jerry taken so far? Any of 'em useful?"

"I don't know. I figure we'll process them, and work out which ones might actually help our case. We'll need the scene kept closed for a while of course."

"I see," said Merrill. He stood heavily. "So, anything I should know?"

Matt stopped dusting "No, not much. I've got competent guys here. Except for—"

Merrill guffawed. "Hey, I'm real sorry about Russell, but that's not my fault. Valerie Herrick twisted my nuts on that one—made me promise to have him on the scene."

"No," said Matt. "Russ White is not the guy I'm complaining about."

"What?" Merrill squinted at him, as if unable to see clearly. "You aren't pissed about Valerie Herrick pulling her favorite lieutenant into this mess? That's a major conflict of interest. Matty, you can be honest—"

"I don't care about Russ," said Matt. "Don't misunderstand. That's not the guy I'm thinking of—Russ is all right. He's the best right-hand man you could have found."

Merrill guffawed and lifted his weight from the doorframe. "Look, Matty, even though you helped him get off on a technicality, you and I both know that Russ screwed—"

"Dammit, Andy!" Matt angrily stripped the rubber gloves from his hands. "Russ didn't know she was underage. He's a damn good officer. Get some perspective, would you? We've got Arlen dead, and you're still worried about politics? About Russ?"

Merrill held up a hand. "Hey, knock it back a notch, Matty—I mean, yeah, just between you and me and the shithouse, I'm always worried about the fuckin' politics. And I'm going to ask you to make sure that Russ doesn't do the press tonight. You can do—"

"Why should I exclude him from that?"

Merrill sighed. "To tell the truth, Matty, it'll look way the hell too presidential just as the filing deadline for sheriff comes up."

Matt threw his gloves angrily in the trash. "See, what did I tell—"

"Hell, Matty, listen—there's another side to it too. I'm not doing my job tonight if I don't worry about the potential conflict of interest. He's married to Valerie, after all."

Matt turned back and glared at him suddenly. "Andy, don't worry your pretty little head, okay? I'll do the damn press conference. How about you worry about the politics and the conflicts of interest, and I'll get the real work done, okay?"

Matt did not wait for a reply. He moved back into the depths of the blood-streaked bathroom and lifted the radio from his belt. He needed two more deputies: one to cover the hallway, and another to finish the fingerprint work.

Russell White looked dirty. His sleeves were pushed up, brown rings around his wrists above the plastic gloves. And he had coffee cupped in his hands, the white Styrofoam smudged with streaks of rusty residue. The steam rose into his face.

"I'll be honest with you," he said. "I'm here because Val is paying me back."

"For what?"

Russ glanced over at the Spokane coroner's assistant working in the same room, a man named Rick Storgen who was studiously ignoring them both. Storgen and one of his technicians were examining the scene. Already they had laid the body out on clear plastic, the pieces on two stretchers.

Russ pointed down at his crotch. "You know," he said. "I been letting the little head make decisions again. Gets me in the doghouse . . ."

Matt shook his head, a great fatigue coming over him. Some things never changed. He glanced away from Russ, he looked down at the stretchers on the floor.

The body lying there seemed oddly unreal. The flesh was wrapped in plastic to keep fluids from draining on the floor, and in the uncertain light, the pieces seemed to have fallen apart accidentally. The flesh was swollen and pale all around the broken edges.

Russ took off his gloves, stripping them wearily from each of his fingers. Russ's hands caught Matt's eye. The nails were rimmed with a dark residue, the spirals on his fingers filled with the brown rust from the body. "Jesus," Matt said. "You're covered in the stuff—we should have been more careful about the crime scene."

Russ shrugged. "Just part of the job, right? Cleaning up messes—it's what we signed up for. There's no being careful about it. No one's gonna live forever, you know."

"Gentlemen?" said Storgen, "Sorry to interrupt—but I think my team might have some preliminary data, and I thought, considering, that you—"

"Yeah, go ahead," said Matt. He glanced at Russ, who nodded and lifted his coffee for another sip. The steam fogged his glasses as the coroner's assistant spoke.

"All right." Storgen held an unlit cigarette that twitched almost imperceptibly. He might have been holding a tool, working it with his fingers. "Body temperature says that time of death was between six and seven. That's inaccurate, of course, because the cavity was opened."

"What do you mean by that?" said Russ.

"I mean that there may have been a long interval of time—as long as a day, potentially—between the time of death and the body being dismembered."

Storgen plucked at the edge of the plastic, pulling it tighter around the torso. Detached from the neck, Arlen Bowman's head was turned to the side, as if he were turning to get up.

"Earlier, you said his throat was cut? Are you sure that was the cause of death?" Matt looked up from the broken neckline. He looked at the dull blue eyes on the stretcher. The eyelids hadn't closed all the way. Water was beaded on the dead cheeks and brow, as if it had sweated through the skin.

Storgen hesitated as he spoke. "Reasonably sure—it's hard to tell with all the trauma of the dismemberment. But I can tell you one thing—his throat wasn't cut here. We don't have enough fluids for a jugular spill here, even though the body was obviously chopped up in the bathroom." Storgen pointed at the deep gouges in the sides of the stalls, the cracked tiles on the floor.

"What else happened to him? Anything before the throat?"

"Oh yes, there was a lot that happened before the blood loss. The skin was cut in all sorts of places, and burned. But you can't see it, unless you take the clothes off."

"But that might not have been the same person—the same time at least—doing the killing and the dismemberment?" asked Matt.

Russ laughed. "I don't know how you come up with this stuff, Matty!"

Storgen shrugged. "We don't know. I can tell you that it was all carefully done. If you look at the face and the wrists—the skin on the ankles, under the socks too, the socks and shoes were replaced afterward—you'll see here this sticky white residue. The skin is slightly abraded in the same places." Storgen pointed to the flesh just below the palms, and around the lips, where it was bruised and dotted with tiny spots of blood.

Matt swallowed thickly and rubbed his hands together to feel the skin move, waxy and smooth, the hair paper thin against his fingertips.

"He was taped very tightly with duct tape to keep him from moving or crying out," continued Storgen. "This kind of tape doesn't come off very easily. That's why the soft flesh is swollen, broken around the mouth. See, the perp ripped it off after."

Rick Storgen held the pale leg on the stretcher. Using a pair of tweezers, he pulled the man's sock carefully down. "There's something interesting here though. Here and there, on the places where the duct tape stuck, there are some tiny bits of foliage."

Matt pointed at the leg. "Leaves?"

"Pine needles," replied Storgen. "I'd have the coroner's office in Spokane analyze them to be sure, but it looks like white pine to me."

"So somewhere outside the building."

Storgen rubbed the stubble on his jaw and grimaced. "Yeah, most probably. But this is kind of tricky. The cut throat and the lack of the rest of the blood—it's odd. The degree of turpitude in the flesh says that it happened after death, a few hours at least. Doesn't make sense."

"Huh—maybe he was killed elsewhere, and then just chopped up here?" said Matt.

Russ guffawed unexpectedly. "That's an odd idea. Why would anyone do that?"

"No, not so odd," said Storgen. "That idea might fit—perhaps the perpetrator transported him. Perhaps more than one person was involved. And if you're considering that possibility, maybe Reverend Bowman could have died hours ago, even a day or two ago. The body could have been preserved somehow?" Storgen considered, rubbing his jaw.

Matt caught Russ's eye. "So maybe you can tell the resort people—hell, just tell Val—that the chaplain probably didn't die here. That'll be a relief, at least."

Russ gave a weak grin. "Yeah, that would be something my wife would be happy to hear. I might get back in the sack, just for passing that on."

Storgen looked at Russ and nervously flicked some nonexistent ash off his cigarette. "Anyway, gentlemen, I think we're done here. After the photographer finishes, you can transfer the body to the morgue." Then Storgen turned to Matt.

"I'll send you my report on Monday." He turned and left the room.

Jerry pulled the plastic aside and took two more pictures of the face. The features of the dead man flashed hot white and then dropped into gray again. The image stayed with Matt, but he saw it in a different context: the eyes closed, the man standing in a briefing room in front of the deputies, the lips moving slowly, hands folded. Something in the photographic light made the face appear surprised, awakened. He remembered Arlen alongside him as they met with a family that had lost their mother in a fire. He saw the same face reflected in his rearview mirror, sitting in the backseat of a patrol car on its way to the annual sheriff's barbecue. He thought of the chaplain talking to his son that time Matt found the pot in his son's room.

And he remembered the last time he'd seen Arlen alive. They'd sat together for hours in Albi's Bar and Grill, Matt doing most of the talking. Now a lot of that evening was black to him—whiskey had a way of wiping the time clean. He didn't even remember leaving the place. Vaguely though, he could remember Arlen's face early in the night, nodding in sympathy. Anyone else, he wouldn't have shared half as much. The man had a way of listening that kept you calm, told you things would be all right. Matt could see him again, smiling, his blue eyes flashing with humor and good will. Arlen.

The face flashed in relief, and faded away again.

A resinous darkness had seeped into the corners of the room. Traces of the black ninhydrin dust, for fingerprinting, still glinted on the handles and doorjambs. He'd been here for six hours, it was almost morning. Russ had left some time ago, along with most of the rest of the shift. Soon the day-shift deputies would arrive and lock down the scene.

Matt pulled on another pair of latex gloves with a snap, and felt for his notebook and flashlight. When he turned the flashlight on, the room seemed to expand into shadow. Under the uneven light, the flat floor seemed concave, curving up to fill the edges with darkness.

Over the intervening hours, he felt as if things had settled into themselves, congealing so that anything that could have been revealed was hidden under the weight of the real. There was only what had always been there. The door, the stalls, the toilets, the tile floor, the faux-marble counter. He shone his flashlight against the walls, the stall doors, the toilets, the tiled floor. The shape of the sinks seemed different. They swelled out at him, the only purely white things in an uneven gloom.

He played his light over the splashed brown drops on the wall, and the taped notations that surrounded the gouges in the walls, the penciled lines around the splash trajectories, showing where the drops had come from. He moved his faint light into the corners of the room. Nothing waited there. They were empty, bare and deserted.

At just after six in the morning, Matt pulled in his driveway and parked beside Sall's Jeep on the verge of the grass. A book had been left in the car. He picked it up. There was no cover, the first page had the title: *Hanging Woman Creek*, it said. Louis L'Amour. A page was dog-eared where Jerry Kelberg had stopped reading.

When he opened the door to the bedroom he could see Sall's shape flung out across the bed. After the fight about Doug, Sall and he hadn't talked for two days. He'd tried not to come home until he had something to say. But he'd never come up with anything.

In the bed, Matt could see the thin blue veins on the insides of her thighs. In the spill of the light a faint pulse moved under her skin. He felt a sudden tenderness. Then an instant later came his memory of the blood in that bathroom, the pieces they had placed on two stretchers.

Matt paused beside the bed. Then he went back to the front door and locked it.

When he came back to the bedroom, he could see Sall's nursing outfit was piled in a rumpled mass against the far wall. He placed his uniform atop it, and pulled the bedsheet down gently, so that her thighs were covered, and turned off the light.

＊ ＊ ＊

SEPTEMBER 1988

THE GIRL was small enough that she could stand in a wheat field, when the stalks hadn't yet reached three parts of the way toward their full height, and be lost in them, her pale hair blending in with the yellow of the fields.

Looking out from the bluff, the girl could see the faint edge of the Palouse Country—it was all fields there, like the dry rustling of the wheat behind her. From Five Mile Prairie, the whole of the Spokane Valley was spread out below her. She could see the river that ran like silver twine through the valley and the buildings, toylike far below. She could feel the wind on her skin.

From where the girl stood, the houses near the Prairie bluff were scattered, like so many blocks. The hills on the other side of the valley were covered by the shadow of a cloud. Her hair drifted and waved in the slight breeze that always came over Five Mile Prairie in the morning. She pushed her hair away from her eyes and squinted. The strands flipped back into her face and one caught in her mouth.

Absently, she wound the strand of hair around her fingers and began to suck on the points, pushing them together with her tongue into one sodden clump.

She closed her eyes and saw her father turn away from her again, held tightly by the man with the dirty ink all over his skin, a blue-black smear. The dragons glared at her as they twisted on his skin. Her daddy was going away forever.

The wind struck the wheat field behind the girl, and the rushing sound of it filled the air, gusts moving across that bright ocean of wheat. The girl closed her eyes. The air struck her a moment later, the wave washing over her, covering her skin with a fine sheen of dust, swirling past her and rattling the scarecrow cans that hung between the house and the garden, slapping the screen door, brushing the windows with bits of grit. She choked on the chaff in her mouth. When she could breathe again, she opened her eyes.

Her dress was covered in the small things left behind by the wind. All over her arms and legs were tiny bits of dead wheat husk, it seemed like a million bugs had landed on her skin. The gust of wind died out in dust devils that whirled across the yard and disappeared among the weeds.

When the man in the uniform came to the house, the girl looked up. At first, she had thought his car was her mother returning. Now that she knew he was in the house alone with her grandmother, she was nervous. Every time someone came to the house, her grandmother was angry with her afterward. She never said why.

The girl let the water from the hose run wild, swirling around each of the stalks and pebbles. Looking down at the running water, she remembered the lake, she heard again the feverish dream of voices all around her.

"You aren't fuckin' with me, are you? Everyone fucks with me."

A hissing voice: "Goddammit—shoot the bastard! Scary motherfucker!"

A groan in her ear: "I got a knife. Big-ass pigsticker."

But her father's voice always echoed in her head: "God will be with me. Anyone can be redeemed."

Then there was the silence of the interior of the other car, the single light glaring at her from the dashboard. The other voice with her, whispering over and over, "I'm your daddy now. I'll take care of you. Just don't worry about him anymore."

"Close your eyes." She pushed her fists into her eyes until there was only a red darkness inside her head. "Close your eyes, your daddy will be right here." The darkness pulsed back at her. "Close your eyes."

O soul, be changed into little water drops
And fall into the ocean, never to be found.
—Christopher Marlowe, *Doctor Faustus*

THE FIELDS were burned in the fall, after harvest. Outside of Post Falls, between the Bitterroot and Spokane, the burn started as soon as the wheat was in the silos. On windy days, the smoke came off the country and coiled around the basin of the Spokane Valley, hemmed in on one side by Five Mile Prairie and the dry heights of Eastern Washington.

On the day that Matt Worthson took his wife, Sall, with him on a visit to Spokane, the wind seemed to follow them. Fed by the hot updrafts of the burning stubble, the breeze brought cinders and soot from burning piles of hay. It filled the sky above Spokane with debris.

Sall's dirty-blond hair swung in around her arched eyebrows as she turned her head back toward Matt, her lip curling with yet another sarcastic remark.

"Some father you were. You never gave a damn about Doug anyway, why do you care that he's left now?" Even after all these years, she was every bit the unstoppable force she'd always been, her derision like acid, eating away at his every failing.

Matt didn't say anything in reply. After Doug had stormed out of the house, the only thing he'd asked her was, "Why did he leave?" One sentence, but she had a lot of answers. It seemed to him that she'd been saving some of these things up to say for decades.

"Twenty damn years you've worked for the sheriff's," she'd said. "Twenty years at the same damn desk job for Merrill. Sure you got the pity promotion after the last election—but where has it gotten you, Matt? Jesus Christ, Matt, the kid has his own life now, and yours is hardly a life to look up to."

But he didn't say anything, and eventually she stopped too. It seemed to Matt that they were always coming back to this place where no one talked to each other. It seemed hard to recall that in the early days of their marriage, they'd spent hours together every Saturday morning, cooking breakfast together. That had been gone for a long time now.

He thought of the time three years ago, after the accident, when he'd stopped talking to Sall at all. Near the end of that spell, Sall had found some comfort on her own. She had been gone from the house for days at a time. When she came back to the house late one Saturday morning he asked her to stay, sitting at the beer-stained table, bloodshot eyes looking up at her.

She didn't give him an answer for half the week. But sometime that week, she began to speak to him, haltingly, as if he had been the one who had left her.

Sall rolled her car window up as the wind lifted chaff off the field and the dusty air gusted across the highway. She sighed, interrupting his thoughts. "These damn fields always screw up the air in the fall!" And although Matt knew that her sigh had nothing to do with the burning fields or the chaff-filled air, he was still grateful. At least she wasn't talking about Doug anymore.

When Kev opened his eyes, he saw red. The light hit his eyes and everything hurt. He rubbed his cheek and felt the blood come back with a sting. He rubbed his throat too, he'd put the necklace around his neck to keep it safe. Then he sat up. The steering wheel was in front of him, it was time to go.

A doll slid off the seat and hit the floor, it made a heavy sound. He started and sat up, rubbing at the grit in the corners of his eyes. He reached down and lifted the doll off the floor. He threw her in the backseat with the rest of the trash. There was a hollowness when he looked at it, something like hunger.

The previous night came back to him in scattered images, a smear of colors and violence and excitement. Fuck, he'd kicked some ass, taken some people apart, goddammit. What the hell had that little priest been thinking? The girl had gotten out of it without being slashed apart. The rest of it was a blur.

His head hurt. He groped in his pocket. And he was out of reddies and weed. Fuck being straight-edge. Maybe he should buy a bottle of something. Somewhere in town.

He rolled down the window and turned the key. Somehow, he'd ended up in the fields outside of Post Falls. He had nothing he'd come for, at least he had the green car.

Now he was going to get the guy, he was going to make him pay.

Kev swerved narrowly around cars and telephone poles. He drove the car like a weapon, designed to hurt everyone he could touch.

The traffic was stalled at the bridge. Far away down the river, past the curve in the direction they had come, they could hear someone yelling loudly, boisterously.

Sall had let go of Doug, she seemed to have exhausted the topic. When she pointed out the window, her voice had changed. "When I was a kid, I went tubing on this river—every summer right here," she said. "The last time I went, you were in college here in Spokane, remember?" There was a pause. The distant sound of yelling, and of water, was fading. Someone revved an engine.

"Oh," said Matt. "I'd almost forgotten that."

Then, without thinking about it, Matt began to talk to Sall about the murder. He told her about the confusion of the coroner's office with the body in the bathroom. He told her about Arlen's missing car, and the man who had been seen driving the car, alone, sometime after Arlen died.

And Matt told her how he wanted to stop dreaming about the pieces of the body in the stalls. It was a dream of terror that had plagued him the night before, a vision of walking back into the bathroom, with the lights off, alone with the wet floor, the walls freshly blooded again.

"Do you ever dream about your dying patients? Or the dead ones?" he asked.

"No," said Sall. "I know they're gone. I think you're still seeing him because you don't know what happened. My patients died at peace."

"Really? You don't have any belief that maybe, just maybe—"

"Matt, you know me. Do I believe any of that? Have I ever?"

"But just last Sunday, you took Pop to church."

"Stan is having a hard time getting out. Going to church means a lot to him."

"Oh, so you were doing it for Stan, not for yourself."

Sall shook her head. "You should call him. You really should. He's getting so old, Matt, and he needs you."

"Yeah, that'll be the day," said Matt. "Pop has never needed me for anything yet."

Sall moved her fingers out of the car window, into the wind, and back toward her lips. She hadn't smoked in five or six years, but her hands continued to mime her habit. She spoke again. "Saw Smitty yesterday at church too. He's a preacher again."

Smitty was an old friend, someone who went all the way back to high school days. After North Idaho Community College, Smitty went and got salvation and became a preacher at Christ's Ordained Baptist Church in Kellogg. He was a preacher for almost fifteen years before he left town with a parishioner. Something happened, and next thing Matt heard, Smitty had been arrested in Boise. He'd gone to prison. That was all Matt knew. He'd received a few phone calls from Smitty on the home machine since then, but he'd never returned them.

He glanced at Sall, suddenly angry. "How could he come back?"

"I asked the same question of Stan. He said that Smitty repented, and the church forgave him." She shrugged. "Lord saved him, said your pop, taught him where he'd gone wrong. Guess you repent, and the church says you're white as snow again."

"That's not what the justice system says—felonies stay on the damn record." Matt spun the wheel, moving quickly into the left lane. "That's the way it should be. Throw the book at 'im."

"Well, few of your friends would be clean, if all the crimes in the book, as you say, were actually prosecuted."

Matt sighed. "Yeah, I know. But at least Russ is honest about his mistakes, he doesn't try to cover them up with some Christian mumbo jumbo. He tells the truth. He's the only guy who's always been honest with me."

"I don't know if Smitty is covering things up at all—he seems to be telling it straight too. He just says he came to Jesus, and he left all that stuff behind."

"Uh-huh." He did not want to hear more about Smitty. Matt turned the radio up, fussing with the dial. Static hissed out, filling the car with white noise.

Sall shook her head at Matt's nervous motion and flipped the radio off. "Smit was talking to us after the service on Sunday—he recognized your pop. Said he's been trying to reach you. He told us Merrill asked him to cover the duties of the Sheriff's Department chaplain, until they find someone new."

"What? Him? Smitty acting as Sheriff's Department chaplain?"

The traffic outside slowed imperceptibly, until Matt found that they were once again waiting, locked in by cars all around them.

"Guess you should have returned his call." Sall pointed at the glove box. "Put your glasses on, wouldja?"

Reluctantly, he pushed the driving glasses on his nose. Now he could see miles ahead. All around was the smoke of stubble burning off the fields. Summer was ending.

"Well, if he's the chaplain now, I guess I'll have to talk to him. Maybe someone from prison was trying to kill Smitty—maybe they hit the wrong priest."

"That's a stupid theory," said Sall. "I think you should look into where the body was dumped. Tubbs Hill is twenty yards from the lake—it would have been easier than the resort. Why did they take the trouble to put Arlen's body in the bathroom?"

"Look into the resort? Val Herrick?"

"Yeah, of course—her hands aren't clean. I can see someone having a beef with the Herricks. Maybe someone wanting to get back at her father, or even her brother, that asshole Will Herrick. After all, look at the reason you and Merrill and the sheriff's bunch were there in the first place, instead of the city police."

Chaff and smoke filled the distant air. Outside the window, the residue from the wheat fields blew toward them. The car edged across a lane, closer to Spokane.

"What do you mean?" he said.

"C'mon, Matt, you told me about Val getting the resort exempted from zoning when she knocked down the Potlatch lumber mill. She couldn't get the city to agree to everything she wanted—so she just pulled strings, got the resort put under county jurisdiction, and built whatever she wanted. Don't tell me you don't remember!"

"So, it was a sweetheart deal. What's your point?"

"She's got a deal with Merrill. They're both bottom-feeders. Geez, put it together, Matt. Someone's out to make the Herricks pay. Finally!"

"But not Merrill," said Matt. "Merrill is helping me out on this. He's the one who assigned me to this case—it could make a career, this case. He's got a good heart."

"Andy friggin' Merrill." Sall rolled her eyes and sighed. "When are you going to learn that Andy Merrill doesn't have your best interests at heart? One thing you've got going for you is that despite it all, you've genuinely got a good heart. Not Andy Merrill. He just doesn't give a damn about anyone but himself."

"But he's behind me one hundred percent," Matt protested. "He's told me how pissed he is that Valerie Herrick isn't helping me out more. Val doesn't want any attention—from the police or the media. Merrill gave me Russ to help out too. They're both helping me work on this, break this case open."

The wind from the window caught Sall's hair, and she leaned into it before she turned back toward him. "See, there you go again with your good heart. Figure it out, Matt—Merrill isn't really helping you, he isn't gonna give you the time of day."

"You really think people would keep things from me? This is a murder case."

"I think the only one who's going to be honest with you is Russ. You said it yourself—he's the only guy who's always told you the truth. He may be married to Val, but he's always been a true friend to you."

"Even when he drinks."

"Yeah, I gotta admit that—even when he drinks, which is when you gotta stay away from him." Sall's fingers went through their mime of smoking once more. Then she turned and looked at him, the wind pulling her hair outside the car, pushing it back in.

"Whatever happens to this case, I do know you and Russ will figure it out. After all, the other thing you've got going for you is that you're stubborn as hell. Makes me love you and hate you. But you'll figure it out, like the damned bulldog you are."

More chaff filtered into the car from outside. Sall rolled her window up.

"Thanks. I think, coming from you, that was a compliment." Matt swung the wheel gently and they eased through a hole in the traffic. "I guess I just find it hard to believe that either of the Herricks would do something illegal—they've both got too much to lose."

Sall made a guffawing sound. Then she flicked a bit of wheat or burnt husk off her skin with the edge of a finger. Afterward, she put the mirror back up. Now he was glad she had come.

Sall looked up from the list, checking things off she wanted to buy. "Anything you want in Spokane?"

He looked back at the road. "No," he said. "I don't need anything."

"Why do you have to do this, again?" asked Sall. "Don't you usually—"

"Yes, we usually notify the family immediately. This time, we've tried to call, but there's no answer at all. Like they've been out of town, or something. Nothing. So I'm going over in person. After all, he was a member of the department. We owe it to him."

Ahead of them, the traffic halted. "Hell," said Matt. "Arlen helped me through. He had a tough marriage too, sounded like. Gave me some comfort in my hard times."

"What, with me?"

"Yeah, with you. And after that last time you left, the only person who helped me was Arlen. He was honest with me. So I want to take care of his family. I owe it to him."

"I never knew he heard about our problems," said Sall. "I thought you just talked to Russell. You talked to Father Arlen too, huh?"

Matt did not reply. After silence, the car began moving steadily through traffic again. Industrial warehouses and open fields gave way to office complexes and mini-malls. He caught a glimpse of the Greyhound sign a few blocks away.

"Maybe the guy used a bus ticket," he muttered to himself.

"What?" said Sall. "Some other case?"

"No, the resort thing." Clouds were blowing over Spokane, drifting toward Five Mile Prairie. Matt tapped his fingers on the wheel. "Someone took the car. Probably the same man who killed him. But why would they connect after the car was initially taken? Maybe they rode a bus together, stopped in Coeur d'Alene, and then the killer came on alone to Spokane. That's what I wrote in my first report to Merrill."

"Did he buy it?"

"Don't know. But now I think it was bullshit. I'm wondering if the Greyhound ticket to Spokane was ever used. Arlen might never have been on the bus at all. I need to find someone else who was on that bus, to check." The wind touched Matt's face, and the driving glasses slid down his nose. Sall looked at him, he pushed the glasses back up.

"What if the perpetrator was on the bus with him? Do you have a picture of the suspect?"

"Yeah, Russ has a composite started. Last thing he does before he retires." Matt waved a hand in the air, dismissing the idea. "That's not my part of it— I'm trying to find out where the man ended up. If the family will tell me, I'd like to find out why Arlen's car was missing—and why Arlen took the bus from Wallace to Coeur d'Alene instead of driving."

"Good luck getting any useful information out of the family today." Sall looked out the window. "I wish we lived in Spokane—the big city," she said abruptly.

"We got out of the Valley at least," he said. "That's what you wanted."

Sall turned toward him, some kind of fury in her. "Jesus, Matt, don't you care that you've been stuck in the same place for twenty years now?"

"I went from hourly security to sheriff's lieutenant. I don't think I've been stuck."

"You're blind to it. You've been mired there ever since Herrick promoted you at the Sunshine." Sall sighed. "Damn Silver Valley mines. They kill every ambition."

"I worked security," said Matt. "After that summer, I never worked in the mines."

"Whatever." Sall turned away from him so she could look out at the burning fields, the brown air over the Spokane Valley. "It could have been us here in Spokane."

"But it's not," Matt said. He took the North Division exit. Ahead of them was the expanse of Spokane's Riverfront Park, the Opera House by the river, and the skybridges that connected the downtown skyscrapers. He stopped the car at a green awning, Auntie's Bookstore and Café. "Thanks for coming with me."

Sall leaned in the window. "Hey, I came for the shopping, remember? Now don't forget—pick me up here at Auntie's. Don't be late, okay?" Then she was gone.

Matt looked in the rearview mirror at the traffic. As he swung the car out into the flow of traffic, he reached up and took the driving glasses off his face. A hazy cloud of husks struck the window, they drifted on the fire-blown air into the car. The gust covered his shoulders with a fine dust.

◇ ◇ ◇

Kev drove the green car out of the rutted lane between the standing grain. The path between the wheat fields turned and twisted with the lie of the land, and it was so deeply rutted it could have served as an irrigation ditch.

Soon he came to the end of the lane, a dirt road. Here there were only turns, one way or another. To Kev's right were the mountains of North Idaho, the lake, the river. He could imagine, in the distance, the river coming out of Coeur d'Alene, toward Spokane. To the left was the distant buzz of the highway and the city. From here he was certain he would come into the city from the rough side, where the warehouses and run-down machine shops were. In among the broken-down contract workers and bar bums, no one would ask any questions of someone who looked and acted like he did.

He listened to the engine murmur and thought of the darkness, the calm, the emptiness of the lake. He turned the engine off and stood up beside the road.

With his free hand, he rubbed his eyes again and wished he'd never woken up that morning. None of it had turned out the way he'd thought it would. Kev could hardly remember how he'd ended up over in Spokane—dropping something off, maybe someone. The tattooed man had even taken the damn blanket. Now Kev didn't have a pad to crash in, he wished he'd at least kept that yellow blanket. He had been sleeping in the car, windows rolled up against the night air.

He didn't care what it took, he was going to get the bastard. One of them should be dead already. And at the end of the day, it sure as fuck wasn't going to be Kev Macht.

Five Mile Prairie rested on top of a bluff that hung above the west side of the city of Spokane. In a large, growing city, the houses with views on top of Five Mile would be part of a suburb. In Spokane, this bluff near the heart of the city remained farmland.

Up on top of the Prairie, Matt found the small house with the prefab walls. The walls were a little higher than the ground, they rested on a mortared cinder block foundation. The steps were of the same cinder blocks, loose on dirt.

Matt stopped at the side of the screen door and checked the address. He was about to knock when he realized there was someone watching him from inside the house.

"Ma'am," he said, and took off his hat.

"You're with the police." She looked at him. "But you're not from Spokane."

"No, ma'am, I'm not. Lieutenant Matt Worthson, from Coeur d'Alene, the Bitterroot County Sheriff's Department. We've tried to call you, but . . ."

The woman waved a hand nervously. "Oh, I'm sorry. My daughter threw the phone across the room last week—when her husband, or soon-to-be ex-husband, called. He's really given her a rough row to hoe."

"I'm sorry," said Matt.

The woman stared at him for a moment. "Anyway, so the phone isn't working. But you drove over from Coeur d'Alene, so it's not about the burning ban then? We've got a Spokane permit for the field-stubble fires."

"No, ma'am. It's something else. No one's done anything wrong here." He paused, took a breath. "May I come in?"

"Oh, yes, I'm sorry. What was I thinking?" She unhooked the screen door from the inside and opened it for him. He saw that she was older than her voice. Her hair was white and frizzed around her face. The lines around her mouth made her look angry, and he wondered what was the cause. She glanced out at the girl playing by the field and closed the screen door behind them.

"Sit down, please," she said, and sat down herself in one of the brown over-stuffed chairs. He stood for a moment, and then shifted his notebook to his other hand.

"I'm Paula Hart. How can I help you?" she said.

He sat down and glanced at his notebook, at the neat lines written there. "I need to ask if you are related to the Reverend Arlen Bowman."

"Well, I'm his mother-in-law. I live here with his soon-to-be ex-wife," she said. "They separated a few months ago. Like I said, the business with the phone. I think he's out of town right now though. Over in your neck of the woods, actually."

"Oh," said Matt. "Is his wife, is Mrs. Bowman, at home?"

"She'll be home in a little while," she said. "Is Arlen in trouble? Is there some problem?" She laughed a short, forced laugh, and he saw that he could not keep the news.

"Ma'am, representing the Bitterroot County Sheriff's Department, I regret, I mean, I'm sorry—I'm deeply sorry to tell you that Arlen, your son here, is deceased. He was found dead, ma'am, in Coeur d'Alene over the weekend."

He saw that nothing had changed for her, her face ungiving. "He's dead, Mrs. Hart. He was deceased before we found him. There was nothing we could do."

"He's not my son," she said. "He's not mine."

"On Saturday night," Matt said, "Arlen was found dead at a crime scene in Coeur d'Alene. From what we can tell, Arlen was not involved with any criminal activities."

"Do you know why it happened?" she said. He could not see that what he'd said was going to have any effect on her.

"We're working on that, ma'am."

She looked directly at him for a moment, and then she put her face in her hands, pushing her hair up, leaning down until her head was almost on her knees.

"I'm sorry, ma'am, I'm sorry," he said. He saw then that she was not crying.

"What can we do," she said from behind her hands. "What can we do?"

There was a pause. When she looked up she said, "You'll have to wait for Betty. You'll have to tell her yourself. I can't." She went into the kitchen. He looked at his notebook, and saw that he had not said most of what he had planned on saying.

From the living room, Matt could look out the front door and see the girl walking back and forth beside the wheat field. She had something in her hands, bright and moving. He looked at it for a moment before he realized that it was a fountain of water. As the water came out of the hose, it splashed to the ground, covering her legs in small mud specks.

The water pooled on the ground when she left the frame of the door, sparkling brightly as the clouds moved, washing indiscriminately across the girl's collection of sticks and pebbles and wheat stalks. Each time she came back into the picture, he could see that the mud puddle had splashed higher on her legs.

Matt turned to see that the grandmother had come back in the room. "I'm sorry . . . ," he pointed out the door. "She's in the mud—I was going to say something to you."

She looked outside, and shrugged. "Thought of something," she said abruptly. "Little Karyn there came back late Friday night—night before you say you found him dead. He was supposed to have her for the weekend. Guess he got rid of her, he dropped her off here. But he didn't bother to come in. And then I guess he got himself killed. Girl came in alone."

"She did?" Matt swallowed, his mouth suddenly dry. "Do you have the ticket she came in on—the Greyhound ticket?"

"Funny you should ask about that—I figure he dropped Karyn off. I didn't think of the Greyhound. How would she get up here?" said the grandmother. "Don't know why she was alone, or who dropped her off. God must of looked out for her. Her father didn't. Irresponsible son of a bitch." The woman shrugged. Her expression hadn't shifted at all, as if her words did not matter. "You want to talk to her, she's out there."

She pointed beyond the screen door, where the girl flitted in and out of view. When she turned and went into the kitchen again, he felt as if she had gone for good.

Matt looked down at the girl, Karyn. Her dress was covered by the small things left behind by the wind. All over her arms and legs were tiny bits of dead wheat husk, it seemed like a million bugs had landed on her skin. The gust of wind died out in dust devils that whirled across the yard and disappeared among the weeds.

When he had come out of the house, the girl had looked up. At first, Matt thought she would say something to him, there was a spark of recognition in her face at the uniform.

But then she returned to building her miniature town, her movements a little nervous now. With her finger, she traced a path that wound between each of the tiny houses.

He sank down on his haunches to get to her level. "Hi, honey, can I talk to you?"

She stopped moving then. The water hose she was holding just pointed straight ahead, the water running wild, swirling around each of the stalks and pebbles, destroying her town. Gently, he moved the hose aside.

"I want to ask you about your time with your daddy last week. Do you re-member your daddy taking you to Idaho, in his big green car?"

At that, the little girl dropped the hose and pushed her hands up to her face, holding them across her eyes like a shield or a charm. Matt stepped back slowly. She relaxed the farther he moved away.

When he reached the porch, she pulled her hands away from her eyes. Her face was streaked with mud. Behind him, Matt could sense the grandmother watching. The angry edge was back in her voice. "Karyn hasn't talked much since she came back that night. I don't think she's said two words."

Outside the house, there was a sound of something lost in the distance—a piece of metal falling, a tractor grinding to a halt. Matt waited, alone again in the living room. He looked at the walls. There were pictures of Arlen with his arm around his wife. In the largest picture, there was a white spot above the shoulders, as if someone had scratched the face off the picture. The scratches were deep. Someone in this house had hated Arlen.

Alongside the pictures was Arlen Bowman's diploma in religious studies from Whitworth College in Spokane. Matt had dropped out of that same col-lege. He wrote down the year of Arlen's graduation in his notebook. After a time he sat down again, settling into the chair in the living room to wait.

Twenty minutes later, when Arlen's wife came in the house, she was carry-ing groceries. She was a short, brown-haired woman. She moved quickly, like a bird. Matt thought of Sall when she was twenty-five. The mother-in-law helped

Arlen's wife put the groceries down, and stood behind her chair while he said most of what he had said before, and held her in her arms and rocked her back and forth, holding on while she wept.

Matt waited a moment and then broke in again. "I'm sorry to bother you any further, Mrs. Bowman, but I need some information to help me in your husband's case. I wonder if our psychologist could spend a little time talking to your daughter. I understand she came back the night before your husband was found. Would that be all right?"

"Sure," said Betty Bowman. "That's fine. She's not talking much, you know."

Matt nodded. "And one more thing, do you happen to have a copy of the registration for his car?"

"No, no, I can't think." Betty Bowman's voice broke and choked on the words. "I don't know. The registration would just be in his car, right?"

"Ma'am, I don't know." He spread his hands out. "There haven't been any personal effects recovered. Nothing has turned up."

"Hasn't turned up?" Inexplicably, Betty Bowman began to cry again.

"It's all right, baby, it's all right." Her mother held on to her. She looked over her daughter's shoulder at Matt, as if to accuse him.

When he stepped outside, he could see that Mrs. Bowman's truck was still full of groceries.

The girl stood near to the sheriff's car. As he came to the driveway, the girl was washing one of her muddy handprints off of his car tire. The shape of the girl was slicked brown with mud. Her fingernails and teeth and eyes looked out from the dark mass, white bones in the wet dirt. After he closed the car door and pulled away, she lifted her hand. The lines of the palm showed bright through the mud and the dirt that streaked her skin.

"Bye," she whispered. "See you later." It was like a promise. When he circled the house, she looked at him, a tendril of unscathed blond hair wafting in toward her eyes.

The road down from Five Mile Prairie was lined with storm windows and stacks of firewood. It was named Honolulu Way. Then Matt turned right on Waikiki Road. Some Spokane city planner must have had a sense of humor.

After Five Mile, Matt felt that he'd caught the family's grief like a virus. He needed a drink. Going dry wasn't all it was cracked up to be, sometimes the only difference was that he could remember the pain. He checked his watch—Sall would not like the fact that he was late. The argument about Doug came back to him. What the hell was it that made Sall tick—and how did Doug get it too? To just up and leave town without a by-your-leave. What he wouldn't give for some of Doug's gumption.

Now he managed investigations, but it didn't seem that long ago that he'd worked for pay-by-the-hour wages. After he'd left college and come back to the Silver Valley, he ran into Smitty, who was then working on Herrick Senior's employment desk. Smitty got him a job, and he worked security at the Sunshine Mine for years before moving over to the Sheriff's Department.

It had never satisfied his father—Pop wanted him to be another mining hero. After all, he had the heavy build, the heft in his chest and shoulders, that made the Wallace High linebackers the terror of the Idaho Football League. On the Valley side of Fourth of July Pass, the muscled solidity of a miner came out in the genes. The valley bred heavyweight men, like marshland breeds mosquitoes. Something in the air, the ground.

Matt reached over to the glove box and took out his glasses. The buildings around him rose from the blur, shapes emerging from a dream. The image of Sall as a birdlike thing floated into his thoughts. It was an echo in his mind of the first time he saw her pull herself into the front seat of his car, years ago, when she was nineteen. Then she opened the car door, and she was there beside him, already speaking.

She was always in a bad mood when they were driving home from Spokane. He didn't understand it. But just like the weather, there it was.

"I mean, how hard is it to keep a conversation with a family to under three hours?" she said. "I should have stayed here at Auntie's Bookstore. Stayed here in Spokane without you. I mean, really, do you need their entire life stories and all . . ."

There wasn't anything that reminded him of a bird any longer.

"It's my job," said Matt. "Just doing my job."

"Goddammit," said Sall. "That's not the point. I wanted to see some of Spokane together. Now the day is gone. Things never change."

"I could be in politics now," interrupted Matt. "If the election had been different—"

"That election can go to hell, Matt," she said. "That's not what I'm talking about."

Far ahead, pipes reached toward the sky. Venting stacks, same as for the mines in the Valley. There was more smoke than even two or three years ago.

The Spokane Valley was fading behind them now. Post Falls, Idaho, was up ahead.

"Look, I'm sorry," said Sall after some time. "How was it? How did it go?"

"Oh, it was shitty," he said. "It always is."

◊　◊　◊

Across the empty three lanes ahead, Matt could see a dust cloud coming toward the highway. In the sunlight, the highway trembled with heat, the dust cloud jumped and flickered against the fields. It was a car coming out of the wheat fields, moving with a dust cloud under it, like an Old West stagecoach coming out of the Palouse country.

As Matt and Sall drove into Post Falls, the green car joined the main road a few hundred yards behind them. The car slid over more than one lane as it turned from the dirt road onto the cement lanes. Then it swerved again, barely missing a road sign.

In his rearview mirror, Matt caught a glance at the car. It didn't seem to have slowed as it hit the highway. The tires squealed and smoked as the driver turned onto the paved road. There was a distance between them, but the car still wasn't slowing down. Matt watched it barrel toward them. He memorized the license plate, and then he saw that even after the driver had straightened the car out, the tires covered part of two lanes.

Something inside the car punched it forward. The green car leaped toward them, chewing up the distance in a few seconds. Every person he saw in a car on the road reminded him of what he'd lost. Now Matt could see a man behind the wheel. He was slumped against the window—a muscled arm rested loosely on the steering wheel.

The realization of the car's lopsided path came a mere second before collision. On that moment, Matt spun his wheel into the gravel on the shoulder. Everything seemed to slow as the left tires spun bits of dirt and rock into the air. He twisted the wheel the other way, fishtailing wildly. As he came back onto the highway, he could see the green car moving ahead nearly a quarter of a mile away, holding its position.

The car under him slid once more. Matt pushed his driving glasses back into place and checked that the shotgun clamp between the two front seats hadn't loosened.

Sall steadied herself in her seat. "What the hell was that?" she said.

He felt underneath his seat for his badge. Matt concentrated on the car ahead of him and began to accelerate. The green car disappeared around the curve of the highway ahead. Matt flipped on his lights. Then behind him he heard a faint, wailing siren. In the mirror now, he could see the red and blue flashing lights of a Spokane County trooper.

In the left lane, Matt slowed down, accommodating the Spokane County car. He watched as the blue and white police car flashed past, whipping around the corner ahead as if it were a few short yards instead of a mile. Matt let his foot entirely off the pedal and merged into the right lanes, ready to pull over behind the officer and lend support.

They came around the bend. On the immediate right, he could see the Spokane County Sheriff's car parked behind a yellow truck. Someone else had been caught speeding. Far in the distance, Matt could see the speck that was the green car. It seemed to him that despite the distance, the car had slowed. Maybe, he thought, the siren had done the trick on the man in the green car after all. He sighed and turned off his lights.

Matt breathed a little slower. He felt his heartbeat return almost to normal. Sall's eyes were now closing again. It was warm in the car. In the bright midday sun, her face was faint against the dark smoke rising from the fields all around them. He thought of the small girl at the farm, profiled against the sky over the Spokane Valley.

Why do you devour him? Tell me the cause.
If we agree his sins deserve this bestial punishment,
I, knowing who you are, and knowing his crimes against you
Will speak of you on earth, if my tongue does not wither away.
—Dante Alighieri, *The Inferno*

THE CITY of Coeur d'Alene seemed to end on the east side of the Tubbs peninsula. Brush and white pine crowded to the edges of the manicured green lawns in the city's historical district. The peninsula was not big, it could be walked in under an hour. A beachhead trail followed the curve of the peninsula and joined the longest boardwalk in North America on the west side. A well-marked trail led up into the foliage. From Ace Hardware on Sherman in downtown Coeur d'Alene it was a short walk into thick woods.

In the morning, Matt and Russ confirmed how close the woods were to town. Matt had found that Ace Drugs was the only pharmacy on the south side of town that sold duct tape. Matt and Russ walked around the bend that the column of the Pillar Rocks forces into the trail. Then they left the trail, working their way from the trailhead straight up into the dry yellow cheatgrass that grew between the rocks. The trees were dense at the top, the ground in deep shadow. Matt could see clear down to the other side of the peninsula. The Coeur d'Alene Resort stood right before them, a few hundred yards away as the crow flies.

Matt's watchband snagged on a branch, and he checked the time before he took it off and put it in his pocket. 11:00 a.m. In his pocket his fingers slid across tiny plastic envelopes that enclosed leaf and soil samples sent back from Spokane. The bits of dirt inside were cold to the touch.

Branches scraped his bare arms and knocked off his hat. He looked over at Russ moving smoothly through the trees. Then he reached the clearing. The light filtered down in shafts as though coming through stagnant water. Someone had worked this clearing: footprints and scuff marks covered the ground.

A great shattered yew deadfall lay half sunk into the forest floor. Matt sat on its crumbled pieces and watched Russ photographing something on the ground.

"Whatcha got there?"

"Footprint," said Russ. "Looks a lot like the one we found in the restroom."

Matt looked carefully across the clearing. Leaves were scattered and broken. The color of the ground was uneven. On top the leaves showed the rich brown of mulch recently turned over the wrong way up.

Carefully, Matt worked his foot under the layer of leaves. The flies rose in a thick, slow cloud off the bare earth. In the same moment, he could smell something rotting, a rank smell that nauseated, like rancid beef.

Under one leaf there was a flash of silver. Folded duct tape, gray and white, with an overlay of mottled rust. He pointed it out to Russ and snapped a pair of plastic gloves on his hands before carefully extracting the tape. Then Matt reached behind him and broke a dry branch off. With the point of the stick he lifted it off, a mat of trampled leaves that concealed all the darker stain beneath.

A breeze came across the lake toward the two men. Although the sky held only a few streaks of high white clouds, the air was brisk and cool. It was nearly fall.

Russ looked at Matt, his gaze inscrutable. "You know, I never did thank you properly for getting me out of that jam with the girl."

The swallows were tiny black cracks in a bright blue sky. Matt looked down at the ground, tracing bent grass blades in the breeze. "You ever tell your wife about what happened, like you said you were going to do?"

Russ laughed nervously, the sound echoing across the water. "Geez, Matt, you cut to the chase, dontcha? Look . . . it's just never the right time. She knows, without me ever telling her. That's why she put me on this case. I can't keep a secret to save my life."

"You still saying that you didn't know she was underage? Was that the truth?"

"I do appreciate you believing me, the first time, when it mattered, and now too. That matters to me, my friend. It matters more than any amount of truth, you know?"

On the lakeside shore, ahead of them, the sedge grass was bent apart, as if someone had walked through, making their own path wherever they went. And there was a flattened, smashed place in the sedge grass and cattails, a minuscule stream ran through it.

Then Russ elbowed him and winked. "But then again, Matty, if I had known, I don't know if I would have stopped—I mean, hell, she was quite a looker, wasn't she?"

"Dammit, Russ," Matt looked up from the grass and glared at him.

"Hell, I'm just kidding, Matt." Russ put a hand on Matt's shoulder, and looked at him seriously. "You gotta make sure they give Arlen some respect. He was a little guy—and they never gave him enough respect as a chaplain."

A bead of sweat came trickling down Russ's face. Matt watched it come out of his hairline and draw a path down his temple toward his cheek, disappearing near his jawline. Russ looked away, sighing. "Jesus, Matty, I feel real bad about his death. He never gave up on anyone."

The midges ran wild as Matt's feet pushed soil into the little stream. Some large animal—perhaps a person holding something—had pressed the grass flat. Other feet had stepped here, the prints of a shoe cracked and distinctive. A black thread and hairs were caught in the grass. Russ carefully took out the tool kit, removing a pair of tweezers.

"I know what Arlen did for us," said Matt. "He visited my pop in the hospital a month or so ago—Pop really appreciated that someone listened to him. Me, I don't know. Sometimes I found Arlen . . . hard to talk to. I told him about . . ." Matt's voice trailed off.

Carefully, Matt pulled the grass apart, holding up a piece of hair caught in a tangle of grass. Russ trapped it in a ziplock evidence bag. Then Russ grinned and pointed at another spot in the trampled sedge grass.

The footsteps went down to the edge of the lake, and then they dragged something up toward the buildings. Matt and Russell didn't follow the prints to the resort. They were interested in where the prints came back out again.

On the side of the peninsula that faced the river, near the overpass, Matt and Russ found the shoeprint again. Near the college, the great concrete pylons of US Route 95 reached down to the shore on either side of the river. The pylons stood twenty feet away from the water, making a shelter of sorts. Matt and Russ looked underneath.

They found the usual, broken bottles, used condoms, syringes, decaying graffiti, and a makeshift latrine. Matt checked a circle of blackened stones—the firepit—for signs of recent burning.

He looked up at Russ. "So, you're due to retire in what—six weeks? What do they have you working on, besides this, as you go out the door?"

"Hell, Matt, it's been a little frustrating." Russ kicked at the grass and the logs around the firepit. "Merrill is giving me nothing to do. Traffic, potholes, paperwork—and old missing persons. Did I tell you about the one that should've been round-filed long ago? Some guy went missing in the Sunshine disaster, and now his family wants to find him."

"My pop was in that mine disaster," said Matt. "We found him."

"I know, I know—your pop came out alive, and he was fine. But this guy—

Larry Clark—he clocked out, we think. He's on the records as having come out alive from the mine, but his family hasn't heard from him since. Nearly twenty years. Ancient history."

Matt moved out on the beach. Here, the trucked-in white beach sand near the water gave way to natural North Idaho grit and dirt. It was easier to follow the shoeprint. And there was something faintly silver there in the grass, something black. Things left behind.

Apparently this was where the man had parked, for the deep ruts of new tire treads moved away from the abandoned beach. The shoeprint disappeared at the tire ruts.

"That heart attack I had back in April—it woke me up, Matt," said Russ. "I want my time here to count for something. Val and I have been talking. If I ran for office—"

"Well, let me tell you from experience," said Matt. "It ain't no cakewalk, running a campaign. Your life will be hell throughout. And sometimes there's hell to pay later too."

"That's why I'm telling you. You've been there—I knew you'd understand. But I have a favor to ask—after I retire, can you keep me in the loop on the resort case?"

Matt whistled softly. "I might be able to do that. But I don't know what I could share. It's not that I don't want to level the playing field—I just don't know if you have a hope against Merrill. He has quite a machine. He'll murder you."

"But you'll help me, right?"

"Basically, you want me to give up information you could use in a campaign." Matt stared at him. "First thing you should know though is that we won't be giving this to the FBI. Andy is pretty clear that he wants the Feds to come in on this, as soon as possible. But I want to solve it here, if I can. I thought you'd feel the same, knowing what Arlen meant to some of us."

Russ sighed. "Well, I hear you. But that's not what Val wants—she thinks it's that Metaline Falls serial killer. Pretty clearly it's—"

"It's always about what Val wants—aren't you the cop here?"

Russ grimaced and shook his head faintly. "Look. On this one, I'd have to concur with her. I mean, the way the body was taken apart is classic. It's the same killer—and the sooner the FBI can track him across state lines, the sooner we can stop him killing again."

"How do you know for sure? Hell, we haven't even got the coroner's report yet!"

Russ gave a chuckle. "Trust me, Matt, I've worked this beat for decades now."

Matt gave him a penetrating stare, Russ's patronizing chuckle finally getting under his skin. "You're not just going off of what Val wants?"

"No, I'm not." Russ looked levelly back at him. "Something in my gut tells me. It's a cop instinct, let me tell you. I know it's the same guy."

Matt looked down and saw a piece of tape, almost invisible against the ground. A swarm of tiny ants covered it, eating at a brown residue. The water was spotted with white flecks of rotted grass that drifted over its dark swell like an infection.

"Guess Andy hasn't trusted me to work the field for a while," said Matt. "Have to get myself tuned up again—get on the same wavelength."

Matt bent down and looked at the ground. Then Russ spoke again. "I think I can win for sheriff. Richard Stanford is advising me. He thinks I have a chance."

"Stanford, that ex-congressman? Isn't a consultant a bit beyond your pay scale?"

"Val's paying for the consultants, for the election."

Matt stood and rubbed his neck. He'd been looking down too long. "Figures."

"Hell, Matty, at least I got good advice. I think you could use some on this case."

"Advice on this case? Just because Andy put me in charge of this thing doesn't mean I can't handle it, and furthermore—"

"Jesus, Matty, hasn't it occurred to you that Andy might just want to have you keep the case so he has a solid scapegoat to blame the mess on?"

Matt held out a hand, stopping Russ from walking ahead. He put on a new pair of plastic gloves. He bent his legs and squatted, lifting the black shape of a sodden sleeping bag out of the rotted grass. It was dripping and ragged. A hair was caught in a fold of the bag. He lifted it out carefully with the tweezers. Brown, with a blond tip.

"You know, I wonder if you're right." Matt spit out over the lake and pivoted on his bent legs to see Russ more clearly. "You think Andy might actually be setting me up here?"

"Yeah, I do," said Russ seriously.

Matt looked at him silhouetted by the light off the lake. "I've always trusted you, Russ. I'll consider it. Thanks for the advice."

At their feet dead specks of sedge swirled into the sump where Matt had made a hole by removing the sleeping bag. In minutes, the rottenness covered it.

◇ ◇ ◇

Walking back along the verge of the bank, Matt and Russ came finally to the stream again. Looking at the bed in the sedge grass now, Matt saw something he'd missed before. There was a slip of paper in the bushes they hadn't seen the first time. He pointed.

"Grab that," he said. "Can you put it in a baggie?"

Carefully, Russ took hold of the crumpled paper with a pair of tweezers. As he lifted it off the weeds, Matt could make out a faint tracing of a dog.

"It's a Greyhound ticket," he said.

"Yeah," said Russ softly. "Nearly falling apart now, but looks like it hasn't been used. A few days old." Carefully, he slipped the bit of disintegrating paper inside a piece of plastic. Afterward, he turned to face Matt.

"You said you trust me," he said. "So I'll trust you with something. Truth be told, I really don't want to run for office at all."

"So why are you doing it?"

"Why do you think?"

They walked up the beach in silence, the toolbox jostling back and forth, the sleeping bag slopping out dank water, a dribbled pattern along the stone pathway. Finally, Matt spoke again. "You've never been able to say no to her, have you?"

Russ did not answer.

"I told you not to marry her."

Russ moved his head, as if to shake off the truth of it.

Out on the water, Matt could see a rowboat. The blades of the oars in the boat rose from the water with their flat sides up, emerging out of the lake with a great splash. Except for the splash of the rower and the buzz of a distant motorboat, it was quiet.

Russ opened the toolbox and slipped rubber gloves on his hands. Carefully, he opened one end of the sleeping bag. There was enough water left in the bag to keep the blood inside moistly rotting. A viscous residue oozed out onto the garbage can. Matt felt nausea clawing its way from his stomach to his throat as he turned his face away.

The wind carried sounds across the water. From a distance, the voices of people came to him. Laughter, distant and removed, a crowd's blind cheer. Some child crying, lost. And as fast as that, Matt saw her again, the small girl with hair like corn silk, staring up at him in Arlen's driveway.

Late that afternoon, Matt spent an hour in Sheriff Andrew Merrill's office. He was supposed to be briefing the sheriff on their progress, such as it was. But as always, Merrill did most of the talking. He was reminiscing about what he'd been doing the evening Arlen Bowman was found at the resort.

"See, I was finishing up a late evening with Will Herrick—over at the lake place on Orouke Bay. In fact, Will and I got in kinda late for dinner. When the call came in, we'd had a few drinks and we'd just got the Copper River salmon on the grill—have you had this year's Copper River yet, Matty, it tastes like a lobster fucked a pâté goose, it's that damn good—and we had the grill going when the call came in. I had to think about Valerie Herrick—she's my friend too, Matty—so I had to think about her interests, of course . . ."

Matt listened as Merrill explained that Val Herrick's worry about the reputation of the resort caused him to take more of an interest. Both of them knew that explanations were in order, because Merrill did not usually do the footwork surrounding a crime scene. He was five feet ten inches tall and he weighed over three hundred pounds. Merrill did as little as possible. His secretary, Phyllis, did most of the heavy lifting: she served as day dispatcher, warrant manager, and often as official and unofficial acting sheriff.

Of course, every two years Merrill conducted well-publicized crackdowns on the strip joints and massage parlors at the Idaho-Washington border, and his deputies kept Fourth of July Pass clear in winter. It was a priority for him to make sure that the Sheriff's Department, and not the city police, got all the high-profile cases.

Sheriff Merrill also cooperated with the FBI when they did investigations on the neo-Nazis, and he assisted the Forest Service in matters regarding the St. Joe National Forest. And as Matt well knew, Merrill spent time going to public events with one or more of the Herricks. He played them off one another as they continued to spar over their father's legacy, launching million-dollar litigation suits at each other every other year. Through the Herrick Trust or individually, Valerie and William S. Herrick Jr. owned the Lakeview Hotel, Restaurant & Gaming Facilities; the *Coeur d'Alene Courier*; the Coeur d'Alene Resort; a fleet of leased tourist yachts; and all large-scale mining property in the Silver Valley. There was little else worth owning in the Coeur d'Alene region.

In the office that afternoon, Merrill seemed to enjoy reliving his rare moment of law enforcement activity. First he reviewed every syllable of the phone calls he'd received and made that evening.

As usual, Merrill had had to appease both Herricks before he could make a decision. Valerie Herrick insisted her husband, Russell, work the case to protect her interests. On the other hand—and mainly because Merrill happened to be at his house when the call came in from the resort—William Herrick recommended an experienced senior officer to offset the conflict of interest. In fact, he had almost demanded that Merrill choose Matt as lieutenant in charge, an oddity Matt did not have time to consider as Merrill kept talking.

Matt yawned. But Merrill wasn't done yet. He seemed to be practicing the story for the next Kiwanis luncheon. "Just between you and me and the door-post," said Merrill. "I'd been keeping up with ol' William on the Jack Daniel's, but what I heard from Val at the resort turned me sober as a . . ." Merrill's voice faltered. He wrinkled his brow, perplexed for a moment. Then his face brightened as he caught the thread of his story again.

"Sober as a Baptist! That's God's honest truth. Sobered me right up. That's when I called you in, Matty. If you can work with the Feds and get this perp nailed, it will be just what I need going into the election."

Matt thought of a way to make Merrill own it, to keep the case close. "Andy, sure, I understand about the election—I know you want me to solve it. But this might be a serial killer, a real one. So now I'm thinking we should just wash our hands—call the press, tell them we're washing our hands of it. Tell them we're going to ask the FBI to do the grown-up work."

Merrill bristled. "C'mon, Matty, you pussy. You want me to tell the papers we don't have any *cojones*? You really want me to call that fucking agent in Spokane?"

"Yeah." Matt nodded. "Agent Clay. That's the name FBI headquarters gave me."

Merrill shook his head. "Dammit, Matty. It'll all go to hell if we call in the Feds. Don't you know that every case we give those damn Feebies goes to hell?"

Matt nodded soberly. "Sure, but it might be the better option. I'm telling you, Andy—"

But Merrill wasn't listening. "You know, it felt real good that evening to be actually doing the job that night—putting the elbow grease in to keep the people safe around here. So I think it's a good thing that you're holding on to the case. We solve it ourselves, looks much better for the media. That's a good decision you made—and I'm making it official. We solve this damn thing ourselves, you hear me?"

Matt gave it one last push, swallowing his grin. "Now wait a minute, Andy, this damn thing might be out of my depth. We've got the FBI right there in Spokane—"

"Like I said, Matty, it's no problem for a man of your capabilities—I'm confident you can handle it. No Feds, no interference. You just keep me informed, as things progress, all right?"

Then Phyllis called down the hallway that Merrill had a call from someone named Butler. Merrill guffawed, and said, "I'll take it. Matty's here—so we'll have some fun!"

He motioned across the desk. "Why don't you shut that door there—just between you and me and the doorpost, this'll be worth a laugh. The reverend is always a hoot, let me tell you. Here, I'll put it on speakerphone for you."

Merrill pushed a button on his desk phone.

"Hello, Andy?" The voice was loud, as if the person thought that you had to shout to be heard. "Hello—did you put me through?"

"Hey, Reverend, this is Sheriff Andy Merrill, what can I do for you?"

Matt didn't recognize the voice. He had the sinking feeling this was one of Merrill's crackpot constituents. Silently, Matt cursed Phyllis for putting the call through.

"Oh. Andy," said the voice. It sank in tone and volume, until it was almost at a normal level. It was a rich baritone—a preacher's voice. "Andy, I never thought I'd want to call you again, but after our last little talk, I thought that one good turn deserved another."

Now Matt recognized the voice. Inwardly, his curses became more colorful. He knew who it was on the phone. Even thinking about the man put a foul taste in his mouth.

"Well, damn me to hell and back," said Merrill. "If it isn't the Reverend Richard Butler. How is your flock in Hayden Lake?"

"Doing well, doing well. God does bless his One True White Flock," said the reverend. "We pray you'll repent and join us in worship one of these Sundays."

"Not likely," said Merrill. He winked at Matt. "Too many Jew folks vote, especially your mother-in-law."

"Now that's blasphemy, Andy. I called in the spirit of helpfulness. I might as well hang up right now, bring this Jew talk to a close."

"No, no, I'm so sorry." Merrill mocked a pout at Matt. "I do apologize, Reverend. Now I'm all ears—what's on your mind, Dick?"

"You remember that little talk we had, Andy?"

"Sure I remember. As I recall, I told you that in felony cases, I would charge the Nations with aiding and abetting, unless you started to help us out here." Merrill nodded at Matt, as if to tell him that he could, under duress, take the law seriously. Then he put a middle finger out at the phone, and laughed silently.

Reverend Butler paused. "Well now, Andy, I remember it different. You said you wanted to support the uplifting activities of the Nations. Didn't want us taking in degenerates unawares. And I appreciate that. So I guess I have one to report—see, this one young man I need some advice about, he grew up in Coeur d'Alene, and was recruited to the Aryan cause a few months ago. Things seemed to go fine for a while."

"Let me guess." Merrill cackled silently at Matt. "He was doing just fine until you discovered he was a Jew *and* a Negro."

There was a snort from the phone. "Now, I can just hang up, Andy. My time is valuable too. I figured you all would be interested in this tip."

"Okay, okay, so you got a name and serial number for me?" Carefully, Merrill wrote down a name.

"I'm sorry about this, Sheriff. We do try to get the best and the bright—but we take whoever the Good Lord brings us. We can't reject one of his sheep, you know."

Merrill glanced at Matt and raised his eyebrows. He mocked a yawn. "Now, Reverend, are you turning in this guy because you owe him back pay for working security? That's what happened last year, you know. I don't need the grief now. I got an election coming up."

The reverend made a sound again, somewhere between a sigh and a huff. "That was just a misunderstanding, that was. I'm calling you just to make sure you don't think I have any responsibility for this boy. He's been antisocial here, despite the Christian Identity training. And I don't want the Nations to be charged for any crime he'll commit."

"Sure, sure, sure, I'll make sure Matty here can put the kid's description in some ongoing case—we can pick him up for you on some charge, get him back in the fold." Hurriedly, Merrill motioned at Matt, handing him a piece of paper. Matt shook his head, disgusted, and pushed it back. Merrill tried again, and the paper moved back and forth.

Finally, Matt stood, the paper stuck in his hand. He motioned that he'd be down the hall. He didn't have time to waste like this on Merrill's games.

As he went down the hallway he heard the reverend make another demand. "Now, the boy is still a member of this church. He's an Aryan. So I need you to swear before Yahweh that you won't give this information to any non-Aryan, to any mongrel . . ."

As Matt walked to his office, he could hear Merrill snort loudly at the request.

Matt was on the phone, talking to Sall, when someone entered the doorway of his office. The door closed with a bang. Matt looked up. First Reverend Richard Butler, and now her.

Valerie Herrick was tall and slim and wore a blue suit. The suit sheathed her body in a new and shiny material, tight as a car's metallic skin. Her mane of curling hair was faintly copper colored. It was set off by the armor-like cloth, jewelry in a shadow box. A pair of glasses in thin gold frames rested on perfect cheekbones.

Matt cupped a hand over the receiver to ask Valerie what she wanted, but she ignored him entirely. Instead, she sat down and took out a small canister that could have held expensive makeup or perfume. As he talked on the phone, Valerie opened the canister. Inside were what looked like small foil-wrapped vials. She peeled one and put it in her mouth. Almond Roca.

She gnashed each piece apart, a certain calculated violence in her movements. As she ate, individual pieces of gold foil drifted down to his floor.

"Yes," he said to Sall. "I hear you. I know I should call him, and I haven't called him . . . but okay, I'll take care of that dang shed in Pop's backyard. I know he's worried about rats in there. I'll knock it down, get it out of there, as soon as I can."

Valerie put another piece into her mouth and broke it violently apart with her perfect white teeth. As he talked on the phone, Matt watched her chew and swallow.

When she was done eating, she put the canister firmly on the corner of his desk and stood from his chair. She left him with a glare and stalked down the hall, her heels clicking on the ancient floor.

Matt could hear her immediately in Merrill's office. The voice was grating, it came through the walls like a saw. "Dammit, Andy—listen to me!"

Merrill's voice was more muted. "Hey, all I said, Val, was that you got one sweetheart of an ass there. Is that harassment, 'cause I just want to—"

"Listen, Andy, you're going to call the union guys on the highway, make 'em pay up. Anything goes south on that deal with the new highway, there's going to be a state audit! You gotta make sure those union bastards finish it. Otherwise, my brother will just . . . dammit, I don't want Will to get away with . . ."

Matt put the phone down and went to the door, intended to shut it against the sound of Valerie's voice. "Hold on a sec, Sall. Got some screamer here in the office." Then he paused for a moment, listening to an unnatural whine in Merrill's response.

Matt went back to his desk, stepping over the pile of gold foil near the door. He could still hear Valerie's voice, all the way down the hallway.

"Why won't your boy just cry wolf? Hell, I'll just go talk to him myself!"

Matt was not surprised when his office door banged open again. But he turned his chair away from Valerie as he spoke to his wife on the phone. "Sall, I really want to hear this—I want to hear what Doug said. But I really gotta go. Can you tell me about what Doug said at dinner? He's okay, right?"

Valerie sat down, clearing her throat harshly, as if Matt were interrupting her, instead of the other way around. Matt's shoulders grew taut against the material of his uniform. "Good, good. Yeah, I want to hear all about what he's doing at dinnertime. Yeah, I'll be home by four o'clock. I love you too."

Then Matt put the phone down. He turned the chair back around and rubbed his large hands across his face before he spoke again. "What the hell is so important?" he said to Valerie. "What do you want of me?"

◇　◇　◇

Valerie Herrick moved her head, the wave of hair shifting in the sunlight, changing color as she moved. He couldn't tell what shade it really was anymore. It crossed Matt's mind that Valerie was like her hair—you could never get a fix on what she was thinking. Somehow, between Merrill's office and Matt's, she'd become calm again. It made Matt wary, as if some unknown color was about to swamp him.

Valerie breathed carefully before speaking. "The sheriff says you are the one responsible for keeping it closed, for making my entire main floor a crime scene. That you don't feel this is a serial killer thing, and that the scene won't open until you approve it."

A tremor ran through Matt, he was tense all over. "Is that what he's telling you?"

Valerie lifted a file folder from her lap and tapped it against her thigh slowly, as if it were a weapon. "Look at the file, Matt. It's so clear that a damn child could—"

"How did you get a copy of the file? From Russ? I'll have his ass."

Valerie grimaced, as if Matt's comment had a bad smell. "No, not from my errant husband. He doesn't show me anything, if you must know. It's from Andy Merrill—he saw fit to let me have a copy of the file, even if you did not." She put the papers down on his desk with a slap.

"As I was saying, look at the file. It's open and shut. It's just a serial killer's body dumped on *our property*, and I want you to call in the professionals. Call the Feds. That's all I'm asking. Every day, I'm losing thousands of dollars in potential revenue. All I'm asking for is—"

"I've got something to ask you for too." Matt spoke in a measured tone. "Why won't the resort give me a list of every employee or contractor? I've asked, but—"

"You aren't listening!" Valerie reached in her briefcase and tossed a stapled stack of paper next to the folder on his desk. "That damn roster is not going to help—my people didn't do it! But I'm paying through the nose for your damn games." She grabbed a plastic pen from Matt's desk and held it tightly between her clenched fists.

Matt sat back. "I don't think you care about who died there. You just don't care."

"Really?" The pen snapped in her fingers with a sudden explosion. She did not seem to notice.

"Yeah, really." Somewhere in his neck there was a throbbing thing, a fluttering frantic and worrisome. "Yeah, really. Just like your father didn't give a shit."

Valerie looked across the desk at him. "Look, Lieutenant, I'm not my father. I know you've still got a chip on your shoulder because of how my father treated the mining union. And I'm sorry your pop lost his lawsuit against Herrick Industries."

"He didn't lose—it was dismissed. On a damn technicality. Men died, you know."

Valerie sighed and leaned forward. "You realize I was in my twenties then, right? What did I know about what the mine was doing? All I can tell you now is—"

"That you're sorry, right?" Matt breathed out, his breath hissing. "Is that all?"

Valerie pulled her fingers through her hair and stared at the ceiling for a moment. Finally, she looked down again. "No. I don't think there's anything I have to apologize for. Look, Russ and I already saved your ass when you were drunk in that accident—the least you could do is act a little grateful now and then."

"Yeah, I am grateful, still." Matt sighed. "There, I said it. That enough for you?"

At that, she stood and threw the broken pieces of the pen across the papers on his desk. "You seem to hate me so much, but there must be something. I mean, all the damn years I've been married to Russ, you've been the only one who's tried to keep him from cheating on me. For a decade now, you've kept him on the straight and narrow."

Matt opened his mouth, the truth about the pandering charges about to come spilling out. Then, slowly, he closed it again. She did not need to know.

"You must have some liking for me, some kind of a—"

"Point of principle," said Matt. "Nothing more. I just don't think that a guy should be screwing around on his wife, even if she's a . . ."

Valerie stared at him, daring him to continue. Matt glimpsed a world of pain underneath the strident glare. Then, she whirled away from him, picking up her file folder and briefcase in one swift motion.

"Look," she said sharply. "We all have to move on sometime. I've moved on, maybe it's time you did. I'll just ask Andy to pull Russ off the case—you don't need his help, obviously, and I don't think we're getting any damn movement on this. Fuck it."

Matt stood as she did, feeling himself suddenly awkward behind his own desk. A tremble came over him, the sense that something had slipped sideways.

"Okay," said Matt. "So you want me to move on. I got that part, I'll consider it. So what else did you have to ask me about?"

"Never mind." Her eyes seemed to settle into him, sharp as talons.

Valerie's hand-tailored coat swung to the side as she went out the door. Matt looked up at the clock, it was an hour yet until four o'clock. He picked up a piece of the broken pen in his hand. The plastic tube in the middle was cracked. He looked down at it. Ink was still welling through his clenched fingers when the phone rang.

Matt took the box of tissue from the shelf beside his desk and wiped his hands clean. They were still trembling, the ink dripping down, when the ringing stopped.

He sighed and rolled his shoulders. Then he glanced at the clock again and pulled a heap of papers toward him. There was a faint note. "Leo / Lenny (?). Urgent. Call him back."

"Don't think I know a Leo or Lenny," muttered Matt, peering at the note.

Then he flipped back to the top of the stack. "Shift discrepancies at resort," read a strident note from Phyllis. "Please see attached time sheets, reconcile officers under your command."

Reconciling Time Sheets was right up there with Latrine Duty and ancient Missing Persons. Matt stuffed the time sheets under some folders and picked up the list Valerie Herrick had finally provided for him.

The Bitterroot County terminal for the National Crime Information Center—the NCIC—was at the end of the hallway, in Phyllis's office.

"Thank God," said Phyllis. To her, it seemed that every use of the machine was an opportunity for conversation. "I've been waiting for someone who can operate that thing."

"I've got work to do. Checking for felonies," Matt said briskly. Then he entered a password and pecked at the keyboard, entering names from the resort list.

Phyllis smoothed the wrinkles in her jeans. "Okay," she said. "But when you got a chance, check my manicurist for me. I swear I've seen his face on a Wanted poster."

"Sure," said Matt. "Whatever." According to the screen he was on, the employees had a few misdemeanors among them, and three unpaid speeding tickets. Dead end.

"I've got something here you might want to look at," said Phyllis. She tapped a piece of paper on her desk. "You aren't really listening to me, are you, Worthless?"

Matt tapped through the menu, looking for a way to search by similar names, aliases, and family members. He put his hands on the sides of the keyboard and took a deep breath, remembering how the program worked. "Sure I am," he answered.

Matt entered the terms of the search. Now there was a result. Brewmer, May. Five years for manslaughter. A cocaine charge had been dropped. Probably a plea. She'd been paroled after a year. In fact, she'd just walked out of Leavenworth three months ago.

Matt did not like the common wisdom about repeat offenders. He liked to believe that people made their own choices.

Brewmer—this time listed as Mary—was a past resort employee. He checked the phone book. There were only three Brewmers listed in Bitterroot County. The name jogged in Matt's memory, the security guard had mentioned someone with a similar name. He checked the transcript from his interview with the guard. May Brue. He searched for the address of record.

Phyllis was still talking. "You know Arlen's green car you were looking for? Your friend and mine, Mister Can't-Keep-It-In-His-Pants, he found it last night."

In September, the case officer's notes said, May Brewmer had ditched out of parole. No sign of her since September. Twelve weeks out, and already in parole violation.

Not for the first time, he thought of how prison stripped the good out of a person. It infected you with something, watching people hang themselves or stab each other with sharpened spoons. An infection—a disease of the soul. Every now and then he tried to change that, to make a difference in one person who might be headed to prison.

His most recent attempt had been only a few months before, a girl named Angie. She was young—so petite he knew on first sight that she wasn't really legal. They found her turning tricks at the Washington-Idaho border. The annual sheriff's raid on the Post Falls massage parlors—only this time conducted without advance notice. She was the one Russ got caught with.

Lieutenant White, of course, claimed to be working undercover. It was a first offense, and Angie was a girl fresh from Scobey, Montana. Matt thought she could change her ways. Tearfully, Angie agreed. So he managed to convince her to own up to her real age, making her file confidential, and getting her therapy and probation instead of prison.

Now he wasn't so sure he'd done the right thing by the girl. Her number had changed and he hadn't been able to reach her since, to tell her that her probation hearing had been rescheduled. Matt had heard that a girl who fit Angie's description might be working in Wallace, in the old Oasis cathouse.

Phyllis bit her nails. A tiny crunching, rats in the walls. "Car crashed into a tree. Looked like someone had been living in it too," said Phyllis.

"Since he's dead, I got an insurance hassle to deal with now."

Matt took the piece of paper, the department log for the car. "Who discovered the car?"

"I told you already. The Ladies' Man. Russell White."

"So, at least someone's still earning their paycheck," said Matt under his breath. "He might have testosterone poisoning, but Russ is still a goddamn good cop."

"Uh-huh." Phyllis gave him a look. "You saw him today, he didn't tell you?"

"He must have forgotten. We had a few other things on our minds."

Phyllis ripped a tiny shard off her finger. "Now you seen the paperwork, it goes back in the file."

Phyllis took the paper back, replacing it in a folder. She used her teeth to tear at a hangnail before she smoothed the wrinkles in her jeans again.

Matt glanced down at his notes. Mary (aka May) Brewmer had been hired three weeks ago by the resort. Night janitor, swing shift. But for some reason, she wasn't on Russ's list of employees to interview. Maybe she'd already been cleared.

He'd left his watch in his jacket pocket. "What time is it?" he said to Phyllis. "Four fifteen."

"Damn, I'm late already." He leaned over Phyllis's desk. "Look, can you get me some printouts, copies of this search? Make me a copy, and I'll find every manicurist in the book for you."

◇ 6 ◇

As he watched, a dark angel came through the light
after him. . . . 'I have loved you, Lord,' he thought.
He wanted to get it on the record.
—Pete Dexter, *Deadwood*

THE OLD man could see the newspaper outside, on the other side of the porch, where the paperboy had missed. The Spokane newspaper was always a day late out in the Valley—but why did it have to be out of reach today, when his picture was in the paper?

The ground moved under him when he went outside. Forever after, that's what he remembered about his fall. He turned the radio on and then he stepped outside the front door. When he let go of the railing and moved his feet onto the concrete steps, everything moved at once. The railing came rushing past and then he was on the pavement, a smear of thin blood on his wrist and on his temple, a throbbing filling his head.

Far away, from inside the house, he could hear the radio. "It's in God's own words," said the radio. "We can clearly see that God owns us. This passage marks us all as God's own property, God's own loved ones—'Oh Lord, you know me, you know all my ways.'" It was J. Vernon McGee on the radio. He listened to J. Vernon every day.

The voice rose and fell. "You know when I sit and when I lie down, you knew me in my mother's womb." The old man moved his head slowly from side to side. His head seemed all right, but he couldn't put weight on his wrist. His arm trembled, holding him up.

Kev ran a hand over the bristles on his head. Unwashed for a week now, they had turned into greasy spikes. And his tattoo was beginning to itch anew under a layer of bug bites.

But all that insurgency training at the Aryan Nations had paid off for him. It hadn't taken a lot to find the fuckin' bastard—Kev just checked on the spots where he himself would have hidden if he were trying to beat a rap. And at the old Route 95 firepit, he could see that the guy had just left.

For nearly a week, he'd been close, their paths crossing here and there. Sometimes he knew he was close, and sometimes he convinced himself that the trail was cold as hell. But he hadn't given up. Kev couldn't shake the sense that somehow, they were connected.

At the St. Joe waterhead, he finally saw the yellow blanket from the bus, the one left behind. It was like a signal to Kev, waiting for him on the porch of a backwoods cabin—one you could only get to by boat, or by traipsing through the woods. When Kev saw the little dock and the cabin with the yellow blanket rolled up on the porch, he froze.

Finally, when a squirrel ran up the doorframe and began to chew on the gutter, Kev was sure the cabin was unoccupied. No one was there.

Inside the cabin, Kev replenished his supplies. He found a bottle of liquor, an unopened bag of potato chips, and batteries for his music.

He still had a bunch of shit he'd hauled away from the car, it slowed him down. He threw it all in the lake that afternoon.

Children's things. Books, toys. A doll. It landed far out in the water. He looked at the cross—but then he put it back in his pocket. He couldn't let go of Arlen's cross yet. He finished the rest of the liquor in one long swallow. Then he lifted the bottle into the air, an underhand toss. He did not watch it strike the water.

Afterward, in the darkness of the cabin, he waited for the tattooed man to return.

The old man pushed himself off the ground until he was sitting close enough to the paper to reach it. He looked at it. Right on the front, there he was, twenty-five years ago. "Mining Memories: Heroes and Heartbreak" said the headline. Under his picture was his name, printed in big, bold letters: Stan Worthson.

Stan's wrist ached now with the effort of reaching out for the paper. The tinny whisper of the radio was there with him. "Now a door stood open in heaven, and a voice like a trumpet spoke to John, saying, 'Come hither, and I will show you hereafter.'"

He considered crawling in the front door. But he could already see his neighbor looking out from between her curtains. He had to get inside before the busybody called anyone, told anyone he was too weak to take care of himself.

His wrist felt as if it was on fire. He glanced at the steps, and was surprised to see blood glimmering there. The railing had scraped him open as he fell. He held on to his wrist with his other hand, thinking that would help.

He thought for a time, watching the light drain out of the sky. The evening was passing him by. He looked at the wide acre of the backyard, at the shed halfway down the yard. It leaned to one side. He thought if he lay here long enough, the rats who had overrun the shed would take an interest in him. He took his hand off his wrist and looked down again, he thought the bleeding had lessened now.

He heard something inside, the faint sound of the radio Bible verses: "The river of the water of life, clear as crystal, flowed down forever . . . On each side of the river stood a tree of life . . . and the leaves of the tree are for the healing of the nations."

Stan looked up at the white pine tree that shadowed the porch. He wondered what a tree of life looked like. A breeze blew through the trees, all the branches moved together, as if the mountain itself was in motion. He remembered thinking about the trees of life when he was mining too. On the outside he would be covered in dust and grime, and on the inside he would be full of the light and life of heaven.

He held on to his wrist, feeling the fire fade there under his grip. In the failing light, he couldn't read the story in the paper, but he thought of the Sunshine Mine, the miners dead around him, in the collapsed drifts. Dead miners, holding their lunches in their hands.

Now the miners were all around him again, holding hard hats in their hands. The miners' union prayer meetings before work seemed so near to him. He looked at his hands. The searing burn of the pain in his wrist washed through. Every time it faded away, he drifted into the past. All around him he could see the dust, the wrinkles in the miners' faces, the worn leather gloves. The miners were waiting for him to open the meeting with prayer. Gently, Stan Worthson put his head down on the concrete steps.

There were moments in Kev's head that never really went away. The past was always behind everything he saw, a vertiginous afterimage that moved beneath the present. It burned in, scarring him like a brand.

The pot he had managed to score over the past few weeks had only blurred the movies in his head. They didn't make that August night go away. Sleep brought all of it to the surface, the memories bright enough to burn anew.

He remembered the man sleeping next to him, Father Arlen. How helpless the little man looked, the cross floating out of his collar, the beard on his chin uneven. Yet he slept in an untroubled way, a naïve child.

The priest had an odd kind of surety, a strength that wasn't connected to any reality Kev knew. Maybe the peace Arlen showed in his sleep came out of that same unreal place. Kev stopped thinking about it then though. He remembered standing up, picking up his bag with his Walkman inside. Always, in his memory, he turned, and the little girl caught his eye.

She moved sideways through the station, her pale dress like a coin dropped in a well of water, flickering uncertainly as it dropped across his vision. There were other children in the station, but she stood out, locked as she was to the wrist of the large man with the tattoos.

She toddled along on her tiptoes, pulled by his grip. Kev saw that she was too tired to keep her eyes open, but she didn't want to fall asleep. Maybe not in the Greyhound station, maybe not with that man. Watching her struggle to stay awake, he saw there was a similarity between her and the little priest beside him. She had the same trust in her, it was written all over her face.

Kev remembered watching the man beside her, his protuberant eyes scanning the station, taking in each person, evaluating them, discarding them. Then the man glanced up at the window, at Kev staring back at him.

Even now, Kev's pulse beat faster at the memory. Those damn eyes would look that way at a piece of machinery he'd bought. The bastard thought he could take him!

When the man looked away, Kev could feel the speed in his veins turn a corner and accelerate. He'd thought at first he needed a reason—that the girl gave him that reason. But then he realized that he didn't need a reason at all. A look was enough.

Kev had decided, then and there, that he would take out the tattooed man. Here he was, still moving from that moment of decision, a ball hit by a cue. He waited in the cabin, trembling still with pent-up rage. He waited for the man to come back and die.

As the blood leached out of Stan Worthson's arm, he sank away from the pain. He sank into the past, back into the mine. The mineshaft he was in had a touch of bad air—you could taste the sourness in the stale tunnels. It was far away from any of the modern ventilation holes. This was where they were supposed to put the files. Deep into some mined-out stope, where they could cover the boxes of paper with tons of fill sand in a matter of minutes. All around them were the marks of ancient dynamite and the distant echo of air blasts from the lower depths. It felt like a place that had been utterly abandoned.

They didn't find out for weeks that they were in the wrong tunnel.

He remembered, too, the second time they visited that isolated drift over at the 910 raise. There was a muck slusher sitting there that time, a big old steel bucket, dragging sand and stone back out of the hole. There was good old Larry Clark working away, dust billowing out of the drift in a cloud against the spotlights he'd rigged, veins of ore glistening in the rock. The stope hadn't been mined out, after all. And along with the ore and dead rock, there were reams of paper tumbling out of the hole in the drift, every move of the muck slusher pulled more of them into the passageway.

He didn't notice at first when smoke started to creep invisibly into the raise where he was working. It was a thin, gray, seething carpet, creeping all across the ceilings of the mineways and the stopes, smelling of coal and cordite, a burn deep in the rock. If only they'd been able to cover the fire with sand as soon as the damn thing started.

In the first hour of the panic in the mine, he managed to find his partner. But his partner only cared about his own skin—about making sure no one knew he had a fake ID.

"Get the hell out of here," he said. "You know this is just going to go from bad to worse. Get out while you still can." But Stan couldn't do that. He couldn't just slip away. So he got everyone he could onto the overloaded hoists. He stayed in the mine, he kept working, until it was too late to get out.

Kev had fallen asleep while he waited for his target to return.

It was a tiny sound that woke him, a noise from the dock. He edged to a window.

A woman had floated into the boat dock, driving a little outboard boat. She put a box on top of the boards. Kev watched as the tattooed man jumped violently from the dock into the boat, his weight thrusting it away from the dock. Then he kicked the woman on the boat. The sweep of his leg carried most of his weight, it slammed her against the bulkhead.

After she was kicked the second time, across the shoulders, she fell against the dock and then into the water. She did not seem able to move her arm on the near side. The kick had broken something inside her.

As the woman fell, her hand grazed the box of papers on the dock, knocking it over. White paper spilled across the dock.

By the time Kev got to the water, the boat was floating out into the lake. The man moved again—Kev saw his tattooed arm yank in a sudden, violent motion—and Kev realized he was pulling at the choke. The thought came to him that the tattooed man did not know how to operate the boat. In that moment, Kev thought wildly of running out there, of jumping on the boat himself, taking the man down with him.

But then the outboard engine revved wildly and the boat leaped in the water, the red taillights blurred by the sleep still in Kev's head. Pieces of paper covered the water nearby.

On the dock, the tattooed man had left something behind. A blackened knife. He picked it up, but then he dropped it again. He would leave that behind.

A shiver came over Kev at how fast the man had moved. He could not forget the smile on the man's face, it had never gone away. And the bastard had slipped away again.

The woman staggered upright in the shallow water. Kev opened his mouth in surprise. She was alive. Her blouse was slick with water and with blood. Her arm hung loose by her side. He watched the water drip down off the woman in the lake, it fell from her face, her elbows, the tips of her fingers, sliding down off the ends of her skin.

Inside the ambulance, Stan felt himself rise to the surface for an instant. The air was thick and blurry, the hiss of a hose going down his throat sent cold air into him. Under the oxygen mask, he waited in a gray world of fog as the sirens sounded all around him.

With a jolt, he couldn't breathe, and he was back in the drift, again. The smell was worse than anything he'd ever smelled underground. There was a seeping miasma of smoke, a stink in the mineway that was more profoundly wrong than the sharp reek of the burned body that came up from the stope. This time, they had packed the stope with sand until there was no way anything could ever come out again. But the nauseous smell of smoke still stayed in the passageway.

Smoke was the worst thing you could smell in a mine.

He knew it. His partner knew it. But the two of them couldn't tell anyone, no one at all. So Stan kept working close to the surface, making sure there was an airhole above him, making sure that he'd get out okay, whatever happened.

He couldn't believe the fire would have smoldered in the mine all this time. He thought it was just a nightmare. But when miners came through the manway, scared and desperate, looking for any self-rescue devices they could find, he knew that the dream had only begun to go bad.

Now he was back in the mineshaft all those years ago, trying desperately to find a ventilation shaft. *Get me out*, he screamed, *Get me out*. The smoldering air was all around him, no matter where he walked, it filled every shaft and raise he came to as he stumbled through the corridors hewn out of rock. *Get me out*. Death was close to him, it smelled like smoke, like an endless burning mine.

Kev reached down to the woman in the water. Her fingers groped across the dock, scrabbling for a knothole or a handle, for any kind of purchase. He didn't understand why she didn't simply take his hand until he saw that she was squinting desperately, fearfully. She'd lost her glasses. She didn't know who he was.

"It's okay, lady," he said. "I'm not him. I saw you get knocked in the water."

Then her hand felt cold in his grip, as if the blood had gone out of it. Her arm trembled as she pulled herself onto the dock, and he saw that her blouse had ripped open on a nail, her skin torn in a line. Feverishly she crawled forward, seeing the papers rising in the breeze, blowing across the water.

"My thesis," she said. A piece of paper fluttered and caught against her temple. It hung there, bending in a gust of air, until Kev tore it away.

She rolled onto the dock, breathing heavily. It was then that Kev saw the metal frame glimmering on the wood by the water's edge. Her glasses had fallen on the dock.

Kev looked back at her. Her eyes were closed. She breathed heavily, recovering her strength. He glanced back at the cabin. Once she got those thick glasses back on her eyes, she'd know what he looked like. He didn't need that kind of grief.

While the woman caught her breath, Kev stepped silently off the dock, onto the porch of the cabin. Hell, it wasn't his fault. The woman would live. And fuck it, he was done with this lame-ass chase. How was he supposed to get a boat?

An hour later he was able to pause and look back through the woods toward the distant cabin. Sirens were coming closer over the water, a battalion of police boats approaching. Seemed like the woman had found her glasses, gotten to a phone.

Far behind him, on the lake, the sun filled the water with light. In the center of that green reflection, a tiny glint was sharp as a knife, it held the sun quivering on the surface.

As Kev moved up the St. Joe River, the flicker stayed there. It was the brown-tinted liquor bottle, thrown into the lake hours before. It turned in the current, catching the light. The mouth of the bottle dipped up and down, filling slowly with water.

Stan Worthson woke in a different world. Nervously, he turned his head toward the dark, reflective window on his right. A white bandage covered the side of his head, obscuring his vision. He looked toward the left. A red bag with a dripping line ran under the sheets. Both of his arms hurt. He pulled the bandage away until he could see the matted red and the needles. It hurt when he pulled.

"Don't touch that, don't," he heard Sally say, and he looked around toward the end of the bed and on the left. There were other people beside the bed, in the room with him.

He remembered a room like this one when he'd come out of the mineshaft. He remembered the people asking the questions, asking what had happened, why he'd survived, and so many hadn't. Now the people would want to know why he was here, why he was in a hospital bed, but nothing in him knew. All he knew was the past.

"Where's Matt?" he said. "I need to tell him something. It's real important. Where's my son, Matty?"

◇　◇　◇

Hours after the ambulance left Stan Worthson's house, Kev Macht crept into the yard. A single bulb flickered on the porch, but all the windows of the house were black.

By the time he reached the street, it was very late. He'd managed to hitch-hike in to the Silver Valley, and then he'd had to make his way by foot up to the center of the Valley. Toward the end of the day, no one would pick him up anymore. He had to walk all the way to the town of Kellogg on his own.

Doug and Kev had spent many hours after school here together, away from everyone. He came to the place in the dark, his feet knew the way on their own. It was Pop Worthson's house—Doug's grandfather's place. He waited in the shadows until past the sunset. Despite the hike up the Kellogg hill, he wanted to be sure no one was home.

Then Kev went to the side of the house and bent down toward the ground, feeling his way ahead with a hand outstretched. He knew the way. He didn't want to end up colliding with the hulk of the old Barracuda, knocking himself out on the manifold.

Finally, he dropped to his knees and crawled along the ground where Doug and he had left the car. His fingers probed the ground. Any minute now, he thought, he'd touch the rounded edge of a tire, or feel the cold steel curve of the bumper against his face.

Kev could feel the ruts deeply scored in the driveway. A stench of spilled oil rose from the ground. Bits of rust from the undercarriage broke in his fingers and he stumbled on a gasket, fallen from the engine well. Then he found the side mirror, screws detached, lying where he and Doug had left it a year ago.

The mirror confirmed it for him. The car was gone. A tired ache filled his bones. He pushed himself into a sitting position and looked at the light on the porch.

Eventually, he went to the side of the house, where he knew there was a window with a broken latch. Inside the house, he didn't turn on any lights. Instead, he stumbled to the kitchen. He ripped open all the cupboards and threw things on the floor, looking for something he wouldn't have to cook. Finally, he found a piece of fruit in the cupboard, and a loaf of bread in the breadbox. He stuffed this in his mouth and left the rest.

On the back of the kitchen door, he found an army greatcoat. He took that with him too. He left the door unlocked. He might need a way back inside.

The yard was even darker than before. He paused, listening. It was filled with the rustling of night noises, the shriek of crickets, and the sounds of rats. Then he went into the familiar dark. On the other side of the yard, when he reached out, the shed door was exactly where he remembered. He pulled it closed behind him.

Inside, he curled up on a rotting feed bag and pulled the army coat over him. He adjusted the tiny headphones to his Walkman. Then he reached in his pocket and pushed the button. The music screeched in his ears. There was a scratching sound to his right. Rats. He turned the music up. Already he was cold on the ground. He had the yellow blanket now, but he was still cold. He'd have to steal a sleeping bag.

Kev Macht shivered for a moment. Then he was asleep.

You got to tell me, brave captain,
why are the wicked so strong,
how do the angels get to sleep,
when the devil leaves the porch light on?
—Tom Waits, "Mr. Siegal"

A FAN turned lazily overhead in the briefing room. The room was stifling, the air stale. Matt began his case review by passing out copies of the file. He reviewed the current progress and existing leads. He was glad to see that Russ White was present, despite his recent retirement. Yet by a half hour into the briefing, most of the sheriff's deputies had sunk into a half-asleep lethargy. There were no questions.

As usual at a briefing, Undersheriff Ward Louden was in charge, in the absence of the sheriff. Matt saw that Louden was alert, but he was unexpectedly keeping his mouth shut. Louden seemed to be waiting for something, he hadn't opened his briefcase.

By three o'clock, Matt had covered his time-of-death conversations with the Spokane coroner's office, and his analysis of the scene on Tubbs Hill. After Matt was through, he turned it over to Russ for an hour. Russ walked through the witness interviews he'd done on the case. So far, Matt and Russ had concluded that there were no real leads, and no clear explanation for Arlen's daughter's arrival back at home, or her silence.

At four thirty, Russ closed his copy of the case file. "And then I retired, gents, so I didn't have to care about this case. But I still hope to hell you catch the perp."

Louden clapped his hands, punctuating the end of Russ's review. "Okay—thanks for showing up for this case review, Russell." He glanced around the table. "Looks like we could use some coffee. Dusty, you got latrine duty, dontcha?"

Hartman sneered at Louden. Then he roused himself and went to the back of the room. He began to collect the industrial-sized vacuum bottles that stood on the sideboard.

"Here," said Matt. "I'll give you a hand with that." Matt walked away from the table and showed Hartman how to pop the top of the vacuum bottles open, to get coffee streaming out of the spouts. Behind him, he could hear the other men stirring and talking.

"So, the case file says there was a composite portrait done," said Louden.

"Sure," said Russ. "I helped collect the witnesses. Guy at that pharmacy where our perp bought the duct tape, one or two of the resort staff who saw the guy in the hotel, and someone who saw him driving Arlen's car. It all fits together, it's good info."

Matt pulled mugs off the shelf.

"So what's been done with the composite?" said Louden to Russell. "I see it in the file, but I don't see any tips from distribution—you didn't get any leads off of it?"

"Actually, that would be a question for Matty," said Russell. "I know it was posted as an internal memo to all officers. But somehow, after I retired from the department last week, it wasn't distributed, never got posted to the public. Matt was in charge."

Matt turned and looked at Louden. "I have a problem with that statement," he began. "I was in charge of it, but there's a history here, and—"

"Y'know, I don't know if that history is relevant," said Louden, glancing at Matt. "We could play the blame game all day. Or we could just get something accomplished."

Wearily, Matt sat down on the edge of the briefing table. He gulped his coffee.

Louden looked up at him. "If you can still get the composite portrait up, do so. Someone knows what he looks like. Do whatever it takes to get it out there, alright?"

For a moment, Matt thought he might protest again. He would have posted it last week, if he'd known it was ready. Then he shrugged, resigned. "All right. Sure. Let's do it now, then."

"Any other questions?" said Russell.

Louden raised his hand. "Isn't there someone who saw him at the station? Arlen was abducted from the middle of a crowded bus station! Why didn't anyone see him?"

Matt nodded. "Bowman left the station with someone, but that's all I can confirm. No one's come forward to identify our perp. As far as I can tell, Arlen went out of there like a lamb. And the place was a madhouse. Hell, I can't even confirm who was in there."

"There must be someone who saw him."

"There is one person," said Matt. "The little girl—Bowman's daughter."

Louden looked sharply at Matt. "Is she talking?"

"No—didn't say a word. I talked to the psychologist about her. Had some advice."

"Nancy Ferreday, the shrink?"

"Yeah. Nancy thinks the girl might have some sort of block—a temporary autism thing. Nancy says she might be waiting for her father to show up. Very young victims sometimes even get triggered by the perpetrator coming back into their lives. Then they can talk. Now they call it temporary, but she might not ever talk again. Nancy will go and check on her regularly over the next few months. Might help."

Louden nodded and looked away. Carefully, Matt filled his coffee cup again. He poured a cup for Russ, who laughed quickly and waved the cup away. "Well, thanks for letting me give my two cents at this briefing, gentlemen. I got something I gotta do over at some of the local churches—so you'll excuse me, Ward, if I duck out early."

"Campaigning," said Louden. It wasn't a question.

Russell gave a quick grin. "Heck, someone has to take Andy down a notch!"

Matt looked up, trying to catch his eye. "I'd appreciate it if you'd stick around—"

But Russell White was already shaking hands, looking to leave as soon as he could make his way around the room.

After the door closed behind Russ, Louden spoke loudly, getting everyone's attention once more. "There's a new lead on this case. Frankly, I'm surprised Russell didn't find it." A malicious grin flashed briefly across his face.

He opened his briefcase. Carefully, Louden lifted a sheaf of photographs out of the case. Next was an evidence bag with a forged iron knife inside. "We had an assault over at the St. Joe yesterday. Some professor had her boat stolen—got banged up too."

Matt gulped his coffee and spoke abruptly. "How does this relate to—"

"I'm getting there." Louden glowered at him. "We brought the lady professor in off the St. Joe riverhead, got her checked out, see if the assault matched any of our usual MOs, and when she was waiting for a lady deputy to check her out, she up and ID's our suspect from the resort—saw the composite on top of the current memos on the deputy's desk. Which as far as I know is the first and only tip we've got off the composite—because it's never gone outside the Sheriff's Department doors, you know."

"No shit," said Jerry Kelberg. "She recognized him?"

"ID'd our suspect on the spot. So that's the connection—answer your question?"

Matt nodded.

"And when we talk to her further, turns out the suspect dropped something when he left, after he beat her up. He dropped this knife." Louden pointed at the bag with the blackened iron knife.

"It's a handmade knife, banged out on a smithy, the old-fashioned way. In the briefing, you guys said that Jerry and Russell cleared a man named Karl Avery. You all know Karl—he's a standard dirtbag with a nutty streak from his mining days. If he's taken in for petty assault, he wants to be charged with manslaughter. A wannabe bad hombre. Well, turns out he's also a wannabe blacksmith. Maybe a wannabe murderer too. So maybe Russell and Jerry shoulda done a better job in their interview with Karl."

Kelberg opened his mouth, but Matt spoke first. "Now look," he said. "That's not fair. You and I both know that Jerry's a rookie, and Russ was in a hurry to get out of here. Jerry reviewed the tape of the guy calling in. Russ told him Karl's a nut job—which he is—and said it was okay to skip an interview. Jesus, guys, I happen to think Jerry does a pretty damn good job, sorting through all the shit we give him!"

Matt heard mutterings around the room. One or two penetrated clearly, the sarcasm cutting through. "Yeah, like hell." And Hartman, close at hand, "If he wasn't supervised by this pair of alkies, he would have done a better one."

Matt ignored the sounds. Instead, he picked up the package with the knife and raised his voice to Louden. "I wish you'd shared some of this while Russ was here."

"Well, he isn't part of the team anymore, is he now?" Carefully, Louden spread the photographs out on the table. "See—here's the lady professor. The guy banged her up pretty good—I think this dirtbag would be capable of taking a body apart limb from limb. Next question is, what's his connection to our blacksmithing boy out in the Valley?"

Matt cracked his knuckles, he could not keep his irritation bottled up any longer. "C'mon, you can't seriously think Karl did this—he's a harmless moron who just knows how to pound an anvil!"

"Well, if he didn't do it, it's clear our dirtbag used a Karl knife. A connection."

Matt squinted at the rough edge of the knife in the bag. "You mentioned his mining history, and I seem to recall that Karl was a tramp miner in the Valley at—"

"So what?" said Louden forcefully. "Personally, I think it was a mistake to put you on this case—and I'm sure you'll be turning this serial killing over to the Feds, just as soon as you can find their number. They can take it. Isn't that right, Matt?"

"No, we're keeping the case. I can solve it." With a heavy clanging sound,

Matt dropped the bag with the knife on the table. "Thanks for this, Ward. Sure, the Feds could do it too—but they've got more important things to do, don't you think?"

Louden glared at Matt. "We'll talk about this later. I want continuing updates."

A mumble of voices rose up from the gathered deputies. Louden looked at his watch and clapped his hands loudly. "C'mon, wrap it up, ladies. There's a new update to the license plate tracking program—make sure to load it. Check the listed cars. Get your butts in gear for the night shift. Briefing is over."

Kelberg leaned over, whispered to Matt. "Barrel of fun and games, huh?"

"Yeah," muttered Matt. "It's a real goat rodeo here in Bitterroot County."

In Smelterville the next morning, the shadow of a minestack cut across the truck. Matt glanced up at the great bulk of the closed mine elevator on the hillside. He thought of the town ahead, of the people he'd see. They were the flotsam left behind after the Bunker Hill closed down and the rest of the mines scaled back in the 1980s. By now, it was beginning to sink in that the Bunker Hill mine might never reopen, and that the Sunshine and Hecla would never scale back up to where they'd been at the height of the boom.

When Matt lived in the Valley, working the mines was always his summer job. By the time he was twenty-two, his inner ear knew too well the shuddering descent of the steel elevator, the rush of an air blast knocking his helmet, the faint cracking sound of pebbles dropping thousands of feet down a chute. To the present day, he often looked around at the sound of a fan, thinking for a moment of himself under the weight of tons of earth again, breathing stale air through a vent pump, feeling the shiver of a biting drill in his hands.

Then he'd known he could breathe in the dust forever, carry home slag residue for the rest of his life. Now when he came to Smelterville, he saw what remained after the mines had closed.

It was early morning, but this apartment building wasn't busy. The old Sheriff's Department 4x4 blended with the crowd of broken-down cars in the parking lot. Few people were rushing off to the day shift at the Bunker Hill or the Sunshine.

On the stairways and in the corridors of the apartment building were big, dull-eyed men with stooped shoulders, overgrown biceps, and swelling beer bellies. As Matt walked past in the dim corridor, some came to the open doors, as if he could offer them something. He saw shadows flit behind the curtains, stringy-haired children who hung around the men like flies, asking, "Mommy, Mommy, where's Mommy?"

"She's at the 7-Eleven," he heard a man growl. "She has a damn job."

Next year, by this time, a lucky few would have gotten on with a mine in Montana or North Dakota. One or two might have shot themselves, or rolled the truck when they were drunk. The rest of them would still be sitting in the same chair, hating themselves, waiting for the wife to come home from her job, the one that didn't quite make ends meet. Smelterville was where they drifted when they finally began to lose hope.

Matt located a door on the second level, at the end of the row. It was covered with grime. He opened the screen and looked closely at the door until he found the number underneath the dust.

The door seemed to open by itself. A large face, pulpy as dough, peered over a security chain. Her eyes were half covered by her hair, her look bleared and uncertain. He had not forgotten that Brewmer worked nights.

"Hang on," the woman muttered, holding up one finger. She fumbled on the table by the door, thumbing her lighter until it caught. Then the cigarette flared.

"You someone I should know?" Her voice was hoarse and low.

"May Brewmer. You go by Mary too?"

She sucked heavily on the cigarette before she replied. "You my case officer? Look, I been meanin' to check in, I just didn't get 'round to it."

"No, I just have a question for you. You get paid well for working at the resort?"

She groaned. "You woke me up to ask me if I like my job?" The child he could hear somewhere in the apartment building coughed hoarsely, once, twice, and was quiet.

"One night. That's all I'm asking about. Did you like your job on August 28?"

"I dunno. Just like any other night, I guess. Like it just fine, long as they pay me." A figure came up in the darkness at May's feet. A small head of hair nuzzled the back of May's knee. Two hands pushed against her clothing and twisted around her leg. As she spoke, May's hand dropped down to stroke the child's sparse hair.

"When you did your job in the bathroom that night, what did you—"

"Ah damn, I knew someone would want that necklace." She let out a breath full of smoke. "This what you're looking for? I shouldn't of taken it outa there, I guess. It was just lying on the floor though—someone forgot it, dontcha think?" May reached beneath her ratty blouse and lifted a blackened chain from around her neck. She held it out for him to take. Then she spread her hands, as if to prove they were empty.

"Look, that's all. I did my job—not that they ever pay me enough for this shit."

Matt held the chain up. It glinted in the morning light. Underneath, it was silver. Something red adhered to the middle, a plastic decoration. "What's on here, on the chain?"

"What is this—a test? Look, he already come talk to me, tell me make sure I don't let on about what I saw. Now you got what I took from there. Now go on back an' tell him that May'll cover your ass. I ain't talking, so you just—" Suddenly, she closed her mouth.

She stared at him for a moment. Then she put her cigarette in a cup and snuffed it out. "You're not with him, are you?"

Matt didn't speak.

"Nothing has changed from before you got here." Slowly, she shook out the pack. "I didn't say anything you can hold me on." She held an unlit cigarette a few inches from her lips, as if it had stopped on its way there, and she didn't know where it was going.

"I don't know who the other man was." He took a laminated card out of his pocket. "But I can start reading the rights to you. Or you can tell me what's going on."

"You can't take me in. I got two." She stared at him again. "All they got is me."

"All right, you think about that. I'll come back later with your parole officer."

Anger flushed her face. She flicked at the child with her hand, drumming her fingers on the drooping head. The hands on her leg loosened a little, slid lower. Her jaw clenched as she glared. "Goddammit, I had to have a lawyer to get them away from the son of a bitch after I come out of the joint. He's addickted, forgets to feed 'em."

"You can make arrangements," said Matt again. "I'll come back later."

"He'd get 'em again, you put me in the joint. And I didn't do anything." She moved into the door a little, pushed by the weight of the tired child holding on to her legs. She lit her cigarette, took another drag. "Someone called me up, hear? I clean stuff up. He was dead already. Don't even know what it was about. It don't matter, in the end. You keep your eyes closed. Get along, go along. You live here too, you should know that by now."

"If you didn't put the body in that bathroom—then tell me who did."

"Get off," she muttered to the child wrapped around her legs. May stumbled forward a step, and left him asleep on the doorstep behind her. Then she spoke to Matt. "Why don't you go ask him? Why dontcha ask that one damned guy from the sheriff's?"

She gave him one last stare before the door slammed shut.

◇　◇　◇

When Matt arrived home, it was evening, far past dinnertime. He finished the last bites of a hamburger. On his way into the house, he threw the bag in the direction of the garbage can. The half-empty paper cup of Pepsi exploded, a wet bomb against the side of the garage. The remains of the fries spread out through the air and scattered over the rear of the car like small pieces of shrapnel. The bag bounced off the can and landed on Doug's old Barracuda, still rusting beside the garage.

Matt slammed the door as he came into the house. Sall was on the couch, watching something on the television. As he rushed in, she jumped and began to speak to him. He continued into the dining room, and through to the bedroom, where he threw his sheriff's uniform on the floor.

He went into the kitchen, poured himself a glass of water, and gulped it down. After that, he went into the garage and got a file box. He glanced at the contents. Outdated receipts, expense envelopes, and old paycheck stubs. He dumped it all near the garbage. Half of it fell on the ground, a snow of white paper. He took the empty box into his study, where he put it in the center of the desk and began to throw duty rosters, case files, and incident reports haphazardly into it. Once it was full, he pushed the pages down until they were nearly flat and resumed shoving papers into the box. Soon he'd cleared his desk at home of everything connected to the sheriff's department. He was done.

Matt could hear Dustin Hartman again, whispering to him, taking his vengeance for Matt's kindness in his moment of weakness. He could see the leers on the faces of the men leaving the briefing, laughing at their own private joke. He leaned over the desk, staring out the window into the bitter dark.

When he looked down at the desk again, the thirst for it came over him again, as if he could taste it, wet on his tongue. He began to take books off the shelves, checking behind them carefully in the dust for the bottles he'd placed there. After the shelves, he shuffled through the desk, pulling papers out and pushing things aside in his haste. He yanked the drawers out, stacking them on the floor and reaching into the structure of the desk, in between the drawers, for the places where he used to keep it. There weren't any bottles left in there either.

Matt stood beside the cabinet. He turned and pushed it. First there was a slow pirouette to the side, then a dull thud as it crashed to the floor.

He picked up papers and crumpled them up, throwing them in the trash. Then he went to the closet and yanked open the door. He took out his windbreaker and stumbled to the front door, feeling the rage still pound through him. Once he was outside, Matt leaned against the doorjamb, wondering if he was up for this.

The meeting was held in the old Moose Lodge near North Idaho Community College. Matt was late, someone was talking already. He sank into a seat near the back.

"So just to keep up with the drinking and the blow, I started taking a little cash from my sister's accounts. She was dying, she didn't know better. And so it was a nasty little racket. You all know where I was going. After she died, I headed down to the bottom like a rocket, like a hell-flamed rocket."

There was a chorus of affirmation from the room.

The walls of the room were covered in dark wood paneling, the white folding chairs and the faces of people stood out, pale against the walls. Black oak timbers held up the ceiling, the voices of the people talking echoed up into the open rafters.

Then the voice of the man at the front cracked and broke, and brought Matt's attention back down to the meeting. "I was drunk half the time, coked up the other half, hated myself anyway, wanted to die. Heck, I nearly wanted to be caught, just to have it all over with. Then somehow I got into a recovery center instead of a prison. Well, this was far short of what I deserved. I saw things there that I never want to see again."

Matt glanced around the room. There were some older men he knew, a woman at the front he thought he recognized. His attention wandered back toward the front of the circle of chairs.

"And in recovery, I met some of them that had gone to prison first, for serious charges. Those were the ones you stayed awake nights worrying about. A guy named Cuz I met in there—real scary guy. And there was this other guy in there that I got to know, a guy like me, I'll call him Jake. Big soft guy. If there's a harmless drunk, Jake was it. Jake was unlucky enough to draw this Cuz person as a roommate. We'll all pay for our sins, but Jake paid double. That he did." Then the man stuttered and stopped talking. He looked down at the podium. After a moment, he looked up again.

It was Russ White, but Matt hadn't seen him talk at a meeting in months. He wondered why Russ was talking. Matt had heard all this before—years ago. Why was Russ sharing it all publicly now? So much dirty laundry.

Russell's voice stopped and started again. "So this lowlife, Cuz, he somehow convinces Jake that he was going to kill him. Some night, while everyone was sleeping, Cuz was going to cut Jake's throat. Cuz told everyone there about it. He told the therapists about it, and I don't know if they thought it was a joke between him and Jake, but all the old hands laughed at it. Short-timers like me and Jake didn't know how to take it. If I was there today, I couldn't take it again. I don't want to do that again." Russ paused, rubbing a hand across his face, as if he could not continue.

"No, you don't," said someone in the audience. "We're here for you, Russ."

Russ nodded gratefully. "Yeah, thank God, I'm back among friends. Thank God I'm back in church, and I'm still here today by the grace of God Almighty. And thank God I got you all to help me stay on the straight and narrow."

Matt recoiled at the religious references. What kind of game was Russ playing? Everyone had a higher power, but he'd never heard Russ be so blatant about it. The problem was, the ones who talked about God all the time hardly ever believed it.

Vic, his old sponsor, used to talk about God until you choked on it. Matt couldn't imagine him being honest enough to come to a meeting now. Come to think of it, Matt didn't really know why he was here himself. Even though he'd been drinking this year, he hadn't felt the need to come. Not in a long time.

"So every night it was like that, said Jake. Every night Cuz would tell him in detail exactly how he was going to kill him. Never a variation, never a change. This went on for three months, and finally Cuz announced a date, the day and time he was going to do it. Then he started counting down for Jake, telling him how many days he had before he slashed his throat. Jake was convinced it was going to happen, but Cuz had said if Jake did anything, he'd just be dead that much sooner. And when the day came, Jake woke up dead, just like Cuz said." There was a mutter of surprise around the room.

Russ shook his head sadly. "But even so, Cuz never touched him. Cuz was found fast asleep—sleeping like a baby. That was the worst." Russ looked down at the floor. "When I saw that all it took was someone convincing you that you were going to die, it made me sober right then and there."

Russell gestured to a large man sitting at the side of the room. "On that very night, I called up Pastor Smitty here. And I was born again."

Matt glanced over and saw a hefty, sweating man with thinning hair and a round face, his skin red in the low light. Smitty, his old friend, and now—according to Sall—the new chaplain with the Sheriff's Department. Matt hadn't seen him in years.

He'd last known Smitty when Smitty was a lush, drunk with Matt most of the time, and screwing anything that walked on two legs. He was as crazy as a man could be and still holding a life together. Now, apparently, he'd gone straight too. Matt couldn't understand how people like Smitty could come back to the church. How could he do that? Wasn't he afraid he'd bring the stink of shit into the church with him? Matt could understand a meeting, but how could the clean people in a church allow Smitty back?

Matt shook his head, and in that moment, Smitty turned his head and winked at him, as if he'd heard Matt's thought. Matt laughed silently to himself, remembering that same wink over a shot glass, years ago.

Russell continued talking at the front of the room. "That was rock bottom for me. And right then, I knew that was the only way I could stay straight." Russ rubbed a hand across his sweating face and looked up again, his expression transformed.

"I've never told that story before in public. But it's been fifteen years now, and I'm still clean and sober. I'm telling you this now because I'm doing something big."

Russell stood at the podium in silence for a moment, his face gleaming. "Tonight, I declare to you that I have decided to clean up this county too, just like I cleaned up my life. I've retired from the sheriff's department, and so I can now legally run for Bitterroot County Sheriff—and I wanted my friends here to be the first to know. I know you'll stand by me. And I thank you for listening to me here tonight." Russ rubbed his eyes vigorously with the back of a hand and looked across the row of chairs.

Matt was applauding with the rest of the room, his hands beating together as fast as his suddenly racing heart. He wanted to believe in Russ. And he found now that something had caught in his throat, and he felt tears come to his eyes. Without warning, he thought of Doug, wishing that his son could see him standing up there. Then, as the applause died out, Matt's hope died with it, a sour taste filled his mouth.

Finally, the tall man who coordinated the Moose Lodge meetings stood up. "Well, I don't know if we've ever had an announcement quite like this at a meeting before. Hope they don't charge us extra for politicking!" There was laughter all around the room.

"Okay, people, there's cookies and lemonade at the back of the room, coffee too. Smoking outside please, for those of you who smoke." They chuckled nervously. Every one of them in this room smoked.

Matt wandered outside with the rest of them. He bummed a cigarette off someone and stood in the shadow of the Moose Lodge, watching the people mill around, little groups of two and three. The taste of the cigarette went straight to his head. He hadn't lit up in years, not since Sall quit cold turkey. He watched the stars, feeling the charge of the nicotine hit him like electricity. He stood there, watching the black trees against the dark sky. Smitty walked out of the building like an evangelist, the Bible in one hand, his other hand already out for the glad-handing. It was as if he had been looking for Matt.

"Quite a story in there," said Matt. "I didn't know you 'saved' Russell."

"Well, I don't know about that part of the story—Russ says his political consultant told him he has to have God to win in this county. I'm just an accessory."

"Is that right? Hell, maybe Russ made the whole damn story up in there."

"No, I was in the same recovery center with him. Lord works in mysterious ways, Matty."

Matt didn't speak. He took a drag on the cigarette, sucking in the acrid smoke.

"So," said Smitty. "Did you know I'm working for your department now?"

"I heard," Matt said dryly. He blew out a lungful of gray air.

"Look, I'm sorry we lost touch. How have you been, Matt? How are you?"

"Fine," Matt said bitterly. "Just fine."

"You ever find out the truth about that accident you were in at the last election? I remember we talked about that. I remember telling you to visit her in the hospital . . ."

Matt looked at him, a tight desperation in his eyes. "Yeah, that's what you said to do. But I could never work up to it. Then she got a complication. She died, two weeks later. She wrote me, but I never read 'em. I got rid of the letters."

"So you still don't know her side of the story?"

"Don't kid yourself, Smitty. I know. Not a day goes by I don't know what happened." Matt ground his cigarette out on a tree trunk. "It's a shitty way to live."

"God can help you, Matt. It made a difference for me."

"Don't do me any favors," said Matt. "I'm immune to Bible-thumping—I got enough of that stuff from my pop already. Valerie Herrick and Russ White already saved me once, I don't need it twice."

"Valerie Herrick? I don't understand. Just because you didn't visit the woman in the hospital . . . What was her name?" Matt looked away, across the darkening lake. He could see cars on the other side of the lake, passing on the road, the reflections of their lights growing larger and then passing, fading away in silence.

"Irene," said Matt. "That was her name. And Valerie and Russell's lawyer made sure her family wouldn't press charges. She's dead, Smitty. What happens when you're the 'Cuz' in the damn story? Go save someone who has a chance of getting out of hell."

"But I believe in you, Matt." Smitty reached out a hand and put it on Matt's shoulder. "You can beat that kind of a rap. Even one you give yourself."

"You really think so, don't you?" Matt looked down at the hand on his shoulder. He stepped back and Smitty let go of him. "You're crazy, I've always said so. After all these years, to have that kind of damn faith in me. Jesus Christ."

✦ ✦ ✦

OCTOBER 1988

CAR HEADLIGHTS floated toward them, little glowing globes in the fog. They were like insects she'd seen the summer before, lightning bugs that couldn't help flying to their death in a candle flame, one light drifting into another.

Pinpricks of mist touched her face as soon as she stepped out of the car. The dampness seeped through her stockings. The clouds that covered the ground blurred the grass into the trunks of the trees. All the way from the car to where the headstones started, she lifted her feet when she walked, kicking the drops off the black toes until her mother told her to stop.

Ahead of them, she could see a blur of white. The sun above had turned into a white, round disk, burning all the haze away. The ground steamed. All the white things floated in the gray air, like balloons. The larger smudge of white in the middle of the green lawn was big and bright, as if someone had made a big cake, as if it was a celebration.

But that wasn't what it was. She saw that when she came closer. The white things were flowers. There was a dirty hole in the ground, big enough for her whole family to stand up in. Above the hole there was a thing like a tent, and underneath it was a white box. All around, as if to cover up the dirt and the ugliness of the square hole, were the white ribbons and flowers.

She wriggled away from her grandmother and went to the flowers. She smelled them all, one by one, but there was nothing. None of them had a smell at all.

After a time, they saw people coming across the lawn, many people, coming to fill the chairs. She looked at them. Most of these people she had never seen before in her life. The fog had melted away, and she was embarrassed for all these people to see her. She squeezed her eyes shut. She reached out and held on to her grandmother's hand. Someone was talking, a deep, loud voice. And then the singing began. It started slow, a moaning sound, and then sped up. "Up from the grave, he a—a-a-rose . . ."

When her mother stood, the girl grew suddenly nervous. The skin on her chest seemed to tighten. For a long time, she could see only her mother's back. "Come back," she whispered. "Mamma, come back to me here."

Her grandmother reached out and held her. She put her hand over the girl's mouth. Her grandmother's fingers gripped her jaw tightly, they smelled like vanilla skin lotion. She opened her mouth, drawing a breath between the gaps in the fingers, and she bit down quickly on the finger in front of her teeth.

Her grandmother kept her away from her mother after the bite. The tear tracks dried after a time. But even an hour later, when she frowned or smiled, she could still feel them there, cracking across her skin.

From far away, the girl watched her mother dab at her cheeks with a tissue. She supposed that her mother wanted people to think she'd been crying, but the only time she'd seen her mother cry about her father was when her father said he wasn't going to leave.

She did not take her eyes off her mother, even though she was only a faint and blurry shadow from this distance. The man came up to her mother, she could see his hair glimmer in the sun like silver as he took off his hat. There had been so many times today that she'd thought she'd seen him, but then someone would turn, the light would change. He would disappear, the same way her pretending would fade away. Maybe this was another one. Maybe she should stop pretending he was here today. She squinted into the sunlight, wondering if the light would change on his face before she looked away.

Someone came up to her grandmother, held out a hand and spoke quietly. Her grandmother's grip loosened. The man leaned close, holding both her mother's hands, as if he were sharing his secret with her too. Maybe she already knew. The light had not changed on his face. Pretending to have him here was not enough this time.

The girl glanced up at her grandmother's face. There was only one way to be sure.

She twisted her wrist back and forth like a broken twig. Then she was moving through the crowd. At first, it was like running alongside the creek. She dashed around each standing clump of black-suited people and pushed her way between moving ladies and uniformed officers. Just like getting through the trees behind their house.

Then her foot struck the white plastic sheet on the ground, wrinkling it, revealing an edge of the dark hole and, beneath it, the white box. She stopped running, it caught at her. When she moved again, it was as if she were underwater, she could barely breathe.

Her grandmother had told her that her father was in the white box in the ground, and so now she wondered how her mother had managed to put her father in the white box. She knew it hadn't happened during their last fight. Maybe her mother had asked the dirty man to do it. And he knew, the man across the lawn. Maybe he knew how it had happened. He was holding her mother close now. Her mother leaned in, as if she would not let him go either. He was close enough that she should know now, but still she couldn't tell.

Cautiously, the girl approached them. Her mother's face crinkled as she said some words. "Thank you. Thank you so much for being here . . . I need you to be here."

The man turned his head, as if something had pained him. "I'll do what I can to be here for you. I just can't do what we planned. I just can't . . . not right now . . ."

At these words, the girl saw something in her mother's face break apart. Her mother made a sudden choking sound. The man walked away from them, never glancing back at her, never seeing her again.

The girl looked away immediately. Someone cried, that's what you did. Her grandmother told her that. She looked down at the ground. The tissue blossomed on the brown earth, a damp, milky flower.

And alien tears will fill for him
Pity's long-broken urn
For his mourners will be outcast men
And outcasts always mourn
   —Oscar Wilde, inscription on his tomb, from *Reading Gaol*

MATT WORTHSON was late to the graveyard service. Near the front, he could see a closely packed group dressed in black and gray. That had to be Arlen's family. On the right the red-clad choir, and the ministers, and the members of the Bowmans' church. Mixed into the crowd were a number of uniformed deputies.

A tall, distinguished-looking man with gray hair glanced back at the news camera at the cemetery gates. William S. Herrick Jr., come all the way to Spokane for the funeral. Somewhere on the other side of the crowd was Valerie Herrick's contingent, resort employees and uniformed officers among them. He saw Russ's gray and bristling head, surrounded on either side by the mayor of Coeur d'Alene and the city attorney. This was an opportunity for him.

Yet on the other side of the crowd were the uniforms—Russ had not won their loyalty yet. Andy Merrill did not wear a uniform, he was in an enormous black suit. And Merrill had won a place of privilege, as the current sheriff and Arlen's supervisor. Like some anchored whale, he drifted nearby the mother and wife, as if he knew them. Surrounding Merrill's contingent was the endless sea of uniforms—Bitterroot County Sheriff, Coeur d'Alene police, Spokane police, and a contingent of north Idaho firefighter and police uniforms, ironed and pressed.

The canopy billowed in the breeze, and the wife stood and went to the front. She looked blankly at the crowd. Her expression still put Matt in mind of a younger Sall. The wife stood near the grave for a moment, carefully taking a blossom from the arrangement of flowers and putting it on the lid of the coffin. The singing started back up again, and the service, for all intents and purposes, was over.

Reverend Edward Smith was wearing a white three-piece suit. Many of the mourners he greeted with a hug. Some of the women he kissed on the forehead as he let them go. To the men in uniform, he gave a solemn two-handed grip, holding their arms in his, looking into their eyes as they talked about Arlen Bowman, their chaplain.

It seemed like years since the night before. Looking at Smitty now in a white suit, Matt still couldn't shake the memory of his fat face laughing at some dirty joke, beet red from the exertion. Now he looked healthier than he had in years, his skin pale and smooth.

Somehow, that disgusted Matt. Underneath, he still thought of Smitty, obscenely laughing. The man had been in prison, after all. Despite their conversation the night before, the white suit had to be just a veneer. Anyone else, once they flushed it away, it was gone.

"Matt! Lieutenant Worthson!" He took Matt's hand in both of his. "My friend."

"Smit, it's good to see you too. Thanks for—"

"Look Matt—I'm sorry if I came on too strong the other night. It was just so good to see you. If you have a chance in the next few days, I'd like to talk to you more about Arlen. I only knew him for a few months. And I'd like to talk more about you, too."

The pity on Smitty's face was more than he could stand. "I'm over that," Matt said.

"I don't know if you are. Let me tell you," Smitty put a hand on his shoulder. Matt looked at his calm face, but he couldn't help from flinching away. It didn't seem fair that after all the nights they'd spent drinking together, all the afternoons poured away, now Smitty was the one giving advice, Smitty was the sober one.

"Hey, it's Matty!" said a voice, and Matt turned in relief.

Merrill winked at Matt and then took Smitty's hand. "You spoke to me, Reverend! Your words—they just . . ." He touched a place on the rounded curve of his vast belly, somewhere where his chest should be.

"Least I could do for him," said Smitty. "He was a good man. A fellow pastor."

Merrill smiled at them both. "Didn't know if you'd make it here, Matt!"

"Car trouble," said Matt. "My engine's running a little rough."

Merrill held on to Smitty's hand, but he glanced over at Matt. "I should tell you both that I feel personally responsible for the case not being solved, for us not having that balm to give Arlen's family today. He deserves to rest in peace. And we should have this scumbag in custody already. That's why we're all here. Responsibility."

Then he stepped away from Smitty. He put an arm around Matt's shoulders as they walked away. "Y'know, that wasn't all bullshit, and I am going to help you solve it."

"Thanks, Andy. Look, do you have Spokane's report yet? Can you let me read it?"

Merrill smiled. "You're sure one eager beaver, Matty! Hey, I haven't even had a chance to check if Spokane sent over their fancy forensics report yet. They probably haven't, they're all backlogged, like usual. So, here to pay your respects?"

"I was hoping to see if he showed up—you know, the old perpetrator at the funeral thing. There's a name for it now. Russ said the FBI calls it a grace note."

Merrill's head tilted. He looked at Matt sideways, seeming to find something odd in his face. "Taking tips from Russell again, are ya? Think he'll be our next sheriff?"

Matt spoke again. "It could happen. You can always hope."

Merrill gave his political grin, an edge underneath. "Hey, whatever floats your boat, Matty."

Then he leaned closer, whispering. "I've been meaning to ask you. You're asking the deputies about this case? You think some deputy is involved?"

"Yes," said Matt. He gulped his coffee hurriedly. It scalded his throat.

Merrill looked down at the ground, and then he chuckled unexpectedly.

"Matt," he said. "You've got a good heart, my man. Good heart. I just have to tell you how much this diligence means to me. But these deputies, they know less than you and I do about this whole thing. Let's keep it that way—not let too much information get out."

"I'm not telling anything," said Matt. "I'm asking. I'm asking easy questions."

Merrill changed expression, and punched him on the shoulder. "And it's impressive that you're here—knowing how spooked you are by funerals. Dedication, that's what it is."

"It's not as hard as I thought it would be. After all, he's dead, he's not . . . ," said Matt.

But Merrill was looking up at the last remnants of mist that curled from the tops of the trees. "Beautiful day to lay him to rest," he said. Then he turned his head toward the crowd. "Hey, Ward," he called. "Look who I've got over here."

When Matt came to Arlen's wife, he was surprised that those in attendance seemed to be avoiding her, clearing an empty path for her through the crowd. She seemed to realize it too. As the people moved, her eyes went with them, back and forth. There was no black veil for her, yet there were tearstains on the cheeks of the little girl holding her hand. The girl wore a wool dress, her blond hair pasted to her brow by sweat.

"Mrs. Bowman?" he said. "We've met before. Bitterroot County Sheriff's Department, Lieutenant Matt Worthson."

"Oh, yes," she said distantly and held out her hand. In its smooth white glove, her grip was dry as a piece of wood. "I saw something in the paper about you a few weeks ago: 'Worthson's Brave Rescue,' I think. Apparently you're a mining hero."

"That was my father, Stan Worthson. It was some sort of historical thing, a retrospective—Pop saved some miners back in the '70s. He's the hero. Not me."

"Oh." She glanced at his face and away, suddenly awkward. "A retrospective. I didn't read it that closely. Sorry, other things on my mind."

Matt reached in his pocket. "I might have found one of Arlen's personal effects. I'd like to return it to you. Did Arlen wear a necklace?"

"Yes," she said. "Yes, he had a necklace he liked to wear. It had a cross on it."

Matt opened his hand. In it was the blackened silver chain, a broken bit of red plastic attached. "Could the cross have broken off—could this have been his?"

The woman grimaced. "Oh no, that's not Arlen's." She touched her own throat. "He had a fiber string, with a simple wooden cross. Nothing heavy and metal like this chain."

Matt put the chain back in his pocket. "I'm sorry," he said. Then he glanced at the girl. The last time he'd seen her, she'd been a clay-covered ghost, splashing water over his tires. But her eyes hadn't changed at all.

"I'm so sorry about that. And I'm so sorry that we haven't solved it, and that we had to wait so long to release the body. That wasn't right."

"It's all right, it's not your fault." She looked at him. "We're fine. I think we buried Arlen a long time ago anyway."

"Right after he died, I'd imagine," said Matt slowly. "I'd imagine you would have to, for peace of mind. For the family."

"Yes, for the family," she said. "But I think we did it a few years before that."

On the other side of the lawn, Matt could see the television camera again. Now it was moving toward them across the lawn. It was following the newspaper reporters toward the Bowmans. He didn't want to finish this conversation here, in front of a camera.

"Betty," said Matt. "Would it be all right if I called you—would that be okay?"

"Sure—that would be fine." She gave a forced laugh. "There was a guy named Leonard called for Arlen too—something I should probably have told you about, I guess. But after Arlen's last phone call, I threw the phone. Broke it, I guess."

She blinked and looked away.

"He left me, but you probably already know that." She picked up the girl. The little body went limp, splayed out against her mother. "He hadn't been around for years, not really. Arlen was a great pastor, he could talk anyone into finding their best self, into not doing the bad things we're all capable of."

She tilted her head back, her eyes wet and dark. Then she blinked and shook her head, and the darkness was gone suddenly from her face.

She went on in a low tone. "The problem with Arlen was that it was his entire life, that damn church work was, and he never gave enough to us. But I had to keep part of myself. I couldn't do what Arlen did. And that's what happened to us, I guess."

She smoothed the girl's hair against her collar. "I didn't care, one way or the other. I figured he wouldn't come through. He didn't. He died instead. That's all there is to it." Carefully, she scanned the crowd. "I was just talking to another officer from the sheriff's department—I just need him . . . Arlen introduced us actually. He's been so helpful to me. I wish I could see him again, today. I need him . . . I need to ask him . . ."

"Who's that, ma'am?"

"Russ," she sighed. "Russell White. Do you know him?"

"Yes, I do." Matt turned and looked over the teeming people. "But I haven't seen him today. I don't know if he's here. I'd be happy to pass along a message."

"Oh, I was just talking to him, I'm sure he's here, I think he might have gone . . ."

"Hold on," said Matt. "Let me get his wife—I think I see her over by the coffee."

"Never mind." Arlen's wife looked out at the crowd blankly, and then her voice tightened. A moment later, she seemed to be talking about something else.

"Arlen was leaving with her, you know," she said. "Stealing my child."

"He was? That's the first I've heard of—"

"He was taking her." She looked directly at him, her face flushed, her eyes bloodshot. "You know, he'd been dead to me—I haven't talked to Karyn about him in a long time. And now I have to pretend I cared, like he's come back from the dead to be dead for real."

Matt shook his head, confused by what she said. "I'm sorry for your loss," he said finally.

The newspaper reporters and cameras crowded close to them. Someone spoke. A flashbulb went off, and then another. Her face was bright and strangely joyous in the flash.

She motioned at them, at all of them. "It'll be in all the papers tomorrow," she said. "How we had to dig Arlen up again for this funeral. He'll be the hero this time, instead of the bastard I thought he was."

Matt looked at the little girl in her arms. Her eyes opened. The girl looked at him as if she had been right about something and he had been wrong. Then her eyes closed again.

"Thank you for talking to me," said the mother. She grasped his hand again.

"I'm sorry for your loss," he said again, and walked away across the lawn.

The truck engine turned over, a choking sound. Then it turned again, and again. But it failed to catch. Matt had been twenty minutes out of Coeur d'Alene when a plume of smoke came out of the hood of the truck. The engine still ran, but after that it wouldn't go above forty miles an hour. Now, after parking for the funeral, it didn't look like it would go at all. He thought it was a busted carburetor, or even possibly a broken valve.

Matt spent a few minutes with the hood up, fiddling with the fuel lines, before giving the whole thing up. Now he'd have to get it towed from Spokane. When he slammed the hood again and yanked the rear open to put his tools away, he somehow managed to run a deep scratch along the side of the vehicle with his toolbox, marring the sheriff's star and the new paint job. It was always something.

Afterward, he sat in the truck watching the television anchors rotate in place at the entrance to the cemetery, all of them doing a variation on the same one-minute summary of the funeral. They weren't interested in him: he wasn't a hero, he wasn't dead, he wasn't running for office either. Then, as Merrill and a phalanx of deputies came through the gate, the cameramen all picked up their gear. The reporters and anchors swarmed together around the cemetery gate, shouting questions at the once and future sheriff.

The day before, Undersheriff Ward Louden had requisitioned the newest V-12 chase cruiser for the ride to Spokane. Already it was filled with officers: Mark Taylor, lieutenant, was riding shotgun. Louden was driving. They made room for Matt beside the rear passenger window, between two sergeants—Dustin Hartman and Bill Bouse.

Louden liked to tell stories in the car. Sometimes they were funny, more often they carried some obscure moral. Matt had heard them all before. He looked out the window and thought about Smitty. How could he come back and act as if it had all been forgiven? Once you'd shit on everything you once stood for, how could anything remain?

"See, there are two kinds of people in the world," Louden said. "The fuckers and the fuckees. You're either fucking or you're being fucked. And if you want to be doing . . ."

Bouse and Taylor were laughing now—they glanced at Matt, wondering if he'd heard the punch line. Not for the first time, it occurred to Matt that he'd been working in the department for far too long.

"Now this works for marriage too," said Louden. "Whoever's holding the reins does the fucking. You let her wear the pants, ain't no way she's going to let you get in—"

Hartman leaned his head back and began to laugh uproariously, a hoarse yelp coming out of him. With a flash, Matt saw the picture Louden had painted: reins going into a man's mouth, a hard bit pulling him this way or that way. Someone was pulling strings.

"Hey!" Matt said. "I'm sorry to interrupt, but I got some time sheets to reconcile for a case—the one at the resort. You know, twenty-seventh of August? So, do you guys all remember who was there? I'm sorry, I just can't remember everything that happened at the resort."

After a moment, Hartman stirred himself. "Maybe if you were doing your job, you'd be able to."

Louden glanced over. "Don't be an insubordinate asshole, Dusty—answer the man."

Hartman sat back. "Hell, that place was a mess, dontcha remember? I had to go to Russell White for direction that night, Lieutenant. Why don't you go ask him? You weren't doing shit all night." He had a smug, satisfied expression on his face.

Matt opened his mouth to call him on the lie, and realized that all he'd accomplish would be to embarrass himself, make his shame worse.

"Look," he said. "It's not a big deal—it's just that I've been informed that a sheriff's deputy was, ah, *credited* with some work before Russell and I arrived on the scene. I need to know what happened there at the Coeur d'Alene. A few of you break out some of that honor bar liquor?" No one grinned. Matt glanced up at the rearview mirror, trying to catch Louden's eye. He was looking stonily at the highway.

"Look, Matty," said Louden finally. "I appreciate your efforts. But fundamentally, something you have to understand is we don't appreciate you covering for Russell. He's—"

"What are you talking about?"

"You're a drunk, sir," said Hartman. "Not to be insubordinate, but—"

"Would you shut the hell up, Dusty?" Louden grimaced. "Look, Matty, it's pretty clear to us that Russell White worked his ass off to take over that case, and now that he's gunning to replace Andy, it's clear where your loyalties lie. You're giving him credit every time you talk to the press about it. And the fact that you haven't solved this thing—that you're trying to point fingers at deputies—is pretty obviously something Russ put you up to. You're making us all look bad. On purpose. Now the fact that you continue to waste—"

"That's a lie! What the hell would make you think—"

Louden held up a hand. "Let me finish, Matty—"

"Russell is just another lush," muttered Hartman. "You're a pair of shit-heel drunks, that's what both you guys are."

Louden whirled and hissed at Hartman. "Enough fuckin' said about Russ too. Now listen! I'll talk to Matty, and you can just shut your piehole. Understand?"

Matt turned toward Bouse. "You agree with this? Is this what all the guys are thinking? I mean, is this why . . ."

Bill Bouse looked uncomfortably around the car and then, without looking at Matt, he gave a tight nod.

"Now listen to me, Matty," said Louden. "I'm only going to be straight with you this one time—"

"Oh gee, thanks for that," Matt sneered. "Thanks for the support." He shook his head and looked out the window at Post Falls passing by. "After all the times I covered your ass, all the times I was your partner on patrol, all the times you and I shared night dispatch duty, all the friggin' work we put in over the years, you and the rest of the guys just up and decided that I would put my friendship with Russ above my loyalty to the department. Thanks for that, Ward, thanks a hell of a lot."

A flush covered Louden's neck; then, in the mirror, it covered his face too.

The car pulled off the exit ramp, and Matt glanced through the car window. Another Sheriff's Department car was there. Nancy Ferreday, the psychologist, talking animatedly to Russ White. Her face was backlit by the sun over the water. As Louden slowed, she looked over too, smiled at Matt. Then she and Russ pulled away.

Matt pushed himself upright, managed to pull a little steno pad from his pocket. "I don't really give a damn what you think of me,"—he glanced over at a cowed Hartman—"my sobriety, or my damn friends. I have a case to work, and I'm going to work it."

He turned to look at the rearview mirror again, at Louden's narrowed eyes. "There's someone who's been taking a little on the side, I think. Something rotten in Denmark here. So I need to find out who was on shift when. If someone else brings your names up as being part of something shady, I can say that you're cleared. I wish I could think you guys would do the same for me, if the tables were turned. I guess you wouldn't. But I don't really give a damn—I need this information, and I need it now."

The deputies slid their seat belts off as Louden turned off the engine.

"Well, you got my statement, at least, sir," said Hartman. "You know what I did."

Louden stepped out of the car, opened Bouse's door.

"Wait a sec," said Matt impatiently. He touched Taylor's shoulder.

"I really don't know anything, Matt," said Taylor. "Besides, I'm on duty in fifteen minutes—there are calls coming in right now. Right now, Lieutenant. I'm sorry. Gotta go."

Matt turned to Hartman. "You hold on. You just said you don't *know* what you did that shift. How about it, Dusty? What did you do at the resort?"

Louden spoke up. "C'mon, Matt, give it a break. This ain't a fuckin' TV show."

"No shit," said Hartman. "You're not some hotshit hero like your dad. Give it up."

The car doors opened, and the men moved down the hallway. Louden stayed there with him. A whisper of sound floated back to him, someone chuckling malevolently. Matt shook his head. An ache started behind his temples as his heart pounded.

"What are you saying, Ward? You saying I shouldn't be doing my job?"

"Maybe so, Matt," said Louden slowly. "Maybe that's what I'm saying, all right. Maybe this job just ain't for you anymore. Like I said, give it up." Louden leaned close to him. "Call the fuckin' FBI in already—those two jokers in Spokane can solve it!"

"No, I don't think I will."

"What the fuck?" Louden looked around the empty garage, as if he'd heard someone else speak. "Let me get this straight. As the officer in charge, you are refusing to release this case to the people who can actually solve it? You're playing right into Russell's hands. The case is an albatross—this damn thing is killing Andy in the polls!"

Matt shook his head grimly. "Look, Ward, I'm pretty sure it's not a serial killing. You think you're protecting Andy, but he feels the same way. All the signs point to the dismemberment being later than the killing. According to the FBI's own memos, the Metaline killer doesn't work that way. Besides, even if I did turn it over to the Feds in Spokane, I don't think they'd solve it either. They don't have the best rep here."

"What a crock. Goddammit, Matt, you are just going to fuck it up—for all of us."

Matt turned his face toward Louden, something rising in him, an unnatural arrogance. "What makes you so sure? I've done a number of cases right over the years."

"Oh yeah? And what was that stunt you pulled a few months back with that slut and Russell—what was that all about? His dick finally got him in the shit, and you just turned around and got him out of it! Talk about something rotten in fuckin' Denmark!"

"Look, Ward, he didn't know the girl was underage—"

"You're wrong, Matty! You made the wrong choice that day—you were covering your damn friend's back, instead of anything else! I don't know how you explain to your old dad the mining hero why you keep sucking up to the Herricks. Weren't they his lifelong enemies and all? Jesus, but you must have a real talent for bullshit, that's all I can think. Maybe you just drink the guilt away, and after that—"

"Dammit—that's totally uncalled for, Ward. Yeah, sure, years ago, I was drinking too much, but I've cleaned myself up since then. I've been dry for a while now. And dammit to hell, I'm still in charge of this case!"

Louden stared at him, as if he'd spoken a foreign language. He came closer. "Matt, you haven't made any progress—and now I have to go dig up leads for you! You're so damn pigheaded, you don't know when to shit or get off the pot. Stop bugging deputies who are doing their jobs about the damn time sheets and do your job!"

"If there is something wrong here in the sheriff's office, who's going to clear any of you, of anything?" exclaimed Matt.

With a grunt, Louden pushed his way past him, out of the garage. Then, unable to resist, he turned back again in the doorway.

"Do the job, Worthless. Even if something did happen, if some deputy fucked up the scene, what does that matter?" said Louden furiously. "Just find the damn guy who cut Arlen's throat. Lock him up, throw away the key. Shoot him in the back, fuck if I care. Sure, you're in charge, God help us all!"

Matt could hear something in his head now, a rushing sound. He imagined blood filling his head, flushing his face. Slowly, he undid his knotted fists.

Louden moved in close and grabbed his shoulder. "You throw this election to Russell White, and I guarantee that I will implicate you in everything you've ever touched. You think it's a big secret, but I sussed out what happened a few years back in that accident. I think I know what happened back then. And so you'll sign your own prison sentence if you throw this election to Russ. Someone will testify—I'll make sure the truth comes out about how you killed that bimbo you were porking. I, for one, am sick and tired of lushes like you fuckin' up major cases, not caring about what's right because what's in the bottle matters more to you."

Then Louden left him and went down the hallway. In Matt's head, the surging tide faded away. He stood there, an inaudible sound in his head, a ticking in his own skull.

> They love not poison that do poison need. . . .
> With Cain go wander through shades of night
> And never show thy head by day nor light.
> Lords, I protest, my soul is full of woe,
> That blood should sprinkle me to make me grow.
>   —William Shakespeare, *Richard II*

THINGS CAME at Matt in a blur. The edge of a cabinet door swinging open. The dark orifice behind it. His arm yanking out the round curve of a bottle. The fluid inside splashing and churning in the abrupt upheaval, glowing amber in the sudden light. The harsh sound of his breathing as he moved like a thief in the early morning, stealing through his own house.

In each bottle, there was enough for a stiff drink. Years in the past, he'd always left an inch. That way he could convince himself he could stop anytime. He had control. He could leave an inch. On the bad old days, he'd drain two bottles down to an inch before he toppled into bed. Now he was done with secrets. His hands trembled as he threw each bottle into the box. Soon his arms were burning with the effort of holding the box as it grew heavier with the weight, a collection of old friends, found in odd locations.

The angular shape of Jose Cuervo, leaning to the side in between the roof beams in the attic crawl space. His buddy Jim Beam, resting behind a stack of magazines under the stairs. A small capsule of Bushmills, lurking inside one of his boots. In the other boot, a half-pint of Absolut. And inside the box with a carton of Doug's cigarettes, more than an inch of rum left in a moldering Captain Morgan's.

Above the box, he remembered to get the bottle of Fleischmann's vodka—the one that hid inside a papier-mâché Indian statue. Wild Turkey in the back of the old barbecue, Jack Daniel's inside a rolled-up newspaper. Jim Beam again, this time sideways, under the Thanksgiving tablecloth.

He'd been up all night, thinking, and his fingers still trembled with rage. Once, he picked up a bottle and swung it around so hard that the cap popped off, spilling some of what was inside over his hand. He flinched, the touch of it on his skin like a wound on the flesh. He touched his finger to it, and brought the taste of it toward his mouth.

Not for the first time, it occurred to him that he could just sit down and empty the bottles into himself. That urge would still be there long after the time he lit a match to it all. He looked at the liquor dripping off his finger, and wiped it carefully on his jeans.

There was another hiding place in the kitchen. The existence of it there had always made him feel comfortable and secure, even when Sall was mad at him. It kept him safe. He reached up and loosened the board above the sink.

Outside, then, he heard a car on the gravel. It was Sall's Jeep, turning in the drive. She was home from the night shift. Hurriedly, he pushed the board flat again, back in its place. He glanced down at the box, its heaving pile of bottles, sloshing with alcohol. He couldn't explain this very well. As far as he knew, Sall hadn't discovered these bottles.

Quickly, he went through the house to the old sheriff's department truck. Carefully, he placed the box on the floor of the passenger seat, out of sight. He could hear Sall on the other side of the house: the squeak of the brakes, the Jeep's door opening.

She came into the garage before he left. "Where are you going?"

"I—I've got some work to do." Then it came into him, something that would satisfy her, and leave behind other questions. "At Pop's place. I decided to finally get rid of that damned old shed. I'll knock it down while he's in the hospital, clean up his yard."

As he drove away, Sall stepped out of the front door to watch him go.

The shed was a mess. It had once been white, but the two layers of paint had mostly peeled off. A miasma of rot seeped up from the damp soil. The lock had broken off, but there was nothing Matt wanted in there. Rat holes speckled the foundation.

The first blow with the axe was aimed at a patch of creeping white mold. The blade went in a half foot—a dull thunking sound—and jammed in a mass of wet wood.

Matt tried again. This time, instead of striking at the rot, he cut down through the edge of the roof. The boards cleaved in half with a shriek, and the axe sank straight through the roof and down toward his feet. A rat squeaked wildly and scurried out a hole in the side. He chopped down again, and again, opening the darkness of the empty shed. Underneath the old veneer of paint, there was dry tinder waiting for the match.

Matt worked for the rest of the morning, taking apart the shed board by board. His first strike all the way through had been a lucky hit; usually, it took more than one swing to slice all the way through. Finally, he stood back, a boxer between rounds.

Everywhere, torn and twisted boards gaped open, letting sunlight into the depths. He could hear himself breathing heavily. Then he leaned his weight against the structure.

Shingles and roof beams began to fall into the hollow center of the building. The walls of the shed bowed out, creaking and snapping as he punched at them with the axe. The roof timbers gave way with a groan and caved in.

Matt poured two inches of vodka and whiskey onto the broken boards. When he brought the barbecue lighter close, there was a sudden inhaling rush. Flames danced all over the top of the broken timbers. The boards were dry, and the alcohol helped. The heat of the flames singed his skin, but still he stayed, feeling the burn.

Inside the shed, he could hear the agonized squeaking of rats trapped somewhere between the blossoming flames and the collapsed lumber. The sound gave him a grim sense of satisfaction: he was taking care of the rats where they lived.

The next bottle that came to hand was bourbon, he smelled the aroma as it hit the bonfire. The next he hurled deep into the flames. It rolled to a halt in the center, and then as the liquor flamed inside, the glass burst upward like a miniature grenade.

They cracked, but they didn't burn. It made him laugh now, thinking he could get rid of the bottles so easily. What the hell had he been thinking? He'd have to scrape up all the glass later. Nevertheless, he kept throwing them in, one after another.

It became an easy rhythm of destruction. Yank a bottle out, pitch it hard into the center of the fire, watch the liquor inside catch on fire, grab another from the box.

When Kev came up the hill, the billowing smoke made him think the house itself was on fire. After getting the greatcoat from old man Worthson's house, and taking a blanket off someone's clothesline, he'd gone to the depot, checking schedules to see where he'd go next. He ran to get his things before the firemen came—they'd probably blame him for the fire.

He came up to the old Worthson place through the trees. The large bonfire was directly ahead of him. He still couldn't make out what was burning. It was large enough to be a slash heap or a junkyard blaze. A man stood beside the fire, his back toward Kev.

Kev concealed his plastic bag—the one with the blanket and his extra tapes—behind a bush and waited. After a time, the man he was watching began to feed old bottles and chunks of wood into the flames. Kev decided that he should simply wait in the shed until the man was gone—either he was a vagrant like Kev or he was doing a burn job for the Worthsons. Either way, Kev could gain nothing from him.

Kev edged toward the spot where the shed stood. Then, as he looked around at the empty half acre, it struck him that the shed was entirely missing. Now he could see, at the edge of the smoldering fire, one of the gray-painted walls of the shed, and part of the shingled roof. He could see a piece of his sleeping bag in the fire, the plastic melting away. Everything else was there too—the duffel bag he'd found, his food, the picture of his mother—all of it being burned to ash. Kev shouted and ran toward the flames.

Matt turned his head, fumbling for his holster, and found that he'd left his gun inside the truck. He stepped back from the fire, and took an empty bottle in his hand. The boy slid to a halt on the verge of the fire, his steel-toed boots covered in cinders.

Matt took him by the arm, dragging him back from the bonfire. The boy jerked out of Matt's grasp, and two small earphones popped out of his ears as he pulled away, a tinny sound at the ends of twin cords. Their absence seemed to cause the boy pain. He shifted, brushing against Matt brusquely.

"What's your problem?" said Matt.

"No problem." The boy stalked away a few paces and stood glowering into the blaze that was consuming everything in the shed. "Why'd you have to burn it down?"

"It's Pop's place." Matt threw the bottle into the flames. "Why do you care?"

The boy was expressionless, his face red from the light of the fire. His eyes glinted from under his brow, deep pockets of emptiness. Yet he seemed familiar to Matt, in the way that people in dreams are familiar. In that half recognition, it also came to Matt that there was a question in the scowl. The boy himself didn't know if the act was succeeding. Intimidation was something studied for the kid, Matt saw. It went only as deep as flesh.

"C'mon, kid—start talking. Did you have drugs in the shed or something?" Matt jingled the cuffs on his belt. "I'm with the sheriff's office—I'm not fooling around."

The boy gave no sign that he'd heard the cuffs. He muttered something inaudible.

"What did you say?"

"You work for Sheriff Merrill, huh? That kike." The boy ran a hand over the ruff of hair on his head. The movement made Matt's skin crawl. "Fuckin' Jews, man."

"What is this garbage? How about I just arrest you now, breaking and entering?"

"I didn't break anything. Didn't hurt anyone," the boy said sullenly.

"Trespassing, then. I can cook up something. What the hell are you doing here?"

The boy's hand came back to its strange movement, caressing the fur on his head as if it were a piece of dead flesh, something acquired from a recent victim. After a moment he spoke again. "I was sleeping here, in that shed. You burned my things, man."

"I'm sorry, Mister . . . ," Matt paused and held out his hand, waiting for the boy to say his name, take his hand. There was no response, and Matt dropped his hand. "Well, I'm sorry your property was burned up—what did you have here?"

"Fuck it. After all, I still got my tunes." He flicked the earphones that hung around his neck and pointed behind him. "I'll just get the fuck outta here. Don't fuckin' worry about it."

"Okay—but I still need to know what you were doing here in the first place."

"Fuck you. Why do you need to know?"

"Well, this is my pop's property, and I can arrest you, and I can—"

"Ah, Jesus Fuck-on-a-Stick, don't give me that shit. Look, man, I just came here for that 'Cuda—the old yellow car parked beside the house." He gave a malicious smile, as if he'd caught Matt in some sort of trick when he'd refused Matt's hand.

"I see." Matt felt a sudden distaste for the boy. It had come with his smile, the slyness of it. "You mean you wanted that old junker I dumped in the lake last week?"

The boy didn't move. His face shifted, but the smile remained, hollow underneath.

"Well, then again, I might not have dumped it. How about you tell me how you knew about the car, and I might tell you where it really is. How you could get at it."

"I met this kid Doug, like a month ago. Bought the car from him." Matt heard the lie in that. Then the liquor in a bottle caught on fire. They stepped back as the bottle spat flames. Matt scratched his head with a soot-blackened hand. "And you had the cash."

The boy shrugged his expansive shoulders. "Hey, man, Doug sold it. I paid him."

"Sure he did. Where's the deed of sale—the papers that prove you own the car?"

The boy gestured at the bonfire, where the coals were red. Despite himself, Matt felt a sudden pity for the boy.

"Look, the car isn't worth all this." He stood and brushed dirt and dust and soot off his hands. "It's just a heap of junk. I had to tow it out of here to get rid of it."

"I like old muscle cars like that Barracuda. I can make it run again."

"All right—have it your way." Matt tossed another bottle into the fire. He watched the flames catch the label and lick the glass slowly black. "So maybe Doug really did sell you the car. I don't know—who the hell knows? I'll give you a ride out to where it is, and you can decide if you still want that piece of crap. That okay with you?"

The boy stared across the fire at Matt. "You didn't tell me where the car is."

"You didn't tell me how you met my son."

In the truck, Matt recognized the boy's reflection in the mirror. It was the shaved head, the sunken eyes, that had thrown him off. "You didn't just meet Doug, did you?"

Kev sighed and unplugged the earphones from his head. "What?"

"Doug—my son. You went to high school with him. Your name is Kevin, right?"

Kev shrugged.

"Yeah, that's you all right. Why, you guys were best buds for the longest time. Both of you have changed a little, I guess, since back then. But I never forget a face. And hell, I couldn't forget your scared faces when I picked you up at the police station."

Kev shrugged again, as if the conversation were about another person, someone neither of them knew. He turned to look out the passenger window.

"Ah, come on," said Matt. "You got arrested with Doug back a few years." Matt accelerated as the car came onto the freeway. "Back when you kids were in high school."

"Junior high," muttered Kev.

"Yeah—that was it! But you weren't here the last year of high school, were you?"

Kev shrugged. The tinny growl of music from the earphones hummed in the car.

"What did you do, drop out? What happened? Why'd you lie to me?"

Matt glanced at him again. "Regardless, I'm sure it was you. Tied up with Doug."

Kev stared out into the blasted landscape of Smelterville as the car moved further out of the Silver Valley. He clenched and unclenched his fists. "I don't remember."

"You don't remember?" Matt shifted savagely, pulling the lever down as the car jumped. "You were the reason he was arrested! You guys were best buds!" Matt shook his head. "Can I take you somewhere other than the car? Where do you need to go?"

"Nah—don't fuckin' worry about it."

"So, your folks aren't around here anymore then? Did they move away?"

Kev shifted his shoulders.

"Okay, so you don't want to tell me. But if Doug is out there, on the road alone, I'd hope someone would give him a hand. If I can, I'd like to help you out a little too."

"Don't fuckin' worry about it."

"No, really—how about this. Doug is gone right now. You could sleep on his old army cot, in the garage. But it's kind of cold without a sleeping bag. You got one?"

"You burned the sleeping bag too." Kev shrugged. "Don't fuckin' worry 'bout it."

"Hey, I'm sorry. Really. Why didn't you say you were Doug's friend? I nearly kicked you off the property." Matt pointed a thumb at the shield between the secure backseat and the passenger area in front. "I nearly arrested you."

Kev shrugged and nodded, as if to agree this could have happened.

"Well, now you know where the car is. It's at my place—sitting out in back of my garage. Heck, we could work on it together like you guys used to. We could get it going."

Kev rubbed his head, pondering. "I don't work with Jew-lovers. Fucking kikes."

Matt slammed on the brakes, throwing them both violently forward before the seat belts caught them. The cab of the truck jerked to a halt, the engine coughing.

Matt looked over at the boy, but Kev just sat upright, facing the windshield, as if he were made of wood. After a moment, he replaced the earphones in his ears.

Matt took his foot off the brake and accelerated again. His voice was tight with anger. "All right, go to hell then. If that's how you want it. I guess I already offered you the garage to sleep in. And you can have the car. But I'm not going to lift a hand to help you fix that piece of junk. Get it running and leave. Just stay the hell out of my house."

"No problem." Kev rubbed his head placidly, as if entirely unperturbed.

At the end of the dream, he would take his revolver
from the drawer of the bedside table . . . and open fire
on the men. The noise of the weapon would wake him,
but it was always a dream and in another dream . . . he
would have to kill them again.
　　—Jorge Luis Borges, "The Waiting"

THE BROWN truck with the scratched gold star decelerated as it came farther up the highway toward Fourth of July Pass. Matt drove warily past flashing yellow lights and somnolent bulldozers, weaving his way in and out of construction zones and blasted rock.

Jerry Kelberg read in the passenger seat. Kelberg's back was flat against the seat, feet planted on the glove box. At the top of the pass, sunlight touched the pages of his book as the truck shivered across a section of gravel-covered roadway. Matt glanced over. "So what's the book about? It's in English, not Korean, right?"

"I don't even speak my mother's damn language anymore," said Kelberg. "You want to know about the book? Here's the first sentence: 'For seven days in the spring of 1882 the man called Shalako heard no sound but the wind.'"

"Bullshit. There aren't any one-man shows like that anymore." Matt snorted and glanced down. "Hey, pick up the posters—they're getting torn down on the floor."

"Sure, no problem." Kelberg scrabbled on the floor of the truck. "See, only the top one is dirty—we can still use it." He unfurled the poster. Outlined on the poster was a black-and-white face, cheekbones finely stroked under slightly bulging eyes. The mouth had a certain sensual tilt to it, as if it had been drawn unevenly. Above was a legend: "Reward Offered—Wanted for Questioning in Connection to Homicide, Kidnapping—Call Bitterroot County Sheriff's Department 208-664-1511."

They had come down from the mountains now—the car moved from the heights into the lowlands. They passed a distant white cross standing in a field of brown. The Cataldo Mission—the only Spanish mission in Idaho. The road slanted steeply downhill before it flattened out on the valley floor. Then they turned off the thoroughfare onto a winding dirt road. The sheriff's truck fishtailed back and forth across the dry-pan gravel.

Matt wrestled with the wheel as the truck caught the ruts. Then he spoke again. "What a waste of an afternoon. Hanging posters up, picking up some dingleberry like Karl Avery. I'd spend my time looking for a transient—someone from out of town. Maybe one of those skinheads up at Reverend Butler's—that's what I should be doing."

"There is some transient who's been stealing," said Kelberg. "Petty thievery. Took batteries and tools from a shed. Stole a blanket off someone's clothesline the other day."

"This is on another scale," said Matt. "Not some kid picking clotheslines. This guy who beat up the professor, he's serious. He's not playing around. And he's on the move."

"So the resort guy could be in another state now, huh? Coulda gone anywhere."

"Maybe." Matt drummed his hands on the wheel. "But the dismemberment says to me it's personal. I think it's someone who knows the Valley. He's still here."

"So maybe he's like those old guys that live under the 95 bridge, and always go to the shelter in Spokane for the winter," said Kelberg. "Homeless types."

Matt scratched his chin, at a spot he'd missed shaving. "Oh, some of them find a place for the winter here in town. There's a kid sleeping out in our garage right now."

"You let these people sleep in your garage?"

Matt glanced at him sharply. "Well, there's a difference between homeless and transient. I know this kid—he's lived here in the Valley his whole life. I found him sleeping outside on my pop's property, he's one of my son's old friends."

"So why is he still in the garage—instead of inside the house?"

In the distance, the thick line of the Sunshine minestack jutted from the mountainside. Matt downshifted. "My son can make friends with anyone, Jerry. Just because Doug's okay doesn't mean I'd trust his friends."

The truck slowed as the ruts narrowed. "Get a map out, wouldja?" said Matt.

Kelberg yanked out an unwieldy armful of maps. "Here," he said, unfolding the one on top. Then he scrabbled a moment longer in the glove box. "What's this?" he said.

He held up a chain with a lightweight pendant, something ragged and worn.

"Huh," said Matt. "That's where it's been. I had the truck at a shop over in Spokane all week, forgot about that damn thing. So you picked it up, what do you think it is?"

Kelberg pushed on the chain with his fingers. "It's silver, with a red plastic pendant."

Matt nodded. "But that's not any pendant. Why's the silver so black, bright boy?"

"I dunno—has it been in the mines a lot? Sulfur makes things black in the mines."

Matt snapped his fingers. "Right on the money!"

"And the pendant looks rounded too—like a thing I saw in the mining museum here in town. Is this thing hanging on the chain an old-style blasting cap?"

"Right—that's half of a blasting cap, about four seconds long."

"Four seconds?"

"You light a spark to it, it would burn for four seconds before it lights the dynamite in the hole. Someone's dumped out the explosive in the cap, punched a hole, hung it on a chain. And you're right, the chain's black from sulfur in the air. No tourist wore this thing."

"Where did you get it?"

Matt reached out and took the chain. "That was given to me by someone who saw the murder scene before someone got in there and cleaned up some evidence. Don't know where the other half of the blasting cap is."

"So if you find that, you can put it all together, huh? Maybe Karl Avery knows something, huh? Something I missed, right?"

Matt shook his head and said nothing. The smokestack from the mine was so close now that it seemed to hang over the rutted road. They were moving into the empty blasted zone behind Smelterville now.

Dust rose in a cloud around the truck, as if the entire hillside were covered in loose, dry dirt. Shapes emerged through the brown fog, things beside the road. In every direction, seemingly random flotsam—broken metal steps, engine flywheels, fenders, cracked steel beams—was joined together in a grotesque mockery of life. Massive figures with eyes made of hubcaps, fantastical twisted flowers, towers as tall as an upended truck. Around the feet of the things, the grass was trimmed, as if they grazed at night.

Kelberg gestured at the hulking things. "This guy, Karl Avery, he makes these?"

"No." Matt shook his head. "His brother does. The brother who takes care of him, makes sure he eats regularly, takes his meds, and all. He's helpless on his own, he—"

"But he called in to confess. We've got the knife, we've got a tape of him—"

"*We* is just Ward Louden jumping to unwarranted conclusions. No one's done any legitimate police work yet on if the guy who ripped the boat off is the same one—"

"C'mon, Matty—they found the knife on her dock, and they know that Karl—"

Matt gave Kelberg a sharp look, but he spoke calmly. "Sure, Karl Avery might have made something they found. But what does that prove? Karl wasn't that bright to start with, and about fifteen years ago, he had some sort of major head injury in the mines. So he's not capable of much now. He makes things. And the fact that he's making pretty lethal-looking knives concerns me, but it would be hard for me to see Karl as a killer."

One tire lifted and the dirt spun out behind them as Matt turned into a side way. Now they were surrounded on both sides by broken pieces of disjoined metal. Something that looked like a disemboweled thresher loomed over their path. Matt gently edged the truck past it. Ahead of them stood a machine shed with peeling white paint.

Matt stepped out of the car and motioned Kelberg to do the same. All around them stood huge metal things, some with grasping hands, others with horns or antennae, some with oversized, flat, large feet. Like sentinels all across the lawn.

Slicked with a thin sheen of the ever-present dust, a gray-haired man squatted in front of the tilted machine shed.

"I see him," said Matt softly. "Just take this one slow and easy. Don't jump to conclusions, okay? The guy's a little jumpy. So nothing too quick."

They got out of the truck and walked toward the man. Something glinted in the man's hand. "Heya," he said suddenly, without looking up. His voice was deep and gravelly. "Glad you could make it." He chuckled, a weird uneven sound. Then he reached behind him. Matt felt Kelberg flinch, and suddenly the boy had his revolver in his hand.

The man chuckled again, sound trickling out of him like a faucet running. He breathed heavily. "Shoot me now or you can shoot me later. It's all the same to me."

Matt stepped forward, his voice slow and gentle. "Put that away," he said to Kelberg. Then he spoke to the gray-haired man. "Karl? We've met before. My name is Worthson—"

Karl seemed to flinch back at Matt's name. Then he stretched his arms wide and looked up at the sky. He spoke loudly, shouting at the mountains, the trees. "There's an end to it—he's come for me now!" he said again. "An end to it—an end to all things!"

Matt continued talking. "Now, Karl, you can just call me Matt. I grew up over in Kellogg, you might have met me or my pop there. I know your brother."

Slowly, Karl looked down from the tops of the trees, and his tone was eerily calm. "Can't say I've met you before—so I'm pleased to meet you fellows, both of you." He put the empty metal pole down flat on the railing and reached out with his right hand to shake. Matt watched Kelberg slip the gun back in the holster before he touched Karl's hand.

"Well, I done it. I did that murder," Karl said. "You come to talk about it?"

"Sure," said Matt. His tone said he didn't believe it, but he calmly motioned them onward, and then they followed Karl into the machine shed. The building was extended and narrow, made to hold three or four tractors and a thresher or wood chipper. Under the low ceiling, the building was nearly full of junk. They followed Karl through a dim corridor. Grimy cardboard boxes sat on every side.

Ahead of them, dirty wet spots of fresh blood spotted the dusty floor. They came to a doorway where a single lightbulb hung and a stack of shoes rested beside the wall and the closed door. Karl knelt down and talked while he unlaced his boots. "I cut open Father Arlen. I seen his insides. You know about that?"

"We don't know," Matt said evenly. "We don't know as much as you do."

Karl thumped his chest with the boot he held. "When I got him into the bathroom, I sliced him from the bottom up. I started down below so he would feel it all."

Matt caught his breath. It was a loud sound in the closed space. "I see."

"You see, huh?" Karl's croaking chuckle broke out. "Let me show you." Karl pushed the door before them open. Then he turned on the light.

Under a floodlight, there was a hanging figure, flayed and muscled flesh. Mounds of offal hung off the blood-soaked cloth on a small table. A large, filthy knife lay on the table. Water pipes ran down from the ceiling to the floor, and an irrigation control system took up half of the wall behind the hanging bloody thing.

Matt pushed Karl slowly in front of them. He kept Karl's arm trapped high up on his back, and Karl turned and twisted when Matt moved, like a puppet. Matt cuffed one of Karl's hands to the pipes and walked forward toward the bloody table.

The sharp, coppery taste in Matt's mouth and nose rose up from the blood. Matt looked at the intestines and the knife on the table, then glanced over at Jerry Kelberg. His eyes were as large as targets in a shooting gallery.

Then Matt stood, hands behind his back, looking closely at the flayed, bloody figure against the far wall.

"Jesus Christ, Karl, stop wasting our time. What is this dead thing?"

Karl paused uncertainly, his uncuffed hand still up in the air, holding a boot. "It's another body—I swear it is. I did a murder. Now you're gonna try to take me in for it, and I'm not going. I'm gonna escape, and you might try to shoot me, you should shoot me down in cold blood, like the murderer I am. I got the body here." Karl grinned.

Matt sighed. "Karl, we are going to take you in. But don't get your hopes up." Matt pointed at the figure that hung from the ceiling. "Because that's a deer. That's a nice side of venison that I'm betting Thomas shot, maybe yesterday. And he was gutting it, and had to go someplace, but you got it out of the freezer, and you're playing sick little games with it, trying to scare us. When did you last take your meds?"

Karl staggered, as if from a blow. "There's nothin' wrong with me. Nothin' . . . " His crying sounded like the chuckle—high and croaking.

"Here, I'll take him to the car," said Matt. "Jer—why don't you put the deer in the refrigerator, before we get out of here. Thomas might want the damn meat, after all."

The freeway traffic slowed as the truck came into old Wallace, where the brick buildings built after the fire of 1910 leaned shoulder to shoulder. The only stoplight on I-90 was working today. Matt coasted slowly to a halt as the light went yellow. He pointed ahead, to a half-built metal figure of a miner holding a drill made from a V-8 engine.

"Sculpture?" said Jerry. "Looks more like a traffic accident. Why are we here?"

"Common courtesy—let his brother know we're taking him in."

Up ahead, a shape was bent over the sculpture. A flash of white light, a welder's mask. Streaks of dirty sweat ran down his face and his shoulders.

When they came close, the small man pushed the welder's mask back on his forehead. Matt was always surprised at his eyes, how young Thomas Avery looked. After he pushed a pair of black-framed glasses onto his face, his eyes were suddenly older. He took one large glove off and slapped it against his thigh. The color of the dirt on his hand was the same as the color of the glove.

"Tommy," said Matt. "How goes it?"

"Mr. Worthson, what can I do for you?" He glanced at their uniforms and their guns and grinned uncertainly.

"We're giving Karl a little trip to the jail. For observation." Matt shook his head sadly. "We just picked him up at the house."

Thomas lifted the welder's mask off his head and set it down on a bench. His head was covered with black hair. When he ran his hand through it, it stood up in spikes from the sweat.

"You can't just release him into my custody?" Thomas looked at the ground.

"Not this time," said Matt. "I'm sorry—he made a phone call, with a threat too."

Thomas glanced up at them. His eyes were full of tears.

"Dammit, Mr. Worthson, he won't take his meds. We took him to Spokane, got him a good doctor. But it doesn't do no good. I mean, my little hobby here is beginning to pay." He gestured at the half-made miner. "I got a commission out in Missoula. Even had some art gallery in Portland asking. I'd like to take some of these opportunities, you know?"

Thomas took off his other glove and pushed it into his overall pocket. He looked up at the sky and blinked rapidly.

"He hasn't ever hurt anyone, has he?" Matt reached out awkwardly, he touched Thomas's shoulder.

"Oh no," said Thomas. "He's afraid of everything. A while back, I accidentally stepped on a cat's tail while I was moving something. The cat was fine, but Karl cried for hours. He's not violent, couldn't hurt a fly." Thomas tore off his glasses and rubbed vigorously at his eyes with one hand. He shrugged Matt's hand off his shoulder.

"So what's it about this time? Did the postman complain about him again?"

"No, Luecke hasn't complained about him since the mailbox incident."

Thomas looked off in the distance.

"Nothing like that."

There was a pause.

"Let me tell you what this is all about." Matt stepped a little closer to Thomas and looked into his reddened eyes. "A month or so ago, you remember that murder over in Coeur d'Alene, in the resort?"

"Yeah, I remember that. What does that have to do with us?"

"Nothing, I hope. It's just that Karl must have read the story in the paper, and while you were gone, he called into the sheriff's office and confessed to the murder."

"Oh my God—you don't really think that—"

Matt held his hand up, like a stop sign. "No, I don't really think so. But his fascination worries me—he tried to tell us a deer was a dead body. He liked the idea."

"Jesus, that deer I shot yesterday? He pulled that out? I got a license, you know."

Matt nodded. "Are you sure that he hasn't hurt anyone? He said something at the house, made me think he knew what he was doing, like he wanted to kill someone."

Thomas spread his grimy hands out in front of him. "You know, I don't know what goes on in Karl's mind anymore, I really don't. But you'd have to talk real hard and real long to convince me that he could change into someone violent. He's not a bad man."

"I know," said Matt.

"I mean, it took me months to teach him how to use a welding torch. It would take a lot of work to teach him anything. Arlen wasn't killed with a welding torch, was he?"

"No," said Matt. "Like I said, he was cut in many pieces. It took a lot of work."

"Well, there you have it," said Thomas. He took a glove out of his pocket and put it on his hand. "I don't think that constitutionally Karl could do something like that."

Matt looked across at Kelberg. "Last thing—Karl have any visitors lately?"

"Well, there's one guy who's been around lately. Name's Curtis—Karl says he knows him from when he used to be a miner, when he could still work. But I didn't ask too many questions. Just figured someone who wanted to see him, that's a good thing . . ."

"Would you recognize him?" said Matt sharply. "Pick him out of a lineup?"

Thomas shook his head. "I only ran into him once, in the machine shed. Karl said he'd been around a bit, but I wasn't sure if he was making up the other visits—the old friend. You know . . . he makes things up."

"Yeah." Matt sighed, looked away. "Don't you worry about Karl. I'll make sure he's taken care of—I'll make sure he comes back home safe and sound, just as soon as they're done talking to him." Matt shook Thomas's rust-darkened hand. "You have my word. He'll be all right."

"Hey, thanks, that means a lot to me." Thomas tore off his glasses and rubbed at his damp eyes. "And Matt—I hope you win your next election. I'd vote for you again."

"I'll keep it in mind. Thank you." Matt motioned Kelberg back toward the truck. As they left the town of Wallace, the sky filled with fog. The day was gray now. On the road back to the highway, Matt thought of the sculptures that had loomed out of the woods at the Avery place. Now they seemed like lost sentinels looking for something long since past, abandoned by everyone they'd ever known.

Above the car, the sky seemed to draw closer for a moment. They could feel the weight of it, thick with moisture, sinking into the Valley, saturating it with heavy cloud.

Then as it began to rain, the foothills echoed with the sound, as if there were myriad tiny fish jumping. The shoreline disappeared as the falling water swept across the lake. Far out, above the deeper parts, the surface simmered and hissed as the drops hit.

We rode to Coeur d'Alene, through Harrison and
Wallace, they were blasting out the tunnels, making way
for the light of learning. When Jesus comes a'calling,
she said he's coming round the mountain on a train.
—Josh Ritter, "Wings"

THE LIGHT on the answering machine beat a tiny pulse in the darkness of
the cold house. Matt stripped off his sweat-soaked uniform shirt, gave a futile
wipe at the venison bloodstains on his work shoes, and wearily punched the
blinking red button.

Unexpectedly, the sound of Doug's voice filled the room.

As the sound emerged, Matt stopped moving. He was not prepared to hear
this particular voice. In his mind, he could hear in the sound of its uneven
timbre the faintest of echoes of every teenage argument, every ten-year-old
utterance, every baby cry. Matt closed his eyes and sank down to the couch.

Matt did not know who his son was anymore. All that he knew of Doug was
past. He didn't even know where Doug was, and he still didn't understand why
he had left. He tried to think back to when his pop had been around, when he
had been a boy Doug's age, but there was nothing solid there for him to hold
on to, it seemed, no emotion that came clear—and besides, he was so different
from Doug. They were light-years away from each other, universes apart. Then
the voice stopped, and Matt realized he hadn't really comprehended a word
the boy had said.

He punched the button again. Once more, Doug's voice filtered up through
months of abandoned cities, distant places far removed from Matt's experience. His voice was like something intentionally lost, now echoing out across
the room again.

". . . just wanted to tell you . . . I've been figuring things out, here in LA. I
think I got a handle on what I want to do with my life. I don't know if you'll
like it or not, I don't really give a damn if you do. I didn't know if I'd be back. I
got a lot going on in LA already, got a job here, got a life. But I miss the mountains there, I miss the high places, the cabin too. I want to get back there when
I get a chance. And Dad, don't worry, okay? I'll be all right. I just had to figure
things out, on my own, without you around. I'll be back, you take care . . ."

As the message ended, Matt heard a sound, a low moaning in the air. He looked around a moment before he realized that he himself had been making that sound.

His cheeks were wet. He remembered with a sudden gratefulness that no one else was nearby. The house was empty, his wife was at work. He wouldn't want to admit to anyone, even Sall, that he was crying his eyes out over a damned phone message.

He was relieved to hear the ratcheting tick of an adjustable wrench continue from the other side of the house, where Kev's work continued, undisturbed.

After dinner, Matt took the kid in the garage a steak. He didn't invite him into the house, he didn't trust him that much. The kid had a little suite set up in the corner of the shed behind the car—on the army cot was an old pillow, that bedraggled blanket, and a poncho Matt had given him. The kid had also cadged Matt's broken-down easy chair for a makeshift living room. By the side of the car was a jug of water. The kid was working on the car in just shorts, shirtless and shoeless. His torso was streaked with grease, and his cot was spotted with old oil. Looking at the boy's dirty skin and the hardening muscles moving under the strain of the wrench, Matt had second thoughts. Maybe he should let him into the house every few days for a shower.

The kid chewed on the steak appreciatively. Matt thumped the rusted hood of the Barracuda. "How's it going with this old heap?"

For the first time since he'd encountered the kid at Pop's house, Matt got to see him smile. "Ah, it's going great," the kid said through a mouthful of potato. "I got the weeds cleaned out—they were growing all over, through the engine, in the fan and the fuel lines."

"Okay," said Matt cautiously. "That's a start."

"Ah, I know, I know." The kid waved his fork in the air and gulped down his mouthful. "I found a battery here beside the car, so I stuck that in—got the juice going."

"Oh damn," said Matt. He glanced inside the engine well.

Out of the corner of his eye, he caught sight of the kid glowering, a renewed sullenness. At the least comment, the kid sank into a state of surly antagonism.

"No, no," said Matt. "I was just kicking myself, leaving a battery on concrete."

The kid brightened a bit, but he still held the sullen posture. "Yeah, I checked for that before I put it in. I know about batteries deionizing. Battery kept the charge."

Surprised, Matt jerked his head upward, banging it into the hood. Gingerly, he felt his scalp for bruises. "Huh, you know that already, Kevin?"

"Yeah, my uncle taught me all about electrical components—like you shouldn't leave a battery on a concrete slab too long, it'll deionize. It's Kev—just call me Kev."

"Hmmph," said Matt.

Kev finished the steak. "I think it's all working. Let's put in the key, start her up!"

Matt took a hose in his fingers and pushed at it, feeling the stiffness and decay in its twist. "Sure, it'll turn over. And it might even run for a while. But all your hoses and fuel lines are filled with dust and old gasoline. That old gas has been sitting so long, it's turned into sludge. Once you turn it on, all that gunk will get driven deeper into the engine."

Kev shrugged. "So it'll run dirty. So what?"

"No, it could end up damaging the engine. Hurt the valves permanently."

There was a frustrated moan from Kev, and he threw a wrench against the wall. After it clattered to the concrete, Matt spoke. "The first thing is to replace all the fuel lines. There's even the right gauge of line here somewhere. You know how to do it?"

Kev grunted. "Yeah."

Matt rubbed the bruise on his head. "But if you really want it to run long-term, you could do one better. You should take apart the engine and wash the fuel system out with denatured alcohol. Probably the last thing a young buck like you wants to do though."

He pointed at a covered bucket. "But if you want to, that's denatured alcohol."

Kev grunted again.

Matt shrugged. "Well, you probably won't get to it. But it'd be the best thing to do." He picked up the plate and the fork and made his way out of the garage.

The witching hour had come and gone. In Matt's head, there was a voice, echoing out from the depths. It was the boy at five, at ten, at fifteen, even at eighteen, with that perpetual cigarette in his mouth. It was the country of memory he spoke from, a place buried so deeply under the layers of dark and buried love, the sand of too many scattered years that Matt couldn't see through anymore, couldn't move aside, couldn't shift, not with the weight and strength of his own life.

I miss the mountains there, I miss the high places, the cabin too . . . I just had to figure things out, on my own, without you around. I'll be back . . .

When the phone beside the bed rang, Matt picked it up automatically. He could still hear Doug's voice inside his head. *I want to get back there when I get a chance . . .*

"Hello?"

"Matty, I'm sorry for calling so late. It's just that your pop, well, he . . ."

"Ruth?" he said groggily.

"Yes, it's me. I'm so sorry for calling so late. It's just that your pop, he's sitting up on his front porch, all the lights in the house blazing away. He's shaking and nervous. He's just not the same since he came back from the hospital. All evening he was sitting over there with his shotgun across his lap. Worried about his kitchen, he says."

Matt sat up in bed. "Did something happen to him? Something while he was gone?"

"Well, he's claiming someone broke into his house while he was gone. Don't know what he's on about, but it had him real scared earlier this evening."

"Dammit." Matt got out of bed, looked for his bathrobe. "It was that damn kid I found on his property. The kid broke in—I know he did. How's Pop doing now? Is he still sitting out on the porch?"

"No, no," said Ruth. "I managed to get him off the porch. He's over here now, having a cup of cocoa. But he's not going to bed, not till he finds 'em. Whoever they are."

"Thank you, Ruth. Sally and I just really both thank you."

"Well, there's no need to thank me. But your pop does seem kind of agitated."

"Let me talk to him. Don't you worry—I'll take care of this first thing in the morning. Let me talk to him, Ruth. I'll take care of this, I'll talk Pop back to sleep."

Kev Macht woke before dawn. He was drowning under the weight of a river pouring down upon him. He gulped in the sudden cold. He shook the liquid off his head.

Then Matt dumped another bucket of water over him.

"You awake yet?" said Matt. "Dammit, how could you do that?"

"What the hell?"

"You broke into my pop's house when you were over there. He was scared all night his first night home from the hospital. How could you do that?"

"Hey, I'm sorry, man," said Kev. The shock of the water was painful on his skin. He blinked water out of his eyes. "I'm sorry."

"He's an old man, dammit! You frightened him half to death, in his own house."

Kev made a sound.

Matt kept talking. "I should have just booked you for trespassing!"

Kev sluiced the water off his face. "I didn't do anything, man. Just ate some food."

"You're going to apologize to him, understand?!" Matt slammed a fist into wall.

"Jesus Christ—I'm coming already!"

Matt sighed. "I'm gonna go make some coffee. Meet me at the truck. Fifteen minutes."

In the truck, Matt handed Kev a steaming aluminum mug. "Coffee," he said. "Y'know, I guess I'm angry mostly because Pop's nearly eighty years old and—"

"Straight-edge."

"What?"

"I'm straight-edge. I don't drink coffee."

Matt yanked the truck into gear and pulled out of the driveway. "Whatever. Drink the damn coffee. It's early in the morning. Everybody needs coffee."

Kev rolled his window down. Matt raised his voice over the wind rushing into the car. "I'm really worried about Pop. He forgets things. He even forgets who I am from time to time." Matt drummed his fingers on the wheel.

Kev sipped from the top of the mug. Then he took the plastic lid off and threw the coffee quickly out of the window.

"Dammit—that was good coffee! And you know what? I was going to talk to you this morning—originally—because I had something good to tell you. I talked to Doug, and he wanted me to tell you hi for him. Goddammit!" Matt knocked the empty mug down on the floor and slammed his foot down on the accelerator, his face flushing with anger.

Kev rolled his window up. He did not look at Matt again, even when Matt spoke.

"You got it? You understand that you're going out there to apologize to an old man who didn't deserve to get scared? After all, I didn't have to take you back to—"

"Yeah," said Kev. "You don't have to spell it out. I'm not some stupid-ass Negro."

Matt raised a fist in the air. "Don't bring that stupid racist bullshit into my house!"

"Okay, man, hey, okay—I'll say I'm sorry. All right, already? Jeezus!"

Matt breathed heavily, and opened his mouth, as if he were about to respond. Then he thought better of it. He downshifted and the truck lurched as they slowed on the grade. New construction had closed off half the highway on the pass. Heavy-equipment trucks blocked the road for minutes at a time. Bulldozers bit into the hillside on either side, enlarging the highway, their massive tires turning on the road in eruptions of mud.

◇　◇　◇

When the rain came, it spread out across the Bitterroot Range and filled the space between the mountains before it moved toward the quiet depths of Lake Coeur d'Alene.

The concrete of the highway steamed as the water slicked it with dark patches of wet. Just before they turned off the highway, Matt switched on the windshield wipers.

The wet slapping sound of them put Kev in mind of the morning. It was the first shower he'd had at Doug's house, ever. Kev had come out of the shower stall slowly, wanting desperately to go back to sleep—but his nest of blankets was soaked with water, and the only place he could think of was in the back-seat of the Barracuda, next to the motor oil and the engine parts soaking in denatured alcohol.

He sensed a threat in Matt this morning. He felt that if Matt found him sleeping again, he would lose the car. The car was the single thing that kept him moving after the shower. The thought of the Barracuda fixed up, painted a bright neon yellow, revving a Hemi engine, that was what got him dressed and out the door.

Something outside himself had moved him to be here now, driving through the rain. When Matt began to talk, he listened for a few moments. He talked about how his pop wasn't close to him anymore. They used to be, or something. Kev tried to tune out the sound of Matt talking. But the batteries for his tape player were running low, and the sound of the voice kept coming through.

Kev closed his eyes. He'd stood there in the shower for the longest time, feeling the hot lines of water touch his skin. He'd stood there drifting off over the edge of sleep, waking only when he felt himself falling.

Pop Worthson walked out of the kitchen slowly, a shuffle in his walk. His head came up to look at them. Kev thought of a turtle pushing its head a little at a time out of its shell. He was surprised how much this old man looked like Matt when he looked up. They were close enough to be mirror images of each other, a few decades apart in time.

Pop reached out a shaking arm to shake their hands. Despite his apparent frailty, Kev was surprised to find that the man's grip hurt like hell. He couldn't crack this old guy's knuckles.

"Good to see you, Pop," Matt said.

"Nice of you to come out unexpected," he said. "Should've called, you know." He turned his back and moved back into the kitchen.

"Ruth been here?" Matt asked. He flipped through the new mail on the counter.

"Oh yes," his father said. "Wish she wouldn't, she—"

"Well, that's what we pay her for."

But Pop didn't seem to have heard him. "You know, she drops by all the time now. Nosy old busybody. Always trying to feed me dinner." They followed Pop to the kitchen.

Kev looked down at the sink. It was thick with grime. Bits of toothpaste and bristles from old shaving sessions were spattered over the tile counter.

Old Worthson turned toward them. His eyes widened and his mouth trembled. "Doug? Is that you?" he said. "I've missed you—we've all missed you around here."

Kev opened his mouth. The lie came up sudden, but then it stuck in his throat.

"No, Pop," Matt said. "This boy is a friend of Doug's—he's Kevin Paulsen. Kevin came over here today to apologize."

Kev tensed as Matt laid a hand on his shoulder. His fists clenched, but the thought of a Hemi roaring in the engine well of the 'Cuda forced him not to flinch away.

"Apologize?" asked the old man.

"Yeah," said Matt. "For breaking in. We talked last night? You were upset?"

The old man's eyes narrowed. "Oh, that? I'm fine. There's nothing to worry about."

"Well, uh . . . ," began Kev. "I just gotta say—"

"Speak up—he's getting deaf," hissed Matt in his ear.

The old man was already turning his back on them. He was heading for the kitchen table. Kev's voice trailed off. "I just got some food that day. Guess it's all right, huh?"

The old man stood beside the table. "No need for you all to come out here. I'm fine. The Good Lord looks out for his own. Don't worry about me none."

Kev sat down. There was a radio on the table. Maybe he could switch his old batteries out for the live ones. All there was on the radio was some preacher anyway.

"Well, I do worry about you, Pop," said Matt. "After all, look at this sink. I should scrub it out while we're here."

"He doesn't even listen to me." The old man stood up slowly and faced Matt, anger in his face. "I told you not to worry about me! Why'dja come out? Just go on home now."

Awkwardly, Matt chuckled. "Ah, we weren't worried about you, Pop! I'll leave the sink alone, okay? I had to hang some posters out in the Valley, I had to get out here anyway. Look—I got one right here. You want to see policemen at work, here it is."

Carefully, he unfurled it. "See," he said. "There's his face. Wanted for murder."

"Curtis Siwood," said the old man, and turned toward the kitchen.

"What's that?" said Matt.

The old man jerked a thumb back over his shoulder. "That there is Curtis Siwood—he used to mine with me at the Sunshine. Was my partner for a while . . ."

He snapped his fingers and turned to look at Matt. "That reminds me, I got something to tell you when you got a chance. It's important." He swallowed hard.

Matt moved forward. "But this guy—you're calling him Siwood, what do you know about him? Did you see him recently?"

The old man shrugged. "I just saw him . . . I mean, it seems like I just saw him—it must have been about fifteen years ago. So he ain't a twenty-year-old greenhorn anymore. Must be forty-something now. Before we get to that, I need to tell you about the mine—"

"Yeah, yeah, Pop," said Matt. "I know all about what you did at the Sunshine—the guys you saved. But this guy on the poster is wanted for a murder! When did you see—"

"Never mind him now," the old man shook his head slowly. "I gotta tell you—"

"Goddammit, Pop." Matt threw the poster to the floor. "This is really important. I need to know."

The old man turned his back again, shuffling toward the kitchen. "So go to heck! Guess your old pop doesn't know anything. Go hang your dang poster. Get out of here!"

Matt sighed. "Okay. So tell me. What's this about the Sunshine disaster now?"

"Nah." The old man grimaced at them. "You ain't ready. You go on. Go to heck!"

"Look, Pop, I'm real sorry." Matt took the poster off the floor and rolled it up. "Can I do anything here? Maybe clean out the gutters, strip the moss off the roof?"

"It ain't necessary," said the old man testily. "House is fine."

"Nope," said Matt. "I never do anything for you. Next time, I'm going to do it. I'm putting my foot down. It's that time of year—things can go wrong. Maybe when I come back, you can tell me what you were thinking about the Sunshine, all right?"

"That time of year . . . ," the old man echoed. He sat down heavily at the table and turned up the preacher on the radio. He rubbed a callused hand across his eyes. Then he reached out and plucked nervously at the material of Kev's shirt. "You're a good one, aren't you?"

"Sure," whispered Kev. "Sure I am."

"You could have been my boy," he said. "I thought you were my own."

It was early in the evening, but the air was already chill. The clouds were closer now, a heaviness in the air. It was as if the earlier rain had only been a warning, the real downpour was yet to come. Kev felt a strange déjà vu, as if he'd come out to the old man's house only to do what he'd done before. His eyes were open, and the car was driving straight and even down the center of the Valley, but felt himself beginning to fall again. There was that sense of weightlessness before one reached out and held on to the solid things. He shook his head and opened the window, and hoped they'd drive a little faster.

"Well, what'd you think of my pop?" said Matt.

"I met him a long time ago. When I was in high school. Doug brought his grandpop to see me in juvenile hall, sign an autograph. Mining hero or some such shit."

"Right, I don't remember that. I keep forgetting you've been around here forever." Matt pulled onto the road and slowed immediately. Construction trucks were mired in sludge and water all along the side of the freeway. The crews were spattered with pale mud, they moved ghostlike through the rain. Dirty water seeped across the freeway.

"So, think you'll get out of Coeur d'Alene by Christmas, huh?" said Matt. "Got a job waiting for you at your stepdad's office and all, huh?"

"Yeah. That's the plan," said Kev. His voice caught, a reminder of his lie.

Matt drummed his fingers on the wheel. "You know, I've been thinking," he said. "There's some things that need to be done—could earn you some parts for that car. A job."

"What kind of job?" said Kev.

"Well, for one thing, my pop is going to be needing help around the place. Maintenance, cleaning the garage, painting the steps, odd jobs."

Kev looked out the window. The clouds were heavy now, oppressive and dark, the feeling washed into him.

"Cutting up firewood for Pop. Things like that. You can handle an axe, right?"

Then it was too late. Anger blew through him, a storm that made every muscle in his body tense. He rode it until it was nearly gone, and then it came out his mouth. "Your pop's an old fart, shoulda kicked it years ago," said Kev. "Let him fuckin' die already."

Matt gripped the wheel tightly. The rain grew stronger. Kev could hear it hit the car over the rumbling sound of the engine and the windshield wipers.

There was a smattering of ice on the freeway now. The windshield wipers slowed as the glass frosted over.

As the windshield cleared, Kev could see a distant green sign. They came around a curve and the sign came closer until he could make out white letters glittering in the wet. The letters emerged, ghostly in the uncertain light. Sunshine Mine Memorial, it said. Historical Marker. An arrow pointed to the right, at the next exit off the highway.

Matt cleared his throat, spoke for the first time in a quarter of an hour. "I want you to take a good look at something."

Kev grunted. He tried to make the sound something accommodating, even grateful. But it came out wrong, it always did.

The sign flashed by as they came off the exit down onto the ground beside the highway. When they reached the memorial and the tall sculpture that stood there, the truck rolled a few feet farther, the wheels crunching on the wet gravel as they came up to the base. Then they stopped.

The rain had turned to sleet. The huge metal sculpture of a miner was streaked with dark wet patches. They could see the man at work, a twelve-foot-tall hard-rock miner, pushing a heavy drill firmly into the empty air above him. "Got any idea what it takes to hold a drill like that up to the rock, eight hours a day?" said Matt.

Kev looked up at the statue, beginning with the heavy boots, the thick heft of the brass legs, moving up to the curved torso. On the man's hip rested a belt clip, the square shape of a self-rescuer, a flashlight holster. Above him rose two lines connected to the drill he held. The roof of the truck cut off Kev's view. He couldn't see the miner's face.

"Those things," he said. "What's in the hoses?"

"Air and water." Matt moved his hands in the air, describing the arc of the hoses. "The air goes into the drill to be compressed and hit the rock, and after the air shatters it, the water shoots out and breaks down the rock. You have to hold on to it the whole time. It's backbreaking work. You know, when I was mining as a kid, the muscles in my back used to get so knotted up, I would have my mom stand on my back for me. The guys I know my age who kept working, they're all bent over now from the work."

"You quit."

"Yeah, I guess I did. My pop was always on my case about being a miner, and I got tired of the pressure. Besides, I figured he had enough close calls, I didn't want 'em."

"What kinda close calls?"

"Oh geez," Matt sighed. "Too many to list. I think he was trying to tell me—again—about one of them. Back in the '60s, he had a drift collapse at Terror

Gulch, with seven guys in it—he managed to save five of them. He was a big hero for that. Then he broke his shoulder when a shaft elevator dropped. And there's the Sunshine too."

Kev looked at the slapping windshield wipers and the statue beyond them. The rain outside was turning into sleet, a froth of white sound.

"You're what—nineteen, twenty?" Matt said. "About fifteen years after I came back to the Valley"—Matt gestured at the statue—"this happened. People still come out here, like we have, to think about it. People every day."

"For what? Talk about mining, working underground, all that shit?"

Matt looked at him. He turned the windshield wipers off, and the rain coursed unimpeded down the window, covering it in ice and water until they could no longer see the statue. Then he opened his door. He stepped out of the car and looked back at Kev.

"Come on," he said. "You come with me—look at the memorial here."

When Kev got out of the truck, the sleet struck with a slap. Matt pointed a finger at the brass writing that stood out on the surface of the stone, covering two sides of the memorial. Rain soaked across his shoulders, a dark and heavy mantle.

"What happened?"

"Ninety-one miners died," said Matt. "There was an accident in the mine— a fire. I don't know how the fire started"—Matt spread his hands out, water dripping off of them—"no one knows. Everyone in there died from the smoke underground."

"What do you mean? I thought this was just about mining." Kev pointed at the words inscribed on the dark metal wall: We Were Miners Then, by Senator Phil Batt.

Matt shook his head, mouthing *No* through the rain. He took Kev's arm and led him around to the other side of the memorial. He pointed at the wall of names there. "This memorial is for these men, these men listed here."

Kev stared at the stone, reading the names.

The rain was turning to snow as it hit Matt's face. He squinted up at the massive arms holding the massive drill. "Idaho's worst disaster—weren't you in grade school here?"

Kev grunted. "Yeah, okay. Maybe I heard about it in school. Ancient history."

"It's not ancient history. For a lot of people." Matt fingered the letters that spelled out May 2, 1972. He touched the Idaho state seal beside the names and date. "It's not."

On the day it happened, Matt remembered, the ore trucks and jammed hoists were filled with collapsed miners coming out of the mine. The men were all still wearing their cap lamps, faces streaked with dirt and soot, as if they'd tried to bring the darkness from underground out with them. Matt worked with others, lifting men onto stretchers, waiting to see someone he knew, waiting to see his father.

A week later, he was working when the protest happened. A group of miners—some of the survivors, and others—came to the administrative offices, to tell Herrick what they thought of the lack of adequate safety measures, the buildup of bad air underground. They were angry because of all these things, and more. The miners stood in a tight knot against the door, keeping anyone from going out or coming in.

Then, when Herrick had to go to Coeur d'Alene, he asked Matt to escort him. To this day, Matt didn't know why Herrick chose him, and why he hadn't turned him down.

Instead, Matt stepped outside into the rising sound of the angry miners, the hoarse shouts, the fists in the air, the threats and accusations. He stood there a moment, ahead of Herrick, unable to move against the arms of the miners. All around him, he saw men his father's age, a helpless rage filling their faces. Finally, Matt took the gun out of his belt, and lifted it into the air. Then they let him and Herrick through in silence, in despair. As Matt walked through the silent group of miners, he did not feel brave. Walking through that crowd made him weak. It sapped every bit of strength he'd ever had.

A week after the mine protest, Matt came to his desk one day and found a note from Herrick. Inside a blank white envelope was a piece of torn paper that said:

> Matthew Worthson—
> Thank you for the help. CONGRATULATIONS to our new security
> day supervisor. You deserve the promotion. Keep that gun handy!
> Good work.
> —William S. Herrick
>   Herrick Industries

When Matt received the note, he wondered if Herrick had looked around at the faces in the crowd, if he had seen men so violently helpless ever before.

The world was full of sleet and snow, it swirled around them, a plague of ashen insects. Matt's finger traced the old names on the brass plate, the long line of lives gone too soon. He'd read a book once where someone visited a nursing home and saw the same faces he'd grown up with, the same ones as in the old neighborhood—old women gossiping over their knitting, old men talking politics and sports over cribbage boards.

This brass plaque on the monument was his old neighborhood. Fathers and brothers. Friends he'd known for years and years. The ones who knew him best.

Kev looked up at the statue. "These guys—they all got burned to death, right?"

"No," said Matt. "They were mostly smoke-inhalation victims. Some of 'em recovered. But if you were caught underground for too long, you didn't recover. You suffocated. Half the guys underground died from the bad air, some fast, some slow."

"Who got out alive?"

"Three survivors," said Matt. "Tom Wilkinson, Ron Flory, and Stan Worthson."

Kev grunted. "That's your pop."

"Right. Stan's my father. He survived. That's part of the reason I come out here."

Kev walked around to the other side of the statue. "Lotta guys here," he said.

"Ninety-one. And there should have been ninety-four." Matt slapped the list of metal names. "There should have been ninety-four, but my pop survived in there for seven days, drinking water condensed on the pipes, eating his dead buddies' lunches, until he was rescued. You know what it takes to do that? To survive?"

"No," said Kev.

Bits of ice danced on the wind. Matt squinted into the cold air. "Neither do I. I've thought about it. Thought about it a hell of a lot, but I don't know. Not at all."

Matt had been to the memorial many times. By now, there were only a few names he did not recognize. Now one caught his eye. He peered at it, and tapped the burnished name on the plaque: Curtis Siwood.

Matt glanced away, looking up at the miner's face with the cap lamp above it, the eternal carbide light shining ever upward into the freezing air.

"What the hell? Why is Siwood on the death list?"

"What is it?" said the kid. "Jesus Christ, are we gonna be out here all day?"

Matt wiped the water and ice from the plaque, sluicing it off with one hand. He scrutinized the name on the memorial. "I just saw this man's fingerprints—and he's listed on the memorial here as one of the dead." He turned and faced the statue, looking up at the ice falling down from above the giant drill.

"And apparently, now there's a fourth survivor. Someone who got out without being found—maybe he wanted us to think he was dead."

"Who? Who wanted you to think he was dead?"

Matt looked at the kid blankly. "Never mind," he said. "Get in the damn car."

"It's about time," said Kev. He ran a hand through his buzz cut. Specks of ice peppered it all the way through.

The wipers became a blur, slapping from one side to the other across the windshield as they came up the spine of the Bitterroot Range. Freezing rain was covering Lake Coeur d'Alene, they could feel it coming toward them, scattered and stinging in the late afternoon.

A presence of the past, the seeds of the madness
and violence that seem to be everywhere.
—David Rabe, *Hurlyburly*

ALL AROUND the lake, the cattails were going. It had begun with the first frost in October. The pollen rotted on the stalk. Then the rounded bolus of the seed stalk fell apart, a building abandoned by its tenants, a rotting mockery of a living plant. After the stalk went brown, the leaves slowly disintegrated into the lake. Masses of the yellowed stalks covered the mud along the lake for weeks after the frost. As the season lengthened, ice mixed with the dead cattails. The lake reeds washed up in sodden clumps of dead matter, forming a barrier that made it impossible for anything from the lake to come ashore.

On the southwest shore, something tried. The pressure of the water pushed it in toward the beach. The mud of the bottom kept it from disappearing under the waves. At first, the rounded whiteness of it looked like a Halloween pumpkin, rotting in the lake. Then the appendages appeared. The arms surfaced slowly, like something living, coming up for air. The tone of the skin maintained this illusion: the flesh was white with a hint of green, as if it had become a creature from deep underwater. The hair that remained was molting off like the cattails. When the solid weight of it struck the shore, the body rolled, and a ruined face came to the air, gray and putrid as a dead fish. The eyes stared up, corroded by minnow feeding, and then turned back again toward the lake bottom. In the evening, the current changed, and it moved away from the shoreline.

The brown 4x4 truck with the sheriff's star drove into the parking lot at the cove in the late afternoon. By the time the truck arrived, the lake had cooled. The cold current had pushed the body out into deep water where it barely broke the surface, a curve like a breaching fish.

Matt walked from the truck across the boardwalk. Gently, the walkway curved around the private berths. The boats waited there under banked blue awnings. The acre of blue shifted in the sunlight, a herd of sheltering whales.

Matt climbed over the arch where small craft could enter the docks. From on top of the arch he could see the offices of Herrick Industries. The office was three stories tall and looked like a miniature tower. William S. Herrick Jr. tried to put as much time in at this office as possible, just to needle his sister, who owned the resort next door and had worked there since it was built. From the water, the buildings seemed mirrors of each other: the small trim office, and next to it, massive and ungainly, its offspring, the Coeur d'Alene Resort.

Matt glanced across the water. In the shadow of the office overhang, Will Herrick's yacht, *Ambition*, swayed in the current. The lights on the third floor of the office were turned low. Matt had given up guessing if Will Herrick was there. You couldn't ever tell.

No one was out on the far end of the boardwalk where it joined the shoreline again. He came around the far end and circled back to the resort. One or two boat owners were moving gear in their boats. He paid the fee and took a rowboat from the dock.

When Matt got out beyond the buoy line, he could sense the current against the oars. If he dug deep enough, he could feel it vibrating, pulling everything down. The weeklong fog had finally lifted from the water, and a hundred people had taken advantage of the late afternoon sun—Lake Coeur d'Alene was speckled with kayaks, canoes, and rowboats.

It was the end of October, but still tourists braved the water in their wet suits and Jet Skis. Because the water was as blue as the north Idaho sky, tourists often seemed to assume it was also safe and warm.

Matt knew better. He had seen too many sodden, panicked Jet Skiers and swimmers rescued from the icy water by a police launch or a passing boat. He imagined the assumption of safety disappeared sometime between the current taking you and the first inhalation of water. The leaving of it would be, he thought, something unexpected, surprising. A pause, a beat of the heart, before the darkness.

As he leaned back again, slicing the oars through the water, a fish jumped off to the right. It was a large fish, and it twisted in the air before it went back in. The splash startled him. He turned to look at the spreading ripples and saw that a young woman in a racing scull was outdistancing him. It had been months since he'd gotten on the water—now the neglect was showing. Matt applied himself to the oars, pulling to reach the pace she'd set.

She was about to put her next stroke in the water when he saw it, just at the surface. Many things collected in the roiling currents at the southwestern tip of the lake, where the Spokane river spilled over toward the Palouse plain. The heavy snowmelt in recent days had increased the strength of the current, and things long concealed rose to the surface.

Matt saw her oar pass over it. A heavy thing, waterlogged and organic, moving in the current. Matt could see the light rippling across the pale thing underneath. It was then that he realized she hadn't seen it, she didn't realize what it was.

"Hey! You got something there," Matt called to her as his boat rolled back and forth in the wake. His shout echoed out across the lake. She paused in her stroke, and then she reached out with a long oar and brought the floating thing to the surface. Matt was grateful that despite her revulsion, she kept it from sinking.

Later he told her that if she had not paused in her stroke, if she had not held on, it would have been gone. The current would have pushed it down and held it until winter covered it, just as it would have held any swimming tourist trapped by the relentless undertow. No one would have found the body until spring, when it came through the ice.

Later that night, Matt worked the graveyard shift. All hands on deck on this night: in the past they'd had problems with vandalism on Halloween. In the time before dawn broke, the shift seemed to last forever. It always seemed to Matt as if he had been traveling forever in the same futile orbit, wearing a circular groove in the county's roads, an endless broken record.

From the hill above Coeur d'Alene, he could see out over the lake. On this evening, the kids with their costumes and their flashlights had gone home. The Halloween parties had ended by two in the morning. Now only the dock lights reflected off the dark water, it brought to mind light refracting through glass bottles on a shelf. The bottles he'd thrown in the fire were buried now. With a surge, the old wave of memory came over him. Desperately now, he wanted his son to come back, to be free to return to him.

Ahead of him, he could see Doug's ten-year-old smile clearly, his Halloween mask askew in the evening light. It was as if the headlights skating across the hillside could project his son's face there on the black earth, could hold him in place there forever.

He glanced at the rearview mirror, and there was his own face, lines creasing back and forth across it, as if every year had scored a mark. His eyes were swollen and bloodshot. He remembered his own father looking just like this when he was a boy—a strong man made prematurely old by work and worry. Matt rubbed a hand across his eyes and squinted at the road ahead.

It was his father's fault he had exactly the same damn face, the same bone-deep weariness. Pop had overwhelmed him, the weight of his heroism too great for Matt to bear. He'd been left with only weakness to give his son, an uncertain love that gave Doug no anchor to tie him to their care, to keep him safe. Doug would never turn into him, but at this rate, it didn't look like he'd ever come home, either.

Matt came around the curve, his headlights illuminating the turn. How long it had been since he'd been drunk, since he'd driven this road in the early morning hours? The faint blue of the sky before dawn was always the same. It was as if no time had passed. He felt as if he could walk into the bar now and not miss a day in between.

Empty cells yawned darkly around them. It was after visiting hours, and the trustee showed Matt the single occupied cell. A hand was clenched tightly to the bars. In the thin fluorescent light, Matt could see a line of blood that ran down Karl's wrist, onto his fingers, and trailed to the concrete. Karl was cutting his arm open with a plastic fork.

The trustee sighed. "Goddamn weirdo. He's been nothing but trouble."

"Dammit," said Matt. "You can't stop giving meds to a guy like this. It'll kill him. He'll kill himself. Look at what you've done to him!"

The trustee shrugged. "Wasn't my call, I'll tell you. Anyway, he was supposed to be asleep hours ago—but he's still kickin' and screamin'." The trustee looked at his watch. "So now I gotta clean the damn mess up before I go home."

"It's all right—I can take care of him. I'll clean up whatever mess he made."

"I really owe you one then, Lieutenant." The trustee tapped him on the shoulder with his nightstick. "Lemme know if he needs a medic. You know the rules—don't get too close to him. And please, he better be calm when you leave." He sighed again and shook his head. "Where'd he get that damn fork?"

After the door closed behind the trustee, Matt waited in the corridor, a rolled-up newspaper in his hand as he watched Karl hold tightly to the bars of the cell with one hand. In the other hand, Karl held the fork and carved into the flesh. Then Karl saw him and looked up.

"Are you for real?" he said in a gravelly voice. "You aren't . . . No, you aren't him."

"Who?" said Matt.

"Him." Karl touched a dented place on his head, as if to indicate something hurtful remaining inside his skull. "Hit me—maybe you did this to me . . ."

"What did he do?" Matt looked at Karl carefully. "I'm with the Sheriff's Department, Karl. I'm not here to hurt you. My name is Worthson, you remember me?"

"I 'member you. I'll always remember you. And what you did to me."

"What I did?" said Matt, nonplussed.

Karl did not say anything. He was concentrating on the task at hand, working the fork into his arm. "Ahh," he moaned. He dug the tines in, the skin twitching with pain.

Matt sighed. "Look, when my friend Jerry and I stopped by before to talk to you, why didn't you say you knew this guy? Jerry showed you the picture, he told you if you had any information, you could come along to the office. But you didn't tell us you'd had him out to your place, and that you'd given him a knife." In one swift motion, Matt thrust his hand through the bars and took hold of Karl's shirt. He yanked Karl's face up close to the bars, and the fork clattered to the floor. "Dammit, Karl, why didn't you tell us then? You had to know him, to know the details about this guy."

The face in front of him wrinkled in sudden pain and fear. Tears poured down the cheeks in a sudden flood. "Nah, nah, nah, you're gonna hurt me. You're gonna hurt me again. Please don't hurt me—let me go home. Please, I wanna go home. Pleeeaaaasssse."

"You can go home soon," said Matt. "But first, tell me, why did Siwood come back here?"

Karl's eyes went wide, but then his face shut down again. Karl touched his head again, as if to indicate the faulty wiring inside, the shorts and sparks that caused him so much trouble. "Nah, not him. You're the killer. You did it, you know you did."

Matt could hear sounds in the walls. Water ran through the pipes—it was like rain in the distance. It occurred to him that he did not know what happened inside Karl's head. Perhaps he could have done this after all, without knowing it was cruel, without even hearing the screams.

"Karl, c'mon—work with me here. Knock off that garbage. Tell me his real name."

Karl stared at him. "You cut 'em open, so they can feel the edge of the world." Karl's tongue came out of his mouth and licked nervously again. A sick sensation came into Matt's throat, it reminded him of the smell of the rotting corpse from the lake.

Nervously, Karl touched the drying blood on his arm. "He was trying to get what was comin' to him from the big money-bags. He took the knives from me, said he'd poison my medication. So I stopped taking 'em, and I got to be a killer."

"Let me get this straight," said Matt. "Your friend had something on someone with money. So he shows up this summer to collect. And someone dies. But why—"

"You gotta leave me alone. Now I won't tell no one you killed 'em, so send me home now, okay? I jes' wanna go home. Jes' wanna go home, home, home."

Karl breathed heavily, as if in pain. His crying sounded like his chuckle, an uneven croak trickling brokenly out. Matt saw that his hand was clamped around his right forearm, digging into the cuts, feeling the edge of the world.

> It was a mystery, although it was right there in a glass
> case for everybody to see . . . a terrible knowledge . . . .
> He could not show the mystery to just anybody; but he
> had to show it to somebody. . . . His blood all morning
> had been saying the person would come today.
> —Flannery O'Connor, *Wise Blood*

THE DREAM was familiar. July of 1968. He was a young man again, and he was rebuilding a car.

A new eight-track tape played inside the garage: Bob Dylan, *Tangled Up in Blue*. Insects whirled and buzzed around the dim incandescent lightbulb that hung above the garage. The car was opened up, a patient on a grease-flecked operating table. He was taking apart the valves, removing the encrusted layers of old oil.

The carbon-stained engine of the decrepit indigo-blue 1939 Packard was spread over the floor in pieces, a great heap of metal fishbones. Sometimes Pop helped him, both of them wordlessly moving the pieces of the engine back and forth, trading wrenches and unspoken understandings of the inner mysteries of the Packard.

They got all the way through the valves, the spark plugs, and the carburetor before the summer ended. They had the car running, the sputtering hulk running on three cylinders in an uneven blast of exploding gas and oil. It turned over, and that was more than they'd had at the beginning of the summer.

But somehow they never finished the work. Eventually the car was junked. Yet part of Matt never let go of it. For years Matt had been working on this same engine in his sleep. In his dreams, he was still tangled up in blue.

There was a click in the late morning. Then another, and another. They came so fast it became one high-pitched noise. It woke him. Matt lay there trying to identify the sound. Then he recognized the ratcheting as an adjustable wrench.

A moment later, the screen door banged with a hollow aluminum clatter against the kitchen door, and then Kev banged on the door itself.

Matt staggered to the kitchen. When he opened the door, he held the boy's fist in his hand, catching it in midswing. For a moment, it was as if the boy held Matt in the doorway by the thrust of his outstretched arm. Then Matt thrust Kev's arm away.

"Goddamn!" Matt leaned against the doorway. The weariness overwhelmed him again. "What the hell are you pounding on the door for?"

The kid's face closed to him as he watched, struck as if by a blow. "Need to go to the store," he muttered. "Thought you'd want to get some parts with me, maybe."

"Auto parts." Matt breathed heavily. "You're pounding to wake the dead."

The boy looked up at him. "You been sleeping late. Sorry . . . I didn't—"

"Yeah, you didn't think at all, did you? Dammit, this is the first regular sleep I've gotten in a whole week of working graveyard, and then you come pounding." He paused for breath. "What did you say? What kind of excuse was that?"

The boy mumbled. "Gotta go to the store. Parts store." He was no longer looking at Matt. He did not speak again.

Matt breathed heavily. "And now you want to go to the store. You sleep in my garage, use my bathroom, eat my food. And now you break my door down, just so you can open my wallet at the parts store—stealing my money for Doug's damn car—and you don't even have the consideration to let me sleep before you do it. Just get the hell off my porch. Go sink the damn car in the lake! So help me God, you won't have any parts left if you wake me up again."

Matt slammed the door. The screen bounced hollowly.

The agony was to know how thoroughly awake he was now. He listened to the pulse throb in his head and prepared himself to stare at the ceiling for an hour, toss and turn for another, and finally rise again, his eyes bloodshot and his head pounding with another of the incessant headaches. It was a pure miracle that as his pulse faded, he found himself slipping off onto the other side of sleep, back into the past.

Although Matt could have slept for hours, when he woke, the fatigue was no longer a desperate hunger. It was the first good sleep he'd had in five days. He took a shower. He pulled the sheriff's truck around in a half circle and stopped in front of the garage.

Then he braked and rolled down his window. The air off the lake carried the acrid smell of denatured alcohol across the yard. In the dim light of the garage interior, he could see the kid dipping the 'Cuda's disassembled carburetor into a bath of alcohol, scrubbing furiously at it. All across the floor of the garage, on the clean concrete, were laid out individual pieces of the engine, each one scrubbed and clean, just as pristine as any of the parts he'd seen in his dreams.

"Hey, get in the car!" he called. "C'mon, we're going—get in the car, kid."

A-1 Auto Parts was filled with winding aisles of parts, each aisle ending in an advertising display—chrome intake valves polished like silver ingots, gleaming halogen headlights, steel wrenches laid out in a swirling wreath of metal spikes.

The kid was talking animatedly about headers and a high-flow exhaust. He had plans to put in scoops on the hood, for induction, and he wanted to add a double-pump carburetor. When he started talking about getting a big-block Hemi engine, Matt just shook his head. "Speed is expensive," he said. "How fast can you afford to go?"

"Whattaya mean?"

Matt sighed. "How much money do you have?"

The kid looked sideways at him, suspicious. "Um, like eighty dollars."

"Where'd you get the money from?"

"My stepdad. He sent it to me."

"He must sure like you a lot—to send you money. Must want you home."

Kev turned away. "Something like that," he said.

Matt spent a few minutes pondering a display of suspension springs, wondering if he could justify a thousand dollars to smooth the truck's ride. Then, as he turned toward Kev, he saw a sign by the register.

"Hey, they're hiring. Part-time guys." He pointed at the sign. "You know what you're doing with cars, and you'll need more cash if you want to get that 'Cuda going."

Kev grunted. "Maybe," he said. "I'll check it out, 'kay?"

Matt looked up at the ceiling behind the counter. "They have factory hoses in stock! Wouldja look at that?" He turned to the boy. "Have you replaced the hoses yet?"

"No, not yet."

"Better do that. If you don't replace the hoses, one of those will blow soon. They're corroded. I wouldn't want you to blow a hose when you hit the road. You won't find good Gates hoses like this everywhere—you should grab some while you can."

"Nah." Kev turned away, looking at the electrical aisle with hunger.

"You know what—Pop is coming over later. We could put a few in for you. Whattaya say?" Matt lifted a long rubber snake down from the rafters.

"Look at that." Matt squeezed the hose, feeling the solid metal spring inside. "A 22597—that's a good hose. That'll be just right."

"Okay—but I'm going out tonight, okay? Hey, what about a new dashboard—"

"Sparkplugs. Stick to the basics. What you need are new sparkplugs."

Kev pointed to a stack of bright-yellow plugs. Matt picked up a set and read the label. "Accel Racing—plated with chromate and triple-layered for performance. The ultimate racing plugs—best in class." He sighed. "You don't need these, you know."

"But it's the original muscle car. The Barracuda was built for speed—"

"Just get the damn car running. You can worry about the bells and whistles later." Matt took a plain brown box off the shelf. "Here—half-price sparkplugs, standard issue. And they're on me, save your eighty dollars. If you get a job or your stepdad sends you more money, you might even be able to get a Hemi engine one of these days."

In the twilight, Stan Worthson felt himself to be bereft of his Savior, without the possibility of redemption. He was finding it harder recently to get to church. Of course, he didn't miss a day of J. Vernon McGee on the radio, but the preacher didn't have the same allure as in years past. The words rang hollow now.

In fact, ever since he'd been in the hospital with the cut wrist and what they said now was a minor stroke, he felt as if his engine were missing a beat. It wasn't a rod through the pan, he could say that much, but somehow he wasn't running on all cylinders.

The past had crept up on him too, just as it had before during bad seasons of his life, but this time it wouldn't go away. Everywhere he looked, he saw the boys dead in the mine, he saw old Larry wondering why he was falling backward into the stope. And he couldn't shake the smoke, it hung on his memory like a shroud now.

He thought he'd decided to tell Matty, when he was in the hospital, but then the moment left him, and now he couldn't seem to do it, no matter what he tried. He still hadn't figured out how to tell him.

He stood up and put the casserole from Ruth next door into the microwave and turned the dial with a savage twist. No cooking tonight, no flames. He'd put Matty and the mine out of his mind for an evening. After all, he had something to look forward to.

There was a nature special on television this evening. Alaska, fishing for salmon. The name of the show came up on the screen and Stan sat down heavily on the sofa, but they'd fooled him. First came a commercial.

"I'm Russ White." The man on the screen turned and pointed directly at the viewer. "And I want to be your new county sheriff." Then the face smiled. The camera slowly panned away, revealing that the speaker was standing on a grassy hillside near the top of Fourth of July Pass. The voice continued as the camera angle grew ever wider, panning down to show the city of Coeur d'Alene gleaming peacefully beside the lake.

"Isn't it too long since we've had a clean county, a responsible county, a corruption-free county? I believe that together we can build a new spirit in

Bitterroot County. I believe that with faith in God, and your votes, we can renew our county."

As the image of the city faded out, a deep baritone voice emerged: "Russ White, a decorated fifteen-year lieutenant in the Bitterroot County Sheriff's Department. Russ White, a new voice for a clean county. With God's help, and with your vote."

At the end was the name again, Russell White, in big, bold, red-and-blue letters: "For County Sheriff. For Freedom, and Security."

There had been a momentary lift in Stan's spirits as the camera panned out, revealing the majesty of the mountains. Russell's smile gleamed at him from the television screen, and it struck him as youthful and naïve. Stan wondered if other people, watching the advertisement, would feel a twinge of hope, some kind of faith in him.

When he turned his head and looked out the window, Stan could see the road toward town. He thought now that he could start over in any new place, and it would be as unfamiliar as the city by the lake was to him right then. He felt he'd only ever known what fit his ideas of the town. He stood up quickly, leaving the thought behind, pulling his dinner out of the oven.

When the phone rang, the camera was circling the Matanuska range, coming in close over white peaks. On the phone, his son reminded him of his promise to help on the car. He sighed and hung up, but beyond the mountains, Stan could catch a glimpse of a glacier-fed lake, and a stream feeding that lake.

Salmon moved underwater, red, undulating flanks struggling against each other, pushing into the churning current. As the camera rose out of the water, Stan could see fishermen across the riffles of the stream, waiting for the salmon.

On the television, the camera panned away to the surrounding wilderness. A skein of snow blew off the top of one mountain, streaming off the edge of the peak like thick, white smoke. Something in the sharp-edged peaks, the whiteness of the snow calmed him.

He pushed a button on the remote, turning up the volume, but instead of the sound of the fishermen, he heard something else. It came like a wind through his house, the old boards resounding with the buzzy swinging in the air, knocking them both flat, the echo of Larry Clark's helmet hitting the rocks as he fell sideways down the stope, the wet thud of a shoulder or a leg twisting in his last agony, and the heavy groan he made as he died.

Stan looked out the window. In the Valley, the houses of the small towns were scattered on the pine-covered earth, white blocks against the dark hillsides, each one separated and alone in a tiny circle of dwindling light. Down on the highway, Stan could see a set of approaching headlights. Matt's truck, a tiny spark coming closer.

Outside with the car, their breaths steamed in the autumn air. The tools gleamed. Pop thumped the curved yellow hood.

"Barracuda. 1968. Slant Six engine. Used to sit beside my garage, right? I think Dougy boy put it there. Who did you say has been working on it?"

"Kevin. Doug's friend. You met him. He came over to your house, remember?"

"Where's the kid tonight?"

"I dunno. Said he had to make a phone call."

Stan pulled the hood up. It took some work, but his arms were still strong. It was just his heart that didn't have the power anymore. His son was talking, but it didn't matter. He didn't care to listen to this again.

"Pop, look, let me do the heavy lifting here. Your doctor said you aren't supposed to exert yourself too much. No heavy physical activity, no emotional stress. Said anything can trigger another one of those episodes, and . . ."

Stan lifted himself on his arms and pushed a flashlight into the engine well. Inside, he could see that the vines and overgrown grass had been stripped away. Even the carbon stains and grease slicks had been scrubbed off. The engine gleamed with work. That strange kid who reminded him of his grandson had put some hours into it, it seemed.

Again, the sounds of Larry's death seemed to echo in his mind. "Poor damn guy, what did he do to deserve that?"

"What was that?" said Matt. "What did you say?"

"Nothing," said Stan. "I didn't say nothing." But he couldn't get Larry out of his head. Poor damn guy went in a mineshaft and pulled sand out of a slushed-in stope, just as he was told. And look how he got paid for it, he got buried in that same stope.

"Okay," said his son. "So anyway . . ."

His son was talking. He'd missed half of it already. "When I saw they had the factory hoses in stock, I just had to grab a set." Matt held out a set of rubber pipes.

"Not the flexall things, are these?" said Stan. "Those never work very well."

"Nope. Like I said, I got the factory-made. With the springs inside. You see?"

"Okay," said Stan. "Let's drain the thing." Without another word, he lowered himself to the ground and slid underneath, his flashlight held ahead of him. With a grunt, he loosened the plug. It spurted for a moment and then began to drain like a plugged-up toilet. The other end was still capped. Fifty-seven years old, and his son still couldn't do anything right.

"Take the radiator cap off, wouldja?" yelled Stan. Moments later, the water gushed out, a steady stream.

Stan had to help with the hoses too. The old rubber was crusty, glued to the radiator by age and decay.

"So, remember I said I had some questions about the Sunshine?" said his son.

Stan grunted and forced a screwdriver into the gap, pushing the hoses apart.

"They gave me a missing persons case recently. You know all the old-timers. A lot of the young guys too, because you helped lead the union for so long. So if I tell you a name, think you can remember him? I'm looking for a tramp miner named Curtis Siwood."

"Maybe." Stan worked the screwdriver back and forth, breaking the bastard loose. Curtis's face filled the engine well in front of him. As he pulled at the hose across the manifold, he could see the distended eyes, the slightly bulbous nose, the rocky jaw, the receding chin under the sullen mouth. He reached out and made the mouth open, he made Curtis talk to him, tell him why he came back after all those years. The face was alive before him. Then the hose slipped off the water neck and it seemed to fall apart in his hand. Gray dust rose up in a gritty cloud.

Matt spoke again. "Do you think Curtis was a miner you knew? He was probably considerably younger than you, because he worked as a tramp miner just a decade ago. He got to know Karl Avery, back when Karl could work. You got any idea who this guy is?"

Stan yanked the corroded hose out from under the hood, a black thing shedding its skin like a snake in his hand. "He's dead."

"What do you mean?" His son's eyes widened, as if the boy had never seen the like.

"Larry Clark is dead. That's all. He's just dead." Stan spit on his finger, rubbing the inside of the new hose with saliva, lubricating it to fit. "You clean the water neck already?"

"Yeah, I cleaned it," said Matt. "But why are you talking about this guy Larry Clark?"

"Checked the thermostat too?"

"Yeah, I got that too. It'll open up at one eighty. But I asked about Curtis Siwood."

"Isn't Larry who you asked about?"

"No, Siwood is who I'm looking for."

Stan stared at him. "Well," he said finally. "You find out about Larry, you'll know about Curtis. Larry died in the Sunshine."

"But Larry is a missing person, still after all these years. How do you know he's dead? He's not on the list. I mean, there were hundreds of men coming out of the Sunshine that day—dead and alive. How do you know that for sure?"

Stan squeezed the metal spring apart. He held his breath and pushed the hose onto the radiator neck. Afterward, he could feel it in his lungs, he gasped as he spoke. "I know. Larry Clark stayed in the mine. I know."

"But you didn't get out. You stayed in the Sunshine after."

Stan turned away from the car, looking for a hose. "You got the antifreeze handy?"

"Sure," said his son. "I got it mixed already. Half an' half. I put a little extra antifreeze. North Idaho is getting colder."

Stan breathed heavily. The work had taken something out of him. "Sure it is," he said. "Look, you know when you brought the poster around—I guess I should have told you then about what Curtis did, about what I know . . ." Stan paused, his throat catching. He glanced away at the darkened house. The only light was the false blue glow of Sall's late-night television. His breath burned in his throat, the truth still stuck in his mouth.

"Tell me, Pop. Tell me what you know."

"That guy you're looking for . . . Curtis worked with me for a while. Back a few years ago, he was tied into the Bunker Hill. He was one of old Mr. Herrick's guys working all over the Silver Valley, finding out stuff about the union, doing petty sabotage."

"I'd heard a rumor Old Man Herrick had guys inside the union, reporting to him."

Stan nodded, the shame creeping over him again, a vast malaise. "I was—I knew that guy you're looking for. I know what he did. I wrote it down. I saw him . . . do things. Cheat guys of their ore loads, mess up the Sunshine books, derail union meetings if things weren't going the right way for Herrick's own Bunker Hill. Whatever it took to win."

"You wrote it down?"

"Uh-huh." Stan nodded and turned, his eyes wet with sudden effort. Somehow, he still couldn't simply tell Matty that he'd stood back and watched a man die. Matt interrupted. "But Pop—how could you know and write it down, and not take action to . . ."

Stan shrugged and looked down at the car. "You already changed the oil. Put a fresh battery in here and all that stuff?"

Matt nodded. "Kevin did that. It's ready. But the fuel pump doesn't show anything. There's no gasoline in the carb."

Stan nodded and reached under the hood. He lifted off the air cleaner. Then he opened the butterfly valve in the carburetor. "You got the gas?" he said.

His son passed him a dropperful of gasoline, which he squirted into each side of the carburetor. After he put the air cleaner back, and the wing nut, he stepped back.

"Okay, let 'er roll." The key turned. The engine gave a throaty cough: gug, gug, gug. Then it caught, and Stan thought he was home free. Then it died again. He stepped forward again. "Nothing in the fuel filter."

Again he primed it. His son seemed to want to ask more questions, so Stan talked as he put the air cleaner back. "Four-barrel carburetor," he said. "Factory Holley carb."

Stan stepped to the car and turned the key himself. Gug, gug, gug. A cough, a roar. "It's a rough idle," he shouted over the harsh growl.

"Well, don't rev the damn thing," said his son. "Let it build up some oil pressure."

"I know that," muttered Stan. "I'm not some stupid kid."

A welter of blue-black smoke came out of the rear. Stan turned the key off. "Is it running too rich? Burning oil?" he said. "Maybe we should check for a vacuum leak?"

His son sighed. "You know something else, Pop, don't you? Just spit it out, okay?"

Stan opened his mouth, but he couldn't seem to speak. Damn his own soul to hell, he couldn't even find redemption right there, at the foot of the cross. Slowly, he closed his mouth again. Then he spoke haltingly, looking at the steam that rose off the cold engine.

As the words came out, he felt something in his chest give way, something from the past slip away out of him. "I remember, back in '72, there were some papers . . . they were supposed to be from the Bunker Hill mine, Herrick's other mine. They got taken into the Sunshine, to be archived under sand in an old mined-out stope . . . that had some consequences. Like I said, you find Larry . . . you find . . . You look into that . . . might do some good."

Stan paused, the breath laboring out of him, the words as if made of sand, he could hardly force them out of his mouth. They were heavy as sin.

The world slid out from underneath him, just like it had before. Distantly, he felt as if a doctor was declaring sentence on him. He could almost hear him saying "stroke, stroke, stroke," as if it were one of his son's rowing competitions. The Barracuda was far beyond his reach, his son was miles away, the sounds from his mouth were incomprehensible. With an effort, he thought he could make out words. "Pop! Pop—my God, are you all right?"

Momentary echoes broke through: the clatter of the gurney wheels on the concrete, the smooth slap of the automatic doors opening and shutting. As if he were being swallowed by a mine elevator, sinking deeper and deeper into the ground.

Stan gulped hungrily at the cold air, but he couldn't breathe it, he couldn't inhale. Something had died inside him, a pump broken in his chest. The mask over his face hissed like a gaslight.

The breath caught in his throat, and he tried to sit up against his restraints, coughing, hacking. Someone spoke.

"Get him immobilized and—"

Stan felt like that poor man must have felt as he fell into that endless hole in the mine stope. A sudden pressure, a pain that wouldn't stop.

Stan could hear Larry falling again, the sound of his helmet an alarming dissonance. In his head was the image he'd seen on the television, a reddened salmon lurching out of the water beside the trawling boat, struggling to breathe in the sudden air.

"Intubate him." Stan opened his eyes to see who spoke, but there was only a white uniform before he was cleaved apart by pain. The darkness blew him out, a flame in the wind.

◆ ◆ ◆

NOVEMBER 1988

THE CORNER of the weatherworn barn was stacked high with old containers and broken furniture. The girl wormed her way between a splitting cardboard box and a wicker chair. She pulled her blanket and the doll's pillows behind her. Then she pushed a piece of insulation into the gap she'd made. No one could see her now.

The water stains and streaks of oil on the floor of the barn were covered with a layer of dust from the field. Carefully, the girl spread her blanket, making an untidy nest on top of the dust. She arranged the bear and the dinosaur. When she curled up with them, she could feel the hollow place under her chin where her doll would have been.

Karyn, the doll, had blond hair like hers, but the doll's hair never got messy, and it didn't blow around. It was always combed and parted neatly, tied back in two braids on either side of her head. Usually the doll wore a red dress with white trim. Underneath, she wore white panties, just like the girl. The girl curled against the pillow, remembering.

That morning, she'd spoken to her mother for the first time in two weeks. "Where did he go?" she'd said. "What did Karyn do wrong for him to keep her?"

The egg sitting unbroken in her mother's hand had rolled out and cracked across the floor. Then her mother came across the room and took the girl into her arms in a suffocating hug.

"Oh baby, oh baby." Her mother rocked back and forth. "Honey, you're finally talking, and you're right here. You're right here with me. No one took Karyn away. Everything's going to be okay. Karyn's right here with me." When she let go, the girl looked up to see the tears freely streaming down her mother's face. Her mother held on to her and tilted her head up to look into her eyes. "Honey, you're going to be okay, and one day soon, we'll be . . . we'll be together with him."

"My dolly," the girl said. "Is Karyn still with my daddy?"

The girl squeezed her hands up against her eyes again, and thought of her missing doll. Like a voice from inside, a whisper, it had come to her that her doll was in the car.

She remembered being in the car with somebody's daddy that night. She'd known where she was, even though her eyes were still closed. The smell of the sweet smoke—a different thing from the smoke itself—filled the inside of the car. When she finally was brave enough to open her eyes again, she thought her own daddy might be driving. But he wasn't there anymore.

Instead, there was the other man. She remembered him only dimly. Tousled gray hair and a smoking stick in his mouth. The one who had taken her in the bus station. He gave her a quick, nervous look. She could tell he wondered if she knew who he was, if she knew his secret.

She wanted to smile at him. But they were alone, and until she saw her mommy, she would not feel like smiling. He would come back someday to get her. That's what he said. So she could smile at him later. She remembered now. She'd left her doll behind, stuffed between the two front seats, so that she could wait to see where he went afterward, to help him come back to her.

The girl opened her eyes. The old scents were all around her. In that corner of the old barn, the aroma was strongest: grass rotting on the mower, motor oil, a vial of incense from a church service, a broken bottle of almond cologne, and nearly buried in the mess of boxes, a forgotten package of his old pipe tobacco. She closed her eyes and inhaled. In the darkness, she could smell her father.

Knowing the pain they keep alive. Feeding my sadness
and dismay. After all those silent years, my father disinherited
me. In his last will and testament, I do not exist.
—Sheila Nickerson, *Disappearance: A Map*

KEV MACHT pushed open the door of the semi. He muttered thanks to the driver and swung himself and his blanket off the side of the cab. As soon as the door was closed, the engine started up again with a roar and the rig pulled around the 7-Eleven parking lot, headed back for the highway. Bits of dirt and gravel and old cans spun out from under the tires, a haze of exhaust drifted over neon signs for beer. Now Kev knew he was alone.

When Kev had started out in the morning, he hadn't known how far away a phone booth would be. After walking for two hours, he'd finally hitched a ride with the truck driver. The truck driver was friendly—he gave Kev good advice about how to tweak the suspension on the 'Cuda. And since he'd recently started part-time work at A-1 Auto Parts, he could actually afford to buy a suspension. Someday.

Against the evening sky, the neon signs were faded and indistinct. The clouds were bright with a dusky glow. He glanced inside the store and saw an older clerk with dark skin. The cashier wore glasses and was balding—and he was staring at Kev through the window. There were two battered phone booths in the parking lot.

Kev pushed the Play button and a furious rush of guitars filled the world. Now he was glad that he'd brought the old blanket and his music. If it took this long to get here, he might be on the street all night before he got back to the Worthson garage.

Kev had already put his money into the phone and dialed the number when he realized that it was broken. Someone had yanked on the metal cord that connected the receiver to the box. The cable inside was splayed out in frayed bits of wire. Then, thoughtfully, they'd put the receiver back on the hook.

He threw the receiver across the booth and punched the button for his change.

He heard the 7-Eleven door swing open and catch. He glanced over to see the balding cashier regard him suspiciously. Kev glowered back. After a moment of looking at him across the empty parking lot, the man went back inside. Kev thought he probably already had his hand on a gun under the counter, just in case Kev were to come inside.

When Kev tried it, the phone in the second booth worked.

The voice on the other end cracked and gargled and hissed out of the depths. It was the same with every public phone in Bitterroot County. The antiquated trunk lines had been rotting since 1933. There was no public works money to replace them.

"I can't hear you," said his stepfather. "Are you calling from the Silver Valley?"

"Yeah," shouted Kev. "I'm in Coeur d'Alene. And hey—I'm coming to Seattle! I want to stay with you. I've been working on a great car and—"

"Oh. Glad to hear it, but your mother doesn't really want you around right now."

There was a pause. Kev closed his hand and squeezed until the tattoo on the back shone against the white of his clenched fist. He did not say anything.

His stepfather sighed and spoke again. "Look," he said. "We've got some friends coming over for coffee in a little while. Is there any way you could call back again later?"

"No," said Kev. "I can't do that."

"Well, I'd really like to discuss this with you, but now is just not a good time. I mean, we haven't seen these friends in a while—they're leaving for a trip to Bali in a week. Do you remember Chip and Jen, from that trip on the lake in '82? Did you know them?"

"No," said Kev. "I didn't know them."

"No, of course not. I'm sorry." His stepfather paused. "Anyway, where were we?"

In the background, even through the static and corrosion of the Silver Valley trunk line, he could hear his mother asking who was on the phone, her voice distant and buried.

"We were talking about me coming out there. Can I talk to my mom?"

There was a muffled sound, as if his stepfather had placed a hand over the phone. Then a muted conversation, and afterward his mother's voice was gone from the room.

"No, look, I'm sorry, Kevin. Gloria is kind of busy. She'd just love to talk to you, but another time would be better. Is there anything you'd like to tell us? Can I ask if—"

"Sure—I'd like to tell you something," blurted Kev. "I have a BMW and a yacht, and I live in a mansion by Lake Coeur d'Alene, and I've just been given a cabin for Christmas by my best friend. I'm going to Europe this year—

Switzerland. And that car I told you about—I'm putting about fifteen thousand bucks into fixing it up, and then I'll sell it for a million dollars." He breathed heavily, gasping. "That's what I'd like to tell you."

His stepfather chuckled, but it wasn't a pleasant sound. "Kevin, Kevin, we both know that's not true. However much we might wish it."

"Okay. But you've got all that already. Can't you just share some of it with me?"

"Well, we did that, Kevin, and you just threw it away. See where that got us to?"

"You weren't there. And it wasn't yours to start with. Let me talk to my mom."

"I'm not playing your game, Kevin. I've sent you enough money for now."

"Let me talk to my mom."

"She doesn't want to talk to you." His stepfather lowered his voice. "Gloria doesn't want to play your games anymore either."

"Man, lemme talk to her. I've got some problems here," said Kev. "Look, the truth is I'm living in a garage at some guy's house. I'm homeless, and I'm working on this car so I can friggin' come to Seattle to see you guys. Doesn't that mean anything to you?"

"Well, I'm sorry to hear that, Kevin. But the truth is that your mother and I have had it with your games, and your slacker friends." His stepfather's voice grew both quieter and more intense. "We don't want you or your friends to come here. Do you understand? I don't want you to come here. And she doesn't want you to come here either."

Kev felt something give way, a thing breaking inside him. He unclenched his hand, and felt the fingers ache with the release, saw the gouges left in his palm by his fingernails closed tight on the flesh. He caught himself gulping, unable to speak for a minute.

"I don't have your address in Seattle anyway," he said finally. "I wouldn't know how to get to your house, you fuckin' jerk. Let me talk to my mom."

His stepfather caught his breath again, as if it were taking effort not to raise his voice. "Gloria has done more for you than you'll ever understand—"

"Let me talk to her. Let me just talk to her."

Then he could hear his mother's voice in the background, and somehow he knew that she'd never left the room. He could hear them speaking to each other, the voices low.

Finally, his stepfather came back on the line. "Look," he said with a sigh. "How much can we send you to just stay away? Will two hundred bucks do it? How about three hundred?"

◇　◇　◇

Kev was kicking the phone booth to pieces when he heard the siren. He stopped then, but it was too late. Inside the store, he could see the cashier, dark eyes wide with fear, the phone still held in his hand. That damned cashier was still holding the phone when the car came to a screeching halt in the parking lot, almost on top of Kev's feet, and two deputies boiled up out of it. It was only later, after they had him spread-eagled and fully searched, that they actually talked to him.

"You check the tattoos, Bill?" A deputy grabbed Kev's hand firmly and held it up. "What kind of a freak draws a Nazi thing on his own hand?"

The second deputy was writing in a logbook. "Yeah, I got him. Tagged and noted."

The first deputy continued. "You come out of Hayden Lake to bother us?"

Kev didn't say anything.

"Hey kid!" said the first deputy. "Did you come down from the Aryan Nations?"

"Yes," said Kev. "I mean—no."

The second deputy bent down so he could look in Kev's face. "Which is it?"

"I didn't," said Kev. "I mean, not recently. I was only up there a little while. I grew up here, I'm from the Silver Valley. Born at Bitterroot Hospital."

"Oh yeah?" said the first deputy. "What's your name?"

"Kevin," he admitted.

"You got a last name, Kev-In?" drawled the other one.

"Macht. I mean, Paulsen."

"You sure about that last one? Paulsen your real name, son?"

Kev nodded, and looked at the ground.

"Stand up when an officer is talking to you," said the second deputy, and Kev slowly got to his feet. Expertly, the deputy grabbed his arm and spun him around, snapping a pair of handcuffs on before Kev could find the energy to struggle. The rolled blanket dropped to the ground, along with the tape player.

"Hey, look at this stuff," said the first deputy.

"Just check the name," said the second one.

The first deputy took him by the arms and walked him back to the car. Then he pushed some buttons on the computer in the car, while holding Kev by the arm. The second one walked to the door of the store and stood there talking.

"Shit, the guy in there doesn't want to press charges," said the second deputy. "Can you get this—the guy says he feels sorry for you, or something. But we've got two broken phones here—that you may or may not have broken. What else have we got on you?"

"Where you living, Kevin?" said the first deputy. "Can we take you home?"

"You aren't going to take me home," snarled the boy.

The second deputy pushed at the boy's knees with his nightstick. "Sorry we offered. Don't worry—we won't take you anywhere but jail," he said. "You living on the street?"

Kev gasped as his knee unexpectedly went out from under him. "I got a job. You can't mess with me like that!"

"We can mess with you anyway we want to. What kinda place would hire you?"

Kev didn't speak. Then his other knee went. "Auto parts store," he gasped. "A-1."

"Right, sure," said the second deputy. "But he didn't answer our first question."

"Where do you live?" said the first deputy. "Are you on the street?"

"No—I'm staying with a friend."

"And what's your friend's name? Whose place is that?"

"It's Matt's place. Matt Worthson's house."

The second deputy laughed. "You are smoking something, kid! Matt Worthson is a lieutenant in the sheriff's department. Worthson is letting you stay at his house?"

"In his garage. I'm a friend of his son's—Doug's friend."

"Damn, I wouldn't pick trash like you for a friend. Just look at you."

The first deputy put the radio down. He turned from the car. "Well, so far he checks out. Kevin is from around here. He's been pulled over before—no adult arrests though."

The second deputy sneered. "No arrests? Or just no adult ones?"

"He's in the database, but record was expunged. Musta been a juvie last time."

"So you have a record," said the second deputy. "What'd you do, little buddy?"

"I'm not your buddy," said Kev.

"Whatever, kid," said the first deputy. "Take it easy. We're going to cut you loose. We'll tell Matt to keep his eye on you, so you don't beat up any more phone booths."

"But you know . . ." The second deputy held up the blanket they'd taken from Kev. "There was that weird robbery at that clothesline a few weeks ago. Didn't they lose some sort of blue quilt—something like this thing?"

The first deputy was loosening the cuffs on Kev. "I say we keep it. Even if it's not the right blanket, they probably need a new one."

The second deputy released Kev from the cuffs and put the tape player in his hands.

The deputy held on to it as Kev tried to take it from him. "What's this?" he said.

"What?" Kev snarled.

The deputy reached out to the cross that hung in the hollow of the boy's neck, fingering the shape of it. Kev jerked away as the deputy touched the soft wood.

"Wasn't there a case recently—" The deputy looked over at his partner. "A cross like this . . . wasn't something like this stolen off a body or something? I can't remember."

The second deputy shrugged. "I dunno. Maybe."

"I'm sure there was—can't remember which case. Where'd you get the cross, kid?"

"That's my business." Kev yanked the tape player out of the man's hands. The headphones fell to the ground. "Dammit—give me my Walkman, my mom gave it to me!"

The deputy let go and turned to his partner. "Hey, didja hear? He has a mommy!"

Kev rubbed his wrists and turned toward the deputies. "Yeah, well, fuck you."

The second deputy walked back to the car. "Sure, kid, fuck your mother too."

"Lay the hell off, wouldja!" said Kev. "You know, the cops s'posed to grab the black fuckers! Here I get harassed just 'cause I'm white—'cause I'm a proud Aryan!"

The deputy opened his car door and glared at Kev. The second deputy tapped the cuffs on the roof and looked over at the cashier. "You got pulled in 'cause you were a jerk. If Mr. Pakistani here was willing to give a statement, we'd be booking you. Understand?"

Kev looked away from them.

"You're gonna start walking now," said the first deputy. "Get the hell out of here."

With an insolent shuffle, Kev began to walk back toward the freeway.

At the on-ramp, Kev caught a semi with a Confederate flag screened across the front. "Fuckin' cool buzz," said the driver. "I stopped for you, man, 'cause I needed to see a white brother. You listen to the Reverend Butler on the radio, right? From the Nation?"

"Damn straight," said Kev. But then there was nothing he had to say.

The driver waited a long time, and finally he started talking. "So I've been thinking about all these greasers comin' in, the mongrels taking our jobs. What do you think about that? You're from Hayden Lake, right, you got some of them wetbacks up there, right?"

"Ah fuck, man," groaned Kev. "Just let me be, man. Give it up!"

"Well, dammit, son, do you care or don't you?"

Kev stopped listening. Finally he realized the driver had stopped the truck.

"You're no proud white man! Get the hell out of here!" But Kev had already moved to the door. As he swung himself out of the cab, he could still hear the driver shouting at him. "Come on, motherfucker, stand up for the white man! You're just a nigger lover!"

By the time he came to the street that he recognized, his legs ached from the walking. Something ached inside too. He went to the left side of the garage where the old hulk of the Barracuda waited for him in the shadows. In the darkness, he strained to see the rest of the car. Then he pulled out the keys and went to sleep in the backseat of the car, curled up under an oil-stained drop cloth.

And even if he absolves himself from his sins a
thousand times, he has lost all capacity of faith in the
true forgiveness, just because he has never really known it.
—Dietrich Bonhoeffer, *The Cost of Discipleship*

IT PULLED him forward that Saturday morning. Sall hadn't woken up yet from her night shift, and the house was nearly silent. Matt turned away from the calendar, shielding his eyes as if ignorance of the date alone would protect him. Even as he swallowed the coffee, it was acid in his throat. Something recoiled inside him, knowing what he had to do.

Outside in the yard, a few crickets didn't seem to realize that daylight had come. They shrieked up at him. He could leave now, lie to Sall about where he was going. Ignore the date. The truck was outside. He could be gone in a moment.

But he knew where he'd be going. It was the anniversary of her death.

The date was like gravity for him. Drawn as inexorably as any body in motion, he would end up at her graveside. He had stopped even trying to figure it out. Was it some penance that would fade with the years? Or did part of him meet her there—did he honestly think that she returned, just for his visit? He took a bitter swallow of coffee and grimaced. Some hope for atonement? He did not know any longer why he did it.

He had missed the anniversary of her death one year, and for months afterward, it was all he could think of. Her face was in his dreams, and no matter how many times he visited the grave in subsequent months, it was never the same. He suspected he did this to himself, that it was some mental game he tortured himself with. But he didn't miss the date anymore. Drunk or sober, sick or well, certain or uncertain, he was always there, no matter how much he wished he could be elsewhere.

Matt looked up at the craggy mountain ahead of him. Vast sheets of ice had pushed them into that formation, long ago, the rock itself twisted and tortured in that glacial grip. He'd read a book about this country once. The power and weight of the glaciers deformed the earth's crust, dug new ocean beds, crinkled the land with a vast wrinkle—the Rocky Mountains. Their work still cut the continent in half, their residue remained in every mountain lake, in every bit of mountain snow.

The ice had trapped him too, it drew him forward, over the mountains, back to her grave. No matter how far he moved away, he still had that stone in him, dragged back to her grave every year, the same cycle as any glacier, a vast arc of ice that encircled the world. No one could break out of it.

Matt's thoughts seemed to keep him deep under water, under ice. And as he came close to the lake, he drove around the construction trucks without thinking. He hardly noticed the bulldozers anymore—the Herrick Industries construction project had been going on for nearly eighteen months now—but the new overpass near the lake's southern edge, freshly cleared of equipment, caught his eye. Something seemed odd about it, although he gave it only a passing glance. Something was askew in his car tires as he passed over the verge of the new roadway. Something unnaturally curved.

It was only when he could see it in the rearview mirror that it was obvious the highway had actually broken in two pieces, the new overpass only halfway there.

At five o'clock on Saturday morning, when the night's frost broke, the wide expanse of the new overpass had begun to melt into the lake. It was a slow ballet of sixty-ton rolling equipment and massive wedges of uncured concrete, all of it slowly sliding off a base of loose sand and broken granite, bending the surface of the road until the asphalt surface was hanging unsupported above the water. Then the roadbed broke in half and the rest of the embankment sank down, describing a slow parabola as it settled toward the water.

The yellow bulldozer moved like something prehistoric. It rolled faintly, pulled by gravity and its own kinetic force, directly to the bottom of the lake. Gradually the bulldozer disappeared, a submerged machine under the surface, sinking slowly deeper.

The second piece of equipment to fall into the lake was the roadbed roller. A half-empty dump truck followed. There was only one bulldozer left, but the embankment was mostly gone by this point, the pylons that had kept the cars off construction now kept them away from nothing except air. The old highway was edged only by a ragged, seven-foot-wide piece of asphalt, on which a wheelbarrow and a bulldozer slumped.

Except for a Montana-bound semi that hugged the inside lane like a highballing freight train, the highway was empty on this morning. So Matt kept going around the lake. Broken highway or no broken highway, some other officer could handle it. He had an appointment to keep in the Silver Valley.

Yet on his way up the mountain, Matt kept his eyes open. Nothing else seemed out of place. The oversized backhoes and graders had all been backed up to the service roads, as they should be on the weekend. Cones were all still in place. Caution signs hung in plain sight on every curve that had construction.

Except for that one curve near the top of Fourth of July Pass. He'd asked them for months to pull some concrete barriers across the edge, place something other than flimsy water-filled pylons. Independence Loop was a thousand-foot drop, and they still hadn't fixed it, despite all the near misses the department had documented for nearly a year. Matt slowed the car, wondering if there was something he could do. Then he sped up again. If he didn't make it there today, things wouldn't feel right for months to come.

It wasn't until weeks later that he thought of Independence Loop again.

When he pulled onto the cracking ice on the gravel road near Osburn, and stopped the car at the rusted iron fence, he felt the same rush of disappointment. He stepped out of the car and headed toward the center, but no matter how often he'd been here, it was always as if he'd invaded from outside, as if he had no right to be there at all.

The first gravestones, from the 1800s, had moldered under the elements, filling the old town cemetery with unrecognizable stumps of stone and mountain brush. Because the words on her narrow marble slab were sharp-edged and clear, it always seemed as if her death had happened only a few months ago. "Irene Closner," the stone letters read. "Beloved Daughter, Friend to All God's Creatures. b. March 31, 1961—d. November 11, 1984."

He stood there a moment in the sunshine and then bent down in the light dusting of snow that covered the graves, brushing away the gathered dirt and dusting of snow. He tried not to look at the dates again, but as always, he couldn't help it. It was compulsive for him to add them up. Four months shy of her twenty-fourth birthday.

He tried to shake the feeling of being unwanted in that place. Yet when he closed his eyes, images came to him, memory developing like film rising in the emulsion: strobing lights, wailing sirens, twisted metal. The weight of responsibility bore in.

"I'm sorry," he whispered to the tombstone. "Dammit, I'm sorry, Irene. I know you and I weren't anything, but still it was my fault I was drunk that day. You were too young to have a drunk kill you like that. I'm sorry, so sorry."

"Hey." Someone was walking across the icy ground, their footsteps solid as they crunched through the frozen clumps of grass. Matt turned and brushed a quick hand across his face, smearing the tears away. "Hey, Matty, I'm here for you, buddy."

It was Russ.

◇   ◇   ◇

The last bulldozer at the edge of the broken overpass was on the verge of collapsing into the lake, but no one was working to stop it. Three pieces of equipment were already fifteen feet down in the lake, and the entire underlayment of the embankment had collapsed.

Tim Morgan, the construction supervisor, should have been trying to halt the carnage. He was responsible for the work site on both workdays and holidays. Typically he checked in for fifteen minutes around nine in the morning on weekends, but by the time that hour came, he'd already been there for an hour in the supervisor trailer, frantically making phone calls, trying to dig his way out of this mess.

He knew that underneath the new overpass, in the spots where there was supposed to be heavy gravel, rebar, and concrete, there were in places only sand and partial reinforcement. The state specs had been seriously compromised.

By the time the news crews showed up, Tim was rapidly reviewing all the paperwork that had been submitted over the weekend, hurriedly scratching in the words "Supported by natural granite" or "Full rebar reinforcement" in any questionable field.

A few hours after the general public had begun to gather, gawking at the slowly submerging hunks of highway and construction equipment settling into the muddy bottom of the lake, Tim Morgan finally got around to calling the sheriff's department.

"Every year," Russ said to Matt. "Every year, I hear from you about how you visited Irene's grave, and how you hate doing it, 'cause you're all alone up here with the dead girl, but you gotta do it. So I figured I'd get here on the anniversary too."

Russ held out his large hands, suede work gloves encasing them in black. "Did you hear I'm ahead in the polls? Looks like I might even win." He glanced at his watch. "I got another campaign event this afternoon. But for now, I'm here for you, my friend."

Matt turned back, blinking at the shapeless stones, the sharp-edged lines of Irene's marker standing in the middle of the moldering ice and dead brush. The whole graveyard suddenly seemed so much smaller, more manageable.

"Well," said Matt slowly. "You want to help me clean up this place?"

"Sure. Glad to be of help," said Russ quietly. "You do more than just her stone?"

"Graveyard was abandoned by the city two years ago when the last of the big mines closed. Osburn city budget went to pot," said Matt. "And Irene's mother died two years ago. So there's no one else now. Only me."

Carefully, Matt rubbed a hand over the inscription on the stone, an icy residue wetting his palm. It was as if he were groping his way through the dark, memories emerging like old fingerprints. The tone of her voice came back, the look on her face when she first accepted a ride from him back to her place in Osburn. He'd never slept with her, but now it seemed almost more intimate to know her. No one else seemed to remember her now, and being here, it was as if he were reclaiming a lost possession.

Russ looked around at the sparse housing on the hillside. "Hey, didn't she used to live around here too? You said once that's why she wanted to be buried here, right?"

Matt continued scraping dirt off a tombstone. Without looking, he pointed a block up the street. "Yeah. Before the city condemned the place, I used to go up there too, look around. Sit there and talk to the dead girl. Can't do that anymore."

Russ squinted at a blackened foundation a few houses away. "Got burned down?"

"Squatters smoked it out," said Matt. "It used to be a little yellow house. She wouldn't have wanted that to happen."

"That's a shame." Russ looked down. He used a foot to clear brush off a grave. "Hey, Matty," he interrupted, and Matt realized he'd been muttering something again. Probably that useless *sorry, sorry, sorry.*

"Look . . . you need to stop worrying about all this," said Russ. "I know that you never got to see her in the hospital, but—"

"It was my fault though," said Matt. His hand trembled for a moment. He stilled it before he looked over at Russ. "And then I was too cowardly to go see her. Went out, drove around the parking lot a couple times, couldn't work up the nerve to go up there and face her. Figured she'd recover, but she never did. Then it was too damn late."

"Yeah, I know, but I told you about when I visited her. I heard her, what she said." Russ threw a rotting branch over the fence into the woods. "What she wanted—"

"You aren't going to feed me some line about her forgiving me after all this time, are you? You're the one who told me the truth about how much she hated my guts."

Russ's face blanched. "Matt, I've kept your secrets. And I've never lied to you."

"Well, dammit, Russ, don't start snowing me now. I already know the truth."

"You think you do, huh?"

Matt snapped out the words bitterly. "Sure, I do. I've heard them enough to know them by heart. Irene wanted to press charges against me until her dying breath. It was only you and Valerie who talked her out of it. Sure, I know at the end, you said she was willing to let go, to forgive, but dammit, that's only because you talked her into it. I owe you . . . I owe . . . Without you, I'd be . . ." Matt wiped an arm over his face. His eyes were streaming, his cheeks wet with tears.

Russ put a hand on his arm, a solid grip. "Look, you need a place to be alone for awhile. You just drive up to our boat cabin, you hear me? You know where the key is . . . you just drive up there, spend an evening or a weekend with our friend Jack Daniel's, okay?"

Matt shook his head and continued between the silent sobs. "That won't work, nothing works. I tried to confess, I really did, but look what happened." Matt felt his shoulders shaking, his body convulsing beyond his control, as if he carried a deep and fatal wound. "I finally worked up the nerve to tell *God* what I did, and Jesus Christ, look what happened after that to Arlen. You and I are the only ones who know. I tried to—"

"Matt, I know," said Russ firmly. "I know all about what happened to the chaplain. And don't worry, I won't be telling anyone. It's between us, you understand?"

Matt looked up at Russ, his vision blurred and uncertain. "I know she couldn't forgive me, but can you? Can you forgive me for that one damned mistake I made? Someone has to—Jesus Christ."

Russ closed his eyes and shook his head slowly from side to side. "Matty," he said. "I forgave you years ago. I already forgave you. Who cares if Arlen never forgave you? And she's dead, what does it matter if she forgives you? I mean, hell," Russ gave a short forced laugh, "Valerie's never forgiven me—for anything."

Matt snorted despite himself, a chuckle choked by grief.

"Look," said Russ. "You're a good man, my friend, and don't let anyone tell you any different, even yourself." Even as Russ spoke, the radio in Matt's truck began to crackle. "Calling five-oh-seven. We need a lieutenant to supervise all available units on a serious situation. We've got a road hazard—more like no road—on the south end of the lake. Potential to shut down the entire interstate. Calling all units in, to meet at new overpass."

At the sound, Russ's eyes snapped open. He looked at the truck and then back at Matt. "Mind if I come along? I know I don't work there anymore . . . but hey," he put a hand back on Matt's shoulder. "You look like you could use someone beside you today."

Two deputies were already out on the open road when Russ and Matt arrived, shepherding traffic away from the gap, moving pylons by hand. Russ pulled on a sheriff's department jacket and began to move pylons as well. Matt went back to the truck and radioed the Bitterroot Fire Department. He also attempted to raise the general manager for Herrick Industries. Matt was in the midst of his seventh attempt when he noticed that the door to the construction trailer seemed to be propped open.

Matt found Tim Morgan inside. Morgan was disheveled and uncertain, but he was certainly present. Matt knew Morgan as a long-time union man, constantly at odds with Valerie Herrick, the ostensible owner of the company he worked for.

"Well, good to see you, Matty," Morgan chuckled nervously. "I expected maybe some overtime . . . but shit. This is a real fuckarow, ain't it?" That was all he said for the first fifteen minutes, as he shuffled papers on his desk. Then Matt noticed that he'd begun to smile. He couldn't wipe the smile off his face as they walked outside and looked over the damage. Outside, in the lake, the top of a cab could be seen just under the surface, looking for all the world like a yellow boat cabin without a keel.

Once the fire engine arrived, Matt took Morgan back inside. "I'm not taking a statement," said Matt. "So this is off the record. But you gotta let me know a couple of things—just to protect the public safety. Is this whole road going to collapse? Is the rest of the highway safe to drive on? How the hell could something like this happen?"

Morgan sat down heavily in his chair and pulled a stack of papers toward him. "Off the record, I don't mind telling you the whole damn story here, Matty. You've been on the inside for a few of these, a few years ago, so I figure you'll understand. This is a private deal I made—but it appears to have gone a little sideways from what we wanted."

"What kind of deal?" said Matt heavily.

"Well, you know Will Herrick wants to buy the company off his sister, see? So although there's supposed to be heavy gravel, I figured out a way to just put sand in there. A hell of a lot cheaper, save the company some money. And rebar is damned expensive too, so we cut a little here and there. State specs say we gotta foot it in natural granite, but I just had them truck in some mine tailings from Herrick's mines over in the Silver Valley, chuck that in there, and I signed off on the granite footings."

"Why? Why would you do such a thing?"

"It'll cost Valerie too much to sustain the company. She'll have to sell the damned construction business. Look at this spreadsheet"—Morgan pointed to a printout—"see that column of numbers? That *was* the profit for Valerie Herrick. And here's—"

A voice from outside the door spoke loudly. "What was that about Valerie?"

Matt sat back and sighed. He felt fatigue settle into him, a heavy weight.

"C'mon inside with us, Russ. How long have you been listening to this?"

Russ came into the room, blinking as his eyes adjusted to the low light. "Just got here. Tell me what you were saying about Val."

Morgan put down the file folders he was holding. "Well, hell, Russ, I didn't know you were still in the mix with the day shift—I thought you were running for sheriff!"

"I am," said Russ shortly. "What happened, Tim? Something got left out of the overpass footings, and I bet on purpose. You're screwing Valerie over again, aren't you?"

Morgan gave him a heavy look, and then as Russ stared back, he seemed to waver. Matt looked back and forth between them. "Look," he said finally. "Isn't there insurance for this kind of thing? Doesn't a construction company carry a lot of insurance?"

Russell did not take his eyes off Morgan. "He knows damn well there's not enough insurance on this deal to cover a catastrophe like this. Val had to take cost-cutting measures somewhere." Russ's voice grew louder. "He knows damn well that—"

"Hell, Russ, I checked it all out four times to Sunday." Morgan shot Matt a sideways glance and held up a sheaf of papers as he shook his head mournfully. "I don't know—"

Russ grabbed the papers from Morgan and threw them across the room. "It's William, isn't it? He's bought you out, hasn't he? He's screwing Valerie with this and—"

Matt pulled Russ back from the desk. "Look, Russ, a judge will sort this one out. There has to be sufficient coverage—it's a state contract, right? Dammit, what a mess."

Morgan began to chuckle. "Russ, Russ, Russ. You couldn't do anything to me if you wanted to. I signed the forms, in triplicate. It's all duly authorized— who am I to know if the company provides material that is substandard? We did our job."

Matt gave him a hard look, it seemed to take hold. "Tim, I don't care about your wheeling and dealing right now," said Matt. "Is the road dangerous? Unstable?"

"No, no, of course not. Just the road that fell in—the new part." Morgan stood and walked out onto the porch, squinting in the sunlight. "Who knows—if the temperature had dropped in time, froze it up, the road mighta been fine. Guess I was wrong."

Russ came out onto the porch right behind them. Violently, he shoved Morgan off the porch. "Goddammit to fuckin' hell! Sure as hell you were wrong!"

Matt whirled around and caught Russ as he was about to jump off the porch down on top of Morgan, who was struggling in the mud. He pulled Russ in front of him, yanking his jacket to hold him still. "What the hell, Russ? I mean, it'll all work out."

But Russell's arms were windmilling furiously, pushing him away. "Fuckin' Will Herrick—he's screwing us over with little Timmy Morgan, just like he screwed us over with you! He just uses all of you—never gets his own hands dirty! Using you!"

Matt held on to him as Russ swung back and forth. "Herrick never used me," he said.

But Russ didn't seem to have heard him. His hands clenched over and over, as if he were squeezing an invisible neck. "Just like he screwed us with Arlen at the resort."

Matt let go of Russ's jacket in sudden consternation. "What are you talking about?"

Russ seemed to see him then. He flushed a violent red, his face going dark. Rapidly, he turned his head from side to side, checking if anyone was near. "Matty," he muttered, "don't worry—I'll keep your secrets. Even about the resort that night—"

"I don't have any secrets about the resort. What about that night—what?"

Russ frowned suddenly, his brow lowering as if at an insult. He ran a hand down his jacket, smoothing the fabric. When he spoke, his voice seemed unnaturally calm, as if he were trying to convince more than just Matt. "Jesus, Matty, c'mon, give it up, would you? You know I didn't have anything at all to do with the resort. Anything at all. I mean, you were there with me, together we—"

"What do you mean? Russ, you better tell me what you mean."

Russ shook his head, pulled away from Matt, as if the glimmer of doubt in Matt's face was something he never expected to see. "Jesus Christ," he muttered weakly, staggering backward. "I can't talk about this now. I gotta go . . . Jesus, I gotta go see her."

"Who? Valerie? I can get the dispatcher to call her office. Who do you have to go see? Who?"

But Russ just looked at him and backed away, moving rapidly until he got to his car. He swung in a wide circle across the unfinished highway, spinning the tires as he swung toward the Bitterroot Mountains.

The first night after the passage, as he slept in the enemy's country, a vision appeared to him. He seemed to see in his sleep the eldest of sons. . . . but he missed the true meaning of the dream, which was sent by God to forewarn him.
—Herodotus, *The Persian Wars*

IN 1912, Shoshone Lumber cut five hundred million board feet of timber, enough to build homes for a city of fifty thousand people. First the company built the Potlatch mill on the shores of Lake Coeur d'Alene, and soon smaller mills proliferated all along the St. Joe waterways. The company filled the lake with floating logs. Timber workers were so much in demand that the company built next to the mill a series of tiny cabins, rent payable directly out of day wages. For a decade, they were filled with itinerant lumber workers.

But by the mid-1960s, there was only one sawmill left from an operation that had once taken a significant dent out of the largest stand of white pine in the world. By 1969, even the flagship Potlatch mill was abandoned. Finally, in the wake of Shoshone's devastating bankruptcy, Weyerhaeuser took over the remnants of the corporation. The equipment and various outbuildings—including the workers' cabins—were auctioned off at pennies to the board foot. The vast hulk of the Potlatch mill itself sat derelict, until in 1982, Valerie Herrick used her father's mining money to purchase the old lumberyard, knocked down the mill, and began construction on the Coeur d'Alene Resort.

All through the foothills of the Silver Valley, one could still find old Potlatch cabins, some fully renovated, most relegated to hunting, fishing, and holiday weekends.

Matt Worthson's family had placed their piece of the Potlatch on a clearing reached only by a winding and unpaved mountain road an hour south of the St. Joe riverhead.

"This is where Pop taught me how to hunt," Matt said to Kev as they pulled off the road and into the clearing. "I'll show you. We got some memories here."

Inside the cabin, Matt took out a pair of books, two feet square. The covers were quarter-inch-thick pieces of cherrywood. Small metal hinges held them to a two-inch piece that bound the pages with a leather strap, wound twice through each page, and tied so tightly that it cut into the wood. The nearly square pages had been cut from some massive roll, each page thickly irregular, a paper as heavy as cardboard.

The covers had once been varnished, and a trace of gold embossment was left on the front of one, some vanished letters. Now they were worn smooth by many hands.

"Cabin books," Matt said. "We take them down for the winter. Left them here one year, and a porcupine got in and chewed 'em." He tapped one splintered corner.

"Damn, how long have these things been around?" said Kev.

"Oh, thirty-odd years. Everyone writes in 'em when they come up here for a visit. I wrote in them, every trip up here." Matt flicked past a page or two. "You can read all about our vacation when I was a kid, if you look. Gotta remember to take these with us."

Kev kept looking through the books. Most pages were covered in writing. Photographs were taped here and there throughout the book, along with other mementos.

"You ever come up with Doug when you guys were kids?" asked Matt.

Kev shook his head. All morning long, Matt had been showing him things at the cabin. He'd woken Kev up early—he'd wanted help up at the cabin. Kev didn't have anything better to do. On the way, Matt had even stopped for a donut and juice for Kev.

Kev didn't know if he should mention to Matt the one time Doug had taken him up here to the Potlatch cabin. They'd smoked a big bag of weed. He simply shook his head. "So what else do we do here?" he asked.

Matt was sifting through the contents of a closet. "Winterize the place. Drain the water, shut off the power, close the chimney, all that stuff. Ah!" He held up a rifle and a pistol. "Found the guns! Now where's the ammo?"

"You guys use this cabin for hunting, huh?"

"Pop and I used to, but we don't hunt much anymore. Could you take these boxes of ammo out to the car?" Matt snapped his fingers. "Oh, and while you're out there, bring back some of the firewood, wouldja?"

At the truck, Kev looked up at a leaden sky. It was close, something about to fall.

He shook the box in his hand, feeling each bullet rattle in its little slot. He opened the box and slipped one out. He looked at the smooth curve of the steel cartridge, the line of copper that surmounted the cartridge, and the dull metal tip, pointed like a missile.

Then he glanced back at the cabin. Matt was still inside.

On the floor of the truck, Kev saw an eye looking up at him. It was sketched in charcoal, and photocopied. He pulled out the piece of paper and saw that it was a poster, torn in half. Even with only half the page and one eye to go by, he still recognized the face. It haunted his dreams. This time, seeing it again, he decided to say something.

"Hey," he called. "I seen that guy. Guy on this poster."

"Yes?" said Matt. He dropped a load of branches and turned. Matt's mood seemed to have lifted now, his smile was back.

"Well, you probably already caught the guy an' all—right?" Kev waved the tattered piece of paper.

"No, it's only a few months old," said Matt. "We haven't caught him. He might match a body we found in the lake, but we're waiting for the fingerprints from the body to come in. Body had tattoos that might be traceable—"

"What kind of tattoos?"

"Miner's tattoo on his arm—Haul Ass or Haul Ore." Matt stopped talking and looked sharply at Kev. "Why do you want to know? He's wanted for murder. Have you seen him?"

Kev thought of the way the man had stared up from the floor of the station, an insistent malevolence overtaking his face. A strange reluctance seized him. "No," he muttered, turning away. "Nothin'. I just thought . . . I just thought I mighta seen him, but it's not him, it's, ah, nothing."

He dropped his load of wood, and let the poster drift down to the ground. Then he looked up at the sky. "Looks like it's gonna snow," he said.

Matt looked up too. "Yeah, I see that. We timed this just right—it might snow on the way down. I nearly forgot to take care of the cabin, what with everything else."

Matt began to wrap the guns up in a blanket. He opened the closet again.

"You leave the guns here?" said Kev. "And take the ammo?"

Matt grinned. "Kind of bass-ackwards, huh? Sall won't have guns in the house, so this is where I keep them. Besides, kids who might break in here can't shoot off the guns unless they have ammo. So I just take the ammo out of here. Bring it back in the spring."

Kev tapped the barrel of the gun. "What do you shoot with this one?"

"Oh, with the .243, I've shot deer mostly. Badger once. Tried to shoot a cougar with the old pistol once. It used to be my Pop's. But I missed." Matt tucked the wrapped guns carefully into the closet and brought out a set of fireplace tools. "I've heard people shoot elk or bear with their deer-hunting rifle, but I've never gone in for that."

"What about the little gun? Can you shoot deer with that one too?"

"No way. The little pistol, I think it just shoots .22 bullets. For squirrels and rats. But don't get me wrong, just because the .22 and the .243 are lighter cartridges, doesn't mean they can't hurt someone." Matt brushed ashes and charcoal out of the fireplace. When he scratched his chin, he left a black mark behind. "When I was a kid, I knew someone who got killed by a stray .22 bullet. That's why Sall doesn't want 'em around."

After he'd finished with the fireplace, Matt moved outside. He took the ladder out of the truck and put a cover over the chimney on the roof. For a while, Kev watched him. "Cover keeps out the porcupines and raccoons," explained Matt.

"Damn," said Kev. "You have to know all this shit to take care of a place. Drain the water, open the refrigerator, cover the chimney. Damn."

Matt shrugged and crawled carefully across the roof. "It's no different from taking care of a car. Every detail counts." He came down the ladder and began to scrub moss off the side of the house.

Then Matt turned and clapped Kev on the shoulder. "Speaking of which— now that the car is running, where are you going to go? I bet your folks can't wait to see you."

Kev glanced up at Matt, weighing the hand on his shoulder. The moment buoyed him up. He opened his mouth. It surprised even him when the truth came out.

"Well, yeah, like, I thought so. But I guess I kinda like exaggerated that one."

Kev had expected Matt to lift his hand, to move away from him, even to dismiss the moment. Unexpectedly, though, Matt was still there with him. If anything, his hand had grown heavier. "What do you mean?"

"I, uh, I really dunno what I'm gonna do . . ." The words began to come in a rush. "I thought maybe my mom—not my stepdad, he hates me—but I thought she might want me around. But I guess they kinda agreed that they don't. Even if they did, I dunno if I want to drive to Seattle. I'm always going somewhere new. I get tired of it, man."

Kev looked at the ground, glancing at the poster that lay there. "I dunno," he finished lamely. Immediately, he felt like a fool for trusting Matt.

"Hmm," said Matt. He took his hand off Kev's shoulder and continued to scrape moss off the house. "Well, with the car running, you've got some choices at least."

Kev kicked at the ground, covering the poster in a shower of dirt.

"Here," said Matt finally. "Take the ladder around the side. What do you want?"

"I dunno," said Kev. "I want to work on cars. That's what I want to do, I guess."

Matt set up the ladder and climbed up to the loft window. Kev squinted at him in the gray light. So far, Matt seemed unperturbed by the news about his stepdad.

"You know," said Kev. "There was this guy who saw me drive in for my shift at the A-1 last week. He saw the 'Cuda. He liked what I did to it—and he has some old cars he wants to get running. Two classic Mustangs and another Plymouth—a Valiant."

"Uh-huh," said Matt. He pounded nails into the shutter. "So, did you tell him to go to hell? Or did you do the work on his cars?"

"I did the work," said Kev. "Fixed the carburetor on a Mustang. Took two hours."

Matt pounded some more. "Did he pay you?"

"Yeah. Fifty bucks."

Matt whistled. "You know, an old car like that—some shops would charge five hundred dollars for the kind of work you can do. He got a good deal."

"Huh, I didn't know." Kev shrugged. "Should I ask for more on the other cars?"

Matt climbed down from the ladder. He looked at Kev until Kev glanced back at the ground again. "You're actually doing a job for this guy? You're doing the work?"

Sullenly, Kev grunted affirmation. "Yeah. Why—you surprised or something?"

"No, I just . . . ," Matt stuttered. "I just—it's a good thing."

"Huh," said Kev. "Yeah, you were about ready to boot me out on my ass, huh? I mean, I've been thinking—since I got some money coming in from more places than my stepdad, maybe I should pay rent, y'know."

"It's just a garage."

"Yeah, but I wanna stop fuckin' with people so much, like live and let live, man."

"Hmm." Matt moved the ladder to another window and pulled out a handful of fresh nails. "You know, North Idaho Community College has a great automotive technology AA program. I took a class or two there myself. They have a good shop."

"I don't know. Sitting in the classroom—it just never worked for me. Always getting on the teacher's shitlist, y'know?"

"They work on cars. They don't sit in the classroom. You do things. Heli-Coils, engine rebuilds, electrical system work." Matt climbed up the ladder.

"You mean, I could do this as a job? Get paid?" Kev carried Matt's toolbox toward the truck.

"Sure," said Matt absently. "I don't see why not. As long as you don't screw people over, you should do just fine. Just stay honest about it."

Kev kicked at the poster on the ground. He thought again of the man in the bus station, the grunting sounds that had come out of him as Kev pulled back his leg for another kick. He flipped the poster over with his foot, and tried to forget the memory of the rage flooding through him, the blood running over the man's eyes. He looked up at Matt on the roof.

"Shit, I dunno," he said. "You think I could have my own shop, someday?"

"Maybe." Matt looked down at him. "But hell, no one hires a skinhead—"

"Fuck you!" Kev threw the toolbox at the side of the truck. "I don't even believe that shit anymore—I don't know if I ever did. I'm not any fuckin' skinhead! Not anymore."

"Well, hell—you sure never told me when that changed," said Matt as he climbed down from the roof. "I can't ever tell what you'll do next. Who the hell knows what you're capable of? Maybe. I don't know."

Kev lowered his brow and picked up the tools from the ground.

Matt pulled the shutter closed and placed a nail into the corner. With two quick strokes, he pounded it into the wood. Then he spoke again. "You graduated high school?"

"Sorta," said Kev. "Took my GED three years ago, sophomore year. Did all right. Got the certificate thingy somewhere."

"Well, that's enough for them." Matt hesitated for a moment. "Maybe."

"I got rid of the Aryan shit." Kev held up his hands, turning them to show off the leather bicycle gloves. "No one even sees the fuckin' swastika anymore."

Kev shrugged and rubbed a hand over his scalp. "I like the skinhead hair though. Damn cool haircut."

Matt pushed another nail into the wood and pounded it in. Then he turned away quickly, but Kev could see something had changed in his face. Something familiar filled Kev's belly, an upswell of resentment. When he saw that Matt was laughing at him, he tried to still the buzzing energy that threatened to fill his head.

Matt took the nails out of his mouth. "Hey," he said. "Would you mind grabbing more stuff from inside the cabin? There's a bunch of crap still in there—stuff I've been meaning to clean out for years, but it's not snowing yet, we may as well get to it, eh?"

"Huh," said Kev. He wandered back inside.

Dust hung in the stale air of the cabin. A pile of old coats and worn gloves waited on top of the plywood window seat. Kev sighed and put them beside the door. Underneath were wormy pieces of wood and a stack of musty newspapers and magazines. He picked these up too, a musty cushion with them.

The damp sogginess of the pad disgusted him, and he dropped it on the floor.

As he turned to go, he saw something in the wood, under where the cushion had rotted away. It was a small, rusted hinge. He reached out and touched it, pushing on it to see what was underneath. A corroded twist of wire broke away in his hand.

The hinge had held the top board down tight. Carefully, Kev put down the newspapers he held. He lifted the hinge. When the board slid out of place, a centipede crawled into the corner, scrambling away from the light. Inside was a square hollow. A place to store things.

He squinted into the dark space. There seemed to be nothing inside except a moldering stack of election posters: "WORTHSON for Sheriff / Vote for Justice & Safety in Bitterroot County in 1984!" Kev flicked rapidly through the mold-spotted handbills. Underneath, there was another collection of paper—a drifted pile of envelopes, each one addressed in the same handwritten ink, to Matt Worthson, c/o Stan Worthson, 101 Pinecrest Drive, Kellogg, Idaho 83837.

Kev glanced at the doorway. Outside he could hear that Matt was still pounding shutters closed. Quickly, Kev reached under the posters, scooping out the collection of letters. Unopened letters, each one still sealed and closed. He flipped the top one over. Carefully, he rubbed at the back of the yellowed envelope. The dried-up glue gave under the rubbing of his fingers. Slowly, the back flap separated from the rest of the envelope. The paper inside crinkled and broke as he bent it open. Inside, words were scratched across pages in thin and spidery strokes.

Dear Matt,

You haven't forgotten about me, have you? I hope you're able to get to the hospital to see me soon. They tell me that now that I've come out of the coma, I'm on the uphill swing, but since I've got one of those infection thingys, it could be up and down for awhile. So I'd sure love to see you before I go 'down,' so to speak.

No pressure though. I know how you are about pressure. I mean, that's why you were running away from Sall, am I right? And you got that election to finish—I was surprised that you weren't sheriff already when I woke up. So I guess you're still running for office. Far be it from me to give you pressure to come see me . . . what kind of claim do I have on you, after all? I just figured it had been three weeks, so I might be seeing your smiling face sometime in the next century.

Kev flipped the page over. There was a lot more, but the letter just ended with a simple "Your friend, Irene." No love letters here. Nothing too juicy. Yet no one had thrown them away—and they'd never even been opened. He reached out and picked up another one from the stack. A miasma of mold had crept across some of the envelopes, corroding the text.

> You were in a good place when this accident happened, Matt.
> You had it beat—you were going to AA, talking to your sponsor.
> Really, I think they keep telling me this lie, hoping that I will press
> charges against you. But there's no reason to do that. Why would
> I? You weren't at fault.
>
> Two-faced bastards. They're playing some game on me. Maybe
> playing one on you, I don't want you to blame—

A spot of mold concealed the final word. Insects had eaten all the way through the paper package, punctuating the text with neat bullet holes. Kev turned to an undamaged page and found the faded thread of words again.

Suddenly, Matt's voice spoke in his ear. "Wondered where you'd got to. What's that stuff?"

Kev felt himself startle, the hair on the back of his neck rising as he glanced down at the broken spot in the window seat, the envelopes and the election posters flung down around the open hole in the wood.

"Nothing," he muttered. He felt his face redden as he looked up. "Old papers."

Matt shouldered him aside, yanking the envelopes out of his grasp. "What the hell are you doing with these?"

Kev watched him stare down at the address on them. "These letters—they're like all from the same person, right?"

Quickly, Matt made to shove them back in the hole, as if the touch of the paper scalded his skin.

"You just gonna put 'em back—not open a single one?"

Matt looked up, bemused astonishment washing across his face. "What business is it of yours? Yeah, I'm just going to put them back. That's why I put them here in the first place—because I didn't want nosy losers like you finding out about them and—"

"A nosy loser, huh?" said Kev. He leaned forward, his pulse shaking in him—something growing out of resentment and frustration, his curiosity becoming a nervous anger. "You ain't hiding them from me. Who the fuck you hiding 'em from—you afraid Sall's gonna find out who you were screwing like fifty years ago?"

Matt turned halfway toward him, the blood rushing up to fill his face. "Look, kid, how many ways can I tell you that it's none of your goddamn business?"

"You don't trust me, man. C'mon, tell me what's up with the letters."

Matt looked at him. "Goddammit, Kev, it's not that I don't trust you—it's just that these are just private papers. It's all in the past. None of your damn business."

Kev felt something spark inside, a fire raging out of control. "Hey, man, whatever you say—I know you're fuckin' afraid." Kev inhaled deeply and twisted his face in derision. "Smell it, man. Like a dog."

"Oh yeah, Kev—you think you can smell things like this? This is just too complicated, too complicated to explain to you."

Kev sniffed the air again. Then he waved his hand. "Hey, whatever, man. All's I'm saying is you stink. You're scared. Shitless." He turned and sauntered toward the truck.

A moment later, he yelled again, an afterthought. "I got shit I know too—an' I'm not afraid to tell you! I got secrets too, man!"

To his surprise, Matt followed, his voice now tight and furious. "Look, kid, these are my private letters. If I choose to hide them, that's my own damn business!" Kev kept walking, and this time Matt sped up behind him. "You got secrets, huh? So what! You're talking about Doug, aren't you—is that what it is? You really think you can tell me something about him I don't already know?"

Kev turned, his back against the truck. Suddenly, Matt seemed larger than before as he propelled himself forward, the envelopes still clutched in his hand. Kev edged around the side of the vehicle and scrambled with one hand behind his back in the truck bed for something heavy—a tool he could use as a weapon.

Matt was still shouting. "You've got nothing on me! Just stay the hell out of—"

"Yeah man?" taunted Kev. "If I got nothin' on you—how come you never opened all them damn envelopes? Huh? You're scared, man, scared!"

Matt slammed a fist against the side of the truck—Kev felt it rock under the blow. Now his mouth was dry and parched. He swallowed and grasped the handle of a hammer. Then, unexpectedly, Matt stopped moving, his head sinking against the truck window.

"Okay," Matt sighed. "So someone wrote to me and I've never had the guts to read 'em. I'm scared of what she wrote, of what she'll accuse me of. So what?"

"Okay, man, okay." Kev nodded. Slowly, he let the hammer slip out of his hand. Then he brought his arm out from the bed of the truck. He spread his hands out slowly in front of him. "It's cool. Hey, it's cool, man."

He waited a moment, feeling the sweat trickle down his neck. Matt stared at him, holding his eyes. Then Matt turned to go back toward the cabin.

When Kev glanced down at the ground, he could see the eye again, the one on the torn poster. "Dude," he said. And it came to him, a secret he did have.

Then when Matt failed to turn around, he said it again, louder. "Dude!" He cleared his throat. "I seen that guy on the poster before."

Matt still did not turn around. "Yeah, I know, at Pop's house. On the poster."

"No, I seen him myself. In the flesh—I kicked his ass." Kev furrowed his brow.

"Yeah, sure you did." Now Matt turned. "Let me tell you—that guy is a serious suspect in a murder case. I doubt you had the *cojones* to kick his—"

"Fuck you!" Kev lowered his brow. "I kicked that guy's ass at the Greyhound station. He was fuckin' with someone."

Slowly, Matt reached down and picked up the old milking bucket that held the cabin door open. With a grunt he shifted it to the bed of the truck. Then he paused and gave Kev a sidelong glance. "At the station? You were at the bus station? Who was he with?"

"I don't know, man. I'm gonna get fucked by the police if I know something. You guys don't play fair. But Jesus, that guy was one freaky mo'fo."

"If you didn't do anything wrong, nothing will happen to you," he said. "If you've really seen him, you'll be asked to give testimony, but nothing will happen to you. Tell me what you know."

"Nah." Kev glanced at him. Then he picked the poster up from the ground and crumpled it up.

"Why? This is a murder case, Kev. Did you hurt someone?"

"Jesus, man, no, not really. It was like this—the guy on the poster was with a little girl and another guy. In fact, I was talking to that other guy forever on the bus. Turned out the guy on the poster and the guy wearing a suit on the bus knew each other."

Matt turned to the bed of the truck and pulled out a worn tarp. Then he spoke again. "When was this?"

"I saw him at the Greyhound station, before we met up at Pop's house."

Matt gathered the loose ends of the tarp together and strapped it down. "Are you sure it was at the bus station? I think this was just something I said."

"Ah, you don't believe me anyways." Kev sighed and let go of his end of the tarp.

"No, no," said Matt. "I'm thinking. I want to hear this. Are you sure it was the night you saw him?" Matt pulled down on the tarp, stretching it taut again.

"Seems like," said Kev. "I mean, I know it was the guy on the poster. He was there with that other guy, the one wearing a suit, talking my ear off 'bout his little girl."

"What color was the suit? Was he wearing a cross too?"

"Blue suit. And yeah, he had a cross." Kev glowered. "Why's it matter to you?"

Matt swallowed, "Well, this could be really important."

"Huh." Kev reached down and picked up a fallen branch. It was bigger than he was. "That usually means I get fucked over when it goes down. Maybe it was a different guy."

"Wait," said Matt. "Tell me when this happened. What was the date?"

"I dunno. Like August. Maybe September something. Before Labor Day."

"Hmm . . . ," said Matt. "It could be."

Kev sighed. "I knew it." He shrugged. "No one ever fuckin' believes me." Savagely, Kev hefted the heavy branch into the woods.

Matt looked up suddenly. "No, I just want to be sure. I just—"

"I don't know why I brought the damn guy up." Kev shook his head, angry now at himself. "Dude, I need a john. You got one in there?"

Matt pointed at the cabin.

"Okay," said Kev. He walked to the door and looked back to see Matt cinching the ladder closed, tying it into the bed of the truck.

Inside, Kev went directly to the window seat. Quickly, he stuffed the bundle of envelopes into his backpack. Maybe he'd read them all.

When they got in the truck, Matt seemed almost happy to have him there. "I want to hear more about this guy you saw, about this man in a suit and that girl. Are you sure you saw them at the station?"

"That guy with the Mustang, he didn't believe I did the work on the Barracuda myself. I had to prove it to him. No one trusts me worth a damn."

"Kevin," said Matt. He snapped his seat belt on. "I trust you. Tell me."

"Okay," said Kev belligerently. "You trust me—so tell me what those damn letters are about."

Now that Kev was closer, he could see sweat on Matt's brow, a twitch in Matt's shoulder. He felt as if the air itself was suddenly charged, everything tense and still.

"No." Then Matt sighed. He held up a hand, flat like a stop sign. "Dammit, Kev." Slowly, he lowered his hand back to the steering wheel. "Okay, so I'll tell you once about this—no questions. Her name was Irene. She was a woman I was with during the last election. I killed her in a car accident. At least, I think I killed her. I guess I'd been drinking heavily, because I don't remember much.

In any case, I lived, she died. Before she died, she wrote me letters, but I just chucked them in there. I just couldn't read her accusations, because I already knew what I'd done, it wasn't worth reading about—"

"Jesus, man, she said in those letters that she could tell you the true story— don't you want to know the truth? What's up with that?"

"Goddammit!" Matt yelled, and pulled the truck back on the road. "You damn kid—I don't want to hear her voice ever again. You don't understand what I went through!"

"See man, see, you don't fuckin' trust anything I say." Kev kicked furiously at the dashboard. "You're scared, so you never read 'em!"

"It's none of your damn business. Fat lot of good it would do if I did read them. Now lay off." Matt floored the gas pedal and Kev was thrown back against the seat.

After a moment, Matt looked over again. "Okay, look, we can't keep this up over dinner. Sall's been cooking hard all day today."

Kev looked out the window. "Yeah, well, you go on an' enjoy your dinner."

"It's Thanksgiving, dammit," said Matt. "Sall has a turkey going. Eat with us."

Kev grunted.

"We'll take some food over to my pop later. He's in the hospital again. He said he'd like to see you—he was real impressed with the work you did on the 'Cuda."

"Uh-huh," Kev grunted. "That'd be all right, I guess."

"He's an old guy, I know, but he hasn't died yet—"

Kev kicked at the floor of the truck again. "Fuck, I said I was sorry for that," he muttered. "Try to help, an' you just get bullshit. No trust. That college stuff prob'ly won't work either. All I get is bullshit. That chick really liked you, sounds like, to me."

"Kev—look, forget the damn letters, they're crap—I want to hear about the bus station, and the guy in the suit, the guy on that poster—"

"Fuck you—so what if I made the whole thing up anyway." Kev pounded a fist on the truck window, and a cracking sound reverberated through the door.

"Watch the damn window!" Matt put out a hand and held on to Kev's fist.

"Okay, okay, I'll watch your damn window." Then as soon as Matt let go, Kev punched the glass again before rolling his body to the side, away from Matt. A stony silence filled the cab all the way back to the house, as the snow began to fall.

He ventures into a labyrinth . . . no one can behold how and
where he goes astray, is cut off from others, and is torn to
pieces limb from limb by some cave-minotaur of conscience.
—Friedrich Nietzsche, *Beyond Good and Evil*

THE COEUR d'Alene Resort glowed in the early morning sun, its fine metallic sheen mirrored on the lake, turning the water of the cove a reflected gold.
To the east stood another reflection—the small stylized building that on first
glance was a scale model of the resort itself. William S. Herrick Jr.'s private
office, the one he maintained as an irritant in the face of Valerie Herrick's
magnificent resort.

Matt waited at the solid maple registration desk of the resort. Matt hadn't
been able to find Russ anywhere in town since he had seen him at the collapsed
highway. Right now, there was no one who fit Russ's description registered as
a guest. Last week, Russ had come into the resort bar and talked the bartender
out of a bottle of Scotch, claiming it was for a corporate function in his wife's
office. That was the last time anyone in Coeur d'Alene had seen him.

Although his campaign roared along at full steam, claiming a new endorse-
ment every week, Russell had effectively disappeared, making no public ap-
pearances. Yet no one seemed to have a desperate need to talk to him. Except
for Matt.

When Matt left the resort, an icy gust lifted off the frozen surface of the
lake, blowing him back against the buildings. He hunched over, holding his
coat close, and pulled his way along the salted walkway past Will Herrick's
office. As he passed, he happened to glance up at the private office level, the
one fronted by windows all the way around. Silhouetted against the blowing
snow, he could see Valerie Herrick, her hands moving in some impassioned
gesticulation. Matt stopped walking.

He'd never seen Valerie in her brother's office in his life.

The vast open space of the office loomed over the lake. On the other side of the
spacious room, next to a redwood filing cabinet and credenza, was a calfskin
attaché, centered in the light of two Italian torchieres.

A tall, solid man with thinning gray hair, an Armani suit, and a rapacious look was staring out the giant windows while Valerie whispered frantically on the phone. The man turned at Matt's entrance.

"Ah," William Herrick said. "A former candidate coming in place of the current candidate. Welcome to my humble suite. I assume you're here trying to find our errant Russell. I do hope we don't have another fatal car accident on our hands, don't you?"

Matt looked at the predatory face, and found that he was too tired to think of a reply to the old gibe. He felt fatigue hanging over him lately, like a disease.

Back in the corner, where the shadows were, Matt could see Valerie Herrick talking furiously on the phone, her hoarse whisper whipsawing across the empty office.

"Do you know where he is?" said Matt. "I have some questions."

"Haven't a clue where he might be. Thing is, neither does his wife," said William sharply. He turned back to look out the window, across the lake. His reflection in the windows showed an expression of unyielding strength. After a moment, William spoke again. "That's where that other gentleman was found."

"What's that?" said Matt.

Behind him, Matt could hear Valerie, her voice rising stridently. "No, Mr. Rawlings, you are not going to run a front-page feature on that equipment collapse. No, I don't fucking care if the Spokane papers are headlining it."

"I saw the man whose body you found. Out there, on the lake." William turned and walked to a bar with bottles that stood by the window. "You want a drink. Gray Goose?"

Matt shook his head numbly. "You said you saw him? Before he died?"

William shook ice cubes into a glass, poured a jigger of liquor over the top. "Sure, I saw him. About two weeks ago, I was here, by the window," he gestured at an expensive telescope that stood erect by the window, pointing toward the middle of the lake.

"No, I've got a story for you," said Valerie. "How does this grab you—Recall Effort Underway for Sheriff. Russ is going to make him just another face in the crowd by the time votes are cast. Merrill may not make it to January. Can you lead with that?"

William Herrick continued talking. "So I saw someone out there in a boat. He was yanking at a rope as the fog came over the lake. Must have been the choke. Anyway, I watched him pull on the damn thing until it broke off. Didn't know how to run a boat. And then, as I said, the fog rolled in. I saw the boat, drifting empty, later. Poor bastard."

William took a swallow of his drink. "Didn't know who I was seeing, of course." He pointed out at the open water. "Unfortunate, but there it is. He was gone."

"Don't write this in the article yet," whispered Valerie. "How about you just put that the recall effort supports White? Cut all this BS about the road falling in the lake!"

William moved the ice in his glass, the sound sharp as a bell. "Truth be told, he's someone I've known a long time. Good riddance to bad rubbish. He was seen near Arlen, hanging around near him, bothering him. I think he's definitely—"

"From who? How do you know this? I've talked to every possible witness."

William shook his head and looked away from Matt. He stared at Valerie. When he spoke, it was in a shout. "Get the hell off my phone—you're done trying to fix it! Okay?"

Slowly, she put down the phone, her demeanor more fragile than Matt had ever seen in her before.

"It's not going to work, Val!" William continued shouting. "Just sell the damned company to me and be done with it!"

Valerie sat back and folded her arms. "Will, I've got some things to sort out—"

William held up a finger, forestalling Val. He looked at Matt, and continued as if Val had not spoken. "The shame of it is that I recommended you. I told Andy Merrill that if he had Russell White on the case, he'd just screw it up. But you, you had some abiding interest here. I figured you could be trusted to do the right thing—"

"What right thing?" Valerie stalked forward, vaulting out of her chair. "Arresting someone for political expediency? Trying to win an election by fraud, simply so you can take my property?"

William glared back at her. "It was mine before it was yours. It's rightfully—"

Matt swallowed, trying to get rid of the taste in his mouth. The taste seemed to come from the water, from the air, from the sky. From the room.

The sudden ring of the office phone cut across William's voice.

"I'm going to answer that," said Valerie.

"It's my office phone," said William. "Mine."

"I told them to route all calls over here." She picked up the receiver with authority, pushed a button on the phone. "Yes, what is it? This is Valerie Herrick."

William Herrick stared at her for a moment. Then he picked up his drink. He spoke quietly to Matt. "Of course, you were lucky in finding him in the lake. I'd recognize those shitty tattoos anywhere. That's your guy. I think you should point the case at Curtis Siwood, and close the damn thing. Perp found dead. The end. You can't ID him for sure, of course, not after all this time in the water. Close the case."

Matt demurred. "No, no, not yet. I figure we'll know for sure soon enough. Fortunately, we managed to get fingerprints. We should have results on any hits by—"

William put his glass down hard. A faint ringing echoed through the room as it landed. Matt glanced down, surprised the glass hadn't shattered. He noticed Valerie had hung up her phone, but she did not say anything.

Finally, William spoke again. "How the hell did you get fingerprints?"

Matt wanted to say something about Russell, to ask a Herrick something point-blank for once in his life. But instead he answered the question. He lifted his fingers, mimed his hand going in a glove. "You slide your hand inside the dead skin—press it down—see. You can still lift prints from a bloated body, if the skin isn't gone."

William favored Valerie and Matt with a thin smile, and mock applause. "Well, Valerie, what do you think? Pretty good work from Mister Boy Scout. Now with fingerprints, you can probably tie Curtis directly to the scene, to the resort that night—"

"He wasn't even at the resort that night, as you well know!" Valerie's voice was shrill.

Again, William simply ignored his sister. "My inclination, of course, would be to go with the dead guy. But truth be told, I think Andy wants to indict someone alive, make more of a public spectacle out of it—have a win just before the election, a collar he can point to, to show he's doing his job."

This time, Valerie's voice carried a hard edge, a cold rage. "Like my husband, maybe?"

Matt whirled around. "What?"

"Yes, you heard right," said William. He did not turn. "I told Val I'd bet her a million dollars, give or take, that Andy Merrill will indict that fucker she married. He's in the shit, he's in deep, and there's no way he will ever dig his way out again."

Valerie stood up from the chair so violently that it crashed to the floor. "He didn't do it, though! He didn't have anything to do with—"

"Shut up!" William shouted. "You shut the hell up. You married the bastard, you deserve to go down with him. At the end of the day, I'll get the resort, I'll get all the properties, you know I will. All of the Herrick legacy will be mine. Dad never liked you anyway, you should have died at birth. Hell, you don't even deserve the same last name!"

Matt glanced back and forth between them as Valerie crumbled under this onslaught, her mascara running down her cheeks, her eyes dripping with tears, her jaw clenching helplessly with anger.

William did not look at her. He pointed toward the other side of the lake. "Hell, I'll even get back the old boat cabin Dad gave to you. I'll get it all, because you allowed yourself, once upon a time, to betray our good name. You allowed yourself to get seduced by that junior-league Lothario! Wouldn't you agree, Worthson, he's just a . . ."

But Matt wasn't listening. He'd been to the boat cabin with Russ before. It was a small place, comfortable for one man to stay for a few weeks, out of the way. Russ had even invited him. *Go to the boat cabin, if you need a place to stay.* Yet showing up might not be enough. He needed some way of finding out the truth while he was there.

"Jesus Christ." Valerie was shouting back now. "You wouldn't dare to do this, Will, if Dad were alive. The least you could do is look at me like a man."

But William did not turn around. His gaze was held by something on the lake, a small swaying dot that might be a rowboat or an abandoned Jet Ski. Out to the west, the old pilings of the Blackwell Logging Company stood high out of the water, above the place where the river joined the lake.

Matt watched William Herrick slowly put his hands on the wide sill, wondering if this was what he had looked like as he watched the man on the boat begin to die. William waited until Valerie was done talking, and then he spoke mildly, giving no response to anything she'd said.

"Well, Valerie, I think we're done here. I no longer need the grief. I've supported you. I've given you rope. You've hung yourself." William stood from the windowsill and put a large hand on Matt's shoulder. "Worthson here will hand the damn case over to Merrill's good graces, and he'll walk away. C'est la vie."

Outside, Matt could see the sun on the lake. Behind them, Valerie stood crying silently, her anger drifting across in waves. The skeleton of pilings stood black on the water. Lake birds slowed in flight, looking for fish in the shallows. They hung motionless in the air, their wings beating.

It came to him that he would have preferred to be talking to Karl Avery today, instead of the Herricks. "I'm not going to do it. Russell isn't . . . ," began Matt. "I'm still working the case."

"Sure you are, sure you are," said William patronizingly. This time he let himself smile, a thin expression, given to Matt in pity. "I'll see you out, Lieutenant. Thank you for coming by," he said in a tone meant to be courteous. "Let me know when you decide to throw in the towel."

Then he gestured at the wall of glass. "Look, the weather is about to turn."

The clouds hung down as if drawn to the land. Then, far enough out that it seemed a different world, their edges were traced with brightness. Out where the sun split the clouds with red, the clouds became separate rafts, opening out in bands of scarlet and purple. Matt looked at the empty room with its expensive furnishings, at Valerie Herrick, crying, her face streaked with thick black tears. It was not the same place that it had been. He watched from a different shore.

The state-licensed liquor store opened at 10:00 a.m. When the door was unlocked, and the sign slid from Closed to Open, Matt looked down at his hands. They were clenching the wheel of the truck so tightly they ached, the skin was slick with sweat. Matt let go and reached in his pocket. He looked over at the kid, who bent his brow and frowned back at him.

"Why did you bring me along again?" Kev said.

"Trust." Matt breathed out slowly, steadying himself. "I don't trust myself."

"So get someone from your work to come along. How am I supposed to—"

"I can't." Matt stared straight ahead. "No one can know about this, about where I'm going today, what I'm doing there. But I need someone here. I don't trust—"

"Yeah, yeah, I know. Yourself." The kid gave an exaggerated yawn. "So now you got a plan, huh? But still, you go in there, you should know, that shit will kill you."

"Right, that's why you're here. I have a job to do here, and I need you. You can help just by being here. You're helping me right now. I'm going to go in there, and—"

"Shit, I don't know if this is a good idea." The kid shook his head ruefully. "What the hell am I supposed to do? I still don't understand why you're buying. Do you have—"

But Matt was already out of the truck. He didn't hesitate once he got to the store.

Back in the truck, the bottle came out of the brown paper bag immediately. The color was amber, the glass heavy and cold against his perspiring palm.

He used to drain these bottles like they were made of air, he used to breathe it in, he used to swim in it. How easy it would be to slip off the lid, to taste that warmth on his tongue. This one didn't even have a cork. He looked down at the ornate label, the familiar words. Not for the first time, he thought of how much easier the world had been when he was draining everything through the same alcohol-fogged filter. A single taste, a swallow. How long had it been?

"Put that damn thing back," said Kev. "I mean, I'm straight-edge, I don't get this."

Matt looked down at the bottle. The memory came back, of his father coming to the rehab clinic the first time he'd tried to go sober, just sitting there, having nothing to say to him. He thought of Louden's voice in the briefing room: *You're a pair of drunks.*

"Yeah," he said to the kid. "That's why I brought you. You don't get it. Thanks. You did what I needed you to do. I'll drop you off at home. I got someone to meet."

Kev just looked at him. "Yeah, well, like I said, that stuff'll kill you."

Matt put the bottle back in the sack. Once the glass no longer touched his skin, the yearning was easier to ignore. It just might work.

Russell White reached out automatically and broke the seal on the bottle. The strong aroma of alcohol rushed into the room, intoxicating in itself. Matt swallowed, feeling his heart leap involuntarily. Russ took a swallow and held the bottle up for Matt.

"Fuck, Matty, I don't know how you found me, but I'm glad you did."

Matt snapped his fingers. "Glasses." He stood and went in the kitchen, filling his own glass with water and ice. He brought back a cup full of ice and the two glasses.

For a long hour, all Russ wanted to talk about was Valerie. He wanted to know how she was doing. He wanted to hear about how she was feeling during his absence. Once he said that they should leave immediately, drive straight back home, let Valerie know that he was all right.

But he didn't move from the couch. Then, later in the afternoon, as his voice began to slur, Matt turned the conversation around, and something more began to come out, in a slow drip like a broken faucet.

"Look, I'm sorry to be the bearer of bad news," began Matt. "But I got to tell you that Will Herrick thinks Merrill is going to arrest you. For something, I don't know what. I'm out here because I figured I should warn you."

Russ offered the bottle back to Matt, who took it momentarily. Then, as Russ rubbed a hand across his flushed face, Matt filled Russ's glass again.

"Russ, it's not fair, we both know it." Matt nodded. "And I'll stand up for you, you know I will. But damn, you disappear like this, I think he'll make hay out of it. It just looks bad."

Russ clinked glasses with Matt. "We've seen worse, haven't we? Hell, thank you for that. Thank you for all of it. Damn, Matt, I owe you. All the time, I owe you."

Russ took a gulp. "Jesus, I'm winning the election. For Valerie—she wanted me to do it! But she can't protect me from this—and this was her damn thing too. Jesus, Valerie told me what to do!" Russ shook his head, the tears standing out in his eyes.

Matt sighed. "I know how you feel." He took a sip of water and waited for Russ. Then he spoke again. "Y'know, I've been having some nightmares. How about you?"

Russ looked down, into the depths of his drink. "C'mon, Matty, you were there. You gotta have figured out already—maybe months ago, you did, I dunno—that Arlen was dead before he got chopped up." Russ gave him a sideways glance, a slyly drunken look. "You knew that, right? Jesus, I'm sorry if I lied to you about that . . ."

Matt looked away, faking a moment of boredom. "Of course, I already knew that."

"So you gotta wonder why he was killed. I mean, hell, it wasn't because that loser Curtis Siwood had something against him. Jesus, I know you told the newspapers that, but . . ."

Matt felt himself attuned to every sound, even to the faint intakes of breath from Russ. In the kitchen at the back of the house, he could hear a fly faintly buzzing against the window.

Russell paused, and gulped hungrily at his glass. "I don't know. That's what plagues me still. I don't know why he was killed. I just know where the body ended up."

Carefully, Matt replenished the empty glass. "On the hillside, up on Tubbs Point."

"No, in the resort!" Russ frowned petulantly. "Dammit, arentcha paying attention?"

Matt held up his own glass, the ice still melting in water. "It's the Scotch—hit me hard. Sorry, Russ."

"Okay." Russ held up his glass and gave an awkward tilt, a toast to him. "That's what keeps me up nights, y'know. Why? Why did I let—why did Arlen have to die?"

"Why?" repeated Matt gently.

"I think it was Will—he has a vendetta for Val's resort business," mused Russell. "And I swear—hell, I know—he had something to do with Arlen dying."

"But how—" began Matt.

Russ kept talking, blurting out the words. "He had us over a barrel. Will knew it would hurt the tourist business, having the body there, on our premises. He needed Arlen to shut his big trap about something, that much I know, but dumping the body on us . . ."

Matt shook his head in sympathy. "It was a strategy. Business?"

"Hell if I know." Russ waved his hand, the syllables blurring more and more together. "You know what happened. You know why Val was pissed at me."

"The massage parlor."

Russ nodded at him, his eyes wide and bloodshot. "Yeah, that girl."

"Look," said Matt. "I know that you had to do what you were told—"

"Of course I did!" Russ shook his head. "I mean, when the body's found there, Val just details me and May to get it off the premises. So we clean it up, get him out of there, and I don't even notice it's Arlen. I mean, May Brewmer and me, we're just mopping the blood off the floor—"

"You're doing the cleanup?"

"Sure, we're cleaning it all up when Valerie comes in. Fucks it up—fucks it up good. Goddamn Val." Russ stared ahead. Perhaps he thought he'd said too much.

"Here," said Matt, holding out the bowl. "I got you some ice too."

Russ nodded in gratefulness and took another swallow. "Goddamn Val with her sharp eyes, she comes in, and when she sees who it is who's dead, she knows immediately why it might have been dumped there—or she thinks she does. She blames it on me. Jesus, I don't know how she knew about my little thing with . . . like a lover would be nuts enough to kill off the husband. I don't know how she knew, but Val was the one recognizes it was Arlen Bowman in there. So because of who he is, Val is pissed immediately, she blames me . . ." Russ gulped noisily at the drink again.

Matt glanced at the heaps of clothes on the floor, at the darkened doorway. "I don't get it, Russ, I mean—"

"She's jealous, Matty. I mean, you ever know a jealous woman?" Russ gulped at the glass, breaking a piece of ice with his teeth. "I'm telling you, she sees it's Arlen who's dead, that I'm cleaning it up, she changes all the rules."

"Russ, if there's a death involved, I mean . . . you got a lawyer, right?"

Russ waved his hand shakily. "I gotta talk about this. Even though she blamed me, Valerie knew who done it, I would swear on my mother's grave. It was her own fault we didn't just dump the body. She made me do it—make it look like something else. But I shouldn't have done that fuckin' thing to Arlen. Every time I think about, I want to throw up."

Russ staggered upright and stumbled to a desk in the corner. With shaking hands, he unlocked a drawer and withdrew a battered gray envelope. Inside were a set of white cards. Polaroid prints. Russ stumbled, and they spilled across the floor, a set of bloody cards scattered across the floor, a body being dismembered.

"What happened? What did she make you do?"

Russ stared off in the distance. Then his eyes tracked across the side of the room as the fly from the kitchen buzzed into the dining room and landed on the ceiling.

"You don't get it yet? Valerie made me do it to Arlen—she made me cut up his body."

Matt felt a dull shock settle on him, holding him to the words. Far away, he could hear the fly stop against the screen door and fly off again, moving in a wide, unsteady arc around the kitchen table.

"Valerie—that bitch made me. She made me chop him into pieces, cover something up. I don't know what it was, but hell, there wasn't nothing I could do. I mean, goddamn, she pays the bills, right?" Russ's glass slopped out, his sleeve wet to the elbow. He gulped desperately at it as his hands shook.

"I didn't want to do anything to him when I realized it was Arlen. I just wanted to put him back in the bathroom where we found 'im. See, you can see in the first picture, Arlen's dead already, peaceful like, his throat cut. Had some cigarette burns on his arms and legs. He was tied up, but hell, a cut throat don't take long to kill you. It didn't hurt him long. Then she says to put the body back, an' next thing I know, Valerie gives me an axe, says 'Chop up the damn body. Serial killing, that's what we'll make this look like. Here, I got some pictures of the other dumped bodies—you make it look just like this shit.' And I already cheated on her, so there was nothing I could say. I had to do it. And I didn't kill 'im. I mean, that was already done for me, I just—"

"But, Russ, why—"

"I'm tellin' you, Matty, 'cause I know you'll keep the secret. Hell, I've always kept your secrets, maybe it's your turn now. I've always kept the secret of what happened with you and Irene." Matt saw something sly flicker across Russ's face, a subterfuge that could not be fully concealed, seeping through the alcohol. Russ would keep what secrets he could.

Matt stared at him for a moment, seeing his face go blank again. How far could he push Russ without pushing himself off the cliff too? How far would his friendship with Russ take him?

"But you're telling me, God's truth, you didn't kill him."

Russ shook his head slowly, that flash of inside knowledge sparking again, as the fly buzzed through the room. In the silence, Matt could hear it turn and curl in the air.

Matt sloshed a gulp of water into his dry mouth. His thoughts ran in circles. But Russ was still talking, his story blurred together now into a sodden mass of syllables. "I thought it would be no big thing, I mean, hell, I've butchered deer before, but this time was different . . . I mean, every night, I see myself jus' lifting the axe, swingin' it over an' over again. Damn, Matty, I wake up every night, an' Arlen's insides are still all over me, like I can never wash it off, like I'll be covered in it forever."

There was a pause. The fly buzzed into a corner and fell silent. Matt swallowed, his mouth dry once more.

Hurriedly, Russ gulped at his glass. He shook his head, and almost fell over from the motion. "And now that I done it, she's still got me by the balls. And I can't . . . I mean, what was I supposed to do? Let that happen? That's why I went an' made sure that May Brewmer would keep it quiet. That's why I did all of this. Christ, what I did for my girl."

Russ looked up at Matt, his eyes hollow and dark with fear. "But we didn't do anything wrong, Matt. I mean, he was already a dead man. I mean, my God, Matt, Arlen was already dead. He was dead, his throat cut. What did I do but help bury him, huh?"

Then Russ leaned his head to the side and a thick fluid rushed out of his mouth. He lifted his glass for another drink and fell sideways onto the floor. Matt could barely hear his last mumbled plea. "I didn't kill him. I mean, I saw him there . . . and my girl, my girl . . . I wish I just . . ." Then a stream of vomit came out, and his eyes closed.

Matt looked at the empty bottle standing on the floor, and Russ collapsed beside it. He gathered the pictures of the body in his hands and put them back in the envelope. Then he put the envelope and the photos in his pocket. He locked the desk again.

In the morning, if Matt was lucky, Russ wouldn't remember much. A blackout. The open window reminded him, there would be bright light filling the room at dawn. He felt strangely tender toward Russ, remembering the blinding pain after a binge. Carefully, he pulled the blinds, draped a blanket over Russ's sleeping body. He closed the door and locked it as he left.

Our torments also may in length of time
Become our elements, these piercing Fires
As soft as now severe, our temper changed
Into their temper; which must needs remove
The sensible of pain.
　　—John Milton, *Paradise Lost*

MATT BANGED the door of the sheriff's office open hard, knocking the sign sideways on the door, but Sheriff Merrill did not look up at him. Matt stood there for a moment, holding the newspaper in his hand. Finally he sat down in the chair across from Merrill. The sheriff's color was ashen, and his hands trembled on his desk. He sat unmoving, as if a shockwave had already broken across him.

"Looks like Valerie Herrick finally turned on you, huh, Andy?"

Matt pointed at the newspaper in his hands, the headline reading "Sheriff Loses Public Confidence: In New Recall Effort, Merrill Faces Anger, Voter Dismay." He tossed it onto the desk.

"So what if Russell is winning? Valerie can get Rawlings to print any damn thing she wants." Merrill pushed the paper aside. "Why the hell are you here?"

"I saw Dustin leave just as I pulled up. Phyllis said you sent him out on a confidential arrest—but I know who he's going to arrest." Matt picked up the phone on the desk. "Call him back. You can't arrest Russ. Will Herrick is just using you!"

"Jesus, Matty—I wouldn't do something that stupid." Merrill lay back in his chair, his arms hanging loosely beside his bulk, as if his body were too heavy for him to lift. He squinted at Matt from across the room. "You really think I'm dumb enough to try to arrest my opponent on the eve of the election? The DA and the election commissioner would have my ass, even if I did have evidence on him. I wish I did. But I don't."

"So you don't have any evidence on Russ."

"Right." Merrill paused, grinned strangely at him. "Not on Russell."

"That's because he didn't do it."

"I know that."

Matt sat down wearily, sinking into the opposite chair. "But you've just sent Hoffman out there to arrest him. You must have a warrant. You must have evidence."

Merrill gave a quick chuckle that was followed by a coughing fit, an awful sound that echoed in the small room. Finally, he looked up, his eyes rheumy from the coughing. "Look," he said hoarsely. "Let's cut the crap. Why are you here, in my office?"

"Because, I told you, I don't think you should arrest Russ. I just got a confession from him and"—Merrill gave that same Cheshire grin and raised an eyebrow, but Matt continued—"I know it looks bad. He *was* involved in dismembering Arlen, trying to cover something up, and I don't fully understand what yet, but he didn't kill the guy, he didn't—"

"Hold on. Just stop talking." Merrill rubbed the palms of his hands over his face. The sweat shone on his skin. He put his face in his hands. "Are you going to tell me who did kill Arlen? Is that why you're here in my office? Because it would save us all a lot of trouble and grief, that's for sure."

Matt leaned forward in his chair. "No, I can't. I don't know for sure yet. I think it was Curtis Siwood, the miner we found dead in the—"

"Yeah, yeah, don't feed me that bullshit. Dead guy in lake, isn't it convenient his fingerprints—which you guys took off his dead body, mind you—are the ones that connect to the resort bathroom, and even to Tubbs Hill. Isn't it damn convenient."

"Convenient? What do you mean?" Matt leaned forward, a sudden uncertainty turning in his gut like a worm. "If you have some other evidence, evidence I haven't seen, I wish you'd share it with me."

Merrill looked away. He muttered to himself, "I've got the damn guy right here, I don't need help." He glanced at Matt. "I don't know why you even showed up today."

"I've got a job to do."

"A job." Merrill looked back at him, he seemed nonplussed.

Patiently, Matt continued. "I am willing to arrest the right person, if all the evidence points there—but Russell just isn't the guy."

Merrill rubbed a hand across the back of his neck, where the sweat stood out like blisters. "Maybe you're trying to ask for God's grace or some such shit, but it's a damn strange thing to do after all this time. Arlen is gone—who cares?—he's dead already."

"He's dead already?" said Matt, rising from his chair. "This is Arlen Bowman we're talking about here! I'm glad I was assigned to this case, and I aim to—"

Merrill held up a hand, motioning Matt to sit back down. He stared at Matt quizzically. "You know the reason William Herrick was begging me to assign you to the resort that night. You know it better than anyone."

Matt paused, his mouth open. He closed it and looked down at Merrill. "What?"

Merrill mopped his hand over the perspiration on his face and sighed, a heavy sound. "I don't know what game you've been playing, Matty, but it's a damn good one. Pointing in every direction except the obvious one. I should have figured it out months ago, but I've been distracted. The election, I guess." Merrill sighed once more. "That's no excuse though. I should have seen through your lies."

It was as if the gravity had been pulled out from under Matt. He sat down slowly, sinking into unreality. "Lies? What lies? I haven't been covering for Russ, I didn't—"

"Now the only problem with your game is that the truth is leaking out all over the place. I talked to people who knew this dead guy in the lake—Curtis or Larry or whatever name he was using—and there's this rumor about Worthson. I keep hearing your damn name."

"Jesus, Merrill, what are you insinuating? What are you trying to say?"

Merrill looked at his desk. He stirred his finger through the jar of paper clips. "Since when did I have to spell something like this out?" Merrill wiped the perspiration off his neck. "Put two and two together."

Matt closed his eyes, trying to see clear. He spoke slowly. "What are you talking about, Andy?"

There was no reply. Matt opened his eyes to see Merrill hunting around in the desk drawer, looking for something. "Cigar," he said finally. "You want one?"

Numbly, Matt shook his head.

Merrill lit a busted stogie, the broken bits at the end burning off with a sudden bitter stench. He placed a dirty ashtray on top of the papers on his desk. "Jesus, Matty, so I see you're not going to pop off right here. I can understand that, respect that even."

Merrill put the cigar down for a moment, placing a hand over his heart. "Honor among thieves, and all that. There is honor, I understand."

"Honor for what? You said you put it together, right? So let's have it."

Merrill sighed, letting out a stream of gray smoke. "You want to see what I got."

Matt looked down at the smoking mass in the ashtray. "Honestly, I don't have a clue what you're talking about, Andy."

Merrill chuckled. "Look at that. Pitch-perfect. And you even have a decoy running for you. Jesus, I had no idea you were so damn smart, Matty. I only wish—"

"Wish what? Are you saying Russ was just a decoy? What about Russell?"

Merrill looked down at the cigar and slowly stubbed it out. Then he put his hand over his heart again, mocking sympathy. "It's heartening to me that you seem so concerned about Russell. So much concern for your fellow man. You were so anxious to make sure Russell wasn't arrested—wherever the hell he's hiding his ass—that you were willing to put yourself in harm's way. Come over here, where you haven't been back to your office in weeks practically. I don't know what you've been doing, but you haven't been here, and you're all worried about—"

"I have a job to do." Matt pounded a fist on the desk, ashes bouncing out over the scattered papers and the jar of paper clips. "I've been working—I'm still working the case."

"Sure you are," said Merrill. It was the same phrasing William Herrick had used, the same dripping sarcasm, as if somehow they knew Matt better than he knew himself.

Merrill continued talking, as a wisp of smoke trickled up from the ashtray. "But for old times' sake, for all the good work we've done together—the sheriff's work, and a few of the other things we've done together over the years . . ."

Merrill winked laboriously, his eye closing slowly. Something in the wink struck Matt as obscene. "I'm willing to give you a little more rope. I just need your personal guarantee that you aren't going anywhere, not out of the county. See, I don't think it would look good to make an arrest like this just as the election is coming. And I'm sure as hell not going to arrest the other guy—my opponent. Even though it's clear to me that you and Russell were tied into this somehow—"

Matt interrupted. "This isn't about who killed Arlen Bowman anymore, is it? You're playing politics with this case, that's what you're doing."

"What I'm doing?" Merrill shook his head, bemused. "Jesus Christ, I cannot believe you both would have the balls to get this case, that you would come here—"

"Russell didn't do this, that's what I'm trying to tell you. Yes, it looks bad that he was assigned to the case, that he had involvement. It's really shitty. But he's innocent of Arlen's death. You have to believe me on this."

Merrill glanced up, a sudden hatred in his gaze. "No, I don't have to believe you. I don't believe a word you say, anymore. And frankly, I wish you'd stop saying them. I think you should have a lawyer here, if you're gonna talk. The only thing is, I can't take you off the force until after the election. It'll look like I don't have control—it'll look like I fucked up. Which I did, in a big way. So I won't do anything to you until after."

Matt rose to his feet again. Something was going sideways. "To me? What are you talking about? Let's allow the evidence to speak, let's convene a grand jury—"

"Ah, quit acting like fuckin' Perry Mason. Sit down, wouldja?" Merrill glanced up at him again, his gaze more weary than hateful now. "Look, let's not do this, okay? Let's stop with the game. Can you promise me not to leave the county at least?"

Matt sank down in his chair, his face still flushed. "I just need to know what you're talking about. I just need to know if you're actually accusing me of something."

Merrill stared at him, his eyes bloodshot and weary. "Jesus, Matty, do I need to?"

Matt felt it come over him then, the realization, a vast tide seeping in around his feet, rushing up toward his heart, his lungs, covering him in a sudden frigid chill.

The breath caught in his throat.

"Me. You really think I killed Arlen?"

Merrill's sleepy eyes did not move off Matt's face. "It's not a question of what I think or feel, Matty. I *know* you did something."

Matt opened his mouth. Then he closed it slowly, a fish gasping in the open air. "Jesus, Andy, you don't . . . you don't even have a motive. Why in the hell would I—"

"Don't snow me like this, Matty." Merrill closed his eyes and shook his head slowly, as if in sadness. "I think Arlen found out somehow, or you told him about it."

Matt leaned forward, the outrage rising in him. "What? Told him what?"

Merrill's eyes opened slowly, narrowed to suspicious slits. "Look, Matty, no one's ever found the real records for that accident you had with that Irene Closner girl. As you well know, Russell was the guy assigned to the accident, and he played fast and loose with the records. Probably as a favor to you—you guys have always covered each other's asses. I have nothing on that thing in my files."

Merrill waved his hands. "Hell, I don't know! For all I know, you raped her and strangled her, and then Russ crashed the car with her body, to cover up . . . the fact that she was in the hospital for weeks. And that you never even went to see her there tells me something too."

"But—"

Merrill held up a hand and spoke forcefully over him. "Oh yeah, Matty, I think you have a motive. Arlen found out something, or was told something, and you killed him to cover up your part in that old accident, that's what I think. But I wish I knew for sure. Maybe you could tell me . . . what the hell really happened in that accident, Matty?"

Matt leaned back in his chair. He could feel his heart pounding, as if it would burst apart. "I wish I knew, Andy," he mumbled. "I wish I could remember. I don't . . ."

Merrill put his hand down. He didn't speak for a moment. Then he began to swirl his fingers in the paper clips, sifting out the ash. "So there you have it, dontcha? In a nutshell, you don't remember a darn thing. Isn't that damn convenient for you."

"Convenient? Jesus, Andy, I didn't—"

"The idea that you've been trying to pin this thing on some drunk miner—an old guy who knew Karl Avery back in the day—that hasn't been a very convincing effort, even though you did manage to substitute in the fingerprints somehow."

Matt caught his breath, his chest filling with indignation. "Andy—those are the real fingerprints. This is the same guy. I don't know what the Karl Avery connection is. I don't know whether he—"

"Matty, you don't know whether to shit or get off the pot. That's the truth of it. And you just haven't done a good job of covering your own tracks here. It's pretty clear to me that you did this." Merrill tapped a thick finger on some papers on his desk. "I have the list here of interviews. It's pretty clear to me where you were, and where Arlen was, in Wallace. Hell, that bartender in Wallace who knows you, he even says you were with him that night! You gotta build a better story than that!"

The breath came hissing out of Matt, a chill coming over him.

Andy Merrill stared at him. "But I'm willing to let you float for a while," Merrill said. "You get me? Maybe you can turn someone, get testimony against that other decoy you've been trying to set up—what's-his-name, that kid who's camping in your garage."

"Kev? You want me to set him up now for . . . this homicide?"

"You already did, Matt. You already did that for me. Just not very well." Merrill took a paper clip out of the glass on the desk and bent it into another shape. "You're the one who must have given him that cross from Arlen. You were probably just waiting until some officer saw it, and then, hell, you could just—"

"What cross? Where?" Matt felt dizzy, the chill sweeping across him again.

"C'mon, Matty," Merrill sighed. "I figured it out already—you did it when you had the body in custody. Hell, you probably had Arlen's cross off him well before then." Merrill traced a cruciform shape in the air at his throat. "All you had to do was pawn that thing off on that Kev kid, and he becomes what you made him—a viable suspect."

"I've been looking for Arlen's cross for weeks. You're implying—"

"It was a little overdone, the way you described the damn kid to a T in your case report." Merrill flipped open a folder. "But even against my better judgment, Matty, I used your description in the warrant to arrest the damn kid. 'Transient, skinhead' . . . et cetera."

"Jesus, Andy, you gave that description to me from Butler. You just . . ."

Merrill looked up at him. "C'mon Matty, don't play dumb. You kept the description in that file, you even added to it, a few question marks here and there. And hell, you never reported he was on your property. For all I know, this kid *did* have something to do with it—you know as well as I do that sometimes murderers can't live with themselves, they give it away, even though they don't want to. An admission, against their better judgment. Maybe that's what you were admitting to—"

"But I don't have anything to admit to, Andy!"

Merrill shook his head ruefully. "If you're playing it like this, maybe that kid was your accomplice—and he's your giveaway. Hell, somehow you got his prints onto the knife."

Matt blinked. Something shifted in his head. "His fingerprints are on the knife?"

"Yeah, prints are all over that blackened piece of shit made by Karl Avery." Merrill guffawed, a hollow sound. "Hell, maybe if I keep the kid long enough, he'll tell us what happened, what he and you did with that knife. Hell, maybe he'll dig himself deeper, but dig you out of it. Could go either way, don't you think?"

Matt felt his mouth to be as dry as a rock. He swallowed hard. "So that's who you're arresting. Kevin Paulsen—the one who calls himself Macht. That's who Dustin was sent to arrest today." Matt looked out the window, the impulse to run taking him by surprise. "Jesus, Andy, you can't—"

"Hell, I'll even let you talk to him—give you access to the prisoner—see if he recalls any other connections to Arlen, find out that hey, maybe there's another way he got that damn cross." Merrill leaned down over the desk, fumbling nervously at the papers. "Maybe he did do it, or at least we can prove he did it. At the end of the day, you walk away clean, I walk away clean, hell, even Russell walks away clean. Everyone picks up a get-out-of-jail-free card. We could play it that way, but . . ." His voice trailed off.

"This isn't a game, Andy. It's life and death."

Merrill blinked up at him, his eyes suddenly wet with tears. "You used to be a good man, Worthson. But they must have put your balls in a vise. That's the only way I can describe it. Balls in a vise. I should know—one of the Herricks keeps handing you hundred-dollar bills, until you scream stop."

Merrill twisted the clip back and forth with his fingers. He spoke quietly, as if he were sharing a secret. "But I've never been able to say it, Matt. I just can't say stop, and I guess you couldn't either. So here we are, aren't we? It's a damn sad way to play."

"That might be you, Andy, but it's never been me. This is my life on the line."

At that, Merrill's face seemed to tighten into stone. He looked at something on the other side of the room, something beyond Matt. "Yeah, don't I know it. And for all you've done for me over the years, I'm willing to give you a little time. I'm going out on a limb for you, Matty. But truth be told, just between you and me and the doorpost, I think the jaws of this damn thing are closing all around you."

Merrill turned his gaze to Matt and pointed, a thick finger shaking fretfully in the air. "So I'd get a lawyer. I'd find a damn good fuckin' lawyer, because my patience will run out pretty fuckin' soon. I'd say just before the election. Then I'll cash in your chips."

Matt blurted out his response. "But what if you're all wrong, Andy—what if that kid had nothing to do with Arlen, what if he's innocent? Hell, what if I'm innocent?"

Merrill stared up at him, his eyes sad and empty. "You should know the score by now, Matty. All you can do is play out that last hand you're holding." He spread his fingers apart, dropping the broken paper clip in the blackened ashtray.

"No one's fuckin' innocent around here."

We all live in a house on fire, no fire department to call;
no way out, just the upstairs window to look out of
while the fire burns the house down with us trapped,
locked in it.
    —Tennessee Williams, *The Milk Train Doesn't Stop Here Anymore*

THE ENGINE made a harsh stutter, a barking choke that caught and held and broke again. When the sound began to roll together into a continuous growl, backfire explosions punctuated the roar. The random rimshots came less frequently as Kev put the Barracuda in gear.

The steering wheel seemed loose in his hands, and the transmission kept slipping, but the car traveled all the way from Matt's house to the parking lot in back of the A-1 Auto Parts store. When the car shuddered to a halt, Kev took a black baseball cap, a pair of bicycle gloves, and a polo shirt out of the box in the backseat.

Kev was already at the employee's entrance, the back door, when a bright-blue 1967 Camaro pulled up. He turned and saw a man step out of the car. The man wore dirty jeans, but Kev could see he had money. The watch gave him away. The man leaned over to look at Kev's car as soon as he'd locked the Camaro. Kev watched him run a hand over the curved air intakes on the hood of the 'Cuda. The metal was curved like the nostrils of some carnivorous animal, straining against the flaking yellow paint. Under the rust and spattered mud, the flanks of the car were curved as well, feral and powerful.

In the parking lot, Kev saw a police car turn tightly, as if circling the building. He scowled and pulled the A-1 polo shirt on over his T-shirt. Time to get to work.

Then the man at his car spoke. He didn't glance at Kev, he looked at the car like a lover. "Saw you drive up in this—Michael said you do good work. Damn, this 'Cuda is running pretty smooth for a '68."

Nervously, Kev saw the police car drift crookedly to the end of the cul-de-sac, coming closer to him every minute, like a fish in the current. "Uh-huh," he said. "Yeah, I got it running pretty tight."

The man glanced over at him. "You do all the work on this yourself?"

Behind the Camaro, the police car slid to a halt, the tires giving a sharp squeal as the officer yanked it sideways, blocking the driveway.

Kev grunted and pulled the leather bicycle gloves carefully over his swastika. He slapped the A-1 hat on his head, as if that would protect him.

The man glanced around for a moment, but then he turned back to Kev. "You got the feel for these things? Y'know, I love cars, and I took classes, but I don't have the damn feel at all. Don't have the magic touch. I gotta hire someone like you to fix up my babies. Michael said you know what you're doing."

"Sure," said Kev absently. He recognized the police officer, it was one of the same ones who had messed with him at the gas station. The officer grinned as Kev recognized him, gave him a false toothy smile.

"Fuck," Kev murmured under his breath. "Fuck me."

"What's that?" said the man with the Camaro. He glanced back and forth between the officer and Kev.

"Move aside," said the officer. "Sir, I need to ask you to step aside."

"Shit," said Kev. Slowly, he edged toward the door of the A-1 shop.

"Is there a problem here?" said the man. "I can't do business with you, if—"

But then Kev was making a mad dash for the door, and the officer had a weapon in his fist. "Don't move! Put your hands up!" yelled the officer. "Get those hands up!"

Kev got the door open. Inside, he could see the light reflecting off the lines of tools, the chrome bumpers hanging from the ceiling, turning in the sudden wind from the door. But he had too much to lose now. So he held the door there longer than he should have. And then the officer was snapping a cuff onto his wrist.

Kev found out there was a protocol for an interview with him. The handcuffs went on his wrists and his ankles. The cuffs were connected together by a chain around his waist. At the waist was the black metal box. After all this, they let him hobble two doors down the corridor to a gray room.

"Now, Kevin—I believe you like to be called Kev, am I right?" She was wearing a purple dress. She didn't look like she worked for the cops. Her blouse was like a flower.

"Macht. It means power in German. Kev Macht."

"All right. Mr. Macht. My name is Nancy Ferreday. We've met before, a long time ago. You've been in and out of the county justice system since you were twelve years old."

"Uh-huh."

Nancy looked down at the papers in front of her. Her brow wrinkled. "I must tell you that I'm concerned. This is your first adult incarceration. Your first adult offense. And they're charging you with homicide one. Do you understand what I'm saying?"

"You're saying juvie was for kids. We ain't in Kansas anymore."

"You might say that." She took off her glasses and looked at him. "You're charged with an offense that will change your life forever. The outcome of the case might end it."

Kev grunted.

She tried to catch his eye again, but Kev wasn't looking at her any longer. "I've been assigned to your case because I have a history with you. The questions I have—"

"You got questions?" said Kev loudly. "I got questions!"

Nancy looked at him. Her eyes squinted as if she did not understand. "Well, I've got your file here, Mr. Macht. We can discuss our questions. Shall we?" She leafed through loose pages. He recognized a lot of the pages. He'd seen these forms before, in juvie.

"In here is everything about you. Your teen years, when you came in and out of juvenile hall here quite regularly. And your minimal employment history, your time at the compound, that Aryan march you went on. There's even some childhood pictures.

"See?" she said brightly, and she held up a yellowed page with a photograph on it. He looked past her, around her. The door on the other end of the room had a metal plate wrapped around the doorframe. On this side, there were rivets that held it tight to the door.

She put the picture back in the folder. He watched her shuffle through the pile again. Her hair was short, but tendrils curled along her brow. The hair made him think of pretty girls. She was not pretty anymore. Her brow wrinkled as she bent over the papers.

"Now that last one is from when you were eight years old," she said. "From school. The next one is from twelve. It's your school picture." She held another piece of paper up.

He did not meet her eyes. The door held his interest. Once that door had been an everyday door, before they brought it in here. The metal plate looked like a recent addition. On the other side of it there must be a knob, or a keyhole—the way in and out.

She waved the paper in the air. "You aren't even looking at the pictures here."

"I know what I looked like."

"But this is when you won a scholarship to summer camp," she said. "You look—"

"Fuck," said Kev tonelessly. "Don't tell me. I looked all happy then, is that it? I was a dumb kid. I didn't know any better. You gonna keep showing me pictures all day?"

She closed the folder softly, like she had planned it, expected him to yell at her. "No," she said. "I'm not. I just thought we could talk about why you're here." Her eyes were green, and around the lower edges were black streaks, as if her mascara had run.

He looked away from her face. Each of the rivets on the door were scraped until they were bright against the metal, as if someone had rubbed them raw, tried to bite them.

"Why do you think you're here, Kev?"

Kev looked down from the top of the door to her face. Her eyes were wide as she waited. He opened his mouth and heard his own voice, unnaturally loud in the small room.

"You're gonna help me, that what you think? I'm prob'ly here because the ideas I got were bad shit! I tried to get rid of Hitler in my mind, Adolf Eichmann, flush that shit. But I guess it was too late, huh? It's a free country, man. But I'm not free."

Kev did not wait for the wide expression of her eyes to narrow, as he knew it would. Instead, he looked down at the floor. It was the color of a blackened fireplace pit, the paint wearing off. There was not a single crack in the floor wide enough for a knife.

Nancy Ferreday picked up an envelope and took out a stack of photographs. She glanced up at him, and the stack fell over, scattering across the table. Nervously, she plucked one off the top, put it down in front of him.

"No, that's not why you're here," said Nancy Ferreday. Her voice was harder now. "You're here because they think you killed this man."

"Killed him?" said Kev. He glanced down and was surprised by the face. The suit on the bus, the man with the cross. "I met this guy! Father Arlen, right? How did he die?"

"Well, I'm here to figure out whether or not you know you killed this man. There's a chance that you might be able to get psychological help. There's an insanity defense—"

"What—now I'm mental? What do you mean, I don't know what I did?"

But her reply was inaudible to him, her voice washed over, unheard. The spilled photographs were mesmerizing, the mysteries of bone and muscle revealed.

"That's what I did?" said Kev in a vacant voice. "You think I did this?"

"The prosecutor's office sure thinks you did it," said Nancy Ferreday. Her hands were splayed out over the photos, trying to put them back together.

As she moved them, he abruptly recognized a head that was not connected to anything else. A quavering sensation vibrated up through him. He turned his head and retched. A clear fluid came out of his mouth and splashed on the floor and the table.

He tried to wipe his chin, and found he could not. Nancy Ferreday reached over with a tissue and touched his mouth. "You think I did this?" he said again. His lips trembled against the tissue.

The kid didn't look at Matt. Instead, he stared directly at the wall of his cell. Concrete block construction, two layers of new green paint. The entire surface was covered with scrawls, absurd field notes scratched on the walls as inmates came down off of meth or speed, a frenetic spattering of words.

"I didn't do anything," Kev said tonelessly. He stared at the indecipherable wall, as if it held a message only he could understand.

"What didn't you do, Kev?" Matt was as close to the bars of the two-man cell as he was allowed to go, but he still had to speak loudly, if he wanted the kid to hear him.

Kev glanced at him dully. "You read those letters yet? Those ones I found?"

"No," said Matt shortly. "We aren't here to talk about me."

"Jesus, dude—that chick really liked you! You should read 'em, you should—"

"Yeah, that's the last thing I need. She liked me, I killed her anyway. Jesus, shut up, Kev. I'm not here about that. I'm here because you've been arrested."

"I didn't do anything," repeated the kid. "I didn't rip anything off, didn't kill—"

"Okay, but do you have a lawyer yet, Kev? Has one been provided for you? Can I call your mom for you? Or your stepdad?"

"Nah." Kev glanced up as the man in the upper bunk rolled over in his sleep. "Everyone is away for the winter. Or Majorca, somewhere like that. Won't do any good."

Matt wrote down a note. "Every little bit helps," he said. "Now I'm going to tell you about the case. I need to know how much is factual. If any of it can be challenged."

Kev stared at him. "How come we ain't in the gray room with me chained up?"

Matt glanced uncertainly down the hallway. "Because I'm not on the record here with you, Kev. The trustee owes me a favor—he got me in to talk to you without logging the visit, you got it? I wasn't here. Be nice to that trustee, okay? Don't give him shit."

Kev nodded, something dead in his look.

"So." Matt looked down at his notebook. "They say you were at the Greyhound station on August 27. They are going to claim that you were the last person he was seen with. It looks bad that you have that cross. So if anyone can provide you with an alibi at the time, I should talk to them. Do you understand?"

The man on the top bunk muttered. But the kid didn't pay attention to him, or to Matt. The words didn't seem to affect Kev, they were like a meaningless wash of sound.

"Fifth amendment, right? Don't say anything, they can't get you. That's what he says." Kev jerked his thumb toward the upper bunk. The man up there was awake now, leaning against the wall. Fresh bruises on his face. Probably caught in a barroom brawl. He was reading a magazine.

"Jailhouse lawyers aren't going to help." Matt lowered his voice even though the man had not seemed to notice Kev's comment. "In two weeks, they're transferring you to Boise. You've got to have a better story about what you did with Arlen by then. If you're going to convince them that you didn't kill him."

"I didn't kill anyone!" Kev's eyes were liquid with fear. "I just talked to him. I rode beside him the whole way, told him I'd do him a favor by giving his girl the cross—and now he ends up dead, and they're telling everyone I took him out?"

"So why didn't you pass on the cross to her? Why did you—"

"I didn't know where she was!" Kev's eyes were flowing freely, his cheeks covered in a wash of tears. "I meant to do the right thing, but I just—"

"So you didn't take the cross from him—he gave it to you, of his own free will?"

Kev nodded furiously and rubbed his face against his shoulder. When he looked up again, his eyes were red and raw. "Yeah, and all he talked about was some story some other guy had told him. Some guy who was in the hospital. Someone from a long time ago had come back, freaked this guy out so bad he had a heart attack, keeled over—and he decided to talk to Arlen, in the hospital afterward. Like, he confessed or something."

"So where was Arlen going? What was he doing with the story he heard?"

"Well, his little girl got taken away from him. Arlen was sure it was connected to this guy. He thought if he talked to him, explained it all, it would be all right." Then he added, as if to explain something to himself. "You know, Arlen was like, a minister?"

"So was Arlen going to talk to someone else? Was he going to the police with it?"

"Nah, he was just tryin' to get his little girl back." Kev rubbed a tearstain off the side of his face, the swastika moving up and down like a tiny spider against his skin.

"Arlen said he had a trump card—something he thought was important."

"What was that?"

Kev waved a hand and then slapped it down against the bars in frustration. "I dunno what it was. But Arlen told someone about it before he died."

"Who?"

"Some guy in Wallace." Kev rubbed a hand over his scalp. "The night before his little girl was taken. He kept going on about his friend Leo, or whatever his name was. I dunno, maybe his name was Leonard."

"In Wallace?" Matt mused aloud and made a note. "Was this someone he—"

"Dammit, I don't know anything else." Kev locked his arms on the bars. "I just—"

"Okay, one last thing," said Matt. "What did you do at the station when—"

"Jesus Christ, I didn't do anything!" Kev exploded, his fists pounding against the bars. "I don't know who that other guy in the station was—I don't know why he drove away with Arlen's little rugrat—hell, I don't know a damn thing!

"Jesus, Matt, I'm getting screwed here, and you're just helping them screw me! You don't want to know the truth about anything. Go to fuckin' hell!"

. . .

THE GIRL pushed her face against the glass, leaving wet spots where her hair and her mouth touched it. She had taken a bath, and her hair was still damp. She stood on the cushions in her good shoes and pressed her face to the big picture window behind the couch, watching the road. She could feel the glass against her teeth.

She stood on the couch only after her grandmother had driven away. Her grandmother had rules she carried around inside of her, she found one whenever she saw a situation that fit a rule. And the girl knew other people had rules inside of them too. Her mother did not. By this time, it seemed her mother only cared about one rule—no one was supposed to talk about the girl's daddy.

For the girl, rules had colors in her mind. There were red ones that people talked about a lot, and green-blue ones that permitted no talking, and every color in between. Once—the only time she could remember her mother talking about her daddy—the very air itself seemed to change, the room tinged with a sudden change in shade.

One of the rules was being clean. That was why she had a bath. Even though she had refused to wash her hair, the bath made her clean. One more rule was to dress for company. And another was not to stand on the couch.

But the woman who was going to talk to her was not here yet. The rules did not matter until she came to the door. After that, every rule mattered, even the ones that had not been told to her yet.

Secrets did not have colors, and for that reason they were more dangerous. No one could see them. The girl had secrets. He had laid a secret on her in the car, after he rescued her. So now she had to keep the secrets invisible, so no one would see them ever.

When she heard the car in the driveway, she sat and smoothed her dress with her hands, so that the wrinkles disappeared. All that was left was the image of her mouth on the glass. Anxiously, she watched the wet spot as the condensation faded away.

◇ ◇ ◇

The girl liked the woman's dress, and her name. It was an old-fashioned name, one from a book: Nancy. And on this visit, Nancy even brought her a Christmas present.

Yet every time Nancy came, she lied. She always said she was there to talk to her. But the girl knew different by now. Nancy was there because she wanted her to talk.

So there was no one she could trust, except her mother, who did not count.

It took most of the evening for Nancy to discover what the girl had known from the beginning of the visits: she could not tell Nancy anything.

Instead, the girl closed her eyes and remembered the sweet smoke drifting around the car, the way his lips moved around the hand-rolled cigarette, the quick glance he gave her as he opened her car door, held his finger up to his lips, smiling at her, keeping their secret.

She opened her eyes again, and everything she'd seen seemed as smoky as a dream. Maybe he didn't exist at all. Maybe it was just her own idea. Maybe she should never have smiled back at him. Maybe it was her fault.

The air in the room became charged with something chill and icy, an underwater blue. She breathed out as fast as she could, and then she kept her mouth tightly closed, not wanting that color inside of her.

Finally, her mother said that she could go to her room.

But the girl didn't. She pretended to go to her room, but she went behind the couch, where she could listen. This time, Nancy's tone did not change when she thought the girl was gone. That made the girl wonder if she'd been wrong not to trust her.

Then, when her mother asked about how daddy died, Nancy said she did not know anything, which seemed to the girl to be more honest than anything her grandmother said. She began to like Nancy for the first time. But by the time she felt she could trust Nancy, it was too late. Nancy was gone again.

Her mother seemed sad after Nancy left, but then that was not unusual. The rule about standing on the couch seemed to have left the house along with Nancy. After they had gone, the girl took the cushions from the couch and threw them on the floor. She took her shoes off so that she could jump on the couch.

She danced on the cushions until her grandmother arrived back at home.

In the thick of thickets, in a wood so dense and gnarled
The very thought of it renews my panic.
It is bitter almost as death itself is bitter.
  —Dante Alighieri, *The Inferno*

EARLY ON in the night, the sheets were twisted and damp with sweat, as if they'd been torn apart in some somnambulant battle. As sleep deepened, something seemed to coil tighter inside him. Later on, his hands clutched tight in imagined pain. He turned on his side, brow creased with distant agony, face flushed with the warm blood of sleep.

Matt Worthson was dreaming.

This time, he stood outside his parked truck, the snow falling in waves, letting him see in mere glimpses through the flickering headlights. There were body parts all over the road, a head staring back at him, blank eyes and a shattered throat, a question in the eyes, a question the dead head had just asked. And he didn't have an answer.

Someone was doing this—in fact, he was doing it, he could clearly see his own hands holding the axe. His arms were streaked with new blood. Bits and pieces of bone and fluid had spattered over his skin, tarring it with gore. All the broken and twisted remnants of a body lay here—chunks of ribs and curled intestines, sickly gray smudged with red. In this strange simulacrum, he grinned up at the camera, filthy with blood and drunk as a dog.

Oh Jesus, he said. *Not another one, not another one.* Through the whirling snow, he could hear a whining sound, something buzzing near to him. He felt himself beginning to cry. All the things inside a human being were out there on the road. *God's plenty*, he thought, *all of god's rich plenty*, and he tried to tear his eyes away from the ripe pieces of body on the pavement. The tears slicked his cheeks.

The curtain of falling flakes became so thick, so thick that the headlights melted into blurred pools. The buzzing noise came again, louder this time. A snow devil spun into him. It took his breath away and left him frosted with snow dust and frozen bits of blood.

He reached out and took hold of the buzzing thing, held it so tight, a solid thing in the uncertain darkness. The headlights flickered against the white, and he couldn't see the road anymore. Then the snow rose around him, over-whelming him. He woke, holding the phone in his hand.

"Hello?" he mumbled. "What is it?"

"Lieutenant Worthson?"

"Yeah. Who is this?"

"Listen, my name is Angie McConnell," she said. "I turn tricks over in Wallace?"

Matt didn't say anything. He blinked his eyes in the dark.

"Hey, are you there? I'm callin' you 'cause about a month ago, I was working in a massage parlor, and you bagged me—along with this old guy."

"What?" Matt opened his eyes, shifted his legs out of the bed. "I did what?"

"No, I mean, you didn't bag me—it's not like that. I mean, you had me in custody, but you didn't come on to me, and you let me go. Jesus, dude, it was six months ago, don't you remember? You were nice to me even though I was fuckin' for a living?"

He was beginning to remember. "I thought I told you to go back home to Montana. You need to quit before you die in a—"

"Fuck you. No, wait, I'm sorry I said that. Jesus, just listen to me, wouldja? Listen to me, dammit—I gotta talk to you about Russ White. He's a fuckin' piece of work."

"You can say that again." Matt stood up, swaying in the sudden rush.

"I'm worried about what he's gonna do," said Angie. "He's got something in for that little girl, he's going to—"

Matt interrupted. "I'll be right there. You want me to come to the Oasis Rooms?" He hung up the phone and pulled on his old windbreaker. It was three in the morning.

The door to the upstairs was closed and locked. The downstairs was empty too, although the door was unlocked and a light shone above the empty bar. This late at night, the chairs sat on the tables like beached skeletons, legs in the air.

On the desk on the landing was an open romance novel and a cigarette smoldering in an ashtray. He walked up the stairs and reached up to knock on the door, when it swung open under his hand.

A large woman stepped out from the doorway, pulling it shut behind her. "Sorry 'bout that. Nature calls," she said. "I'm Margot—you pay here. Got an appointment?"

"No, but I got a call from one of your girls. I need to see her in a private room."

She sat down heavily and flipped open a small book. "You got a name for me?"

"Angie."

"Huh," said Margot. "Take a number. She's had a lot of her old friends come by to visit. She already worked something like eight of 'em last night. She's off for a while after this one. I think he's still up there, but you could maybe work out a deal with her—"

"No, listen, I'm not a client. I just need to talk to her and—"

"You gotta pay regardless, you understand? You use a room with one of our girls, you have to pay. I don't care if you're talking up there or screwing her eyes out." She considered him briefly. "If you're really just gonna talk, you can wait in the room next door, if you don't mind hearing 'em. She times 'em pretty well—done in ten minutes."

Matt made as if to walk up the stairs, but she held her hand out. "Sorry. No cash, no room. You could be the pope in person, I still take my pound of flesh."

Matt scrounged in his wallet, and found three twenties. "It's fifty bucks, right?"

"Love," she said flatly, as she made change. "Exciting and new." She picked up her cigarette and book and waved him toward the door at the top of the stairs.

The bed in the room was broken, the sheets twisted in skeins of unkempt white. He closed the door and walked to the window. The neon sign for Albi's Bar and Grill glimmered across the street, its light flickering across the rumpled bed. The street was empty of people at three in the morning.

When he turned from the window, the room tasted suddenly sour. An odor of old bodies, the human stink. Matt leaned over and yanked the window up an inch. Then he smoothed out the bedclothes awkwardly. The Oasis wasn't what it used to be.

On the day the Oasis building opened in 1895, a brass band played and a large sign covered the front of the building: "Silver Valley Oasis: Wallace Winery and Women." The classic Oasis building even escaped the 1910 fire that turned most of downtown Wallace from wood to ash and then to brick. A century ago, they'd had maids, and a wet bar in every room, regardless of the hour. Yet by this time, all the Oasis had left was the reputation.

He sat down heavily on the dirty bed. Three in the morning and he was waiting in a worn out Wallace bordello.

The residue of dream had stayed on him, a hallucinatory narcotic that colored everything he saw or touched. If he could simply close his eyes for a moment, he might be able to answer her inarticulate question. He let his eyes drift closed, but all he saw was Arlen Bowman.

The chaplain's dead eyes moved, and he too asked the question the girl had been asking. But Matt had no answer for him. Matt trembled in the depths, shuddering awake.

Through the thin lathe and plaster wall came a cry of sorts. An artificial mewing. The woman sounded as if she had been practicing some instrument too long. By now she could only make the barest attempt at a proper tune. The sound grew louder. Matt checked his watch. According to Margot, the guy had three minutes left. It wasn't all bad that he could hear the girl next door, at least he'd know when she was free to talk.

He stood to keep his eyes open, and began to pace back and forth across the creaking wooden floor. Forcibly, he turned his thoughts from that to the vision of the dead.

When the door to the room opened, Matt saw that Angie was still little more than a teenager, wrapped in a pink corduroy bathrobe two times too big for her small frame. He sat down cautiously and showed her the badge.

"You look different," she said. "You're Matt?" The girl looked up at him, wide-eyed, her bruised mouth twitching nervously.

"It's been a while," said Matt. "You look different too—did your hair blond, got those track marks on your arm. You trying to hide from probation? Where've you been, Angie?"

She pushed the hair back out of her eyes again. "You're bugging me at three a.m. about not showing up for rehab or probation?" She flicked the hair back off her forehead and glared at him, a weary glaze over her eyes. "Why are you really here?"

"You called me." Matt stepped back, uncertain. "At least, I think you called me. About him. About Russell White."

At the name, she looked around nervously. "I called? About Russ? Isn't he running for office now? Is this about—"

"Yes, but I'm here because you said you owed me a favor, had something to tell me. Can you help me? I'm thinking he should pay for something in his life finally."

"That's what you think, huh?" she muttered. The girl looked away from him, searching through the pockets of the bathrobe. "You got any fuckin' cigarettes?"

Matt shook his head.

Angie sighed and yanked the bedclothes closer around her. "Yeah, okay, I remember calling you now. I musta done it when I first shot up. They got courage in a needle now, you know that shit? Jesus, I shouldn't have called you about Russ—"

"Look," said Matt, reaching out a large hand to touch her shoulder. "I can protect you if there's a crime involved. If you'll agree to police custody—"

"No!" She pulled back from him. "Shit, Russ told me all about the cops in this town. That's the last damn thing I need. He already told me what would happen if—"

"Okay, calm down," said Matt. "You don't have to go anywhere."

"All right, all right." She gulped air in, quieting herself. "You got me out of the shit the first time, so I guess I should take a fuckin' gamble on you, huh? He lied to me, he's probably lying to her too. I don't know why I care." She plucked at the sheet, pulling it into tight circles all around her legs.

"What did he lie about?"

Angrily, she flicked the hair back off her forehead. "You can see I'm still fucking like a bunny rabbit for money. I just, I guess I just . . . hell, the honest truth is he talked me into it. I thought he'd leave his wife and move in with me, but he just wanted me out of the way. Didn't want to lose his fuckin' marriage or his job for screwing someone underage. So here I am—and there he is, Mister Fuckin' Future Sheriff, huh?"

Matt shook his head. "So he told you he'd leave his wife for you?"

"Yeah, that same old story. Only thing is, I'm so young and stupid I bought it. And now he still comes to see me, and I can't tell him to get lost. Hell, he needs me."

"He needs you?"

She sighed. "I dunno. He says he does, but maybe he's just screwing with me. I don't give a fuckin' damn about me, you know. I just . . . I'm worried about that girl."

"About who?"

Anxiously, she pushed her lip in and out of her mouth. "Jesus Christ, I don't know. She's just a little girl. Russ said she knows something." She began to cry.

Matt waited until her cries grew softer. "Is this the little girl tied into the resort business? The one whose father . . ."

Angie glanced over at him, her eyes narrow, leaking tears. "Yeah, that's the one. Preacher guy got killed, she belonged to him. For some reason, she really gets Russ going. Every time he talks about her, I'm worried that he will . . . After all, Russ knows who her real father is—and what he knows fucks with his head. The preacher didn't—"

"Wait a minute—you mean Arlen Bowman's little girl wasn't really his?"

She squeezed her eyes shut and spoke all in a rush. "What keeps me up nights is that he could do it again, don't you see? Him or his fucked-up friend . . . All of Russ's shit freaks me out, I can't hardly sleep. He's always talking to me about his bad dreams, about this screwed-up job thing back in September, when he says his friend—I dunno, maybe it was him—he says they chopped up that preacher just because he knew . . ."

She shuddered. "Russ says he can't get that body, that blood, out of his mind. He keeps talking about it. I'm afraid he's going to do it again—maybe to her, maybe to her father this time, if he can find the guy. It's personal to Russ somehow, that girl. I'm telling you, he wants to take care of her." In a rush, she turned to him, leaned forward, her eyes wide now, the pupils tiny as pinpricks. "You think I'm making this all up, don't you? I'm telling you, it's the truth."

"I believe you." Matt sighed, the sound rushing out across the empty room. "I already know what Russ did to the priest. I know all about it."

"You already know what he did?" Angie picked up a glass of water off the table and took a drink. She quivered as the cold water went down her throat, nervously glancing at Matt, seeming to shrink back against the headboard.

She trembled on the bed, pulling the bedclothes tight around her. "Blood and fucking. Fuck me, fuck me to hell," she muttered. Then she pulled herself to her feet, lunged toward the side table. When she turned around, she was holding an oversized Buck knife. Warily, she held it in front of her chest, pointed at his heart. "You already knew, but you haven't arrested him? Christ, why am I talking to you about that little girl, she's gonna be next! You're just gonna kill her—hell, why did I trust you?"

"No, wait. He lied to me too." Matt moved slowly away from her, feeling the doorframe behind him, under his feet. "Look, you don't understand. It's not like that."

Angie staggered to the door and yanked it open, pushing him backward by the point of the knife. "Jesus—you need to get the hell out . . . Russ said he knows the guy did it to Arlen, maybe you're him! You're in the shit with him! Christ, what have I done?"

She held up the knife, the tip trembling. "You gotta leave, please, you need to leave. Right now."

> How could I trust my father less than you
> Believe yours? Or conversely, how could I
> Demand that you should charge your ancestors
> With lies to avoid contradicting mine?
> —G. E. Lessing, *Nathan der Weise*

STAN WORTHSON was thinking of his wife again. She'd been dead for ten years, but Martha's face was always there. It was her scent that was with him. A warmth in the air.

He opened his eyes slowly, and was not surprised when he saw that slow grin of hers. He wondered what she made of him now. He'd never been much to look at, but now his hair was mostly gone, his skin blotchy and wrinkled. She understood. She'd gone on ahead. She'd gone when her hair was still there, when her color was still good.

It came to him that if someone talked to her, God would keep her here. So he opened his mouth, to ask Martha to stay. But the words slurred, and she disappeared. The hot tears sprang to his eyes. God was too tricky for him, he didn't let people tell his secrets.

"Pop, I'm here. Is everything all right?"

Stan looked to his right and was surprised to see his son sitting in the place that Martha had been, moments before. It was as if she'd brought him there, just then, to hear him say what he had to say. As if she knew she had to get his attention first.

"Matty," he gasped. "I gotta talk to you."

"Sure, Pop, just take it easy. Do you want a glass of water? Something to help you calm down—I can get the nurse in here for you. Is everything all right?"

Stan nodded wordlessly. Matt settled into his chair again, watching his face anxiously. Stan thought of words he should say. It was hard, after so many years.

"I have something to tell you too," said his son. "Something important. That miner you recognized on that poster—the man named Curtis Siwood—we found him dead in the lake. We positively identified his body. So I thought I'd let you know. God rest his soul."

So this is where Martha wanted him to start the story. With Curtis. He would have started elsewhere, but when you're telling the truth, it all runs together. You can't pick and choose, separating the bits you don't like from the bits you do, the silver from the dross.

"Christ be with him." Stan raised his fingers, making an awkward sign of the cross in the air. It was hard to talk, but not as hard as he'd expected. "Curtis was a good man."

"You really know everyone around the Valley, Pop. So I got a question for you. You know anyone in Wallace named Leonard—or Leo? You know anyone by that name?"

Stan squeezed his eyes shut again. He remembered the blur of a face handing him a drink, the blue fug of cigarette smoke, the click of pool balls, the neon-lit glow of a bar. "Bar," he finally said. "Albi's Bar and Grill. That's him."

Comprehension dawned across his son's face. "Oh, I'd forgotten that. Albi's real name is Leonard, isn't it? Bartender at Albi's—Jesus Christ, I've known him for years."

"Yup," said Stan. "So have I." Again, he saw the hardened face that had seen everything, and the solicitous tenderness in the expression every night as Leonard handed another one over the bar to his regular drunks. For a long, long time that was his son.

But Matty was talking more. He'd missed half of it. "So this guy, Curtis, you worked with him at the Sunshine, right? What was he like?"

There was a twinge in Stan's chest at that old name. Sunshine. But he could answer this one too. "Sure, sure," he said evenly. "Young guy, sharp little Herrick brownnoser, that was Curtis in the mines. Always suckin' up to the big boss." It was an old habit, avoiding his own part in it. And if Curtis had lived, he would have told this story himself, and he would have told it different.

But Curtis wasn't around now. No one knew how it had been. No one except him.

His son spoke confidently, as if he had any idea. "I know how it worked back then. The bosses—Old Man Herrick and his friends—they owned the Sunshine, the Bunker Hill, the rest of them. And they hated each other—constant competition."

Stan gave a brief little nod. So far, so good. His son continued. "I've read that it was vicious—the competition, trying to outdo one another, recruit the best guys. Undermine the union. A whole lot of infighting, betrayals, backstabbings. What did you do?"

Stan hesitated, and then he avoided the whole question. "Well, Curtis . . . and his friend . . . got paid under the table by the Bunker Hill. Even while he was supposed to be working a regular mine shift at the Sunshine. Of course, often enough Herrick was doing things I didn't approve of—but I couldn't open up Curtis's business without letting people know about the sabotage he did at the Sunshine, which actually helped the union."

"And you cared about the union?"

Stan nodded slowly. How much could he keep back? "Curtis was real up-and-comer for the big boss—made things happen. Usually bad things." Stan shook his head from side to side. "I hated that bastard. Still do, I guess. He caused no end of grief to us, day after day, week after week, and I guess he's still taking the piss out of us today, huh?"

"Well, he's caused no end of problems in the Silver Valley recently." Matt sighed, his face seemed drawn and pained. Something had happened to him. But what?

Stan knew now how he could make Curtis pay for this, after all the years. He could make him pay for all of it. Just change the story around. "So, one afternoon, Curtis tells me that we're supposed to take a bunch of files deep into the Sunshine. It's another of his little shady jobs from Old Man Herrick, he tells me, but of course I never am supposed to know about these jobs. Since I'm his partner on shift though, I get roped into helping him out from time to time—whenever he thinks it's something I'll stoop to, something that I won't consider reprehensible. You know how I feel . . ."

"Right." His son nodded. No question about it, for him. "You wouldn't do anything wrong."

Stan nodded his head solemnly too. If only he knew. "Right," he repeats. "So Curtis tells me that they're just papers. So I give him a hand. Carrying papers can't be too bad, and we get to carry them in a mine train. Turns out we're supposed to put all these boxes of files in a mined-out stope. They're gonna get covered by two hundred feet of sand."

"What kind of papers were these? What was in them?"

Stan shook his head slowly. Could he play dumb convincingly any more? He'd bought a moment of silence, and then he tried, "Well, I snuck a look while Curtis was taking a leak. I couldn't make heads or tails of it. Lists of numbers and chemical readings—you know, typical crap from mine engineers, all gobbledy-gook to a guy like me."

Then he moved forward quickly, before more questions could arise. "The only problem was that we screwed up. I don't know who actually picked the stope that we were putting them in—it was near the old Number Five main-shaft, which was hardly touched any more. Heck, the air was turning bad in there, you could taste it. So we figured we were in the right stope, and we dumped all the papers down, and then we filled it all with sand, and into the tunnel too. We were done, the papers were gone."

"So what was the problem? I've been near some of those old shafts—they haven't been touched in decades. I think they're filling with water now."

"Right, it would have been fine—only I helped him put 'em in the wrong shaft. Turned out that particular shaft had a bunch more high-grade ore in it. The ventilation hole had been closed that week, that's why it smelled stale, but it was the next tunnel over that was due to be plugged up with sand. Anyway, Curtis was there with . . . . with some other guy he uses for dirty work. Not me. Anyway, it's a few days later, I guess Curtis is walking by the Number Five shaft, and he and his friend sees that there's hoses going down the hall to that stope, there's equipment and lights in there.

"And down there, at the stope we thought was safe to fill up, is a guy named Larry Clark. Good hoistman, from time to time. It's a lunch break, and all the guys are out of the tunnel, except for Larry and another guy. These guys are sitting down there alone with their muck slusher, working like eager beavers, digging out all the stuff we'd put in there.

"I got upset—then Curtis, I mean, he got upset—and shit, what happened then, I just . . ." Stan blinked his eyes, they were full of water.

"What?" said his son. Stan shifted gears. Pull it together. Back to something safe.

"See, turns out the reason those papers are deep in the Sunshine Mine is that Herrick needs to get them off-site. There's a group of federal inspectors coming through—and Herrick must have thought these documents were too hot to remain over at the Bunker Hill."

"Pretty damn sensitive documents. So why didn't he just destroy them outright?"

"I dunno—this was before those newfangled paper shredders, of course, so maybe it's just that it would have been too obvious that he was destroying documents before the inspectors arrived. There was file box after file box—a whole man-train full of them, I swear."

"We checked in on the stope later in the day, to make sure they hadn't been found—but of course they had been. I mean there were reams of files, boxes and boxes of documents." Stan lifted his arm—but there was a needle tying it down, so he used the other arm, wiped it across his sweating face. "What happened next, I wish I didn't even know . . ."

But he kept talking, the memories flooding out of him. Stan had made his choice. He would follow the vein of ore wherever it led, as close to the truth as he dared go.

◊ ◊ ◊

Stan's headlamp spotlighted Larry Clark and Karl Avery in their dust-covered clothes, stacks of white office paper clutched in their grubby hands. Larry looked up at them as they came around the corner: "I got all the high-grade stuff out of that stope—don't know who filled it with sand. Look what I found too—some technical stuff ..."

"Shit," snapped Stan, pushing past Curtis. "What are those lousy guys doing?"

"What?" said Curtis. "What's the big deal?"

Stan whirled around in the mineway, to face that dumb-ass Curtis, his face shadowed in the weird gleam of the worklights, the flash of the headlamp sliding over the dark stone. "Jesus, Curtis, you just don't get it. What the devil do you think Herrick is going to say when our friends Karl and Larry here start wagging their tongues all over town? Larry might not understand 'em, but he knows someone hid a shitload of papers."

At that moment, both of them shuffled forward in the darkness. "What's this stuff, guys?" said Karl. "I can't read, I can't read at all, but Larry here said it looks like something from the Bunker Hill. Right, Larr? You know anything about this here stuff?"

"Yeah, I know that," muttered Stan. "I put 'em in there."

Larry looked back and forth between them, holding the pages in his fists. "Well, hell, then you know there's stuff in here about the Bunker Hill that they wouldn't want to get out. So it looks like someone finally got proof of your dirty work for Herrick, Stan."

Larry grinned, a gap-toothed smile. "This proves you work for Herrick don't it? I got you dead to rights. C'mon, Curtis, Karl, you gotta back me up on this one—he's worked against the union for Herrick for years, I know it. Finally, we got the proof."

Karl looked at them both, uncertain as to what was going to happen next.

"C'mon, are you with us, or with Stan?" said Larry. "If you don't help me out, who cares how many years seniority you got, Curtis? Your hide will go up on the wall!"

Then Stan pulled back his arm, made a fist and hit him. He didn't go down at first.

"What the hell are you doing?" Larry reached up, and felt where the blood was trickling off of his ear. "What—"

Instinctively, Larry swung back at Stan. It was too late for him though.

"Wait a minute, guys," said Karl nervously. "Wait a minute—what are you—"

Stan lifted the heavy power drill off the floor, swinging the buzzy into both of the men. Karl collapsed backward against the wall. Larry's helmet popped off his forehead on impact. Stan would always remember the ringing sound of it hitting the floor, something final in it, the lid being pulled off of a man.

Stan sighed, his voice breaking. He looked around at the white walls of the hospital room. Behind him, there was a soft beeping, like a mine train running underground, the constant blinking light. It was faster now though, as if it accelerated along with his heart. He looked at the concerned look on his son's face, and he realized he couldn't tell the rest. It would hurt him too much—it would wipe all the rest of the innocence out of him. And dammit, his son had already been through too much in life. Matt didn't need this burden.

But he kept talking. "Only one man was injured, of course. No one else was there."

"Right," said his son. "So this guy Larry was the only witness to Curtis . . ."

Stan sighed again, his voice breaking. "Yeah, and Larry paid for it. I don't know what the big deal was—it was all scientific stuff, so why did it matter to anyone? But like I was saying, he just blew a gasket. It was Curtis. He did it. He hits Larry, hits him with a buzzy, with one of them heavy drills, knocks him right back down the stope. It was all Curtis's fault. And I feel guilty still about it because—"

"But you didn't do this thing, Pop, you didn't—"

"No, you're right, I had nothing to do with hurting him. But I've felt responsible."

Stan hadn't said anything about the other man. Karl's eyes were closed. He was down for the count. But the agonized look that Karl gave him as he fell had burned into Stan's memory, something he could never forget. A questioning look, like he didn't understand what was happening to him, he could never understand again. And Larry beside him, he staggered and fell as his neck shattered, broken by the weight of the buzzy.

"Jesus," Curtis whispered in the darkness of the mineshaft. "Look at 'im lying there. I think Larry's dead, Stan—what'd you do to him?"

Stan reached down, feeling at Karl's throat. The man's eyes were fluttering, a weak rasping breath still in his chest. "Karl here ain't dead though. He's banged up, but he's still breathing. Get him back around the corner. Make sure he's far enough away he won't come back here, if and when he wakes up. I'll take care of Larry."

Curtis stood up to him then. "What the hell are you doing? I won't stand for this." That's what he said. Stan didn't even pay him a moment's notice though. He took the unconscious Karl down the mineway himself. Then he came back and began to riffle through Larry's pockets. The body was already losing heat, getting cold in his hands.

Finally, he found it. "Here's Larry's damn mine ID. We'll need that."

Then Stan took the body by the belt and pulled it back along the mineway. He could see the wet streak of blackness on the dusty rock, the leak coming out of Larry's head.

Curtis said it again, yelling the words, as if he were trying to wake up from the nightmare: "What the hell are you doing?"

"Hand me the acetylene torch, wouldja?" said Stan calmly.

Mechanically, Curtis handed him the torch he was holding. Then, Stan lifted Larry's limp body and shoved him forcefully into the open stope. They could both hear the man falling down the thirty-foot shaft, his body striking the sides of the crib as he fell.

Stan stood up and wiped his hands off, as if he'd just finished a job. "Okay," he said. "Give me your wallet."

Numbly, Curtis reached in his pocket, handed over a dirty canvas wallet.

Stan put it in his own pocket. "Listen to me now. You don't exist anymore. You look enough like him, no one will ever know. And you never saw me here—after all, I'm not clocked in on any shift. See this ID?"

Curtis glanced over at the stope where Larry had fallen. It had all happened so quickly.

"Pay attention, Curtis!" Stan shouted. "See this ID, this one here in my hand? You're gonna become Larry now. I'm gonna clock out as you today, and then I'll throw your ID away—that way there's no connecting us on the shift or this level to these two. Hell, no one can tell who we miners are anyway, underneath all the damn dirt an' our rotten clothes. When we're dirty from working, we look enough alike, both brown hair, lil' bit of a beard. You understand? After we get outa here, you're gonna disappear forever, and anyone asks you, I'll say I never met you. We'll go our separate ways."

Curtis shook his head numbly, he didn't understand, and now he seemed afraid.

"Dammit, pay attention, Curtis. Here's the deal. Now you're Larry. You came into the mine with me, you came out of the mine with me."

Curtis gasped, as if he had just begun to grasp what had taken place. "What about—what about Karl?"

"I don't know if he'll ever come back and bug us. After all, his head is pretty banged up, especially after those rocks I piled on top of him fell down so naturally."

"You piled what?"

"Now shut the hell up and listen!" said Stan. "You can't ever forget this part of the story. Throw your ID down here, right above where he went down the shaft, and they'll be sure to think you're the dead guy. The guy who's down there, he's nobody now. He's down a mineshaft now, and no one's gonna ask about him, right?"

Curtis gasped, and stuttered. "What—what if someone finds Larry? What if Karl turns out all right, and he can tell them who did this? He knows who you are. Who we are."

Stan grimaced, something between a grin and a frown. "Karl is not gonna be all right. I hit him already with the buzzy, you saw his damn head. And Larry here is never gonna be recognizable again. See?" Then Stan tossed the acetylene torch into the hole. There was a wet sick sound as it struck the body far below. He gathered the rest of the files off the floor of the manway and threw them into the depths of the stope. Stan could still see them, papers drifting down, white and gray in the headlamp's glare.

Stan flipped a switch then, and the gas hissed suddenly in the line. "Got a light?"

Curtis shook his head. "What the hell!"

"Never mind," said Stan. "You're a pansy." He ripped a blasting cap open and shook the contents into the stope. He held up the empty red cap in the light. How close they'd come to being caught. After all the jobs he'd pulled, this one was too damn close. Worth remembering. Fuckin' nosy guy. He threw half of the cap to Curtis. A souvenir.

Then he tossed in a pack of wrapped dynamite, hooking it to a fuse line. "Might want to back up a little," he said. "Fire in the fuckin' hole."

Then Curtis ran back up the mineway like the coward he was. Stan bent down and lit the end of the fuse. He stood there, watching the fuse sparking, popping, hissing and burning, all the way down into the stope where Larry was. Stood there like an idiot for a moment too long. There was a sick feeling in his gut. Something in him wanted to get blown to kingdom come.

His feet moved on their own then. Without thinking about it, he had dashed around the corner, back where Karl was lying half covered by rock. Just in time.

A rushing sound like an air blast filled the tunnel as the gas went up, but the explosion wasn't immediate. He thought it was a dud. They both looked around the corner. So when the place blasted apart, it sent Curtis flying against the wall. Broke his nose, it turned out later. Stan waited, thinking. They were filling the stope next week, and no one would ever find it again, the stope filled with two tons of sand.

When he looked at Curtis again, he was holding his dripping nose. Stan could hear a continuing crackle as the papers went up in flames. The smell came to him a minute later. Something roasting. Larry. Or the man who would be known as Curtis Siwood on the brass monument of the Sunshine Mine Memorial.

Stan coughed at the memory, the smell still sticking in his throat. He choked in his hospital bed, and his son was beside him in an instant, handing him a glass of water. "Goddamn," muttered Stan. "Goddamn, I thought I'd gotten over it. I thought . . ."

After Stan had caught his breath, he found his son was talking. "So what happened then? Was Larry Clark ever found? Were murder charges ever filed against Curtis?"

He looked up at his son, his eyes empty and dark. "What do you think?" he said.

Unexpectedly, Matty stood up. He reached slowly into his pocket and lifted out a blackened silver chain. On the end swung a familiar thing, the twisted red plastic end off a four-second blasting cap. Stan felt surprise sweep across him, his head was suddenly light.

Matt spoke as he held it up. "So I wonder why Curtis left this behind—left it with the body, for Valerie Herrick to find? What was in those damn papers that was so bad about Old Man Herrick?"

"I don't know," Stan muttered. "I just don't know."

"Hell, and you said you weren't even down there when this happened! Who told you about all this?"

"I don't know." Had he really said he wasn't even there? Fear shuddered over him. The web of lies tightened. Then a sudden flash of possibility came to Stan. "Karl. He was the one who told me. Ol' Karl was down in that shaft with Curtis."

"Jesus Christ," said his son. "Karl Avery?"

Stan nodded sorrowfully. "Poor guy's never been the same since . . . I guess Curtis took revenge on him later. Hit him with a mine drill, that's what I think happened to Karl."

Frantically, his son scribbled notes. "So Curtis did all of this. Where did the other half of the blasting cap go—what did Curtis do with it?"

Again, that fear nearly overwhelmed Stan's thoughts, freezing him tight in his bed. He breathed deeply, and finally he could speak again. "I think it was split between the two guys who murdered Larry. I think Curtis gave it to the other guy who killed Larry too . . ."

Stan could not say anything else, there was a pain coming into his temples, draining his thoughts away. He turned and closed his eyes, the pain worse inside than it was outside. He didn't know how much longer he could keep going. He sighed, trying to get it out.

"Then we went on a mine strike." He held up two fingers, to keep going. "Two weeks we were out of the mine, before we got a chance to fill the stope back up with sand. After those weeks of the strike, we all came back, just in time for the Sunshine fire."

The next part would be the hardest thing he'd ever done. He could already see in his son's eyes that the fortress that had been his life was breaking apart. His heart was pounding, he could feel the pulse throb in his head. The rock that had been Stan was turning into sand. Goddamn, how could he wash the rest of it away? What would his son have left to stand on? His whole history was a lie, and they hadn't even got to the worst yet.

How could he tell Matt about what they knew had happened when they checked on the Number Five shaft after those two weeks were over? The seeping smell, the smoldering miasma, something more profoundly wrong in the mineway than the sharp stink of the rotting, burned body that had come up from the abandoned stope when they got too close. They covered their faces, and filled the stope up with sand. But that smoky smell stayed in the shaft, regardless of the fresh sand tamped down into the hole, sand that eventually filled the entire mineway. He couldn't say anything about that.

Stan shook his head, an inarticulate moan coming out.

"Don't worry about it," said his son. "I know what happened next—you helped a lot of men get out of the Sunshine Mine fire. You must have felt tremendous guilt over Larry's death—but I think you made up for it, Pop. You saved a lot of lives that day, a lot of 'em."

Matt gripped his shoulder with a strong hand, and Stan knew tears were falling down his cheeks. He could almost feel them carving furrows across him, cutting through the mine dust on his cheeks, he could see eyes gleaming at him under the headlamp's glare. They were all around him now, every miner he'd known. Stan knew it was true—he got them all out. He saved them. Yet now it was too late to save himself.

"It's all right, Pop," said his son. He bowed his head, pulling Stan toward him. "It's all right. I forgive you—and it wasn't your fault, really. And you saved a lot of folks."

Stan tried to pull away, his face streaming like a little kid's. "I gotta tell you . . . ," he stuttered. "I . . . I . . . gotta tell you . . ." He sighed. He'd let it wait a bit, settle in. The next day he'd have more strength. Maybe the overpowering need to tell the truth would go away, maybe he'd never have to talk about it. He sighed again, a sound from the depths of his being. That was unlikely. He wiped his face with the back of his trembling hand. "I'll tell you the rest of it tomorrow, Matty, all right? I want someone to know. I'll be stronger tomorrow."

He could feel his son's grip loosen, letting go of him, allowing him to take his time. But Stan didn't know if he'd ever have the strength to take away his son's faith in him. He could hope. He'd come to the brink of it. Tomorrow was another day.

"All right," said Matt. "All right. Now you rest, okay? We'll get the nurse in here, check you out. Sall and I will check in on you first thing in the morning. You rest now."

When he opened his eyes, things were somehow askew. Martha's sheets at home were always patterned faintly with small flowers, and the sheets in his room were a gentle cream color. But these sheets—they were bright white. There was a strong scent of antiseptic, something urgent in the scent. Faintly, on the edge of his hearing, there were beeping and humming machines. Hoses running into him, needles in his arms.

"Do you know what happened?" they asked him.

He turned his head, as if he could not hear them. But their words came through the fog anyway.

"It was another stroke," they said. "A week ago. A larger one. Doctors don't know for sure, but it might have hit your brain harder than your body."

Finally, he tried to say something. He thought he asked for Martha.

They looked at each other, like frightened children keeping a secret. Stan twisted his mouth in frustration. Half of it worked. The other half didn't seem to belong to him anymore.

His son, Matt, continued. "They think it could happen again, at any time. The next one could be fatal. So they're going to keep you in the ICU here. Under observation."

Stan tried to move his mouth another direction, but his throat didn't move right either anymore, and he began to choke. People in white and blue rushed into the room. And by the time the nurse got his airway straightened out, he'd forgotten the question.

He was getting shot full of holes, each stroke a bullet. Incoming fire, just like when he fought the Japanese—but this time, he had no idea who was shooting at him. It sure as hell wasn't a little Jap sniper in the trees. Maybe it was God, shooting little rips of heat and pain and death into him? Every time a stroke hit him, it took him longer to recover. Maybe God wanted to kill him slowly, for what he'd done.

Now that his son was here again, Stan knew what he had to say. The difficulty was in getting the words together. He had thought of how he would admit what he'd done for a long time. Decades. But now that he had the courage, the language wouldn't form in his mouth. He began to cry from frustration and motioned for a pen. His arm didn't move right either, the scribbles illegible.

Yet there was still strength in his arms. It occurred to him that he might be able to reach the side table. He wished he hadn't given up the notebook—that would have told the story for him with no effort at all. But that was gone, he'd given it away.

There was something else in the side table though. He'd put it in there, smashed flat at the bottom of his wallet, hidden for all these years. He could show Matty. Then his son would know. Beyond a doubt, he'd know.

Stan moved his arm again. An inch. He could get there. He would, even it if took him all night. Sall reached out and took his hand from off the cover. "Stan, are you worried about us? I want you to be at peace." She looked at Matt, who just nodded.

Stan shook her hand off. He would get closer to the truth before the end, if he could just figure out how.

There are many things from which I might have
derived good by which I have not profited, dare I say.
—Charles Dickens, *A Christmas Carol*

THE BITTER air went through Matt's clothes and cut into his skin. Quickly, he pulled a greatcoat close around his neck. He reached under the hood and unplugged the extension cord for the engine heater that kept Sall's Jeep from freezing. Then he scraped the frost off the windows of the Jeep. In a few hours it would be colder still.

Clouds covered half the mountains. As they came into the foothills, the moon rose, illuminating the bulk of the range. They ascended into the fog, and Sall spoke again.

"Okay," she said. "Tell me about it. So, we're going to see this thing with Sherrill and Patricia—their play. But what happens afterward? Is this like that time when we had to spend all evening with your informer? Remember? That bum threw up all over me."

"No, no, nothing like that," Matt said. He reached in the pocket of his greatcoat and pulled out a folded copy of the composite poster. "A man I know in Wallace—Old Albi—knows something about the case. He said I could come tonight."

"But why are we going to Sixth Street Melodrama?"

"Albi is in the play. He was surprised to get my call—outside of work, he doesn't like attention. So he suggested we see the play. Then we have a drink with him, afterward, and it's not like we planned anything. He's a pretty secretive guy."

Her voice was soft now. "I wonder—Oh, wait, slow down! I love the view here."

Matt carefully slowed the Jeep. From the top of Fourth of July Pass, they looked for a moment over a land of racing clouds torn apart by towers of ice projecting from the mountains. The Jeep pushed through the cloudbank toward the Valley. Then the wind kicked up a screen of blown snow, and the mountains were gone.

◇   ◇   ◇

"Of all good days in the year, on Christmas Eve, Scrooge sat busy in his count-ing house." One spotlight came up slowly on an old man sitting center stage, a bank register before him. "Scrooge was hard and sharp as flint. The cold within him froze . . ."

Sall leaned close to Matt and whispered. "That's Patricia Grounds."

"Are you sure?" said Matt. He looked closer, and recognized Doug's old public speaking teacher, a longtime actress in the Valley. "She's playing a male role?"

"She's the star," whispered Sall. "Her husband, Sherrill, is playing all the spirits."

"The clocks intoned the hour. Fog came pouring in at every chink and keyhole."

Matt had last seen Doug's speech and drama teacher ten years ago. He'd gone to see Doug in a play—and although he thought Doug was an atrocious actor, he'd loved seeing the joy on his son's face after the performance. Al-though Doug's teacher had always used a wheelchair, Matt remembered her as a cheerful, youthful presence. But he could see that this evening, the lines drawn to make her into Scrooge were sketched on top of existing wrinkles.

Seeing her brought Doug back into his mind. Back before the accident, be-fore he lost the election, he'd used Doug as an excuse, a cover. He made him lie. Almost every day, he made him lie for his father. Whenever the election tension or some sheriff's case got under his skin, he'd buy a bottle of Jack Dan-iel's or good Scotch and disappear for a while. He always told Pop and Sall he was working on some car with Doug.

But he never was. Yet Doug, like a good son, always backed him up. And he must have gotten damn tired of dishonesty. It sickened Matt now, to think of the endless rounds of subterfuge he'd created to conceal his not-so-secret drinking sessions. He quit, finally, but it was too late for Doug. Of course he had to leave. He wanted a life that wasn't a lie.

A wind machine filled the room with a white wash of sound. Matt looked at the stage again. The actors all approached a frozen center, a man who could not move. The wheelchair-bound Pat was an inspired choice to play Scrooge.

Albi's face floated in the frame of a door. It was lit from below, a frozen leer. Matt nudged Sall. "That's him. I guess he's playing Marley."

"Humbug!" said Scrooge.

But Marley shouted, "I am pursued by a legion of goblins, all my own making."

"Humbug!" said Scrooge again. He sounded less convinced.

The audience jumped as Marley bellowed, "I wear the chain I forged in life. I made it, every link . . . Of my own free will, I wore it."

"I don't know about meeting him, Matt," Sall whispered. "He's pretty convincing."

"Look to see me no more before the changing of the hours," bellowed Marley. "And look that you remember what I have told you, this night!"

After Marley was gone, they turned off the wind machine, and the fatigue of the last week finally caught up to Matt, he found himself falling asleep. When he woke up to random lines, all of it seemed part of one continuous dream, where Matt himself, wearing the bloated body of the drowned, held Arlen's severed head aloft at center stage. Someone screamed in the background as the theater flamed. Matt shuddered awake.

Outside the theater it was cold enough for their breaths to steam in the night air. Underfoot, tiny granules of hardened snow crunched and shifted like sand. From the front door of the theater, they could see the cars moving endlessly on I-90. The red taillights seemed festive as the cars stopped and started at the stoplight. From the intersection came a faint, tinny clanging, a bell and a charity kiosk on the highway corner.

"Hey!" called a booming voice from across the street. "Got time for a drink?" It was Old Albi, faint streaks of macabre makeup still on his cheeks and collar. Carefully, he unlocked the Bar and Grill next door to the Melodrama.

"Albi's is closed," he said. "But I've got a key." Albi flipped the lights on over the bar and gave a mocking laugh. "Matt would know—you used to practically live in here."

"Yeah, well," said Matt. "I've been dry a few months now. Look—"

"You'll never really go dry, Matty." Albi expertly made a drink for Sall and poured another shot glass, pushing it to Matt. "You can have one for the holidays, can't you?"

Matt pushed the glass away and looked at his watch. "Let's cut to the chase. We still need to drive back over the pass, and I'd prefer to get going before it freezes up."

Albi pulled the shot glass back and took a sip himself. "No need to get high and mighty, Matt. Better folks than you been here. Just last week, Jerry Dolph was in here—"

"The governor?" said Sall.

Albi nodded. "Yup—he came through on that special Centennial train, and then he stopped and spent two hours back there with the slots. C'mon, Matt, what'll you have?"

"Got any coffee?"

Albi shook his head. "Damn, Matt, now you're a fuckin' Boy Scout." He flipped on the coffee percolator.

Sall glanced between them, as if she sensed the edge of frost in the air. "May I?" said Sall, gesturing at the dimly lit back room where the slots waited.

"Sure," said Albi sullenly. "But we don't rig 'em for you, and there ain't no refunds. Even for cops."

Albi lifted his shot glass from the counter and held it in front of his mouth for a minute. He glanced toward the back room. Sall was out of sight. The faint rolling sound of the slots could be heard. Albi took a tiny sip before he put the glass down on the counter and leaned forward over the bar.

"What the fuck are you doing here, Matty? Highway over the pass is frozen harder than a wedding dick, snow's pissing down. No one comes over here from Coeur d'Alene in the fuckin' winter. What the hell do you need so bad that you couldn't ask for it over the phone?"

Matt stepped back, as if struck by the blow. "Someone who talked to the chaplain, the night he died, said he was talking about you. Called you Leonard."

"Jesus, this is about Arlen Bowman." Albi breathed deeply, and seemed to brace himself on the bar. "So what—Arlen called me by my given name: Leonard. So what?"

Matt leaned forward. "I want to know what happened to Arlen. Why was he being followed? Who was after him? We found a guy dead in the lake—mining tattoos all over him, fingerprints matched for a Curtis Siwood. Yet his name is on the memorial for the dead from the Sunshine Mine. And I don't know why this guy with Siwood's name was after Arlen."

He waited as Albi swabbed out a pair of empty glasses that sat on the bar.

"At least, I think he was a miner," said Matt. "That's all I know."

Albi stared at him. "I can't figure out what game you're playing, Matty."

"I'm still trying to figure it out—about why Arlen died. Who could have—"

"Well, hell, are you here because someone told you I catalogue my tapes?"

"Tapes?"

Albi cocked an eyebrow at Matt. "Videotapes. I got a security camera, got everything on tape—everyone who comes by here, every day. So when your poster came out, I found a segment that looked interesting. I showed that piece to a couple of my barflies. That must be why you're here. You want to see that same segment?"

Matt shrugged. "Sure."

At first, the images were ethereal, a mesh of lines and magnetic static from a tape that had been used too many times to count. The lines overlaid each person who walked along the street. Then Matt saw two small white boxes that moved up and down, coming into resolution as they approached closer to the camera. Small white food boxes.

"See?" said Albi. "Here he is—your guy comes out of Wah Hing Restaurant, carrying take-out Chinese. Then he walks up the freeway off-ramp with his little boxes, like there's someone waiting in his car."

Matt took the remote. As the man approached, Matt slowed the tape. There was a wariness in the man's eyes, as if he were afraid of being watched. And now Matt could recognize the face. In the blotchy version on the videotape, the eyes tracked nervously.

"This is him. But there aren't any answers coming from that quarter anymore."

"Dead?"

Matt nodded. "Found in the lake. We're going to bury him in a pauper's grave, no family we can locate. We think his real name was Curtis Siwood. By all accounts, he was a bastard and a half." In blurred slow motion, the man on the video screen turned his head, showing a profile. Around his neck hung something, a red blotch.

Matt looked sharply at Albi. "You talked to Arlen the same week you recorded this video, didn't you?"

Albi crinkled his brow and touched the video remote. "Who said that?"

Matt shook his head. "I can't tell you."

The coffee bubbled and hissed behind him, and Albi reached for two mugs, poured black coffee, put one of them in front of Matt. "There are more angles in this town than a damn pool table. What's yours?"

Matt ground his teeth together in frustration. "I don't know if it's safe to tell you, Albi. Dammit, you've known me for years, can't you give me some help here?"

Albi put a set of clean glasses on the shelf behind him and pulled down an unopened bottle of whiskey. "You said you stopped drinking."

Matt sighed and looked away, toward the wall. This again. "Yeah." he said.

"How long you been dry?"

"Four months. But this time, it's for real."

Matt felt a sense of connection, some hope that he could be trusted again. Then Albi sighed too, and the moment went away as suddenly as it had come. "Dammit, Matty, I've heard that line before, from every drunk in the world."

"Look, what do I have to do to prove to you—"

Albi held up a hand. Flat, like a stop sign. "You don't have to prove anything to me, Matt. I'm in it for me. You watch your own ass—I sure as hell ain't doing it for you." He looked over the rim of his coffee cup. "But you know, I am curious about one thing. I sure would like to know why you stopped drinking at the end of the summer. Why then?"

"Jesus, Albi, they're tying me into it too, they claim they've got something on me too, and I just—" Matt's voice dropped as he glanced toward the back room.

"Your wife doesn't know this yet? Doesn't pay to keep secrets from your wife. Let me tell you that from experience—I had three of 'em." Albi held up a hand, touched the thick gold ring on one finger. "I'm stringing along number four right now . . . don't know if she'll go the distance, frankly. But hell, if you're digging Sally's grave, if you—"

Matt slammed his mug down with a sound like a hammer landing, a splash of black hit the table. He turned his back to the bar and gazed out at the tables sitting empty. The sound of the slots was a tinny echo from the back. "You want me to tell someone the truth—I'll tell you then, Albi. Back in August, I know I was here at the Bar and Grill. Jesus, I remember waking up in the morning, feeling like hell, and with a vague memory of telling Arlen some of my secrets, what I . . ."

Matt paused and turned back toward the spilled coffee. "Only problem is that when I look at the record, it was the night before Arlen was found dead, the same night things went wrong for him. I don't know."

Albi opened a bottle and pointed at a corner. "I remember—you talked to Arlen for hours in that booth over there. Got all weepy an' shit, as I remember."

Matt turned quickly around. "You saw me? You remember?"

"You're a mean drunk, Matty." Albi held up a shot glass of whiskey and poured it into his coffee. Then he glanced up at Matt. "Arlen liked to say that Albi's Bar and Grill was his church in the Silver Valley—and it seemed to me that usually Arlen didn't mind confessions. But that night, he did mind. After he was done with you, Arlen looked like something the cat drug in. Before he left, he asked for a drink. He didn't have a drink here very often. So I guessed, over the years, that he only did it when he felt dirty after talking to someone. So I figured you confessed to some nasty business that night—"

"But, Jesus, I just told him what happened with—"

Albi waved off his answer. "I don't want to hear it all over again, Matty. So you told him something you weren't proud of—maybe you cheated on Sally or something like that. And when you left here, I'd swear you were more drunk than I thought a man could be and still stand up. Arlen left right after you, maybe he met you outside, he's not drunk, but he looks like hell. I'm worried for both of you."

"What happened after that?"

"You have your secrets, Matty. I've got mine." Albi raised his coffee cup in the air, giving a mock toast before he drank.

"Jesus, Albi. I'm asking you—I'm begging you—not as a sheriff's officer or anything, but as a . . . as a friend. Please, please level with me. Save me."

"Why the hell should I do that? You don't even know if you need to be saved."

"You know, truth is, I always disliked Arlen. I don't like folks who turn to God to solve their problems. And he always seemed too high and mighty for me. But hell, I wouldn't kill him, would I?" Matt's voice trailed off.

Albi raised his coffee cup and drank from the steam. "You tell me, Matty. You had a God who lives in a bottle, didn't you? I don't know what you could have done."

Matt leaned across the bar, his voice softening as he spoke. "Jesus, Albi, I'm beginning to doubt myself what happened. Afterward, I don't know what I did—did I see him again? I went home and drank more. I don't know what I might have done."

"You're saying you had a blackout. Another one. You're sticking to that story?"

Matt shook his head slowly. He took a drink of his coffee and looked away, not trusting himself to meet Albi's accusing eyes. "Will you testify for me?" he said. "Will you tell the prosecutor I was here all evening? That Arlen left long before me?"

"What's it worth to me?"

"Jesus, I don't know. I need a break here, Albi. I can't sleep, I can't think—I just keep seeing him dead, and everywhere I turn . . . If you talked to Arlen after that, if you saw him alive, or might know anything more about this guy on the video, I need that on my side. I need some breathing space to find out who did actually do it. I know for sure that the kid they arrested—Kevin—he didn't do anything here. I want to know the truth. I think we deserve the truth, even if it points back to me. And truth is, this kid is innocent. Don't you give a damn about the truth anymore?"

Albi didn't seem to have heard Matt's question. Slowly, he poured another shot of whiskey into his coffee. He held the shot glass in the air, the whiskey dripping into the steaming mug, the aroma drifting into the air. Slowly, he put it down and spoke again.

"Shit, Matty, I can't believe the truth matters anymore. But maybe you're the one with the straight flush. Because if you knew the truth, you wouldn't be asking me."

"What truth?"

"I think I made the phone call that got the whole shitstorm rolling. Back in mid-August, Arlen comes in here and he pulls me aside, and then he tells a humdinger of a hypothetical story. First, he asks me if I happened to know what caused some mine deaths, and if I could finger someone with serious dirty money in this town, what would I do? I know he's thinking of Herrick—

he's the only money player still in town. Maybe Arlen thought he was being damn tricky, but I saw right through it."

Albi breathed out, and Matt could smell the whiskey. "After Arlen leaves, I make my phone call. Now I make a call like this every so often, keep myself in his good graces. Make sure William Herrick knows me, pays me. And after I hear this from Arlen, I make my little phone call for that month."

"You called William Herrick? And told him what?"

"Jesus, Matty, I cover my ass, same as anyone. I keep my ear to the ground for Will Herrick—or the other side, if that bitch would pay me. I send 'em both dirt, if I can. That night, I told Will Herrick that there were allegations floating around about mining sabotage, things his father may have done."

"Why would you do such a thing?"

"Hell, Matt, those are some serious allegations. Could really affect his business—and of course at the time, I'm thinking it has to be bullshit. Anything like that would have come out years ago. And Herrick pays good money to shut down gossip like that."

"You did it for the money?"

"What do you think, Matty? C'mon, besides, it just can't be true." Albi swallowed his drink in one gulp. "And if it is, I figure Herrick will cover his butt—maybe get proof out in the newspapers or something like that, that'll be the end of it."

"But that wasn't the end."

"No. I surely didn't expect that Arlen would end up dead. I mean, goddamn, you think I'd make a call like that to kill that little priest, do you? I don't cross some lines."

Matt looked at him and took a sip of his own coffee. "You really think Arlen's death is connected to the mines? If Herrick was covering something up, it would give him motive. If you'd say that, it could exonerate Kevin. It would save him."

Albi looked at him sharply. "It would cover your ass. That's what you mean."

Matt squeezed his eyes shut tight. "Jesus Christ, Albi—no. I really care about this damn kid. He hasn't done anything, he's absolutely innocent here. No one else cares about him, except me. He doesn't deserve any of this. He's been shanghaied into—"

"Jesus fuckin' wept, Matty."

"Leonard, the kid is going to fry for this. He didn't do it. He has no other help."

Albi stared at him, drinking his coffee slowly. "Cry me a river. Jesus wept."

"Don't you care that someone who didn't do it is getting set up? Don't you?"

Albi looked away, at the sound of the slots in the back room. "It's a real fuckarow, ain't it? Jesus, Matty, I'm in this world to take care of me, myself, and I. Not you. Not your fuckin' friends. Me. And I can't see a way for me to get ahead, helping you, helping this damn kid with a rap sheet as long as my arm. But I can see plenty of ways I could get fucked, knowing what I know. But dammit, you came all this way. I'll do you one favor."

Albi reached underneath the bar. In his large hand was something rough-edged, small, and square. "I'm just going to wash my hands of this damn thing. Your secrets."

Matt swallowed hard. "What secrets? What do you have on me?"

"I didn't have anything on you before August. But it turns out Arlen did. So maybe if I give you this damn thing, you'll go away."

Albi lifted his hand from the counter. Matt looked down and saw a tattered notebook in a leather binding. "This little book was given to Arlen during a hospital confession. Someone saw a ghost—that's what they thought—and the nurses called the chaplain on duty—Arlen—and this guy in the hospital confessed the whole lot to Arlen. Then, to wipe his conscience clean, he gave him this. This proves everything Arlen told me about Herrick. Yeah, it was all real, and you're right there in the middle of it all. If you're serious about wanting to help the kid, this is the only thing that will help the damn kid. But if I know human nature, you'll just bury the damn thing."

As Albi spoke, the sound of the slots came to a halt, and the rear saloon doors swung open. Sall looked back and forth between their intense faces. "Sorry, what did I interrupt?" she said. "I smelled the coffee."

Albi looked down at the tiny notebook, a quick secretiveness in his eyes. Then it was gone, almost as soon as Matt had seen it. Without speaking, Albi poured a cup of coffee for Sall.

Matt glanced at Albi again and pointed away from the counter, toward the frozen image on the screen. Curtis Siwood holding white boxes. "Albi here has got a video of the guy on the poster. He was here in town, the night that Arlen disappeared."

Sall looked between them, her mouth open in surprise. "A video? Jesus, that's great, Matt! Now you have a witness, don't you? With his testimony, Kev could go free and—"

Matt nodded. "That's true. But we don't have a witness to Curtis being alone with the girl. That could be important too. The kid in jail—Kev—he's told me that. But we need another witness. In fact, we don't have any proof that Curtis took the little girl."

Albi clicked the remote, and the face on the screen shrank down to a dot of light. "You can take the videotape, Matty. But you know, I can't testify . . . I just can't."

Sall spoke up. "You aren't going to testify? What about that innocent kid, in jail!"

Albi finished off the shot glass. He did not say anything.

Matt put his hand on Sall's shoulder. "You have to understand, the business Albi is in—there are consequences for getting involved. It's a tricky place to be—"

"What? He's a bartender. What's so tricky about that?"

Albi put his hands together again, flexing the fingers. He did not say anything.

Matt fumbled for words. "Albi takes care of things for people—anything you need in the Silver Valley, Albi can get it for you. He usually doesn't talk to cops though, takes care of everything himself."

Sall looked back and forth between them. "But the kid's innocent, isn't he?"

"She has a point," said Matt. "And think about the life you're wasting, Albi. That's a murder one charge. And if someone could say they saw this Curtis Si-wood guy alone with the little girl, it might get someone out from underneath a rap they don't deserve."

"I couldn't do that, Matt," said Albi. "I made one mistake already, I'm not going to make another." He looked up and shook his head.

"Jesus, Albi, make an exception for once in your life. My life—this kid's life is gone, he's hanging on by a thread, and you don't know anything for sure. You know what I'm fighting for! One good man is already dead, but don't trade another good man for him too—heroics aren't going to bring Arlen back!"

"Jesus fuckin' wept." Albi sighed, and looked up at the black television screen. Only his reflection looked back at him. He took a swig of whiskey from the bottle.

After a long pause, he looked up again. "Okay," he said finally. "I don't know if the facts support the version of events you're asking to hear, but you put me in front of a grand jury, I'll testify that you were here for hours that night, long after Arlen left. That's what I'll say, just for you. And that's all I'll fuckin' say."

"But how will that help?" Sall began. "How will that help Kev in the case?"

Albi ignored her. He pointed a thick and shaking finger at Matt. "You just make sure any lawyer doesn't ask about Herrick or this other thing—you never heard the rest of this damn story. If I stand up and open my mouth about that, everyone who ever trusted me is going to wonder if I'd sell them out too. My business would be gone."

Matt put his hand on the counter. Without speaking, Albi slid the small book over to him. He poured himself another shot from the bottle. He downed half of it. He seemed relieved to no longer be touching the notebook.

Then Albi leaned over the counter, close enough that Matt could hear his whisper, low and hoarse. "You want me to help the kid—this damn thing will help the kid. It may not be what you want to hear, and you may choose to bury it, but this is his only hope. I'll testify for you, but I won't be holding on to your family's damn secrets any longer."

In winter, Fourth of July Pass at night was a fearsome sight. The Bitterroot Range was the last bulwark of mountains to hold back the Pacific weather as it spun toward the continent's heart. Every winter, acres of trees buckled under the strain of tons of hoarfrost as the wind blew across the Palouse into the Big Sky country. As snow fell, the Bitterroot Range grew craggy cliffs and vast undulating spines of ice.

The chains on the Jeep's tires bit into the icy road, and Sall moved closer to him. "When did you start caring again, Matt?" said Sall. "You haven't cared about anything in a long time. Not since that accident. I've been waiting for you to come back."

"It's what we're supposed to do—care about the cases. It's my job."

"C'mon, honey, for years now you haven't cared about the job. What happened?"

Matt grinned. "I guess when I started moving forward, I just didn't stop."

"Well, I like it. You got Albi on your side, I think. What's this book he had?"

Matt glanced down at the small, square notebook on the car seat. "From what I understand of this, someone had a heart attack and gave this to Arlen as a deathbed confession, in the hospital. Somehow, this explains things, what happened to Arlen."

The Jeep slid across the ice. Matt pulled at the wheel, gritting his teeth. "Now I gotta talk to the prosecutor's office. We have a witness to help me and Kev out of this."

"Good," said Sall. She leaned against his shoulder. "You know, despite your work stuff tonight, I think we should do more plays like this one—I really enjoyed being together with you again. How long has it been since we went out like this?"

"Too long," said Matt. "Too long."

There ain't much living here inside.
Lately, I don't know what I'm holding on to.
Wished I could run away to Coeur d'Alene,
Take nothing with me, not even my name.
    —Iris DeMent, "My Life"

IN THE morning, the sheriff's car was cold. The starter chewed and spit slowly. The weight of the cold oil held it back. It was still dark out. He'd forgotten to shut the garage the night before. The snow had blown inside, drifting and melting in the corners.

He swept a pile of snow out of the kid's empty bed and off the 'Cuda. He thought of the sheriff's car he'd drive the kid down to Boise in today. He would keep the shield between the backseat and the front seat down. There was no need to make Kev feel worse.

The spines of frost on the windows were barely shaken when the starter caught. The engine turned over with a concussive thump and the heater began to mutter in the chilly air. Eventually, he came to the road that led to the Bitterroot County Jail.

Matt tapped on the bars of the cell. "Hey you," he said. "Up an' at 'em."

Kev turned sleepily on his bunk. "Fuck, man, I got a cold. Feel like shit." Then he seemed to see Matt for the first time. "Jesus, it's you. How'd you get the transfer, man?"

Matt glanced at the closed cell block door. "I still have connections. And I used 'em, so I could get the job driving you down to Boise. I wanted to do it so I could talk to you. We're going to get you a good lawyer—these charges won't stick."

Kev looked away. "Still, I wish it wasn't you with me. Wish it wasn't you, man."

"What? Kevin, listen, I used a lot of favors so I could get in to talk to you. Last night, I got a witness. Some testimony that will help you, and if you can just tell me—"

"Yeah, whatever. I don't have anything to say. Don't feel like talking." Kev coughed hollowly.

"Listen, we're going to get you out of here. You can beat this rap, we'll just—"

But Kev just let out a choking burst of sound, a series of deep, sobbing coughs that left him helpless afterward, wheezing for air.

In the car, the kid didn't say anything at all. When Matt asked a question, the boy caught his breath, as if he couldn't hear Matt through the sound of his own lungs. Then, just as Kev started to speak, something rasped. He coughed continuously.

"Son," Matt said. "Listen, I'll get you a nurse or someone like that for that cough when we get to the Boise facility. Right now, though, you've gotta listen. You listening?"

"Yes," Kev said hoarsely.

"Look, our psychologist says that she might be making progress with the girl," Matt said. "If that girl talks, will she tell us that you didn't do this, you didn't hurt her dad? I mean, this witness I found, he—"

Kev coughed again. Afterward, the breathing was harder, as thick as a whisper. It had an exhausted quality to it that was hard to take inside the closed space of the car.

Matt tapped his fingers nervously on the wheel. "You'll be free soon. Believe me."

Kev coughed again. "Snowball's chance, man." His head lolled against the window. "In hell."

He looked at the kid's face. In the uneven light of early morning, Matt could see that something had come back to the surface, a morose desperation he'd thought was gone.

The boy closed his eyes, coughing harshly, and Matt was reminded of the other face he'd seen on the videotape. He thought of the eyes, staring out at the viewer, slightly oversized, and the cheekbones, fine high lines traced all the way to the sideburns. That tiny shifting sign around the neck, blurry and red. He imagined the mouth twisting and smiling and speaking to him. He could not understand what was said. It faded as he saw it.

He made the lips on that face in his mind lie still and flat and silent, and when he spoke to the kid again he was not reminded of it at all.

"There's hope, that's what I'm saying. There's always hope."

Matt turned his head to look back at Kev. The kid had collapsed into himself. His feet and hands were still chained together, but his head was down, buried in his arms. Matt adjusted the rearview mirror so he could see Kev in the backseat.

"Are you all right?"

Kev coughed, and moved, and Matt squinted at the mirror. Then there was a shift in the feel of the wheel in his hands, a wet sharp sound from the tires. The car was sliding over a patch of ice. Matt couldn't hear the rasping cough any more. He twisted the wheel, and the car moved straight again. But the mirror was still awry.

He straightened the mirror and listened. He couldn't hear the kid breathing now.

"Hey—are you all right back there? You sure you want to stay back there? Kev?"

There wasn't a sound from the backseat. The boy seemed to be asleep, his head against the window, his breath against the glass melting a half circle on the frost.

"You'll be okay," Matt said. "I know the heater doesn't work as well back there. But you're going to be okay. Just give me a minute." There was the glitter of neon against the snow on the right side of the road, red and yellow, wrapped around with tiny sparkling white lights—holiday lights. A service station. He pulled in beside a half-ton red truck with a Russell White for Sheriff sticker plastered across the chrome bumper.

When Matt opened the car door, the cold came in like a flood. He put his gloves on before he took hold of the frigid metal pump handle and began to fill the car.

The service station speakers broadcast loud Christmas carols and static. Against the predawn gray, the dark woods, and the rutted snow, the sound was tinny and strange.

The man at the other pump tried to talk to him over the music. "Hey, sheriff, that boy gonna be okay?" the man was saying. "You got a problem with the jailbird?"

Kev was moving inside the car, rocking slightly, as if he were being buffeted back and forth by an unseen attacker. A spasm of coughing erupted out of Kev, the sound ripping out of him, high and hard.

The man beside the truck talked on, even as Kev coughed. "What a time a' year to be in trouble," said the man. "Sure feel sorry for anyone like that—"

"Kevin?" said Matt.

Kev spoke in the husky murmur of one enfeebled by a long fight. "I'm okay."

The man was still talking. "You need help on the road, I'm right behind you."

Dawn was coming. An hour before the gas station, the road ahead had been five feet of grainy black pavement under a veil of airborne snow that danced like rippling surf above the road. The pavement, the slush at the verge of the road, the drifted snowbanks and the near shapes of the trees had all been vague shadows falling away from the headlights, into darkness. Now between the grains of windblown snow, Matt could see an expanse of dark road in front for hundreds of yards. In the distance, the edge of the sky was washed in pink light. The road glimmered with a thousand lines of glare ice.

Matt could see the boy in his rearview mirror, his head lolling against the window, his cheeks flushed with what looked like a high fever. At a wide spot, he pulled over, and let the tires crunch over a patch of frosty gravel until they came to a halt.

"C'mon, Kev," he said. "Doesn't seem fair to have you dying of strep throat or whatever in the back of a car. And it's not the worst I've done, having a prisoner in front."

Matt moved the kid's backpack and his police computer off the front seat. He put the computer in the trunk and the backpack on the floor. He unlocked Kev's feet from the leg irons and helped him move out of the car, and back inside, to the front seat.

Kev's eyes were closed, and he shivered and murmured as Matt moved him.

"No one will mind," said Matt. "I'll move the cuffs from back to front too. Keep you comfortable. Who the hell needs to know? At least I can keep an eye on you."

He seemed to be talking more to himself than to the kid. He looked back over the road behind, where the headlights of the distant truck behind them were approaching.

The sky melted into an ashen gray. The clouds covered part of the mountains around them, they rested close down upon the hillsides. They seemed about to cover the entire road. The trees on either side were wreathed with mist. The road gleamed as the gray light came over it. It steamed with a haze of fog in the sudden warmth, as if it were on fire.

Kev seemed comatose in the passenger seat. He breathed in a strangled way. Every now and then, he took a normal breath. Then his body seemed to remember what he was struggling with, and he pulled air in as if from deep underwater, choking out the air.

Matt put a hand on the boy's shoulder. Kev was warm to the touch, his brow wet.

"Have they been treating you all right in the jail?" Matt said.

Kev opened his eyes halfway. His head moved slowly, as if it caused pain to move his neck. His eyes slid over the seat toward Matt. "Yeah," he said. "I'll be okay."

Matt patted the package on the seat between them. "Hey, I got your personal things—your backpack and your tape player. It'll be held for you in Boise, for when you get out."

The kid's eyes nearly closed again, and he began to cough, starting weak, and growing louder each time. A tiny tattoo on his neck pulsed with each spasm.

"All right," said Matt. "Just take it easy. Lie back, take it easy. I'll turn the heat up."

Kev settled back against the headrest, his eyes slit open to see the morning come.

Matt drove for another twenty minutes. Then he looked at his watch. "Only two more hours," he said to Kev. The boy didn't reply. His eyes were open, but he was dead to the world. If things kept up this way, there would be no new evidence, no explanation from Kev. Most of Matt's hope was gone now too, it had evaporated with the dawn.

Matt looked at the road ahead, and at the sky. The clouds were a sickly dark gray. They were coming into the St. Joe National Forest. Small yearling trees advanced through the snowbanks toward the pavement, making the road narrower. The sky was as bright as it was going to get. The clouds were near now. It had all closed down all around him.

When they hit the ice, Matt felt the car's momentum shift first, the weight of it moving unnaturally to the left, the thrust of the engine sliding out from under his control as the tires began to spin. He wrestled with the wheel, willing it to the right. Then he could hear the skidding sound of the car turning wholly sideways, sliding in a dizzying circle over the line in the middle of the road. The mass of the car itself seemed to lift off the tires and float sickeningly in the opposite direction before there was the sound of something cracking. Matt's elbow struck hard against the shotgun in the middle of the seat, and he felt Kev seem to lunge against him, thrown there by the car's whirling rotation. His temple banged hard into the driver's window, shattering it.

Suddenly, they were facing back the way they'd come, and then just as quickly, he could see the snowbank on the right rushing toward them as the tires scraped over the frost berm at the verge of the road. He heard a ripping thud before he felt the car collide with a sapling and the hard ice inside the snowbank. He saw the hood of the car crumple, and his shoulder hit harshly against the roof of the car and then back against the empty frame of the driver's window. The skidding sound stopped, and he could hear the car engine shuddering and rattling, but it didn't die. He reached up to his temple, and felt a patch of warm, sticky blood begin to spread.

Then, quicker than his hand felt the warmth, there was a sudden cold weight at the point on his throat where his jaw met his ear. His head flicked to the side involuntarily, as if there had been a shot. But the gun did not move when he flinched. The barrel of the gun stayed where it was. Afterward came the knowledge of his holster being jerked open quickly, his belt moving with it in the moment his head had hit the car roof. And also came the sense that his hand had dropped to the seat, trying to catch it before it left the holster. He'd been too slow. Now he could hear his own breathing. Something in his throat fluttered fast against the weight of the cold metal hole on his skin.

Kev's breathing had changed now too.

"You bought it, man—I knew you would," said Kev. His voice was hoarse, but all of the labored fluid in his lungs had seemingly disappeared.

"Always been a soft touch," he said. His hand shook as he held the barrel of the revolver against Matt's throat. "No one's gonna take care of me. Make my own way."

Behind them, the red truck slid to a halt. The cold air carried every sound through the broken window. Footsteps came crunching across the snow toward them as the man approached. He paused for a moment, pulling a green scarf tight around his neck.

"Everything okay? Anyone hurt bad? Should I call the cops?"

Kev's eyes flickered toward the shape of the man behind the car.

"Don't do this—" began Matt. He tried to turn his head to look at the boy.

Then Kev pushed the barrel back into Matt's face until Matt was facing the snow-spattered window again. The shivering sound of the engine ran through the car.

"Over here," said Kev in a panicked voice. "He's hurt—front seat. Help me out."

The man came around the corner of the snowbank. Carefully, he leaned down toward the window, peering in. Like a shot, Kev lunged against the door, banging it open against the man's midriff, knocking him across the ice. The man's head hit the pavement, a sickening sound. His limbs flailed as he tried to find footing.

"Kevin," said Matt. He turned his face to the gun, so he could look in the boy's eyes. "Kev—they'll track you down, shoot you. Remember when you said that buying that Scotch would kill me? This stuff will kill you too. I'm telling you, as your friend."

Kev looked at him. His pants were ripped and his skin bleeding from lunging against the door. Sweat stood out on his forehead. "Fuck you."

He moved the gun again, and pushed the barrel against Matt's throat. Tears stood out in his eyes. He thrust the gun against Matt, and choked as his cheeks begin to shine with tears. The sight on the front of the gun caught Matt's skin, scratching him. Kev pushed the gun hard under Matt's jaw as he took the cuff keys off Matt's belt. It felt to Matt as if the kid was unhinging the keys to his soul. A moment later, the kid flung the cuffs down onto the snow and took his backpack from the front seat. Then he was gone.

Matt heard the truck start with a roar and move past him. He still felt as if his soul had been cut loose from him, it was floating somewhere up above, in the frigid air.

His neck and head were filled with pain. He put his head down gently against the wheel. Outside the open door, grains of gusting snow swirled into the car, melting on the place where Kevin had been. Every crevice and wrinkle in the twisted car hood was covered with white snow. Before it all went dark again, he saw the man on the pavement lift his head, a new expression on his face now, as if he had just realized there was a gun lying on the ground, where Kev had dropped it after getting the keys.

He couldn't see for a moment, but Matt reached blindly for the microphone of the police band. He shivered as the car engine died. He pushed the microphone button. It had been only minutes since they came onto the stretch of black ice. He could feel something missing in him, a hollow place inside his head.

"Five-oh-seven calling in," he said. "Five-oh-seven. I'm calling in a seventy-seven. Escaped prisoner in a Dodge Ram on Route 95, near St. Joe National Forest. No injury to officer."

A multitude of voices erupted from the handset, the radio crackling with sound. "Seventy-seven," he said again. "No injury to officer—should *not* be considered armed."

He keyed the microphone off, and touched the tender places on his neck and ear where the gun had hit him. He rubbed the spot of blood where the window had collided with his temple. His head throbbed with pain, the snow outside seemed to pulse with light. He closed his eyes for a moment. In a moment he'd have the strength to tell them more.

The sun touched the treetops with light. From above the expanse of the forest, there was only the sputtering smoke from the car concealed in the trees and the form of two men on the frozen ground.

Far below, on the road itself, there was only the shattered snowbank, specks of glass from a broken window, and the scored lines of tires burned into frost.

Burn me with fire, bury me in earth, or give me as a
sacrifice to the demons of the deep, but I beg you to
begrudge me not these prayers . . . conceal not from me
what I am to endure.
    —Aeschylus, *Prometheus Bound*

THE WIND blew in the open car door. Long minutes later, the frost on his face
woke Matt. His breath had collected against his chin and his chest while he
was unconscious. Now it was frozen against his chin and lips. His skin tingled
with cold.

Then he noticed the man with the green scarf in the front seat of the car,
shaking him roughly, a panic in his eyes. "You okay? You okay?" the man kept
saying. "You okay?"

For a moment, Matt didn't know where the man with the green scarf had
come from. All that occurred to him was that he didn't know where Kevin had
gone. The man had a red ice burn across his cheek and a deepening bruise on
his jaw and ear.

Then an image of the man lying in the road, the green ends of the scarf
splayed around him like dead limbs, came to him, and he reached up, feeling
the hand on this shoulder as hot as fever against Matt's frigid skin.

"It's all right," said Matt. "I just got a headache from the accident. Let's see
if the car runs." He put his head down against the window and rested for a
moment. Then he slapped his cheeks until the frost shook off, and they burned
with the fresh blush.

"We're okay," he said. But the man did not look reassured.

Matt reached toward the ignition key, and hit the dashboard with his arm.
The car hadn't seemed to stop spinning for him. Matt corrected his aim and
took hold of the key.

The engine shuddered awake, and then the radio burst to life. "Charlie Delta
Alpha four six five. Truck last spotted northbound on Highway 95," said Phyllis. Matt reached for the microphone. He swallowed, and a throb of pain ran
through his forehead and his neck.

"Is that your license?" Matt said to the man in the passenger seat. The man
nodded.

Matt put the microphone back on its hook. He picked his gun up off the ground, and checked the safety. It seemed heavy in his hand now. Then he shifted the car into gear. The engine shuddered, but the car stayed together. In the background, the radio droned on.

"See?" he said. "They're on top of it. We'll find the kid—get your truck back." He turned the radio down. Then he jerked the wheel to the left. The car moved unevenly across the road. Steam billowed out from the broken radiator. The car hood was a crazy landscape of snow and twisted metal, and the wheel swerved to one side whenever he shifted gears. But by forcing the wheel in the right direction, he could still drive.

He swung the car in a half circle, scraping over the broken tree and the scattered snow. Then he shifted into low gear. The engine revved, and they lurched up the highway.

Matt dropped the man at the gas station, telling him to call the police with a statement. He would drive on ahead. He had an idea where the kid could be headed.

Kev could feel the growl of the engine reverberate in his chest as the gearbox shifted into fourth gear. The leather inside was the color of coffee and cream. He couldn't stop touching it—it was smooth and velvety brown. New leather, new tires, new engine. He'd managed to steal a brand new Dodge Ram 4x4, in bright red. It was unreal.

Drifts of fresh snow lifted off the road and flurried into the air. For a moment, the truck seemed to float in a world of blown white.

In the truck cab, his legs and arms were still shaking, a spasm of nerves running uncontrollably up and down the length of his body. He pushed down on the gas pedal, holding the wheel tightly, willing his skin to stop shivering. The melting snow left dark, discolored spots on the leather.

Kev downshifted and took the truck onto the backcountry road that led up the mountain, toward the Indian reservation. There were sirens on the distant highway.

When he turned the truck off, steam rose from the hood. As long as Matt didn't get back on the road soon, they'd never think to follow him here. Even so, he'd just pick up what he needed and take off.

The cabin was shrouded in icicles and hoarfrost. Webs of frost slicked the brown, unpainted boards. He reached down to the ground and shoved his fingers deep into the snowy sludge. The ice balled up in his fist, and he rolled his hands together before he threw the ball at the cabin. It floated through the falling snow, free and alone as a bird.

Just as the ice ball hit, he heard the sound of the siren, closer now. A car was coming. From the edge of the cabin roof, an icicle fell with a tinkling echo. His target.

The siren gave a final distant burp and stopped. But they were closer now, on the side of the hill, engines working to get up the road. Shit, how did they get here so fast?

The key was still there, hanging on the nail under the eaves. Kev locked the door behind himself. He found the pistol in the chest under the window and unwrapped it. Then he got out his tape player and batteries. He tucked the earphones in, and flipped the switch. The exultant metal rush of guitars gave him confidence.

He could not see any cars outside yet. Maybe they'd think that he'd taken off into the woods. Especially if the cabin was impossible to get into.

Even if they stayed here, he knew what to do. At the Aryan Nations, they'd taught him. He took the axe and widened a gap by the door, making it into a peephole. Then he took the two-by-fours by the fireplace, and he began to nail them over the doorframe and across the windows. The front picture window couldn't be covered, and it was too wide for the boards he found beside the fireplace. He covered the rest of the windows with wood.

After the entrances were barricaded, he could hear them outside, driving to the other side of the clearing. Someone opened a car door, and then there was the growl of a bullhorn, the sound barely audible through the nailed layers of lumber and the rhythm of the music in his ears.

The snow obscured the men in the clearing. Matt could make out a scattered handful of four or five deputies. There were several cars parked in a loose half circle around the cabin. Their headlights broke up in the whiteness, picking out individual flakes like flecks of silver or mercury, freezing them in the air for a moment.

The words from the bullhorn were washed away in the wind that had begun to blow over the ridge, until only a few sounds broke through: "Sheriff's Department . . . You are surrounded . . . Come out . . . hands up!"

Matt walked toward the deputies, and almost stumbled over Bill Bouse, spread-eagled and half covered by snow. He was pointing a long-range sniper rifle at the cabin.

"Put that fool thing away," said Matt. "This is your commanding officer."

"Hell, you sure don't look it," said Bouse. "He banged you up good. For once, I'd think you'd be standing with the rest of us."

Matt glanced down at his uniform. His shirttail had pulled out, it hung haphazard all around his waist. Both of his arms were covered with a black-vinyl residue from his impact with the dashboard. His shoulder was stained with blood from the blow on his temple, and somehow his right sleeve had ripped. He had no idea where his hat was.

"Don't shoot that kid. He's unarmed, and we can get him to surrender."

"Even if he surrenders, looks like the kid has the place barricaded—who's to say we could even get him if we tried." Bouse shrugged. "Let's just burn the damn place down."

"Jesus Christ!" said Matt. "You want a firefight that bad? Why don't you go find Nancy Ferreday's number? We need a shrink up here, not trigger-happy knuckleheads!"

The sound of the wind and the thick falling snow obscured Bouse's reply. Matt went toward the cluster of squad cars, hearing the bullhorn bellow again. "Any offensive action will be responded to. You must come out with your hands up! Come out with—"

Matt interrupted the man with the bullhorn. It was Dustin Hartman. "Let me have that, Dusty. I think we can talk him out of there. When he agrees to come out, I want—"

"Agrees to come?" said someone incredulously.

Matt motioned toward the cabin, and turned toward the others, hoping to encourage them to close the loop. He got Mark Taylor to listen, and then Hartman. He told them about his plan to make a rush from either side, and wrestle the kid to the ground. They could take the kid without difficulty, he tried to say, no need to fire a shot, but the words seemed to wash away in the wind before anyone could hear them.

Jerry Kelberg began to move toward the cabin, awkwardly shuffling through the drifts.

Moments later, there was a muffled snapping sound, an explosive pop in the white world. Matt looked up at the trees, thinking it was a limb falling, the snapping of frost.

Anxiously, he glanced around. New cars were pulling into the clearing. Bill Bouse was out of sight. Kelberg was still moving forward, but on the other side, Hartman had lost interest. He had faded back to the cars. Quickly, Matt held up the bullhorn. "Cease fire!" he bellowed. "Cease fire!"

From far away, Matt heard another voice. "Belay that!" He turned to see Ward Louden stepping out of a squad car. Now Taylor paused too, uncertain in his direction.

"Belay that!" said Louden once more. "Keep firing, dammit! Keep that kid cornered!"

Matt ran toward him, and again Louden spoke, this time into the microphone in his car radio. "Look, guys, we've got the dirtbag locked in. Take him out. I'm in charge now."

Matt lunged through the snow. "What the hell are you playing at?"

Louden glanced at the men. He spoke in a low whisper. "Matt, he assaulted an officer!" Louden closed his car door with a ferocious shove. "This is just what we need—a manhunt in the middle of winter. It's fuckin' winter, the snow is five feet deep. Weather is still pissing down on us. We need to take him out now! Hell, you're the one he clocked to get out of the squad car—for once in your fucked-up life, I'd think you'd get it!"

"I don't care about what he did." Matt pointed across the snow. "We were going to get the kid without a shot! Jerry's out there. What the hell are you doing about cross fire?"

"Jesus Christ." Ward shielded his eyes from the glare and squinted across the meadow at the cabin. He stumbled through a drift, and shook his head. "You must really believe that damn kid is unarmed! Damn, Matt—you sent that rookie out there alone—"

Matt raised the bullhorn, snowflakes dotting the black barrel. "Down, down!" he shouted at Kelberg. "Goddamn it—get down!" But Kelberg kept on through the thickening drifts.

"You were really trying to rescue that bastard, weren't you?" said Louden. In the broken cabin window, a curtain swung aside. A shape moved. Someone trying to climb out the window. Another shot came from the group of deputies. The shape disappeared inside.

"Dammit, Ward. You're just going to allow them to fire at will? The kid is just—"

Louden leaned toward him, pushing him backward into a deep drift of snow. "You know Matty, I used to respect you, but that damn kid crossed the line in my book—and it's your fault he's here!" Louden grasped his shoulder and yanked Matt around in one quick motion. "I don't know what fuckin' strings you pulled to get car duty today, and I don't care! And you know, I don't really care whether you let the kid escape or whether he shot you in the gut. Andy is going to take your badge as soon as he gets here."

Matt stared back at him, a jagged tremor running through him. "And you want to watch the kid die, don't you? That's what you want. You're going to kill him outright."

Louden's mouth quivered as a snowflake touched it. "I don't have to, Matty. That's the beauty of it—the deputies saw Arlen dead, they think they got his killer cornered. So they're doing the Lord's good work, you see?" Ward grinned. "It's hopeless for the kid."

With a frantic motion, Matt threw the heavy weight of the bullhorn against Louden, pushing him into the drift. "It's never hopeless," he said. Then he was running forward, the sky covering him in a deluge of white, his shape swept away in the wind.

◇   ◇   ◇

The picture window collapsed as another shot hit it. The glass fell inward in a rain of glittering ice. Kev cowered by the door and felt the cold rush in.

He thought he'd climb out the window, and he lifted his backpack, tossing it lightly out. But someone had seen the movement. When it hit the snow, there was the whining concussion of a shot breaking into the room, puncturing the far wall. And another, and another, they came in an explosive barrage.

He crouched back against the wall under the window and cranked up the volume on his tunes. For a long time, he waited at the windowsill. The chorus echoed in his head: *I've got a fear of enclosed places, Crowded rooms and unknown faces.*

He put his trembling hands in his pockets, keeping the cold away. On the floor in front of him was the empty pistol. His only bullet was in that damned backpack with those old letters now, and it was forever out of reach.

The wind from the open window cut through his jail coverall. His teeth were chattering now, his skin rigid with goose pimples.

Carefully, he edged his way across the floor to the fireplace. Even without more bullets, he could not let go of the pistol. He clutched it with one hand while he stuffed paper and wood chips under the fire irons. He glanced toward the window before he pulled the trigger on the lighter, checking that no one could silhouette him against the light of a fire.

After the paper was aflame, he piled logs on top, hoping the draft would catch soon, and stop the smoke that poured out of the firebox. He staggered backward as the choking cloud filled the small room. The pistol clattered against the chair as he waved his hands in front of his face. Belatedly, he remembered the covering they'd locked over the top of the chimney. Billows of smoke came out of the fireplace.

He pushed the logs apart, separating them, yanking the smoldering wood out of the hearth space onto the floor. Then the fire sprang up anew, the fresh air from the broken window rushing in to reinvigorate the flames. The room was suffocating him.

Frantically, he grabbed at the flat bulk of the cabin books, beating at the smoldering spots on the floor, the blazing hulks of the logs. As he lifted one of the books for another blow, he saw that the pages had caught flame. He held a massive torch in his hands. With watering eyes, he flung the cabin book toward the open window. The books collided with the remaining shim of glass and slid down the wall, the thin curtain bursting into flame.

Matt moved forward, his feet lifting rapidly in and out of the deep snow. The sound kept coming, louder now and more percussive, as if the shooters had found their range. The closer they were, the louder the sounds seem to come, a sudden low bark followed by a whine. Matt's head still pounded from the accident, a solid pain in his temple, hurting with every step. Just ahead was the gray curve of Kelberg's back. He reached out, but a sudden splash of darkness erupted from Jerry's shoulder on that moment, the sound of the shot a moment later, as Jerry spun around, his mouth opening in the silent *oh* of surprise.

Matt drove through the air, colliding with Jerry as he fell. He rolled over and looked at Jerry. It was a shoulder wound. Jerry screamed in agony, and then the fractured syllables of an Asian language spilled out, gutteral sounds twisting into the air.

Matt's hand moved automatically. He felt the wound, suddenly sticky and warm in Jerry's shoulder. He held it there, pressing down against the muscle, feeling the boy writhe under him. After a moment, Matt lifted his hand. The bleeding was only on the surface.

Jerry sat up to feel the ripped jacket, the torn flesh on his shoulder. His skin lost all color, and sweat broke out like a disease across his face. A flurry of snow closed in again, covering them in a veil of white mist. Matt pushed him back down. He took his jacket off and wrapped it around Jerry's shoulders. "Keep a hand on that wound—apply pressure. It's just a nick, but it's still bleeding. Stay down—we're in a free-fire zone."

There was a lull in the wind, and now Matt could see the cabin. In front of them, the meadow was windswept and empty: a clear killing field that led directly to the picture window. On the lee side—the side with the door—the cabin was shadowed with trees.

Matt barked instructions into Jerry's ear. They struggled forward, aiming for the trees and the door. Behind them, Matt could see a thin red streak behind Jerry. It extended across the snow toward the cabin, growing longer with each forward lunge. Smoke was billowing out of the window-sized hole in the cabin wall. It leaked out around the door and the chimney lock, a gray sludge against the white snow, as if the cabin itself was dissolving. "C'mon, we've got to get inside," said Matt. "Help me kick this door in."

Kev scrabbled backward, his feet slipping under him, his head ducking down near the floor, where he caught a sudden breath of good air. He struggled to his feet again, breathing in the stifling smoke. He staggered backward against the barricaded door, desperately pulling the nailed wood from the frame. The music kept pounding into his ears. But the earphones were burning welts into his shaven head now. He tore them out, flinging them across the smoky room. The snarl of the fire filled the room with a roaring darkness.

With a tortured gasp, he tried to pull the locked and blazing door open. Then a bitter smell filled his nostrils, and he realized the fuzz of hair on his head was burning. He heard a crack from the window.

Something hit his chest, a shattering pain as a bullet pounded into him, and a sudden choking sensation came into his throat, taking his breath away. As he fell onto his back, he was surprised to see the door break apart, a pair of shadowy angels pushing through it as a curling mass of flame blew across the room.

Matt pulled the boy's body over the snow. The muscles seemed to shift under his hands, smoking and sliding away from his grip like rotten meat. The arms were blackened and tortured with heat. Red flesh steamed under his hands: the skin was burned away. Quickly, Matt let go of the burned limbs. He took hold of the boy's torso under the arms, hauling him once more toward the cars, lifting him above the knife-edged drifts.

Matt could see Kelberg dragging Kev's feet. Every time he moved, Kelberg staggered forward, his one strong arm gripped tightly around the boy's smoking legs. Matt thrust rearward through the heavy snow, and his head became a continuous pulse of pain. Matt was stricken with a flurry of sudden sensations. They were rowing backward across an endless white lake. He was at the side of a road again, crying as Irene screamed in pain inside the twisted car, the snow falling over him. The car was spinning as Kev took his gun. He pulled again and again, a white light filling his head, shooting through him, as if he would never stop moving, as if he could never let go.

Then he looked up to see a van with a flashing red light pull in. Matt sat down in the passenger seat of a squad car, his arms quivering with effort. Someone opened the car door, wrapped a blanket around his shoulders. He watched from the car as they slid Kev onto a stretcher. Matt shivered, and saw that a book had fallen out of Kelberg's pocket. *The Daybreakers*, by Louis L'Amour. The snow covered it slowly.

"I should feel sorrier for you," said a voice next to him. It was Andy Merrill. He was standing next to the open car door. In his hand was a soot-streaked backpack. Kev's pack.

He dropped it in the snow next to the car, a sneer marring his face. "That damn kid was dead by the time you got him out of the cabin, I guarantee it. And the boys tell me they just found a gun too. Kid was armed, looks like. So we've got an open-and-shut case on him. I should feel sorrier for you," he repeated. "But you no longer work for me. You're done. I'm informing the DA you're under immediate investigation."

"I'm going to fight this," Matt muttered. "On what grounds can you suspend me?"

"You just don't get it, do you?" Merrill's voice rose. "I'm not putting you on suspended duty, I'm not doing a disciplinary hearing, I'm not giving you any pension.

"You're fired! I can tell the law enforcement board a whole raft of reasons. Insubordination, concealment of evidence, violations of policy on prisoner transfer!" Merrill paused, his face flushed in the cold air. "I am tired of the corruption, of the—"

"I'll appeal!"

"Sure, Matty, you can appeal. But you can't spin your way out of this one. I may be losing this election to Russell, but I can still take this damn thing out of your hide."

Merrill breathed heavily, and then leaned forward into the steam that was rising off the hood of the car. "Oh, and there's one more thing—Will Herrick has taken an interest in your situation. I would think he wants his pound of flesh too. Apparently, he doesn't want you to kill yourself just yet. I won't arrest you until Monday—so you've got time to hang yourself after you talk to him, got it? It's imperative you go down to Herrick's dock tomorrow."

Matt shook his head wearily. "Why? What would Herrick want from me now?"

But there was no answer. Other cars had come into the clearing while he was pulling the boy's body out of range. The light on the windshield and the snow pulsed with light. The wind rose, pushing a drift of snow into the open front seat of the car. The radio crackled with sound and voices. It was all white noise to him.

Numbly, Matt reached down and took hold of the boy's backpack. Merrill had left it behind. Then Matt closed his eyes for a moment, just a moment.

When he opened his eyes again, two deputies were helping Jerry Kelberg, his shoulder bandaged, toward the backseat of the car where Matt sat. Jerry's face was contorted behind tear-fogged glasses. The brightness of the snow covered Matt's vision with white. People came up to him through the falling snowflakes, but all of them were ghosts.

Matt could still smell the smoke as he took off his jacket. Tiny bits of ash fell from his shirt. The sleeves took forever: his arms ached as he raised them above his head. He sat down on the edge of the bed and began to remove his boots. The fingers were solid, but his mind was blurry. It was moving too slow. And it was dark in the room, despite the open curtains. It was still snowing, and the gray sky had turned deep green with the reflected lakeside lights. He went over and closed the curtains and finished undressing. When he sat down on the bed, lightly, so as not to disturb her, her fingers reached out. They took his hand and pulled him in toward her. He could feel the heat rising off her skin, and then she brought him in close to her, and he could feel his hand against her thighs, and then softer, touching inside her. Her fingers left him there and slipped away to stroke his back as light as a moth trying to land. She touched his skin all over, with her hands, with her lips. She pressed her face into his neck.

He could feel her below him, the length of her pressed against his body. He could not speak. She was still moving around him, pulling him in. She lifted him up by the muscles in his legs as though she was holding a glass that might break, holding his weight into her like the slightest thing might spill him, as if he himself were fragile. Then he held to her like a falling man losing his grip, thrusting into her in desperation. He went into her like a man who would be lost if he let go, holding on until sleep came over him.

◇**25**◇

> It was now the hour that turns back the longing
> of seafarers and melts their hearts, the day they have
> bidden dear friends farewell, and pierces them . . . he hears
> in the distance the bell that seems to mourn the dying day.
> —Dante Alighieri, *Purgatorio*

AMBITION WAS a forty-three-foot custom-built yacht. It was a Farr-designed racing vessel and had cost a small fortune, but William Herrick had never used it for racing.

Two miles out into the lake, with the *Ambition* heeling under the press of its powerful mainsail, William put the helm down. The sail crackled with the violence of the turn as the boat pushed itself aggressively upright. The mainsheet whipped around the cockpit, and Matt nearly dropped his coffee.

The turn of the boat seemed unintentional for a moment. Matt hung against the side railing, a few feet above the water, and gripped the thermos tightly with one hand. The papers in his hand fluttered forward against the pull of gravity and wind.

"So what are you doing now? You got plans after leaving the sheriff's office?" shouted William from the helm. Matt turned, unable to speak over the sound of the sail snapping over them. The mainsail caught the wind on one side, then the other, as the hull came to a halt and began to slip backward against its rudder.

William made a sound Matt could not hear. Then the sound quieted as the mainsail caught the wind and the boat surged forward onto a new course. Herrick came forward and leaned over the mainsheet track, putting a piece of paper into Matt's hand. "You shouldn't worry about this, Worthson. I'll have my accountant take care of your pay for the next few months—and your pension too."

Numbly, Matt opened the envelope flap and glanced at the top page. A figure with many zeroes was printed on a check that fluttered in the wind. Quickly, he put his thumb on it.

"Now, I hear that Andy Merrill is trying for some sort of grand jury indictment on you." William sighed. "But once Russell is elected, you'll be fine. I'll lean on Valerie and Russ, and we can just get that wiped off the books. You'll walk away from this."

Matt looked up incredulously. "You'll work with Valerie to protect me?"

"Look, my sister and I may disagree on nearly every matter. But blood is always thicker than water. Both of us know that our fortunes rise and fall on the foundation our father laid—and I think I am correct when I say that both of us would use any possible method to preserve our father's legacy. Ultimately, this is self-preservation."

Matt gathered himself and closed the envelope. The movement of the boat was smooth now, nothing to throw him off balance. "I'm not going to cash this check, Mr. Herrick." William glanced up at the curve of the sail and shook his head. "Look, Matt, we've known each other a long time. My father was the first one to promote you, right?"

Matt nodded. "That has no bearing here, Mr. Herrick. I need to know why you—"

William held up a finger. "Ah, but it does. I've known you long enough to be straight with you. I'm talking to you because you can help my father once more."

"Your father's dead. He's been dead for nearly ten years."

"Too true," said William. "But his legacy lives on. All the work he did here in the Silver Valley, laying the groundwork for Herrick Industries. And now there's a very simple story to be told, and there's a less flattering one. You know both of these stories, and I want to ensure that you keep telling the right story."

Matt sighed. "Jesus Christ, why all the secrecy? What game are you playing?"

But William wasn't listening. "Look!" He pointed at the sky. "They're out. I had hoped to see them here. Sad, no?" Against the clouds fluttered small black specks. They moved erratically, up and down.

"It's the middle of winter," said William. "Bats hibernate. Yet here they are. And the weather being cold, occasionally they hit the lake. Let's see if we can find a downer."

Matt looked down. The boat's reflection was fading. The wind had dropped and the *Ambition* slowed its forward motion. Behind them, barely a ripple of wake scored the lake.

"What story are you telling?" said Matt. "Some fairy tale about Curtis Siwood?"

"See, there you are." William turned from the lake. "You and I both know who did it—Curtis Siwood, that deadhead in the lake. Your problem is to prove it, and I can help you do that. I can help you prove it beyond a doubt."

"You believe in the story I'm telling?" said Matt incredulously. "You believe Curtis did it? Finally someone who believes the story that—"

"Well,"—William's eyebrows went up—"there's little sense in being coy about it. I did, after all, tell Curtis that he had to talk to Arlen. He did get a little bit more adventurous than I expected, it seems. I don't know what got into his mind, but he was very angry when he finally caught up to Arlen, and I think that poor preacher paid for it."

"You hired Curtis Siwood—you, you knew who he was the whole time?"

William nodded sadly. "Curtis always was a sadistic fucker. Of course he would be the one who did that to Arlen. I didn't exactly hire him to do that, but I knew it was always possible. Anything was possible with Curtis. That's why—back in the '70s—I recommended Curtis to help out my dad's saboteur in the Silver Valley."

"Jesus Christ, your father had a saboteur? Someone assigned to do this job?"

William gave him a strange look. "Yes, of course. And I thought by now you'd know something about sabotage. I would have assumed that you knew."

Matt moved away from the mast, approaching William face to face. "Jesus Christ! If I had any standing at the sheriff's office, I'd arrest you! You're confessing all this?"

William stared down at him, as if surprised to see him on the boat. "No, of course not. I'm not confessing anything. It was, in a business sense, entirely unavoidable. I regret it, of course. Yet Arlen's death was unintentional. Collateral damage, so to speak."

William looked away from Matt. He pointed down. "Look. In the lake."

Matt glanced down at the black water, at the thin bits of ice that swirled against the side of the boat as it passed. Something was moving. An animal. It was a small thing, no bigger than a mouse. For a moment he thought it was swimming, except that its head seemed too big for its body. Then he saw the almost transparent wings, floating on the water, and he realized it was a bat. Somehow, it had slipped out of the sky.

Matt had only seen a bat up close once before. That other time, the bat had been sitting on the porch swing at their house, all wrapped up in its wings, as if it were cold. It had been a little thing on the porch, its fur a soft gray brown, its eyes small ink spots of life.

Most of the fur on this one was wet. It stuck up in spikes, like a tiny soaked rat, part of it already under the surface of the lake.

"We should rescue it," said Matt. "So it can fly again."

William looked at him, a blankness in his face. "Why? It's the middle of winter. It doesn't belong here in the first place." He shrugged, a slow and uncaring movement. "But it might save itself after all. Life continues to be unpredictable."

Matt stared down at the floating bat. After a moment, he could see that the bat was not really struggling against its death. It was staying in place, not moving forward or back. He could see that it might be some time before it sank. He saw that if the bat fought harder, it might sink faster. In its perpetual uninterested action, it would stay above a long way before it sank. The chill in the air brought a shiver over Matt.

The bat was staying afloat, but barely. It lifted its head out of the water to breathe.

Then Will Herrick spoke again. "I was sorry to hear about that boy's death," he said. "I hear they worked on him for a long time. I did not care for his life either way, but I know you wanted him to make it. For your sake, I wish he had lived."

"Thank you." Matt looked up at him. It was impossible to read William's expression before he looked away again.

"My problem—" began William. Then he put his hands together, as if he were praying. "But perhaps it's not right to think of it as a problem. My concern—is that in your attempts to 'clear your name,' you may inadvertently make public statements I'd regret. If the story were told in the wrong way, it could be quite hurtful to me and my business. Incidentally, it would also, of course, hurt you. So I don't think you'll do so. And in fact, let me be clear with you, Mr. Worthson, I won't permit you to endanger—"

"You're making threats now? I want this on the record!" shouted Matt. "You should know there are people who know I'm with you—Richard Stanford, my wife, they both know I'm out here with you. You can't—"

"Calm yourself, Worthson. I'm not about to do anything callous or rude." William glanced down at their darkly pulsing wake. "Just a friendly chat between old friends."

Matt glanced back. The shoreline was farther away now.

William came closer, was almost whispering to him now. "I gather you already know much about Siwood's activities in the Silver Valley. You may not know that after this man Siwood got back to the Silver Valley, he also talked to me, and he said—"

"What he said will go on the record," said Matt shortly. "If you're connected to him, you may be culpable too. I discovered a notebook that names illegal activities done for Herrick Industries in the 1970s, payments made by your father. I will sink your entire—"

"You won't be sinking anything." William's tone did not change.

"Goddammit, Herrick, I'm going to find out who wrote this notebook, who did all this dirty work for your father, for your company. I'm going to find out, and then I'm going to nail you. I'm going to clear my name too. Why did you do this? Why . . ."

William held up his hands, as if surrendering. "You tell me. You tell me. After all, when Curtis Siwood visited your father in the hospital, the nearness of death seemed to wake some latent flicker of conscience in him, didn't it? He told the whole story then, I fear. That's what I regret now, in fact. That was the first hole in the dike."

"Pop?" Matt's mouth opened slowly as he stepped back against the rail. "Curtis Siwood visited my pop? What story did he tell? You need to stop this damn boat and—"

"Sure, I'll stop the boat," William said mildly. He seemed unperturbed. "I'll just go below and engage the diesel engine, so we have some heat and light here. Care to join me for a drink? I have a good bottle of Scotch below decks—shall I warm your coffee?"

Matt brought himself off the rail. "I quit drinking," he said. "Or didn't you hear?"

William raised an eyebrow. "More coffee then. I'll get it from the cabin."

After William poured the coffee, he spoke again. "Let me tell you something—a parable, if you will."

"Goddammit, Herrick, I need to know what you are saying about Pop—about—"

Herrick continued speaking, his voice rising over Matt's interruption. "Listen to this. A parable: Imagine with me that you are serving on a mining board of directors in the Silver Valley. You have a problem. I know you're not much of a businessman, Mr. Worthson, but I will pose the question in a simple way so you can be sure to understand."

Matt took a drink of coffee, sloshing the bitterness around in his mouth. "I'm sure I can understand a lot more than you think I can, Mr. Herrick. What's the problem?"

Herrick nodded. "All right—you're on the board, as I said. Lead and silver prices have jumped up to—what was it at then—fifteen dollars an ounce. Now keep in mind, Mr. Worthson, it hasn't hit those levels since, not in the fifteen years since." He looked away, muttering to himself. "I think we made the right decision. It was the only thing we could have done . . ."

Then he looked back at Matt again. "So you, of course, have your miners working around the clock—you remember a time period like that. The boom time in the Valley. In the '70s. Every miner had a new four-by-four, every mining family had a roast on the table. And that was due to the fact that all the mines were working overtime, getting that silver and lead out of the ground and processed to be sold on the world market."

"Okay, I got it so far. I'm a mine owner, have a successful run in the metals market," said Matt. "Look—we're close enough to save it now." He pointed at the bat.

In the pulse of the water's motion, the bat turned its head slightly, and looked at them with tiny, glittering eyes. Then the eyes moved away as the bat lifted its upper body out of the lake. "What about giving me a hand?" Matt picked up an aluminum boat hook by the toe rail and reached out, touching the surface of the water. "We can get it out."

"Listen to this—I want you to answer a question." William pursed his lips and spit at the bat in the lake. "I want you to hear this story. In the middle of the boom time, the baghouse thimble room goes to hell. The smelter bag."

Slowly, Matt put the boat hook down on the deck. "What is a smelter bag?"

"Hmm, I'm glad you asked. That's critical to my little parable here. The smelter bag keeps lead oxide in check. It's the primary air recovery system. With that very important piece of machinery broken, the air system doesn't do jack-fucking-shit. Now, we know the government says you have to have that smelter bag in place, but we can't get one right then. A factory has to custom manufacture it, and that'll take five months. Bottom could drop out of the silver market by then. It's happened before." William leaned forward so he could see Matt's face. "Here's the choice: either we shut down for the winter, or we keep making money."

"That's the only choice? What does this have to do with—"

"That's the choice, Mr. Worthson." William put a hand on his shoulder. There was pressure in his grip, and suddenly Matt sensed the cold of the open water a few feet away. "And that's the question: what would you do?"

Matt thought it through. "Keep digging. That's what I'd do. But what does this—"

William took his hand off Matt's shoulder and walked toward the foredeck. "Right you are," he said. "Hell, we've got hundreds of miners and their families dependent on us for income, for development in the Valley. Keep digging." He chuckled. "Damn the engines, full speed ahead. Damn the twenty years of lead oxide we're going to drop on the people here. Keep digging." He chuckled again, but it didn't sound happy.

"You didn't mention the lead oxide," said Matt. "On the people in the Valley?"

"Ah, but I did. You just weren't paying attention, just like most people who smell money. You're a good man, Mr. Worthson. You'd just keep digging. Keep making the money."

Matt placed the boat hook back on the deck, and William turned at the sound.

"But in all seriousness, I should have been more clear. Sure, the lead had real consequences. Twenty years' worth in three months. And it bothers me, even today, I must admit, even though I recommended the same course of action to my father. It bothers me, even after all the good that came out of it. I mean, look at what it did." William pointed at the small, furry shapes that moved in the night sky.

Matt looked up at the dark specks fluttering. "What do you mean?"

"Look," said William. "There are bats out here in the middle of winter—but they're supposed to be hibernating. As near as I can figure it, something toxic in the mine tailings has caused their wires to get crossed. So they come out now, and die quick deaths in the cold. For all I know, that unfortunate boy who was burned in the cabin fire and shot by those overzealous deputies also had toxins in his head that impaired his judgment." He sighed. "I can tell you honestly, it's enough to make one cry."

Matt steadied himself against the shrouds, looking out at the lake. The bat was still in the water near them. He saw it took no notice of him any longer, and realizing that, he saw it was better that the bat did not have a purpose to move toward. It was less complicated this way, reflexively moving, back and forth on the rippling water.

"You know, the liberals, the troublemakers in the Valley, they think I'm not an environmentalist. That I don't give a damn about the lake's beauty, the animals, the people. But I do. Yet sometimes there must be a sacrifice, in trade for our livelihood."

"A sacrifice?" Matt looked down at his shivering hands. He didn't know if his hands shook from the cold or from the anger.

William shrugged. "Whatever you want to call it. In trade for the greater good."

Matt looked out at the water. Close at hand was the bat. It gasped air in again, a repetitive motion that he saw was something like flight. The wings moved the body like arms would move in a butterfly stroke, pushing it down and then lifting it up. In between breaths, the bat kept still. The bat had nothing else in its deepest parts except that sense of staying in place.

"I brought you out here to prove that the mine had to keep operating. After all, it is only by development, by having money in the system, that we're going to be able to clean up the Valley. The only way is by being on a sound economic footing. As you said, we had to keep digging. That's the choice you made."

Matt watched the bat and felt himself calm. There was no anger in the bat's movement. Animals did not feel sorry for themselves or their purposes. Yet already the color of its fur was nearly indistinguishable from the dark water. The tiny, sleek head was hardly moving, as if the bat realized that struggling would also bring it to drown.

Matt could hear William walk aft to the cockpit. The engine came on, and the boat turned in a circle. The sail hung loose—they were under power. William was at the wheel, moving them back toward the distant dock. Behind them, the sky was turning into ash.

Slowly, Matt walked back along the length of the yacht. He felt as if his own words, his own thoughts were twisting in the wind, wound up by William Herrick and tied in new directions. The boat vibrated gently with the engine sound as Matt approached the hatch. William took the engine out of gear. "Can you give me a hand with the sail?" he said.

William went forward in the cockpit. He loosened a coil of halyard and laid it on the cockpit floor, then released the cleat lever and eased the sail down until the boom dropped against its topping lift and the sail began to lay itself over the deck. With Matt's help, William pulled the folds up over the boom. Then he went below to get the sail cover.

When he returned, Matt spoke. "This story about the Bunker Hill mine— what game is this?"

William reached over the boom and tied the folds of the sail in place. "It's not a game," he said. "It was a business risk. Unfortunately, if we'd let the general public know what happened at the Bunker Hill, the government might have stepped in."

William snugged up the mainsail sheet and began coiling it in long, easy loops. He stepped back behind the helm and put the engine in gear again.

"Fenders and docklines are down below," he said. "Can you get them for me?"

From the cabin, Matt pushed the fenders out into the cockpit, uncoiling the heavy rope as he went. William took one of the heavy lines from him and began to uncoil it on the deck. When he was done, he spoke again.

"So, we made the best calculation we could. We weighed the considerations of a few lawsuit-happy people against the greater good—all the economic benefits we'd bring to the Valley by continuing to operate."

Light was washing out of the clouds, a deeper darkness emerging from the depths of the lake. Matt shook his head, as if to clear it. "What do you mean? What lawsuits?"

William stood and looked out at the lake as the boat moved under its own power. "The self-serving lawsuits that we'd assume would happen once the lead levels came out. Frank Woodruff calculated that the liability cost would be only about $6 to $7 million, if we had to settle with each one for $10,000 per kid, if their parents wanted to cause a ruckus.

"Fortunately, no one ever sued us, despite a whole bunch of kids who can't think too well. It turned out all right. The Valley gained, we gained, and Herrick Industries gained. The mine made profits of about $26 million that year.

And look what we've done with my father's legacy—just look!" Ahead of them, the city lights flickered in the breeze, the many skyscrapers and the great lights of the Coeur d'Alene Resort glowing into the night, jeweled spikes reflecting across the water.

"But your company was doing something illegal—you were poisoning the—"

"C'mon, that's how the world works," said William. "Laws are like spiderwebs. If some little person comes up against them, he's caught. But the bigger ones can always break through and get away."

"What's that—some private code of ethics you made up to benefit the Herricks?"

"No, Mr. Worthson, I didn't make it up. The philosopher Solon said it first, over two thousand years ago. You should read more, broaden your horizons. The world has been this way for a long, long time. You should understand these things by your age."

"But . . . but . . . but why didn't the lawsuits happen? Why didn't anyone sue?"

William raised both eyebrows, it made his face look innocent. "Why, because none of them knew. Your father buried the records. In fact, all I had to do was merely suggest it—I can take no responsibility for what happened after that. In any case, they still can't pin down the origin of that lead in the local ecosystem. It's only this year that a doctor duplicated the tests we did in Kellogg in '72. They discovered that heavy metals aren't indicative of longevity either."

William's face broke open, revealing a sadness underneath. "Bunker Hill's gone bankrupt now. All the directors took a cut and shut it down. Now no chance of a lawsuit. Assets are scattered to the four winds." He turned away and stepped down behind the helm, then put the engine back in gear. The stern settled slightly as he opened the throttle and steered them toward the moorings.

Matt stepped into the cockpit. "I don't know why you're telling me this. But I do know that Herrick Industries was involved with the Sunshine somehow."

William grimaced, as if he'd smelled something unpleasant. "I had nothing to do with that. The Sunshine fire was a sad tragedy. But I'm surprised you brought that up, Mr. Worthson. This may be more fruitful than I thought. After all, you would have kept mining for silver, remember? I think your father always said the same thing."

Matt clenched his fists. "You keep talking about Pop, but my pop never—"

"I can't believe he never had the courage to tell you." William nodded his head gently, as if remembering. "When Curtis last spoke to him, I understand your father had no question as to his own guilt."

"That's a lie!" But Matt felt his conviction waver, remembering the look in his father's face in the hospital room, a terror in the eyes after he could no longer speak.

William paused momentarily, and then continued speaking. "As to the kind of assistance he provided to Herrick Industries through the last fifteen years—"

"He wouldn't sell out the union like that! My father was no rat!"

William held up his free hand, as if testifying in court. "I personally would not call him a 'rat' at all. Your father was a principled man who helped Herrick Industries with a few tidbits of information. Judiciously chosen. In fact, often my father and I did not know what information he withheld. We greatly appreciated his assistance, as it helped to destroy that irritating union. I have the proof, but even now, I would honor his memory, his secrets."

"What secrets are you talking about?" said Matt. "Dammit, get to the point, Herrick!"

"Hell, you don't know anything, do you? I got you put on the resort case because I figured you already would know everything your father did—I thought you'd easily discover Curtis Siwood's involvement, and you'd know immediately that Curtis was connected to what your father had done for me."

"You thought I'd already *know* this—and then I'd do what?"

"Obviously, once you saw all this, you'd shut down the investigation, find a scapegoat. Perhaps you would even go so far as to close the file, an unsolved case. I thought that was the point of that kid Kevin, but in conversation with Andy Merrill, you seemed to be fighting his arrest. When I heard that, I did take the step of suggesting his arrest. And, of course, I managed to throw Andy Merrill off the scent by convincing him that you were the guilty party."

"You were the cause of—"

"Mr. Worthson, your own life is such a mess, convincing Andy of your guilt wasn't at all hard to do." William looked over at Matt, a sneer on his face. They had reached the marina. William cut the throttle back and steered in among the slips. "Frankly, it never occurred to me that you would chase this case to the source without understanding your self-interest. Hell, in my family, blood is always thicker than water, but I should have foreseen this contingency. Of course, if you didn't *know* anything about your father . . ."

William aimed the *Ambition* neatly between the finger docks and pulled the engine into reverse, jabbing the throttle as they came to a stop against the dock. "I never expected to have this conversation with you. It seems that instead of your father, I am now the one forced to help you. I have no doubt that once you understand, your self-interest will make clear only one course of action. Your father is implicated in—"

"Dammit, you keep insinuating things, but what kind of proof do you have?"

William stepped close to Matt and whispered to him, "Before I show you the proof of what your father did, I want to express my hope that you will not break our trust. The proof is ironclad, but I've never broken your father's confidence before this moment."

William stepped down inside the cabin hatch, taking a green file folder off the chart table. "That's why I'm giving this copy of my records to you, Matt. You'll find that every entry here correlates with that notebook you found. I believe that notebook was your father's record of our transactions. These documents prove that Stan Worthson worked for years to cover up the misdeeds of Herrick Industries. This is your father's entire legacy, your history in the Silver Valley. You're part of it now, you always have been."

Matt felt something give way inside him, a tide breaking over all, drowning him. He took the folder with a quavering grip. "Jesus . . . Pop, Jesus . . . ," he whispered.

William looped his line under the horn of a dock cleat, snubbing it gently. He turned toward Matt, his eyes steady. "How is he, anyway? Is he at peace?"

"Yes, at peace," whispered Matt hoarsely. "He just went to hospice. Not long."

William put his fingers together, again as if he were about to pray. "It's touching, the way he's become so religious, isn't it? A fine affectation, at the end."

The boat settled into the slip. William stepped to the dock. He wrapped the rope carefully around the cleat and made up the bowline. He said nothing more to Matt.

Quietly, William Herrick began whistling as he locked down the boat. As Matt stepped off the boat, he recognized the tune. *You are my Sunshine, my only sunshine . . .* Matt saw that on the horizon, there remained a touch of the flames that edged all the western rim of the world as night came.

In darkness, Matt reached out to the side table. There, he fumbled for Sall's sleeping pills. The sound of her breathing rose and fell as always beside him.

His throat was parched and dry. He saw the same images every time he closed his eyes, as if they'd been seared inside his eyelids. Pop's rheumy eyes looking up at him, the red talisman nested in his palm.

When the pills put him back to sleep, Matt had nightmares. Infinite mine corridors in flames. Mineways, stopes filled with choking smoke. Men falling, dying, all around him.

The previous afternoon was the last time Matt had seen his pop alive. Pop had been at home again, a hospital bed and a half-ton machine crammed into his tiny living room, a nurse visiting him every hour before he died. When

Matt sat down beside him and began to talk, a groan came out of him, the sound like an engine turning over.

With an effort, Pop lifted up his arm. He opened his fingers slowly, as if they were being pulled apart by pliers. Matt looked down to see a red thing, the other half of the blasting cap on Curtis's chain. Pop looked up at him, pleading with him to understand.

Matt woke, surprised to find his face wet, his eyes full of tears. He was awake again, at two in the morning. He couldn't stop remembering the contents of Will Herrick's file, all of the pages detailing payments made over the years, information shared, confidences broken. Payments that bought Matt a new bike, that paid for health insurance, money that paid for Matt's only year of college, that paid for a down payment on the very house that Matt and Sall lived in now. The legacy of that inheritance would always be with him, the memory of when he first read the file. The knowledge caused his heart to race, an urgent terror running through him again.

He could see his father's face, coming out of the mine that day all those years ago, after seven days underground. He imagined the choking smoke inside a drift shaft, the miners searching desperately for air. He saw his father reaching down to him on the wrestling mat, rescuing him after injuries.

His father was gone now. His son was gone too.

The snow fell endlessly outside the window. He seemed unable to break the sense of moving without volition, a train on the tracks. He walked to the kitchen.

Matt reached up above the sink and gently shifted the molding that hung askew above the cupboards. He reached up to that hollow that was as familiar to him as a cavity in his own body. He drew out a miniature bottle, from an airplane trip. It wouldn't help him, he knew it wouldn't, but all he needed was a little taste, enough to fill the wound inside.

The glass of the bottle was warm from its storage place. In the dim light, he could barely see the amber fluid that remained inside. He unfastened the screw-top lid and the heady scent of the alcohol rushed into the room. He held on tight to the table, not daring to move.

Then he saw it in the corner of the kitchen, exactly where he'd dropped it the night before. Kev's old backpack, the stains unchanged since his death.

Gingerly, Matt put the tiny bottle on the table, placing it steady so it wouldn't spill. The little pack made him remember the smoke, the frantic stare Kev had given him before the wind moved into the room. All around him now were the memories of the flames, the walls seemed to tremble as he looked. Not knowing why, he stood and picked up the pack. Something rattled and crinkled inside. He fumbled with the zipper and the seam nearly came apart in his hand. A sheaf of old envelopes, the secret Kev had tried to give him.

Something in his mouth trembled. He sat down at the table and closed his hands around the papers before the tremble hit them too.

CHAPTER

◇ **26** ◇

He understands; but now there is other pain
That he must bear, the bitter torment
Of seeing his own hand's mischief,
The guilt that none can share.
—Sophocles, *Ajax*

THE HOUSE was empty of light. From far away the shadows of passing cars swept across the room. In the front room, a breeze gusted across the heap of old letters on the coffee table. The contents of each envelope had been carefully revealed, the shards and scraps of moldering paper pieced together laboriously in the late night, perused for every syllable of meaning.

Even though the story was composed of uncertain sentences, pieced together by a dying woman undergoing a long and useless convalescence, these letters had found their intended destination at long last. The ink seemed to have grown stronger in the last four years, aging like a rich wine. For the reading of them had worked some change in Matt, a change that was near to intoxication. After reading through all of the scattered letters, he had only just managed to stagger to bed, exhausted and perplexed.

In his dream, a broken yellow house stood slanted on the hillside above Osburn, a block above the abandoned graveyard. Sunlight flickered on its surface, the rest of the world floated in an underwater gray. A woman sat on a straight chair against the far wall, the heap of letters piled about her feet. He saw that she was smiling at him. In her lap was a ball of yarn. She was crocheting or knitting.

Her face was different. It was as if he'd never seen her before.

"Irene?"

She laughed, a small girlish sound, and Matt felt he should explain. "Faces take a while for me to remember. Something that happened to me."

"The accident," she said, a chuckle still in her voice.

"Yes. Of course, you'd know about that."

She lifted a hand from her lap. "You look different now too," she said. "Older."

He was not frightened by the woman in the chair, not in the way that he'd thought he would be. Instead, he felt himself drawn by her vulnerability.

He was close enough to see her fingers on the roll of yarn. "They told me that you visited while I was in a coma," she said.

"I wish. I did drive to the hospital a time or two, but I could never work up the courage to get out of the car. I guess I couldn't get over what I did to you."

"Anyone can have an accident."

At her words, he felt something lurch inside, some dark beast crashing through empty rooms below. Déjà vu. The same sensation he'd had when he'd read her letters that night. His mouth was dry and parched. He swallowed hard. "Could I get a drink?"

She smiled gently at him. "It's all dry here, Matt. Nobody drinks."

"Right." Again, he felt out of place, nodding dumbly. "I should have known."

There was a tremor inside him, something recoiling. He turned his head toward the door, hearing the crickets shriek. He could leave now. He could be gone in a moment.

Matt looked at the woman in the chair. The sweat broke through his skin, his fear rising to the surface. "Where are you now?" he asked. "Where are we?"

Irene fumbled with the yarn in her lap. "You do need a drink, don't you?" She held up something, in his hand it felt like a glass, cold and wet. "I'm sorry I brought up the accident," she said. "You haven't seen me in four years, first thing I do is remind—"

"No, it's all right, Irene. Sounds like you never knew." Matt drank. Ice clanked together as he put the glass down. "You didn't wonder why I stayed away from you."

"Well, I thought I was a liability. You were trying to win the election, I thought."

Matt found that his hands were trembling. He picked the glass back up, giving them something to hold on to. "Even at the cost of being a friend to you?"

"Well, I don't know how politics work. Someone told me that maybe people would think you were cheating on your wife, if you stayed too close. Having an affair."

"Weren't we? Having an affair? That's what Russ has always told me."

"No, not as far as I remember." She looked down at her knitting. Her fingers moved around on the yarn. "I mean, we were just casual acquaintances. Coffee now and then, if we happened to need it. Not that I would have minded if we had slept together, but you weren't interested. You had a marriage, you said. You just needed a friend."

Matt leaned back. He sighed. "Jesus, why were you friends with me? A sad-sack drunk. That's real amusing."

"Well, at first I think I felt sorry for you, Matt." Irene picked up his glass from the table. With a loud crunch, she cracked an ice cube in her teeth. "You were like some big lost puppy dog or something. Really confused. Drinking too much. And really nice to talk to. You never tried to come on to me. And I guess I was lonely, far away from home.

"But you were funny too—you made me laugh. Even though you were kind of numb to it all. Sally was thinking about leaving you, you said. You remember how we met? You gave me a ride one day in your sheriff's car when my car broke down. That's how we met. Then we kept running into each other, we had coffee. We were just friends."

"You wrote that I never loved you and left you. But I don't know." Matt sighed. "I hit bottom after you died. After I was told about a woman I was cheating with, drinking with, and how I killed her, I tried to die too. The whole year after that alternated between blurry hangovers and drunk blackouts. Sometimes I still live that way."

"Someone lied to you."

Matt rubbed a hand over his glass, condensation wetting his palm. He groped his way through the dark, dead memories emerging like old fingerprints.

"Matt," said Irene. "Look at me. I was your friend. Like I wrote, that's all it was. Until you fell asleep at the wheel, and then I fell asleep forever, because of that accident."

"What do you mean?"

"I mean when you weren't visiting me, before I died." She grinned.

Matt sipped at the glass, and felt only ice against his teeth. "No, I mean the other thing you said. What do you mean—I fell asleep at the wheel?"

"That's how I got banged up. How I lost my life?" She gestured sarcastically at the gray wall, the surrounding room. "That accident—the one we were talking about?"

"Oh no, I understand. I just don't know what happened." Matt put his glass down. "I mean, your letters seem to know me—but how well did you really know me?"

"Well, like I wrote, there was one deep dark secret we shared. You told me about your drinking, and you told me when you quit. And so I asked you, every time you drove me home. You swore you hadn't had a drop that night—I put it down in a letter to you. I figured it might give you peace. And it was true, Matt. You never lied to me about that."

Matt looked outside the open door. Here, it seemed, the mines were still running, time had shifted back. A faint haze from the Bunker Hill smelter gauzed the towns of Wardner and Osburn in a translucent sheen. The faint lights of the town seemed to float in the evening smoke.

"I must have lied to you that one time," said Matt. "At the scene, they said they could smell it, even before the test—blood-alcohol level of three point five. I was drunk as a skunk."

"Who are you going to believe? I remember. There wasn't anything to smell."

Matt coughed. He could feel his throat constrict, his voice grow hoarse with the effort of what he was trying to say. "I guess—I guess I'm here to say I'm sorry. Sorry for all the pain I caused you. Finally. I'm sorry it took four years. I know you can't forgive me. There's no way you could forgive me. But I'm sorry for lying to you."

"But Matt, what are you apologizing for? What do you remember?"

The despair rose in him, a nauseating flood. He was lost in the dark now, there was nothing else to grope for. "I don't remember any of it anymore. All I have now are these damn letters you wrote me. I tried to drown my memory. Blackout. And it worked."

The woman leaned forward, her face insistent. "But Matt," she said. "You hadn't had a drink in a month. You were so proud of yourself. You said that after you got elected as sheriff, you weren't planning on ever having a drop again. And if Sally left you, even that was okay, you said. You were going to make it. You were in a good place, Matt. You had it beat—you were solid with the guys at AA. I just can't believe you were on the bottle. Read the letter again. There's no way you were drinking that evening."

"You don't want to believe it," he said bitterly. "I'm sorry. I'm sorry for it all."

"I know you," she said gently. "Or at least I knew you. And I forgive you, Matt."

Matt started in his chair, glancing up at her face. "But if I was—"

"Even if you were drinking. Even if that—I can't believe that—but even if you lied to me." Irene leaned forward, touched his face with her slight hand. "I forgive you."

Matt moved back, stunned. An unreal world swelled out at him. The force of his feeling hit him like a wave passing, something immutable and astonishing. He felt overcome, cleansed and fearful at the same time, alive in its terrifying power. Irene was smiling, she could not stop smiling.

He closed his eyes, a sudden vertigo overwhelming him. He had made a horrible mistake, he wanted to beg for forgiveness, but it was too late for that now. There was nothing to be done to redeem the time. Maybe he could do the next best thing.

When his eyes opened again, Irene reached out to the phone on the table and spoke to him. "She knows something."

"Who?" he said. But then he was looking out the window. Her house was floating over Lake Coeur d'Alene. And he knew that Arlen's little girl was waiting for him down there.

In the sky were small dark specks, bats that flitted over the surface of the lake. He watched them move against the fading light in the west. Darkness covered his vision as the phone buzzed under his hand. He turned back once more, but Irene had disappeared.

Flickering in a submarine light was the little girl who had waited for him on Five Mile Prairie, who had been at the funeral. Arlen's girl. The phone buzzed under his hand again, but he questioned her insistently.

"You aren't dead, are you?"

"Not yet," the little girl whispered. "Not yet."

Then she said something else to him, a question he could not understand. Sall stirred restlessly beside him in the bed.

Matt lay there for a long hour, waiting for sleep to return. Finally, he got up again and went to the kitchen. The little bottle was right where he'd left it. He could go back, like no time had passed at all. Go right back where he'd started.

He was so sure that he was going to take a drink, that for a moment he didn't feel her hand slip onto his shoulder. Finally, as he brought the bottle toward his lips, she said his name.

Sall's voice calmed the shiver that had come to his face. His body burned with a sudden heat. When he opened his eyes, desperation overwhelmed him, as if he were falling off a cliff. He tried to pull himself into the present, gripping the edge of the table hard enough to hear his knuckles crack. He did not look at her, staring instead at the small bottle in his hand.

"Matt," she said, whispering to him. She rubbed her hand across his shoulders.

Matt began to cry, groaning as each spasm cut out of him.

"All those years wasted. I just read Irene's letters. She didn't—she didn't hate me when she died. I did nothing to her. It was an accident. I thought I killed her. But . . ."

"Jesus, Matt, you carried this around—you lived with this, and you never told me?"

Matt turned toward her, his face streaming. "I couldn't. I thought I had an affair, or something. But I didn't—it was all a lie they told me. I lived a lie. I thought . . ."

Sall shook her head, shock breaking across her face.

"Coffee," she said. "I'll make us some coffee." She ran water in the sink, poured ground beans into the filter. The aroma of it was sharp, it cut through the anxious fog. Sall put a hand on his shoulder, quieting him as he sobbed.

"And Pop—how could he have lived like that for decades? His whole life, a lie."

Matt stared blankly down at the tabletop, his eyes fogged with tears. "And now it's mine. I have to live with Pop's goddamned secrets forever."

Sall took a swallow and pushed a mug into his hands. There was a pause as he gulped hungrily at the coffee.

"No," she said finally. "You don't have to."

"What do you mean?" Matt took a breath, the air painful in his lungs.

"You've made it this far." She turned toward him. "I'm not going to let you fall now. I know you."

He shook his head and stood from the chair. He curled his hard arms close around her warmth, pressing them into the soft places, holding on as tight as he could.

"You know me." Matt looked into her face. He rubbed an arm across his reddened eyes. "And damn, you still believe in me. Jesus Christ, you are beautiful."

She laughed hoarsely as he cradled her in a rough and desperate grip. Her mouth tasted sweet and bitter, sugar and black coffee.

If now the dead of this fire should awaken
and I should be stopped beside a cross,
I would no longer be nervous if asked
the first and last question of life,
'How did it happen?'
    —Norman Maclean, *Young Men and Fire*

OUTSIDE THE church, the crowd moved in an unseen current, clumps of black-clad bodies drifting together and apart. The soul of the Silver Valley was here: every remaining man who had mucked out a stope in the Sunshine, every union organizer who had held a picket during the Bunker Hill strike, and every mine boss who had ever negotiated on the other side of the table. The crowd was full of men with rough hands, most of them wearing suits that hadn't seen the light of day in ten years, tiny holes eaten by moths in the elbows and at the hems, the insidious grit of the mines still caked minutely in creases on their necks, behind their ears. There was a subdued hum as families met each other in the street, sounds of mutual consolation.

As the throng poured into the church, Matt saw Betty Bowman. She seemed to be caught by the swell of the crowd, confused as she looked from face to face, recognizing almost no one. He saw that in her confusion, she was slowly losing her grip on the small girl by her side. Quietly, Matt stepped around the family section and into the aisle, avoiding for a moment the many outstretched hands and expressions of sympathy that immediately surrounded him. As the throng eddied back and forth, the small girl stumbled, and then he almost lost her behind the pews. When he reached down, she took hold of his rough woolen coat immediately, with relief. She knew him from before.

"Mamma?" she said. "Where's my mamma?"

"Hi there—we'll find her." Then he blinked in surprise. "You're talking now."

She nodded. Then, as Betty Bowman came up to them, the girl was suddenly embarrassed. She reached out and grabbed hold of her mother, burying her face in her mother's shoulder.

"Oh, thank you," said Betty. Then she spoke to the girl. "You remember Lieutenant Worthson, don't you, honey?"

Matt felt something give in him at her words, his eyes crinkling with the momentary pain. "I'm not a lieutenant anymore. But I do thank you for coming," he added. "You didn't have to drive all this way. Thank you."

"We came, like all these others, out of respect," Betty said. "You've been so helpful to us, Lieutenant."

"No." He shook his head again. "No, I haven't really been much help at all to you. But thank you, thank you so much for coming."

Then she waved good-bye as the crowd moved again. Matt began to shake hands with people, but he didn't feel a thing, he was talking without caring what he was saying, listening to words he didn't comprehend and then nodding in agreement as he took his cue from the tone of a voice. He hardly heard a word anyone said. He watched the remainder of the Bowman family move away into the crowd, watched all the people find their places. Sall and Doug were already sitting near the front, talking quietly to other relatives. His son had flown in the night before, along with a cousin from Oregon, but even that had not lifted the sense of numb unreality that enveloped him.

Yet when he saw Russ sitting serenely on the left side of the church, something got to him. His heart seemed to catch for a moment, and he couldn't seem to take a breath. What had Russ done to him?

Russell White had won the election, and he looked it. He had a fresh haircut, a sleek look. His suit was freshly pressed. The new sheriff. Yet Russ did not look anywhere near Matt's direction. He acted as if he had other things on his mind. Valerie Herrick was whispering urgently in his ear, under the newly trimmed sideburns. He glanced from side to side as she spoke, recognizing political players and corporate friends, grinning vaguely when people approached him to shake his hand, offering their congratulations and support. Russ was here, but he was not here.

The church was full, but Matt felt himself to be suddenly marooned, stripped of all words. He stood there alone, struggling to catch a breath. From their seats in the pews, people looked up at him strangely as he stood.

The minister came to the front, the organist began to play, and gradually, the people subsided around Russ and Valerie. In his last glance around, before he took his seat, Russ saw Matt staring at him. He gave a desultory smile, a grin and a shrug, and then—as if remembering belatedly Matt's place here today—a solemn sudden nod, a grimace Matt wondered might be his substitute for sympathy. Valerie touched his arm, and Russ turned away once more, giving one last handshake to a supporter before he sank into his seat.

For a moment, Matt was on his feet alone, looking around at the sea of mourning black, the bright glow of the colors in the church windows, the myriad faces that already seemed strangely faded in the stained glass light, and the worn haggard face of Pop, resting now placidly on a cream-colored pillow, surrounded on four sides by the darkly burnished wood of a coffin. Underneath the box, the floor was filled with flowers.

Finally, as the organ swelled in prelude, Sall pulled him down into his seat.

It seemed hours later that Smitty rose and began to talk. At first, his voice was tinny, it echoed through the underpowered speaker.

"My name is Reverend Ed Smith. Most of you know me as Smitty." He spread his hands out, as if to apologize. "I don't know exactly why Stanley wanted me to officiate at his funeral, but here I am. I'd like to thank Father Mel for letting me speak here, for letting all of us take over St. Alphonsus this afternoon for this very special service. And now that I've thanked the Catholics, I've just got to take off this monkey suit."

A nervous chuckle ran through the crowd as he shrugged off a sports jacket and rubbed his face. His eyes were bloodshot. He laid his jacket over a seat and then walked back to the lectern.

"I gotta tell you, it's a hard thing for me to do, being here in front of you all. As some of you know, I've had a long road coming back to the pulpit. And Stanley knew it would be hard for me to do." The man paused and sighed. "But I think he wanted me here because Stanley believed in second chances. He served the God of Second Chances."

Matt felt his thoughts begin to wander at Smitty's last words. Would Pop have a second chance? Would he get up again and start over? Where was he now?

Smitty seemed to know what he was thinking. He stepped out of the lectern and moved toward the flowers. "I want you to know something," Smitty said. He walked across the steps and came close to the cream-colored cloth where the old man lay.

"Stanley would want you to know that he's not here right now. His body may be here, but he's not." Smitty pointed. "Right now, he's standing before that most merciful of judges, his Savior Jesus, who gives him both judgment and grace. Without deceit and without shield, he stands now before his Lord and Maker. He's up there."

Surreptitiously, Matt glanced at the ceiling. Pop was somewhere, but he sure wasn't up there. The wood was too dark to see. It looked to be the same wood as the coffin.

Why couldn't he focus his thoughts? Could he still say what he had to say, with Russ here? All the years of lies seemed to be folded on top of him, they wrapped him like a shroud.

Smitty was still talking at the front of the church. He was moving his arms now, starting to raise his voice, animating himself as he came toward some kind of glory. Matt could see damp circles under his arms, and he wondered if he'd sweat too, when it came his turn. Smitty talked for a long time, then they bowed their heads and prayed. Afterward, Smitty looked at a card he held in his hand.

"Now I'd like to introduce several who will give remembrances of Stanley," he said. "Mr. Tom Dexter will speak, followed by the mining union's local chapter president, Roger Jorgensen. And then Stan's son, Matt, will conclude our service today." He looked at the audience and nodded when someone agreed with him. Then he took a deep breath, and seemed to look straight at Matt, an edge of concern in his gaze. "First will be Tom Dexter, operational manager for many years of the Sunshine Mine, and now serving Hecla Mine over in Silverton as vice president of mining operations. Mr. Dexter, sir."

Someone clapped in the pews behind him. Neither Matt or Sall raised their hands in applause, and the scattered clapping died quickly. The mining managers could speak at the funeral, but they did not speak for Pop. No one could now. Except for his son.

When Smitty called Matt's name, it seemed to him that his stomach had turned into lead, a heavy thing that weighed him down. He could hardly move, and when he stood, the windows swam in his gaze, all the colors bleeding together, darkness threatening to cover him.

He closed his eyes and hesitated, breathing deeply. But then he put one foot in front of the other, and when he got to the black microphone, he steeled himself, holding on to the cold metal, tapping a finger nervously on the mouthpiece. He could not look at the crowd. All those expectant faces would make him change what he had to say. Then he began to talk, and gradually he lifted his eyes to take in the people in the church.

"I haven't always had my father's faith," Matt began. "I don't know if I believe as deeply as he did, or as faithfully, or pray as strongly. Few of us do. Yet Stan would say that winning the Purple Heart in the Pacific didn't make him brave, he would say that dragging a miner out of a collapsed chute after an air blast didn't make him brave, surviving the Sunshine disaster and helping others out of that hellhole didn't make him brave, and he would even say that holding the picket line strong with the United Mine Workers union, even that didn't make him brave. He always felt that the bravest thing you can do is stand up for what is right. That's what he would have said."

Matt paused, and felt his voice crack under the strain of what he would say next. "Yet that was not what his life was about. I'm here today to tell you the truth about Stan Worthson.

"I know many of you revered my father for his courage in surviving the Sunshine Mine disaster." Matt paused and looked around, feeling the air of the space close around him, constricting him, suffocating him in its fearful embrace. "But since my father did survive, I feel as if I should tell you what I now know about that disaster in which ninety-one members of our community perished: fathers, husbands, brothers.

"Sixteen years ago, my father was credited with saving nearly two hundred men by getting them out of the Sunshine Mine ahead of himself, at great risk to his personal safety. He worked as a hoistman all during the time the smoke was pouring through the mine, and then when he went back down to get one last load, we thought we'd never see him again. Yet there is more to the story. A man you all know here in the Silver Valley, Mr. William Herrick, he knew the truth as well, and he has corroborated this for me. In fact, my father helped to cause the Sunshine Mine fire."

Matt was startled to hear people gasp around him, a sound he had not expected. He waited until the sound died away, and then he looked down at his notes, held tight in his trembling fingers.

"Before he died, I discovered—partially through my father's attempt to share it with me—that Stan worked secretly for many years as a saboteur for Mr. Herrick's mine, the Bunker Hill. In 1972, my father concealed a series of incriminating documents inside the Sunshine Mine. In the process, he killed a man, and for some reason, he started a fire deep in the mine. It happened near the Number Five shaft—and that fire was not put out for several weeks."

Again, Matt heard the people take in their breath, a muttering coming across the crowd, as if there were a distant wave approaching. "This secret fire—fed by the boxes of documents—smoldered deep in the mine, and eventually, because my father did not raise an alarm about the dead man and the fire, it became a deep ground burn. My father's mistake—his greatest crime—was that he caused the Sunshine Mine disaster."

Matt wiped furiously at his face, rubbing his eyes, pushing himself onward against the rising tide of sound. "It's true that my father saved many men as a hoistman that day, but they wouldn't have needed saving except for the fire he lit weeks before. Before his death, Stan was not able to tell me everything about what he did or why he did it, but I was able to discover every detail on my own. I know him now."

Matt gulped. If he paused now he would start to cry. "My father must have felt terribly guilty about his actions his entire life. I can only believe that because he followed that mistake by betraying his fellows in the union, paying back a debt by working secretly for Mr. Herrick his whole life, breaking confidences that were not his to break, and breaking trust with nearly everyone he knew. Yet I feel certain that in his last days my father wanted to admit to these terrible mistakes—both to the fire, and also to providing the information that helped destroy the union here in the Valley. I am certain that he wanted to say this, but could not do so because one of his last strokes left him unable to communicate. So I'm left here today, in his stead, to tell you the truth."

As he kept speaking, Matt felt something solidify in him, a flooding rush of strength. He looked out at the crowded mass of the Silver Valley. They were listening to him. He wasn't afraid anymore.

"I know as well that the man who killed Arlen Bowman was also in some way involved in setting the fire that caused that disaster. I know this fact because last summer, after his first heart attack, my father called up Reverend Arlen Bowman, as many of us have in our times of need. Last summer, my father confessed to him his involvement in the Sunshine fire, and because of that confession—because of a story Arlen held in trust—Arlen was killed. Yet now, my father is dead, Arlen is dead, the man who lit the fire with my father—and killed Arlen—is dead as well, and so are others who may have shed light on all this. It is time to forgive. Forgive them all, both the living and the dead."

Matt was surprised by the sudden tears that came over him. His mouth twisted as he spoke, a sob shattering his words. "In the end, I am here today to tell you that I have forgiven my father for what he did, and for how he did it." Matt looked down at the floor. He did not know how he could go on.

"Lieutenant?" someone said softly. He looked up through his blurred tears, and saw Smitty standing there solemnly, holding a handkerchief. He wiped his face with the handkerchief, blew his nose. He glanced out at people. Many of them were also crying. No one looked away from him.

So he continued. "Because my father cannot say it today, I am here today to say that the time has come for all of us to stop living in lies. My father lived in a lie for nearly twenty years, and he was a lesser man for it. In the Silver Valley, we've lived for many years in lies—we've lived with the lie that we can only make a living if we sacrifice our children to the mining gods, and allow pollution to destroy this beautiful country. We've lived in the lie that our elected officials, in their corruption and deceit, are only as good as we deserve. And we've lived in the lie that we have killed ourselves, that the past cannot be redeemed, that people cannot be forgiven for what they have done. To move forward, we must be willing to forgive those who have lied to us, those who have tried to kill us and have failed, we must forgive even those who have profited from our destruction . . ."

Without thinking about it, Matt found his eyes drifting to the left, to where he imagined Russ still sitting so sedately, untouched by all of this. Yet Russ was no longer the confident player he'd seen at the beginning of the service.

Matt stuttered as he caught sight of Russ's agonized expression. The color was stripped out of his cheeks and his forehead, the sweat stood out in drops. The lines on Russ's face seemed as if they were etched deep in gray stone, and he blinked furiously, as if in some subtle Morse code, some plea for mercy.

Matt looked away, the tears leaping to his eyes again at the memory of the lies. But this time, he continued speaking. He did not pause as he felt them course down his cheeks and mar his voice with pain. They were part of what he said.

"For I could not go on from today without telling the truth. Even though I've forgotten much else that Arlen Bowman told me, he said one thing through the years that I'll always remember, and it's something my father repeated before he died. Father Arlen always said, no one's irredeemable. And so just as Arlen told my father, told me, and told you, I urge you to—"

A sudden movement caught his eye, a man pushing himself rapidly out of his seat, nearly vaulting over the people all around him on his frantic rush to leave the building. Matt drew in breath and turned his head. It was Russ White, thrusting his way through the crowd, getting free finally to the aisle and striding down the aisle toward the rear door.

"Wait," said Matt. He moved forward, away from the lectern and into the aisle, pursuing him. And when Russ didn't pause in his anxious stride, he dropped the microphone as it suddenly buzzed and squealed with feedback. He was going after Russ.

◆ ◆ ◆

JANUARY 1989

THE GIRL saw the man at the front of the church stop talking. Moving quickly out of the front of the church came a man with silver hair. He wore a shiny black suit. The crowd rustled like a wave as he passed. People knew him, he was some-one important. The man who followed him seemed to know him, he called after him, but the silver-haired man never paused.

Then the girl knew him too. He had walked in her dreams.

The silver-haired man moved from the front of the church like someone had him on a string, pulling him right out toward the back doors as fast as they could. His face was blotchy—white and red—and streaming with tears and sweat.

She stood up in her seat, opening her mouth in desperation. She remembered now—she could see him—the thick, bristly hair, the warm smoke coming out of his mouth. The very air seemed to hum and blur around his face as she looked at him. It was the same kind face she saw in her dreams. He was the one who always rescued her. It was really him. He was real, here with other people. Her other daddy wasn't pretend after all.

The other daddy came even with her, and then he was past, and soon he'd be gone again. "Daddy," she said. Then she said it again, shouting it this time. "Daddy!"

Then the other man, the one who had been talking to all of them, he was coming down the aisle too, running after her other daddy. It was Lieutenant Worthson, but why was he leaving too? People turned, surprised by the sight of the two men leaving the church.

Her mother pulled her down into her seat, but she whispered it again: "Daddy!"

He would save her.

But then he kept going, moving away into daylight as the doors of the church slammed shut behind him. The look on his face as he disappeared was something she knew well. He was afraid.

She closed her eyes, the memory bursting apart inside her chest, as if her very soul had torn open, there in the darkness behind her eyes. She could not stop crying, her voice broke into a keening wail.

It is easy to go down into Hell; night and day, the gates
of dark Death stand wide, but to climb back again, to retrace
one's steps to the upper air—there's the rub, the task.
—Virgil, *The Aeneid*

THE CB radio in Sall's Jeep crackled and hissed, every rock in the mountains magnifying the signal until the static reverberated sinuously with the shape of the mountains and the lake.

Matt had been following Russ White's car for the last hour. At first, Matt had tried to catch him, but Russ accelerated every time, slowing down when Matt dropped behind. Finally, Matt turned on the radio, hailing on every channel until he managed to get a terse acknowledgment on one channel from Russ. So far he'd only heard a few short responses—a "roger" here and there—but Matt kept hoping.

The microphone crackled unexpectedly in Matt's hand. "Why the hell are you following me, Matty?"

"Jesus, Russ, come back with me, talk to people. You drive away this way, it looks like you're admitting to things you didn't even do."

"I know what it looks like." There was a moment of radio silence. "Jesus, Matty, you gotta understand, I never meant to lie to you."

"Why?" said Matt. "That's all I want to know. Why did you do it?"

Russ did not reply for a long moment. "I figured it was a little white lie—tell you that you'd been drinking, that it was your fault. You'd swear off the white lightning, and you'd be clean. Dammit, I did it for you. I figured I was doing you a favor."

"You did it for me?" Matt said tightly. "Who asked you to tell me that?"

"Jesus, Matty, this is all coming out wrong—" Russ's voice broke. When he spoke again, his voice was hoarse and desperate. "By the time she died, it was too late to take back what I'd said—you had convinced yourself that was the way it happened, and no amount of talking could get you to stop drinking. You heard me try, I tried to tell—"

Matt punched the button, his fingers trembling with suppressed rage. "Irene died. You told me I killed her. You sure as hell didn't do her any favors. You didn't try hard enough to tell me, you didn't—"

The radio clicked as Matt spoke. Russ was trying to interrupt. "But that accident told you something I thought you needed to hear—something you could never hear from anyone, least of all your old drinking buddy. Dammit, Matty, the whole thing just spiraled out of control. By the time she died, it was impossible for me to take it back, I couldn't do anything . . ."

Matt spoke softly. "You let me live in a lie."

Matt could hear him pull away from the microphone. Russ blew his nose, the sound small and pathetic over the radio.

THE GIRL remembered the bus station. It was the middle of the night, the people moved as if they were old or drunk or asleep, sliding sideways into walls and sinking heavily onto benches. None of their eyes stayed on her tears. Instead, they talked to one another. The girl tried to listen, to hear if there was anyone she could trust, but it all seemed to turn to babble, dirty syllables splashing back and forth across empty spaces.

On the other side of the echoing room, she saw a gray-haired man with kindly eyes. He watched as she slapped the dirty man's hand away from the top of her head. The tattooed man had brought her out of the car into the station, but he never let go of her. He lifted his tattooed hand and put it on her hair. She pushed at his fingers, but he never seemed to care that she squirmed under his touch. Gradually, his fingers slipped to the side in a weary torpor. She would not settle into him, but her movement slowed to a tick.

When the station's loudspeaker squawked out a sudden surge of static, the dirty man startled, looking around wildly. His eyes had been heavy, he was almost asleep. The girl pushed forward in that moment, worming out from under his heavy grasp.

THE CB radio crackled as Matt tuned the channel. His car followed in Russ's wake, along the narrow and twisting Bitterroot Mountains highway. Matt knew this ground better than his own skin. He imagined tracing the route in a map drawn in flesh on the back of his very own hand, the curves and undulations lying like tendons and veins over a solid terrain of basalt and bone. The granite of the Bitterroot Range emerged like a jutting skeleton through the etched-on carcass of soil and snow that just barely concealed the lower regions of the range before the rock broke through at the top into a region of frost and wind.

Matt pushed the button on the microphone. "Let me tell you something, Russ, and I want you to listen to me. I forgive you for all of it. I forgive you for lying to me about Irene. I forgive you."

"Bullshit," said Russ immediately. "People don't forgive lies like the ones I fed you. People don't forgive that kind of betrayal, that kind of—"

Matt pushed the microphone button furiously, cutting Russ off. "Listen, Russ—there's nothing you could have done to me that would hurt worse than finding out about what my Pop did to all of us. After I found out about my Pop, Jesus, it was easy to forgive you. What you did was nothing, small potatoes."

"Hell, I hadn't thought of it that way." Russ gave a strange laugh. "Small potatoes? This wasn't small. I've shot a man in the line of duty. Maybe in the big scheme of things, that was small potatoes. This wasn't—this is big enough to kill me."

"C'mon, let's stop driving these damn cars. You're going over eighty, you know. It's gonna get dangerous in the mountains here. Let's stop, take a break, get some coffee or something. Chew the fat. I forgive you, Russ. That's what I've been—"

"It doesn't matter how many people you kill, Matt, or how many people forgive you. In the end, you still have to live with yourself. And what if you can't do that?"

THE GIRL had pushed frantically between the suitcases and the legs of sleeping people. She did not look at him, but she knew where the gray-haired man with the kindly eyes was standing. It was hard to push through the crowd. No one saw her coming. When she glanced behind her, she realized it cost the dirty man no effort to follow her, people simply moved when he glanced at them. This was true even though he did not look angry yet, only bemused, irritated.

Ahead of her, she could see the gray-haired man had something heavy in his jacket pocket, he fingered it with one hand. He watched her and glanced at the dirty man moving through the crowd behind her. His kind eyes were weighing something.

She came close and held up her bedraggled doll. "My baby don't feel well."

"Ah," said the man. His voice was nice too as he reached out to the doll. "Maybe I can make your baby all better. What's your doll's name?"

"Karyn," she whispered. "That's her name too."

The man crouched down on his heels and stroked the plastic head, wrinkling his brow in concern. He leaned over her. "Do you remember me, honey?" he said.

The girl did not know. "Baby wanna go home," she said in a singsong voice, pretending to be younger than she was. "Hungry, and tired, an' she's scared. She's real scared, but I can make her better. Karyn needs her daddy."

"That ain't your daddy," he said quietly. "Where's that daddy your mommy got?"

The girl shook her head and leaned into him. "I don't know," she said. She lifted up her doll again. He wrinkled his nose and she knew he smelled her panties, where the pee had dried. She whispered hoarsely to him, as if it was pretend.

"That's not baby's daddy. Baby need a real daddy. Karyn go home."

"Ah, a real daddy." The man laughed, as if the girl had said something funny. He reached out and tousled her hair, but she did not mind his hand on her head. As he stood, the dirty man reached them.

There was a momentary pause before the gray-haired man spoke again. "Hi there, Curtis. Mr. Siwood, sir. My name is Russ. I thought maybe we could talk about—"

The dirty man leaned close to them, the stale stink of sweat overwhelming her. "How the fuck do you know my name?"

"I was just talking to Karyn here and—"

As Russ spoke, the dirty man pulled his foot back and aimed a kick at the girl. She sprawled across the floor, so that he missed. When she got up, he kicked at her again. This time, she staggered backward, one arm over her head, to ward off another blow.

"Dammit!" Russ shouted and lunged forward. "What the hell are you doing?"

The dirty man jerked her off the floor. "I don't care who you are, or how you know who I am. Don't touch my girl!"

Russ reached forward. "She isn't yours," he hissed. "I'm telling you, I've got—" His arm shot in his pocket, clenching a fist, but then nothing came out. The girl was yanked backward, and for a moment she did not see the knife that the dirty man had pulled when he kicked her, the knife that made Russ pause, his face red with pent-up rage.

The dirty man pulled her across the floor, flinging back words over his shoulder to Russ. "Whoever the fuck you are—get away from us. Don't touch her again!"

And the girl was sure that no matter how nice his eyes looked, no matter how many words came out of him, the man named Russ would not help her. The dirty man had won again.

THE MICROPHONE clicked, as if Russ were speaking. There was a hiss, and then Russ's voice came from far away, the words catching and ripping on the static.

"Matt, there's one thing I know for sure now. I know you didn't kill Arlen—"

Matt keyed the microphone. "Russ, why would you ever even think—"

"Even you wouldn't publicly announce your pop's connection to the Sunshine thing, and to how Arlen got killed, if you had done it yourself. That's why I know."

"I didn't know for sure, until last week. Will Herrick told me about my pop."

"That damn Will Herrick—he keeps screwing me up. Keeps rubbing my nose in it. So fine!" Russ sighed, the sound breaking up over the channel. "So you're clean."

"But Russ, if you'd simply believed me all along, if you'd—"

"I needed to think you'd done it."

"You needed to think that about me?"

"Anyone," sighed Russ. "For the longest time, I needed to believe anyone else was responsible. I'd told you lies long enough that I could lie to myself this time. For months I lied to myself, thinking somehow Arlen got away, somehow you did it to him. But now I know for sure that Curtis killed him—and it was my fault."

KARYN REMEMBERED *her daddy coming down the stairs of the bus. When she saw him, something rose in her, but whether it was terror or hope she could not tell. He wore sleep like a drug, it slowed him down.*

He reeled forward, the weariness in him vaulting him toward the ground. When he stopped walking, the girl was sure he would fall to pieces all over the floor.

But then he lifted his face to look at them silhouetted against the bright lights inside the bus station. She saw that the fatigue didn't reach his eyes—they were as sharp as ever, the deep and peaceful blue she knew from her bedtime stories. A tight wire inside her let go as her daddy squinted up at the tattooed man.

She saw a boy standing in the shadow of the bus doorway behind her father, a thin fur on his head, his shoulders clenching reflexively, bloody snakes and dead girls on his shirt. The dirty man still held her wrist, pulling her high off the floor. The girl turned her head, her feet scrabbling for a purchase against his thick legs.

"I kept my promise," her father said to the dirty man. "You didn't have to take my daughter to get me here."

"Dammit, you're right. Hell, I didn't want to do this." The dirty man's fingers dug into her shoulder, as if to take a piece of her with him. "Besides, I didn't want her. The lil' ones die too fast!" Then his voice broke apart, a hacking sound came out of his throat.

Behind her father, she saw the boy with the shaved head move forward, as if to hear better. Her father came close, his eyes sharp as agates. "We had a deal, Curtis."

The dirty man made the sound again, and the girl realized he was laughing. "Jesus, Father, it's a joke." He took the car keys out of his pocket and shook them, jangling. "See, here's the car—an' I didn' hurt her—here, take a look, huh? You hurt?"

The girl made a sound, an uncertain moan. The dirty man glanced down at her, and his fingers released her slowly, as if he had little control over their action. His voice sank, as if to get inside her. "I didn' touch you, right? I wasn't gonna hurt anyone. I don't mean to hurt your daddy. I didn't mean to hurt you."

The girl tried to squirm away from him. Unexpectedly, the man released her, so that she collapsed on the concrete. He held out his hand, a dragon tail coiled down onto his wrist. "Here she is—now where's that damn notebook?"

There was a sharp pain in her mouth. She could taste it in her mouth, something gritty and wrong. As she pulled her feet under her, she wiped her hand over her mouth, and found a streak of red. She'd bit her lip.

Then she saw the man with the kind eyes—Russ—he was watching them too, from across the room. He put a finger up to his lips. He was still holding a heavy thing in his pocket, he lifted it so she could see the metallic gleam. It was a secret now, something between them.

Her father did not see Russ, far away across the room, and her father did not move, but his voice came to her, a low whisper, "It's all right, honey, I'm right here."

He spoke aloud to the dirty man. "I'm sorry, Curtis—I planned on bringing along that notebook, to give to you. But I can't reach the man I left it with."

"Dammit!" The dirty man swore loudly enough to turn heads all around the station. "You fuckin' left it with someone!? What the fuck do I get out of this deal? What you got I can use? You got credit cards? You got a bank account? I'll fucking do—"

Her father put his hand up in the air. "It's all right—it's in Wallace. The guy who has it is trustworthy. He'll give to you as soon as I make a phone call."

The dirty man lifted his arm, his fingers clenched in a thick fist. "You're fuckin' with me—goddammit! I'm gonna fuck you up!"

"Have I ever lied to you?" said her father. Then the girl was shocked to see him reach out and put his palm on the man's dragons. "We can go get it tomorrow. You aren't going to have to go chase this on your own. I can promise you we'll get it back together, and then you'll be done with this whole game."

"All right," sighed the dirty man. "You made it here, damn straight. Everyone fucks with me—oh yeah, just fuck over ol' Curtis, he can handle it—but you're not doing that, are you? You made it here, I guess that's proof nuff you ain't fuckin' with me . . ."

Her father cupped a hand around the man's rough-colored shoulder. "No, I'm not, Curtis. Not at all."

The dirty man put his arm down, a slow movement, as if it hurt not to punch something. "So what's gonna happen? What's gonna happen, huh?"

"Well," said her father calmly. "We'll get the notebook, and that'll be an end to it. You've done your part. If you're ready to acknowledge what you did, we can end it. If we can find proof he did this to them, to you too—the police can talk to the Herricks also."

Then her father calmly took out his wallet and put a bill in the machine on the *wall. With a gush and a hum, a cup dropped down and filled with dark fluid. Her father picked it up, held it out for the dirty man.*

"Here, have a cup of coffee, okay? Take a load off."

He looked up at the dirty man with his calm blue eyes. "You don't need to worry about running away, Curtis. We'll be able to take care of this thing. You'll be done with the whole burden. Just give it to Jesus."

Suddenly the man looked nervous, as if he had become aware of her again. The coffee shook in his hand. The girl looked down to see black drops spatter on the smear of blood her lip had left on the floor.

"You won't hold all this on me?"

"No, there really won't be anything against you, Curtis. You'll be free."

The dirty man seemed reassured. He lifted the cup and swallowed from it. He took another drink, and the girl thought he was about to leave them. When he was done, he wiped a hand across his mouth, just as the girl had.

"I got a knife," he said abruptly. "Big-ass pigsticker."

Her father paused at what he said, something changing in the way he stood. "What were you going to do with that, Curtis?"

Behind her father, the girl could see the boy with the shaved head move close enough to touch. There was some bond between the two of them she didn't understand.

"I don't know," the dirty man said in a bemused tone. He took another swallow of coffee. "Stick somebody? You, maybe your girl, someone who fucked with me. Stan maybe. Someone's always fuckin' with me—tell me go do this job, do that job."

"But that's over now, right? Can you give me the knife, Curtis?"

"Sure, that'd be okay," the dirty man said. He lifted his jacket and took out a knife. To the girl, the shiny blade seemed two feet long. As he turned it to give the handle to her father, he muttered something again. "You aren't fuckin' with me, are you." This time it was a statement, a bemused moment of wonder.

THE HIGHWAY was incomplete. Beside the road, Matt began to see water-filled pylons instead of the heavy concrete barriers that bordered the lower reaches of the road. A few hundred feet above them, the waiting fog hung down, an empty gray morass.

Cautiously, Matt punched the microphone. "Where the hell are we going, Russ?"

"Just tell the truth, Matty, are you part of the Herricks' dirty little game? Is this your job—talk me off the ledge, so they can take me apart on the ground for sport?"

"Russ, you know I've always been on your side. But right now I'm driving blind, and I wish you'd give me some answers. Why are you doing this, why . . ."

There was an answering hiss, and then nothing for a moment before Russ spoke again. "I should have known that the past would catch up with me. It catches up with all of us. You can't avoid it."

"Now wait," said Matt. "Just slow down, Russ. What did you do that was so bad? So, you messed with Arlen's dead body. How could it be your fault that Curtis—"

A jolting stab of static punched through the fog. "I was there, Matty. I was there in the station that night that Arlen was abducted."

"What do you mean, you were there? You saw him? Just slow down a sec, Russ."

"Matty, I was there in the bus station—before the body was found in the resort. I was there because I had a job to do for Val. There was a leak, and it threatened both Val and her brother."

Russ kept talking as the fog sank down on the mountainside all around them. "Will found out first, and he was the one who told this guy Siwood to go get answers—find the evidence and destroy it. But Val didn't trust them—she didn't trust either Will or his hired gun. So she sent me to take care of it, finish it off, shut down the source."

"Who were you going to shut down? Curtis or Arlen?" said Matt, but the radio just kept hissing with the sound of Russ's voice.

"So I was there in the station, that's where they'd agreed to meet, and I was waiting there for him. I saw the guy pull a knife, and that could have easily been the reason I shot him. I could have done my job for the Herricks, and walk away with a clean story. But it didn't work out that way. That damn kid interfered."

THE BOY with the shaved head moved forward with a sudden, violent shout, his hard boot swinging up in the same moment. At first, the girl shrank back, thinking that he was kicking at her, but then she saw the boot strike into the belly of the dirty man.

She reached out for her father, but the dirty man staggered backward at the boy's kick. In that moment, she looked in the other direction. She reached out toward the kind-eyed Russ who had said he'd make her baby all better. She twisted out of the rough grip and ran across the room.

The dirty man turned, as she darted away, and held up his knife so it flashed like a flag in the air. She nestled into Russ's chest and arms. Russ was breathing hard, yanking frantically at something in his pocket, a hard metal thing. There were voices all around her. The engine sound of a bus pulling in, a rush and a rumble.

Everything seemed to slow in a sickening moment as the dirty man pivoted, swinging his arm violently in the air, grasping her father and lifting back the blade of the knife. She screamed, the sound high and piercing as a dying animal.

The boy with the shaved head did not seem to care about the knife. He moved forward with a slow insolence, hitting quickly with his fists. His face didn't change at all, as if the fight bored him. Yet he broke the hold the dirty man held on her father.

When he struck a third time, she saw the dirty man suddenly stagger backward. The boy kicked out, and there came the sodden thunk of the man's head hitting the floor, a set of keys falling off his belt, jangling on the floor.

The boy picked up the keys. Then he kicked once more and the knife went spinning across the concrete floor.

Russ held her tightly. "Close your eyes," he whispered. "Close your eyes, honey."

But her eyes were locked on the dirty man. He stared at her, looking deep into her soul as the boy's thick boot struck him over and over again. Across the blue-black arms, a bloom of red started.

The man scrambled onto his knees, curling into a ball as the boy picked up the keys and kicked him one last time. The man stared up at her, a forceful hatred thrusting through the pain to center unblinkingly on her. Slowly, the blood on the dirty man's face became a dripping scrim across his eyes. Finally, his stare was broken.

A THIN film of water covered the broken gravel on the road. Already it was freezing. Matt felt Sall's Jeep slide under him as he corrected for the turn. Suddenly, he knew that Russell was counting on the fact that they'd never fixed the broken barrier at Independence Loop, despite all the accidents and near misses documented up here.

"Wait," he whispered. "Wait for me. Goddammit, Russ, just wait and talk to me. Whatever you've done, we can get through it together. Wait for me, talk to—"

As if Russ had heard him, the CB radio in the car suddenly crackled with sound. "What you did today, you took away the guilt for a lot of things, but you can't lift this burden off of me, Matty, no one can. I'll never be free of what I did. There's only one way to—"

Frantically, Matt pushed the button. "Jesus, Russ, you're scaring me here. Get some therapy—go to counseling, do something for how you feel. I'm telling you, you haven't done something you should beat yourself up about, you haven't done anything—"

"I don't think you know shit about what I've done, Matty." Russ sighed, his voice as empty as a whistle. "This is not your fault, you know that. All you did at the funeral today was point out what I've been thinking for weeks now. We have to let go. Let go or die. That's the damnedest thing about life—you got to go on living with yourself."

"But I don't understand what you could have done, Russ, you didn't hurt—"

"I killed a man, Matty. A good man. Oh, I may not have pulled the trigger—or in this case, cut his throat. But I knew what was going to happen to Arlen. I knew what this guy Siwood was there for, and yet I gave him up. I betrayed Arlen. I let him do it."

"You let Siwood kill Arlen? Why would you—"

"I thought it was the way to get the life I always wanted—but after it was done, it felt all wrong. I couldn't enjoy it, and I still can't live with it. The worst is, she knows. I can see it in her eyes."

"Who?"

"Every time I've seen that girl, I can tell she knows what I did to him. The blood doesn't come off my hands. Jesus died for thirty pieces of silver—but hell, I got Arlen killed for something a lot worse than that.

"I took away the only daddy she had ever known . . . I don't think some things can be redeemed."

The last word Russ said seemed to echo in the car. Quickly, Matt put his foot on the gas, skidding around the icy corners, coming as close as he dared to Russ's car. Matt turned on the Jeep's high-beams, they glowed uselessly against the encroaching fog.

SHE BOUND herself to Russ with her heart and her mind. With him was the only way she would ever get out. She squeezed her eyes shut and held to him as tight as she could, the frantic breath rushing in and out.

His voice was deep. It came from inside his chest and reverberated against her ears. "Stand up, you—dammit, face me when I shoot you. You're no coward, are you?"

She slit her eyes open and saw that Russ's other hand was holding a squat black thing pointed at the man on the floor. The dirty man scrabbled to get to his feet as the boy with the shaved head swiveled around, staring in sudden consternation at Russ's unwavering grip on the gun.

"Close your eyes," Russ whispered to her. "When you open 'em, it'll all be okay. Forget about all this. Close your eyes, cover your ears, honey."

The dirty man stared out of a mask of bruised and broken skin. He glared at her face, unblinking and unafraid. She glanced down at Russ's hand. His fingers were tightening on the dull black metal, his knuckles growing white.

There was a flurry of motion, and her father was abruptly standing in front of Russ and the gun. "No," he said quietly.

"Goddammit, shoot the bastard!" yelled the boy. "He's a scary motherfucker!"

Her father flinched at these words, and she could barely hear his response. "I gave my word. I should go with him, take him where he wants to go."

"Sure," said Russ. "You believe that? Then you go with him. You do that."

Her father's answer echoed always in her dreams. "You don't understand his story. God will be with me. Anyone can be redeemed."

Russ waved the gun to the side. "Curtis—you should know the truth, we planned it like this. Arlen and I set you up to be caught, and now I'm gonna shoot you dead."

Her father turned, a sudden shock on his face. "No, it wasn't like that."

The dirty man had an answer for that. He looked at Arlen, saying, "This is just between you. And me." Then he moved rapidly toward her father, pausing only when Russ gave a low whistle, as if he were calling a dog.

Russ lifted the gun again, pointing it at the dirty man. "You got any last words?"

"No!" Her father waved his hands frantically. "In God's name, you can't do this!"

The dirty man paused and looked at the girl and Russ. He wiped a swollen hand across his bloody face, his eyes narrowed with loathing. "Fuck you—whoever you are."

"I'm an angel, Curtis, or didn't you know? I'm an Angel of Death." Then Russ smiled, a strange expression on his face. "But it seems I'm taking a vacation tonight."

Russ pointed the gun at the ceiling. "Bang. You're not dead," he said. "Someone else can do the dirty tonight, because I'm off duty, as of Father Arlen's request."

She saw her father step back, a sudden uncertainty in his step. When she saw that, she stopped listening. She watched him speak without hearing the words, watched him take the cross from off his neck and give it to the boy with the shaved head.

Then her father said good-bye, said he'd see her later, and even as he spoke, the girl knew that it was a lie. She began to cry.

"Don't worry, honeybunch." Russ took her face in his hands, made her listen to him. "It'll be alright—Curtis here just wants to ask your daddy some questions. That's what your daddy wanted. Right, Arlen? I'm not doing it for me, right?"

Her father did not seem to be listening either, but Russ continued talking to him. "I'll wait here, Arlen. I'll take care of Karyn until you get back. This won't take long."

The girl watched something clench in Russ as the dirty man took her father's *arm in his grasp. He stared at them until they went out of the building, and then they were gone. A moment after her father was out of sight, Russ took the girl to a different car. "Let's go."*

Then she began to cry again. "But my daddy . . . he . . ."

"Get in the car, honey."

"Why do you call me honey?"

But he didn't seem to have heard what she'd said. He helped her into the car, locking the belt of the front seat gently around her. She had forgotten her doll in the other car, and she was about to tell him that when the boy with the shaved head came up to the car.

"Hey, dude—"

Without pause, Russ had the black gun back in his hand, it was already pushed into the boy's chest. "What the hell do you want?"

"That dirty bastard . . . he dropped the preacher's car keys. What do I do with them?"

Russ stared at him coldly. "You took my kill away from me. Now you got the keys for your efforts, so take the damn car. I don't give a shit what you do with it."

"But what about Arlen? Isn't he coming back?" The boy's voice rose into a whine. "What's going to happen to him?"

"Why the fuck should I care?" said Russ. He shrugged, and the girl watched him sink down into the car seat and close the door. Carefully, he rolled down the window and put the gun back into his pocket. He started the engine as he spoke to the boy outside.

"If you care, you can track 'em down. Otherwise, get out of my way. I gotta go to Spokane. See you in hell."

MATT COULD see Russell's car dead ahead, it drifted back and forth across the lanes. Matt hoped there were no other cars in the higher elevations this time of day. The headlights scraped from snowy verge to center line, the fog seemed to sweep aside as the car cut through it.

Matt accelerated across the ice, driving as fast as he could. A sudden helplessness came across him—what could he do, after all, if he did catch Russ? Why had Russ betrayed Arlen at the station? What secret was Russ killing himself to hide?

He pushed the microphone button on the CB radio. "Russ, I'm going to be here for you, come hell or high water. Come on back, you don't have to do this, you don't have to go here."

"Matty, it's too late for that. You don't know where I'm going. You never will." There was a strange sound over the channel, and Matt realized Russ was crying. "See, the problem is that here in Bitterroot, people know only one story about my life. I thought I could go on with life, but this isn't the story they know, and I can't change it anymore."

Matt could hear the blustery air howling over the pass, a monstrous howl as skeins of distant snow were lifted and thrown by the wind. "But you can change, you can survive this, you can."

Russ didn't seem to hear him over the roar of the wind. "Y'know, Arlen asked me not to kill Curtis, but it was my choice to send him away with the bastard. When I gave him up, I knew I'd signed his death warrant. Yet I was happy when I was doing it. I was happy—that's what I'm telling you. I did it because I wanted that life. I broke my life, Matty. I did it to myself, and no one can ever forgive me."

A pleading note came into Matt's voice. "Why were you happy about that? What life? For God's sake, Russ, just talk to me, please tell me *why*."

Russell muttered something he couldn't understand. The radio clicked off with a horrible finality.

SHE REMEMBERED *Russ glancing over at her while he drove. This car was different, and somehow worse. It smelled so sweet it was close to rotten. When she first sat down in the car, her fear was like a poison eating at her heart and her bones, a heavy leaden thing eating away at her lungs, until she felt she could not breathe any longer, as if she would suffocate under its weight. When she took another breath, she was surprised by the lightness of the air in her mouth.*

She glanced up at Russ, and then something in her released itself. It let go when she saw the wrinkles around his mouth, the kindness in his eyes. "It's going to be all right, honey," he said. "See, there's a secret your momma never told you. Your daddy isn't really . . ."

She could see spittle on the edge of Russ's thin, narrow lips. Some of the spit came out and touched her face as he spoke, his hint of a smile somehow dangerous, like a warning or a badge.

Her fear welled up again, leaking out her eyes in hot tears. "Where's my daddy? I want my daddy! My daddy . . . where is he . . ." She gasped, the sobs bursting out of her.

Nervously, Russ reached across her, pulling a plastic bag out of the glove box. Without looking at her, he took a small piece of white paper out of his pocket and put a pinch of something inside it. Then he put the paper up to his lip and rolled it back and forth. A moment later, he was holding a thin white stick.

"Sorry, honey, I just . . ." He held up his hand, and she saw it quivering in the air. "I've been waiting for this moment for a long time, honey. I just . . ." He held up a lighter and struck a flame in the dark.

Time seemed to stretch out as she watched the smoke drift out of Russ's mouth.

The strong smell of the smoke was hypnotic, the musk scent took the fear away again.

"Listen to me," said Russ finally. "I call you honey because you're mine. Your momma and I—we made you. Five years ago. An' after that, since I couldn't leave my wife, your momma met Arlen there, and they got married just before you were born. But you're mine. You'll always be mine." He sucked in, the stick pulsing redly in his mouth. Then he blew the smoke out and looked down at her, his eyes watering.

Then he seemed to see the thin stick of smoke. "I guess that's enough of that. If I'm a daddy, I better start acting like one, eh?" Carefully, he emptied the bag of green stuff out the window. She could see the moving flicker of cars on the high-way. When he flicked the small stick outside too, it burst apart, making a flower of sparks against the black road.

"You can't tell your momma you know this yet—it'll be our secret, you under-stand? Just don't tell her." He rolled up his window and gave her another smile, but this time it was nice underneath.

"I'm your real daddy, your other daddy," he said. After he said that, every-thing seemed to fragment and break apart. Nothing made sense anymore.

All these months later, she could only recall isolated phrases Russ had said in the car, as if everything she'd heard had been spoken to her from a distance, drifting into her mind from miles away. "I'll always be here for you."

She had been drifting in and out, the weariness in her bones taking her under every other moment, but she could still recall things he had said. "I'm coming back for you, as soon as I can figure out how to move to Spokane . . . your other daddy, he left you. He didn't really love you like I do . . . I'm your daddy now. And your momma and I will be together soon . . . because I'm your real daddy."

Russ kept saying that part over and over. "I'm your other daddy, your real daddy."

She remembered his face coming closer as he kissed her, whiskers rubbing her cheek. She woke up when they reached Five Mile Prairie. "I'll be back," he said. "Don't tell your momma, you understand? But I'll be back as soon as I can. I'll be your daddy for real as soon as I can, you hear me?" When she went inside the house, her mother and her grandmother were on the couch, they'd fallen asleep in front of the TV, waiting for her.

THE RADIO was dead. Matt rolled down his window and tried to shout ahead to Russ, but his voice dwindled against the high-pitched rush of the wind. In the ghostly light of the fog, it seemed a vast pack of hounds were baying up the mountain, running ceaselessly alongside their cars.

Russell took Independence Loop at the same speed he'd been driving up the mountainside, he didn't slow an inch as the front tires edged off the road. Matt swerved away at the last moment from the Loop as Russ passed through the gap where so many cars had caught themselves before, spinning their wheels wildly on the edge of disaster. Without pausing, Russ bumped over the gravel verge and left the highway. The car slowed for a moment before it leaped forward, bumping aside three water-filled pylons.

The barriers split open in front of Russell's car, baptizing the car, blurring the road with a cascade of water. Matt slammed his brakes on and twisted the wheel of the Jeep, sliding across the ice, to land finally on the opposite side of the highway, as close as he could get to the solid rock of the mountain.

A clump of hoarfrost dusted the Jeep, and then Matt yanked the door open and ran wildly to the side of the road, looking down to where Russell's car was still airborne, a thousand feet above the Silver Valley. Matt's stomach rose, a heavy thing inside. It came to him that the last thing Russell murmured had been a prayer: *Forgive me, this isn't how my life was supposed to go . . . Forgive me . . .*

Matt watched the car drop horizontally through the cloudbank. The rear fender lifted silently, as if the engine were revving. It hit a rock outcropping a few hundred feet above the Valley floor. Snow exploded into the air, the cracking sound came a moment later. Then the car corkscrewed violently end over end and disappeared into an icy fog.

WHEN SHE woke in the car, the sun was going down over the distant lake. The funeral was far away now. All the people in the church were gone.

Only faint traces of the fog remained, a creeping condensation on the road. She sat up. The ground outside was wet and black. All the buildings had a darkened, scuttled look.

She wondered at the way time had slipped away, the past shifting in and out. It seemed suddenly that all the houses they were passing were empty, as if the town itself had emptied while she slept. She felt like a leaf caught in a current. She reached out to her mother, holding her tight in her arms. "Where is he?" she said. "Where's my other daddy now?"

"I don't know," said her mother. "I don't know if he's ever coming back to us."

Far away on a distant hill, there was a signal pulsing over the water. It blinked on the top of a radio tower, shining for the pilots of planes. She turned and watched the beacon on the tower float, suspended, above the darkening trees, caught in a moment of light.

This is the first day of the rest of your life. Live it Safely.
—Entrance sign, Sunshine Mine, Idaho

SNOW BLOCKED Fourth of July Pass for only nine days that winter. By March, the foot-thick ice had melted all across the southern end of the lake. The snow was gone and the first green shoots were breaking out of the ground before the days lengthened. Spring had come early to Lake Coeur d'Alene.

Every day of the week now, Matt woke early. On weekdays, he rowed, and on Saturdays, Sall and he cooked breakfast together. For five years or more, they'd tried to avoid each other. Now he found himself seeking her out. Breakfast together was something he'd missed for a long time, and when he finally mentioned it to Sall, he was surprised to discover that she'd missed it too.

Awaking before first light, he looked out at the darkness. A white frost traced the edge of the lake. It felt like the middle of the night, it felt too early to get out of bed. Summer couldn't come quick enough for him. But soon enough, he put on his jeans and a sweatshirt.

Sall already had coffee brewing, the scent had seeped into his dreams. When she woke him, she had a serious expression on her face, and for a moment, Matt thought something else was wrong.

"This morning," she said. "I'm going to remind you of your lost art."

"My lost art? What's that?"

"Cheddar cheese muffins. You used to make a pretty mean one."

"All right." He grinned hopefully. "But I've got to have my coffee first. You sure I can still do this?" Matt held out his open hands, the palms thick with calluses, the tips of his fingers scarred from chopping wood and wrenching bolts out of engines. He looked down at the heap of shredded cheese, the measured cups of sour cream and flour, brown sugar and dill. Everything was blurry in the half-light before dawn.

"Of course you can!" Sall set a steaming cup of coffee next to him. She reached in the bag and carefully scattered white flour over his hands and the cutting board. The sensation of the flour falling tickled, it made him want to sneeze. He gulped a breath.

"No, no, don't sneeze!" laughed Sall. He turned his head toward the window.

The lake was deeply black around the dock. Across the water, he could see fingers of light beginning to touch the dark surface, a glimmering of dawn across the water. Winter was almost over, the year was turning toward the sun.

"Okay," said Sall. "Now what you've got to do is put all of it in the bowl, and then mix it up with your hands until the consistency is like, um, oatmeal, and then—voilà!"

"Wall-la?"

"Well, then you put it in the oven, and we've got cheddar cheese muffins for breakfast." Sall laughed. "C'mon, Matt, you act like you never made these before. It's only been a few years since you did it. Ah, honey, I know it's early. You'll wake up."

"Thanks," he said. "So, you still think I can do this . . ." He took a swallow of black coffee. Then, gently, he began to knead the cheese into the flour and milk.

Sall cracked a pair of eggs into a bowl and began to whip them together. "Hey," she said. "I've been meaning to ask you, what did they get from the little girl?"

"Karyn, you mean? The Bowman girl?"

Sall nodded.

"She's a waterfall of information now. It won't be admissible in court though."

"Why not?"

"I guess because of how long she took to talk," Matt pushed down hard on the dough. "Nancy says the lawyers can argue that I set her up—that we're prompting her or something, after all this time."

Sall took a drink of her coffee. "Did she see—"

"See who left the station with her father? Oh yes she did." Matt paused to pour cream in his cup. "Curtis Siwood is definitely the one who abducted her. He's also definitely the one who took Arlen. I mean, Karyn nailed him out of a group of composites. Positive ID."

Sall turned the onions and peppers into the pan. A slow sizzle rose, as she stirred them. "A couple of national reporters have called here about him, you know. Once the Spokane papers published what you said at the funeral, the floodgates were open."

"Yeah, but who would have thought *Time* magazine would care? I thought those talking heads were on short leashes on the coasts, didn't know they'd give a damn about Idaho. I guess they do. Someone does."

Matt pushed balls of dough into the muffin tin, patting them down. "There, I think they're ready to be baked. Just sprinkle the dill on top, eh?" He paused and took a gulp of coffee before passing the tin to Sall.

Sall closed the oven door and clicked the timer on. "So you can prove that you didn't do anything—and that Kevin was innocent." said Sall. The scent of the sautéed onions and peppers filled the kitchen. There was a hiss and a sizzle as she slowly poured her eggs into the saucepan.

"Looks like it." Matt dried his hands slowly, his face shifting to something else, sadness and disbelief. "All along, I guess I was right after all."

"Of course you were. You were right." Sall stirred the eggs. She took a cloth and wiped the flour off the counter. "Almost done," she said.

When they sat down, the muffins were steaming hot, the cheese inside soft as warm butter. Matt chewed slowly. "Just enough salt on the eggs," he mumbled. Sall smiled.

"Hey, I almost forgot to tell you," he said. "Richard Stanford called again."

Sall shook her head. "Trying to get you to head up Tri-State Security again?"

"No," said Matt slowly. "Something else. I already turned him down on Tri-State."

"Right. I think that was mostly courtesy anyway." Sall wiped her mouth with her napkin. "So what was it, Matt?"

Matt stood and went to the refrigerator. He took out a bottle of orange juice and squinted at the lake. Outside, the sky was brilliant with sunrise. Brown specks were winging into the beach. The birds moved awkwardly up from the sand, into the sky, and back down, bits of rag in a current of air. Beyond the birds, the lake shivered under a gust of wind. It shone in sudden glints of light.

"This time he was calling on behalf of the County Commissioners. He wanted to ask me to take over as interim sheriff."

"Are you going to accept?"

Outside the window, a bird with feathers like frail brown leaves came through the air toward the windowsill and landed there. It stood there for less than a second. He could see its wings tense a moment before it turned and pecked blindly at a spot on the inside of the glass. Its head turned toward him like a flicker of mica. When it gathered itself and flew away, back toward the beach, Matt spoke again.

"Yeah," he said, and turned toward Sall. "I think I am."

"But what about Andy Merrill?" said Sall. "Isn't he still technically sheriff?"

"Yes, but he was already on administrative leave, because of the corruption charges. Now they've just extended his leave until they can figure out what to do. I think the Board of Commissioners may just ask for an early resignation—once the inquest into Russ's death finishes, that is."

Matt closed the refrigerator, but still he stood at the window, gazing out. The window seemed to vibrate with light off the water. The breeze caught the water, sounds came to him from far away.

Matt shook his head slowly. "Will Herrick has failed to release anything, and the prosecutor is making no headway in getting new information. I think the investigation is basically over. There are just a lot of questions left behind. Questions that will never be answered." Matt brought his coffee back to the table and sat down with Sall as the light from the lake filled the room.

Matt picked up a slim file folder from the kitchen counter and opened it. Inside was a copy of *Time* magazine, folded back to Siwood's picture. "See," said Matt. "Here he is. And we still don't really know why he came back here. Was it really to collect on the favor he'd done—or was it for some other reason? If Russ was alive, I could ask him, but . . ."

Sall looked at the magazine in his hands. "But you're sure Curtis Siwood killed Arlen? Somehow to get back at Herricks, or under Will Herrick's direction? Which is it?"

Matt shook his head. "We'll never be able to prove it. We do know that Will Herrick and Curtis were connected. None of it admissible in court, but we know. For sure, in April of '72, Curtis and Pop were following Herrick's direction by burying the files. Now we have Karl Avery saying that Curtis said he caused the Sunshine disaster with his accidental fire, and Will Herrick claimed to me—privately—that Curtis helped Pop cover that up. But that's hardly proof. Who's going to believe the village idiot and some off-the-record hearsay?"

"But what was in those files—the ones they were supposed to bury?"

"There's the rub." Matt sighed. "Curtis and Pop did their jobs too well. We'll never find out what was burned that day. What kind of incriminating evidence was there? Toxins released, laws broken, under-the-table deals? We'll never know the extent of the damage."

"So, try to find out. Open the case back up!"

Matt shook his head wistfully. "Oh, I'll try, but with Russ dead and Valerie Herrick keeping her mouth shut, there's precious little the grand jury can do. Will Herrick will probably weather this one. He manages to weather everything else."

Sall finished her eggs. Then she glanced at her watch. "Are you sure Doug wasn't going to be here for breakfast? He said—"

Matt held up his fork in gentle admonishment. "No, he said he *might* come. I think he's still figuring some stuff out. At least he's doing some good in the world."

Sall wrinkled her brow. "How do you know?"

Matt broke a muffin apart, and handed half to her. "I talked to the Bowmans."

"The Bowmans?"

"Yeah, Betty and her daughter—you know, the little girl. They told me Doug's been over there near every day since he got back, talking to Karyn. I don't know what he says, but he's definitely not on drugs. And a time or two, he's had dinner with them. Told them he's been fixing up the cabin. And he's been sleeping at Pop's old place."

Sall sucked air through her teeth, a low whistling sound, as if she'd found something worth breathing. "Is he going to stay in the Valley then?"

Matt gulped at his coffee. "Yes, he did take the 'Cuda up to the cabin too—said he was going to finish the job Kevin started. But then he's going to leave again. Said he was going to take the car to Seattle, on his way back to California."

Matt chewed and pointed his fork at Sall. "I asked him why he came back. And it was just for the funeral. He just said he had to be here with us, at a time like this."

Sall nodded in disappointment. "So he has his own life. What did I tell you?"

Matt opened his eyes. He could see the clouds hanging low over Lake Coeur d'Alene, as if drawn to the water. Their shadows covered it immensely, the last faint traces of their light limning the current as the river flowed endlessly away.

IT WAS only on the bad days that Matt felt as if he should simply walk away from Coeur d'Alene, leaving behind all that he knew, all that he didn't know.

In the end, Matt felt he might not ever know what demons had haunted Russ, what final act was irredeemable. For that reason, he felt he should be angry at Russ, for not being able to tell him more, for not being able to save himself. Yet the anger would not come to him. Something in him had let go of that obligation.

In fact, since his father's funeral, the need to resolve things had diminished until it was no more than a murmur. Now the past was in focus, he wasn't afraid to look back to things he'd left behind long ago. Often, it was as if he were looking through cloudy water that clears as a current passes through it.

For that same reason, he had not spoken to anyone about Russ's final words in the car. When he got around to it, it seemed to him that Arlen's little girl might be the best place to start.

There was no hurry, the dead would wait.

The speech he'd given at his father's funeral had left a lasting impression. Weeks later, his father's former colleagues, and even those who had not attended the funeral, continued to stop him on the street to thank him for what he'd said that day. They seemed to see him in a new light. Increasingly, he saw himself that way as well.

One month after his father's funeral, Matt became interim sheriff for Bitterroot County. Andrew Merrill was due to leave office officially in a few weeks, and a special election to replace Russell White was scheduled for the following year.

"I can think of no better person to fill the office during this time of uncertainty," said Richard Stanford. "We can use your insight and experience. We owe it to you."

On his first day back in the Sheriff's Department, Matt was surprised to find his office untouched. Only the resort files had been riffled and removed. Phyllis simply showed him to his desk, as if no time had passed. There was a huge backlog of bookings and case reports to review on top of his filing cabinet, covering his in-box with paper.

Despite the work he had ahead of him, Matt couldn't seem to get the resort off his mind. Although Russ and Curtis were both dead, technically the case of Arlen's murder had not been closed. All information related to the case had been effectively purged by Andy Merrill before his departure, but there were few secrets remaining in the files anyway, and there were also few of the answers Matt sought.

When he'd worked through half the backlog, he located Curtis Siwood's mother in Phoenix. Mrs. Siwood had little to say. Her son had always been distant and vindictive. Recently, Curtis's landlord had called, wondering why rent had not been paid. She found his apartment full of the broken wet boles of cactus plants and the rotting parts of dead animals.

Matt offered to return Curtis's remains to her, but she was not interested. "Leave him be," she said. "He always loved it up in the Idaho country. I seen pictures of your lake—looked mighty peaceful to me."

Matt had kept the letters written to him by Irene Closner, he reread them frequently. In some letters, she talked about the Silver Valley. In others, she wrote about their friendship and things he'd told her. The worst passages to read were always near the end, when she begged him to visit her in the hospital. But the letters he searched for were the ones that would tell him details about the accident and its aftermath, events he could only dimly remember even yet.

He never found what he looked for—there were only hints and warnings of Valerie's involvement, of how Russ had managed to convince Matt of his guilt. It was now impossible to get the full story—but Matt supposed he didn't need that now. Irene had forgiven him, at least, and that seemed enough, most days.

Often, he thought of her, as she had traveled in her hospital room on her lonely path toward death. He thought too of Kev's furrowed brow, that deep hurt he masked so well with anger, and the wind that had filled the cabin in a sudden gust, covering the boy's burned corpse with a scattering of snow.

Matt tried not to make too much of his past mistakes.

It also helped not to think too much of the future. Richard Stanford was urging him to stand as a candidate in the next election cycle and keep the office. Yet Will Herrick might find it in himself to recover from the public disclosure about the Sunshine disaster and the many newspaper articles about his company's past activities. And one of these days, either one of the Herricks might fund an opposing candidate, more amenable to their will. Matt was not concerned. He simply took it all one day at a time.

As was now his habit early in the mornings, Matt rowed a half mile out in the lake and back again. In that time before the day took hold, a light mist sometimes dropped into rain as he worked his way across. The sound of a car on the other side of the cove came across as something distant and scattered. The splash of the oars, like other sounds, was distorted by the water in the air. The waking city was muted by the mist.

Recently, he'd noticed that the cattails were in bloom, it was almost summer again. He watched them growing beside the lake, pathways carved through the sedge grass.

The paths were made by animals, but every time he saw the grass bent apart, he thought someone had walked through, making their own way wherever they went. Without fail, it came to him, a memory of the day he'd tracked footprints through tall grass, the soles cracked and distinctive. Sometimes the memory of that day spent walking the lakeside with Russ White was conflated with Pop's desperate stare, the blasting cap held in his wrinkled hand. Often, Matt seemed to remember both dead men in the same moment.

And when a mist rolled across the lake, he thought of the ghostly static of the videotape, that strange, haunted purpose in Curtis Siwood's gaze. Then he imagined that someone came walking across the lake, footsteps ghostly and unreal on the water: he could almost see him stepping from the fog. Sometimes he thought it was himself, someone finding their way. At other moments, it seemed to be the drowned man who came.

Yet always, memory spoke to him out of the depths, the words coming clearer every time. *Forgive me, this isn't how my life was supposed to go . . . Forgive me . . .*

The thought always faded back into the fog, whispers dropping away before Matt could understand all that he had to say. Matt always imagined that the apparition walked silently over the water, past the splashing oars across the lake. He edged into mist and was gone, headed back into the past.

When he rowed in the early mornings, Matt would stay in the stillness for whole minutes as the quiet rose off the lake, wondering who waited for him out on the water.

COEUR D'ALENE & THE SILVER VALLEY

THE "Bitterroot County" portrayed in this story is a fictional one, although the events that transpired in the 1970s and 1980s are very real events with very real consequences.

The Silver Valley devastation described in this novel is historically accurate. The only organization actively working to clean up this wonderful wilderness is the Silver Valley Community Resource Center. You can donate to this organization at **SilverValleyAction.com**.

The Sunshine Mine in Kellogg, Idaho, was once America's richest silver mine, producing over 300 million ounces of silver in the course of its history through 2002.

The 91 men who died in the Sunshine Mine disaster in May of 1972 are memorialized in a permanent shrine built beside the I-90 highway outside of Kellogg. The shrine was built by a miner.

After the 1972 disaster, the Sunshine Mining Company could not be sued for lack of safety gear. Idaho law states that employers may be held liable only for workers' compensation claims. The average family received death benefits to equal two years of a good miner's salary.

To this day, the mystery of the fire that began the Sunshine Mine disaster has never been solved. Miners Tom Wilkinson and Ron Flory were the only two survivors found in the mine.

During the winter of 1973–1974, the Bunker Hill mine smelter broke, dumping some twenty years' worth of undiluted and unfiltered lead oxide emissions on the communities of the Silver Valley.

In August of 1974, the highest lead levels ever recorded in human beings were found in children tested in the town of Kellogg. Bunker Hill mining operations produced record profits of $25.9 million in the same year.

In the late 1980s, it was revealed that the Bunker Hill board of directors had calculated that it would be profitable to operate the mine, despite the dangerously broken baghouse thimble room and smelter. The poisoning was just a business expense: their calculations included liability of "$6–7 million/$10K per child," for planned settlements to families permanently damaged by lead.

The Bunker Hill mine went into bankruptcy proceedings in 1989. A variety of government studies have demonstrated continued toxic effects, although no person or company has ever been brought to account for their flagrant lead, cadmium, and zinc poisoning of the entire region.

To this day, lead levels in Silver Valley children run twice the national average, and a plume of heavy metals extends 200 miles downstream from Lake Coeur d'Alene into Washington State.

The region around the Bunker Hill mine was designated a Superfund site by the Environmental Protection Agency in 1991, although federally mandated warning signs regarding environmental toxins are not consistently posted in the area, due to the desire not to alarm tourists and other visitors to the region.

The Coeur d'Alene and Silver Valley destination resort areas today constitute some of the most successful tourist destination regions in the United States, despite the many tons of lethal mining residue that still cover the basin of Lake Coeur d'Alene and the lake's tributary waterways.

READERS MAY find it useful to know that I drew on past events and real locations for much inspiration. All of the locations in Coeur d'Alene and the Silver Valley described in this novel really existed in the 1980s and '90s, including Albi's Bar and Grill, the Oasis Brothel Rooms, the Sixth Street Melodrama, the old sheriff's office, the Sunshine Mine, the Coeur d'Alene Resort (built on the site of the Potlatch mill), the office next to the resort, and the cabin where Kev died.

A trip to the real Silver Valley is mandatory for those interested in the region, especially a visit to the Wallace District Mining Museum, curated by the able and helpful John Amonson. I also recommend these books: *Fire in the Hole: The Untold Story of Hardrock Miners*, by Jerry Dolph (Pullman, WA: Washington State University Press, 1994); *Wyatt Earp and Coeur d'Alene Gold! Stampede to Idaho Territory*, by Jerry Dolph and Arthur Randall (Coeur d'Alene, ID: Museum of North Idaho, 2008 / Eagle City, 2005); *The Sunshine Mine Disaster* (poems), by James Brock (Tampa, FL: Florida Gulf Coast, 1998); *Steamboats in the Timber*, by Ruby El Hult (Caldwell, ID: Caxton Press, 1952).

Further helpful information came from Robbie Burrows of the Seattle FBI Field Office and Father Tom of St. Alphonsus Catholic Church in Wallace, both of whom I thank for their assistance. The assistance of Kootenai Health (formerly Kootenai Memorial Hospital); the Thurston County Sheriff's Department in Olympia, Washington; and the Kootenai County Sheriff's Department in Coeur d'Alene, Idaho, has also been invaluable.

I will take this opportunity to point out that every one of the sheriff's deputies, law enforcement officials, and citizens of Shoshone and Kootenai Counties who assisted me in research for this work were kind and noble persons. In particular, I recall with pleasure my time in Kellogg with Sherrill and Pat Grounds, who are the only real people to appear as characters in this story. I hope to honor Pat's memory with a book that I think she would have greatly enjoyed.

Pat and I both knew that no Idahoan would undertake the unsavory and unethical activities I describe. Thus it was necessary to invent a completely fictional place—Bitterroot County—of wholly imaginary persons who were less noble and more suspect, all in the service of an interesting novel. I do hope that the people of Coeur d'Alene and the Silver Valley will forgive my depredations on the good character of their delightful communities.

ACKNOWLEDGMENTS

Thank you to Jill and to Kate and to Nick for helping me write late into the night and early in the morning. Thanks also to my parents, Carl and Tressa Hayes, for their support, and to George and Joy Rittenhouse for their help. Thank you to Pete Dexter for his personal encouragement.

Thank you to my amazing copyeditor, Kyra Freestar. I also thank Jeff Gerecke, who represented this book to publishers for several years. I give my gratitude to Vic Bobb of Whitworth University in Spokane and Steve Vander-Staay of Western Washington University, both of whom encouraged me along the way. Thank you to my early editor, Anne Dubuisson Anderson, and to my early readers Larry Clark, Molly Brown, Katherine Ropp, and J. E. B. Thornton.

My gratitude is owed as well to the following friends and reading companions, all of whom graciously read portions of the book in draft form: Katherine Wallace, Dean Bonnell, John Turnbull, Daryl Thul, S. Mackenzie Glander, Jeff Bond and Cheryl Murfin Bond, Ross TenEyck, Nina Naberhaus, Tom Osoki, John de Turk, John Stroeh, Emily E. Kelly, Ken Efta, and Marinell Simpson.

Thank you.

ABOUT THE AUTHOR

NED HAYES conceived the story of *Coeur d'Alene Waters* when he was nineteen years old and living in northern Idaho. It is his first novel.

Mr. Hayes graduated from Whitworth College in Spokane, Washington. He has subsequently been the recipient of graduate fellowships at Western Washington University in Bellingham, Washington, and Luther Seminary in St. Paul, Minnesota. He studies writing in the Rainier Writing Workshop MFA in Tacoma, Washington. His forthcoming novel, *Sinful Folk*, also a historical novel, is set in the medieval period.